"Co...
Drop to your knees and place
your hands on your head!"

A dozen Starfleet personnel in black commando uniforms had emerged from concealed positions along the corridor, and ten more looked down from the level above. They all aimed their combat rifles at Data, and a clatter of running footsteps behind his back told him that he was surrounded. Civilians scattered, screaming in panic, as the Starfleet security force advanced on Data, slowly shrinking their perimeter around him. A male Bajoran seemed to be the one in charge. Data froze as the man shouted, "Commander! This is your final warning! Drop to your knees and place your palms on your head!"

With careful, slow movements, Data lowered himself first to one knee, then he tucked the other knee under himself. Before removing his hands from his pockets, he clutched the quantum transmitter he'd concealed in his pocket, and which held a prerecorded message he'd saved in its transmission queue as a hedge against an unforeseen emergency. A single tap on the finger-sized metallic cylinder sent the SOS to the one person Data knew he could trust to answer it. Then he took his hands from his pockets and placed them atop his head.

"Hold your fire," he said. "I surrender."

STAR TREK

THE NEXT GENERATION®

COLD EQUATIONS

BOOK II

SILENT WEAPONS

DAVID MACK

Based on
Star Trek® and
Star Trek: The Next Generation
created by Gene Roddenberry

POCKET BOOKS
New York London Toronto Sydney New Delhi Orion

Pocket Books
A Division of Simon & Schuster, Inc.
1230 Avenue of the Americas
New York, NY 10020

This book is a work of fiction. Names, characters, places, and incidents either are products of the author's imagination or are used fictitiously. Any resemblance to actual events or locales or persons, living or dead, is entirely coincidental.

First Pocket Books paperback edition December 2012

POCKET and colophon are registered trademarks of Simon & Schuster, Inc.

For information about special discounts for bulk purchases, please contact Simon & Schuster Special Sales at 1-866-506-1949 or business@simonandschuster.com.

The Simon & Schuster Speakers Bureau can bring authors to your live event. For more information or to book an event, contact the Simon & Schuster Speakers Bureau at 1-866-248-3049 or visit our website at www.simonspeakers.com.

Manufactured in the United States of America

10 9 8 7 6 5 4

ISBN 978-1-4516-5073-0
ISBN 978-1-4516-5076-1 (ebook)

For John, who got me into this mess

HISTORIAN'S NOTE

The events of this story take place in 2384, approximately four years and four months after the events of the movie *Star Trek Nemesis*, and two months after the events of *Cold Equations*, Book I: *The Persistence of Memory*, in which legendary cyberneticist Noonien Soong (who was not so dead as the galaxy had been led to believe) sacrificed his life to resurrect his android son, Data—who has now undertaken a personal mission to bring back his own lost child, Lal.

Mundus vult decipi, ergo decipiatur.
(The world desires to be deceived, so let it be deceived.)

—Petronius,
Roman satirist

PROLOGUE

It had been three days, nine hours, and eighteen minutes since Federation Security officers Kohl Chamiro and Treg mor Glov had embarked on their patrol of the Komatsu Sector's most desolate star systems, and it would be three days, fourteen hours, and forty-two minutes before they could chart a course back to civilization. Kohl stared with sullen boredom at his reflection in the *Sirriam*'s cockpit window. He noted with dismay the first hint of a doubled chin on his otherwise youthful face and the slow proliferation of gray hairs above his ears. Despite his best effort not to disturb the silence between himself and his partner, the disgruntled Bajoran man succumbed to a heavy, dejected sigh. "I'm not trying to point fingers or anything, but this is all your fault."

The rust-maned Tellarite swiveled away from the helm console and looked down his snout at Kohl, his brow furrowed with reproach. "We've already had this discussion."

"We could be at the game *right now*, Treg." The harder Kohl tried not to think about missing the long-awaited championship *fútbol* match between Pacifica United and Royal Betazed, the more stubbornly rooted his resentment became. "Do you have any idea what I went through to get those tickets? We had *sideline* seats, Treg. At midfield."

Glov's solid black eyes betrayed no sympathy. "I won't apologize for doing my job." He shook his head and frowned at Kohl's resurrection of this sore subject. "It's unfortunate that our recreational plans were affected, but that was beyond our control."

"It was completely within our control. If you hadn't been so gung-ho to chalk up another arrest, we could be kicking back at the stadium with cold drinks and an unobstructed view."

A low growl of irritation rumbled inside Glov's chest. "I did what the law required. Just because young Mister Nolon's father is the governor of Tyberius Prime, that doesn't exempt him from responsibility for his actions."

Kohl wondered why this was so hard for Glov to understand. "I'm not saying it does, but it's not like he killed someone. Letting him make restitution would have been a perfectly—"

"He tried to drive a hover vehicle while intoxicated. It was only good fortune that his accident resulted in no injuries or fatalities. Reducing his penalty to a mere fine would hardly have been equal to his offense. I doubt such a sum would even seem significant to him."

"So, because his family's rich, we have to put him in jail?"

"No, we put him in jail because that's what the law instructs us to do." Glov shot a disparaging glance at him. "The fact that Governor Nolon abused his authority to punish us for performing our duty reflects upon his character, not our judgment."

The rant drew a bitter chortle from Kohl. "Your judgment, pal—not mine."

A tense and uncomfortable silence fell between them for a long moment. Then Glov mumbled under his breath, "No one forced you to come with me."

"Excuse me?"

"You heard me." The Tellarite aimed a sidelong glare at his partner. "The director put my name on the duty sheet for this patrol, not yours. If you'd really wanted to attend that *fútbol* match, you could have let one of the rookies ride shotgun for me."

Kohl pinched the ridges above his nose, then rubbed some crud from the inside corners of his eyes. "Nice try, Treg, but you seem to be forgetting one important detail."

"And that would be . . . ?"

It pained him to say it, but it had to be said. "I'm your partner. If you're on dust patrol, so am I." He sighed. "Besides, it's not like I'd enjoy the game half as much without you."

His admission coaxed an embarrassed smile from Glov. "Thanks."

"Don't mention it." A small flashing icon on the sensor display snared Kohl's eye. "Hey, look at this. Guess we're not the only ones roaming the galaxy's ass crack."

Glov checked the command display between their seats and tapped it a few times to call up more detailed readings. "Wow, that's big. What do you make of it?"

"Hang on. Scanning it now." Kohl trained the interceptor's sensors on the ship, which was maneuvering into orbit above Tirana III. "It's a Trill design, a *Mardiff*-class industrial ship." He paged through some secondary screens and read a few of the highlights aloud. "Crew complement ranges from as low as twenty-five to as high as sixty. Says here they're used mostly for mining, heavy salvage, and refinery operations." Troubled by suspicions he couldn't name, he keyed in a new series of commands. "I'm running a check on its transponder."

As the onboard computer processed his request, Glov plotted and executed a short-range warp jump. After a momentary blurring of the heavens, the *Sirriam* cruised into orbit close behind the hulking mass of the Trill industrial ship, which looked more like a floating factory than a vessel capable of crossing interstellar distances. "Coming up on their six," the Tellarite said. "Quick scan shows they have no weapons, no shields, and a skeleton crew. I'm reading only twelve life-forms on board—humanoids, species unknown."

"I've got a hit: the *S.S. Basirico*, an excavation-and-recovery ship. Registry . . . Ramatis."

Glov frowned. "That figures."

Kohl inferred his partner's meaning. In the three years since the Borg invasion had laid waste scores of worlds within sixty light-years of the Azure Nebula, criminals had made a practice of fabricating ship registries from worlds on which there no longer existed anyone or anything to corroborate or refute their authenticity. "What do you think? Smugglers?"

"Could be. Or it might be an illegal mining op." He nodded at a console showing a geological profile of the planet below. "Gallicite, kelbonite, noranium, boridium . . . no shortage of minerals worth stealing." He powered up the interceptor's weapons. "Hail them."

With a tap on the comm controls, Kohl opened hailing frequencies. "Attention, mining vessel *Basirico*. This is the Federation Security interceptor *Sirriam*. Please respond." Several seconds passed. Kohl looked askance at Glov, who was locking the interceptor's phasers onto the *Basirico*'s prodigious impulse drive. Glov nodded, and Kohl pressed the transmit key again. "Mining vessel *Basirico*, this is the Federation Security interceptor *Sirriam*. You are ordered to respond and prepare to be boarded. Please acknowledge."

"I hope they try to run," Glov grumbled. "I've got a lock on their warp core. First sign of a power-up, I'll put a hole through that thing so big it'll—"

An alert chirped from the forward console half a second before a thundering blast rocked the *Sirriam* and sent it spiraling toward Tirana III. Sparks erupted from blacked-out consoles, and outside the cockpit canopy, the airless world whipped in and out of sight as the interceptor wheeled and tumbled out of control.

Kohl shouted over the screeching of the fragged impulse drive. "What the hell hit us?"

"No idea!" Glov struggled with the helm controls in a bid to arrest their uncontrolled plunge. "Patch in the backup thrusters! Try to—"

A flash of white light was the last thing Kohl knew . . . and then there was nothing but darkness and silence, forever.

1

Few things vexed Hilar Tohm as much as being kept waiting. Ever since her youth on Trill, all through her years at Starfleet Academy, and since then as an analyst and now a section chief for Starfleet Intelligence, she had prided herself on her punctuality, and she took it as an affront when others failed to extend to her the same degree of professionalism and courtesy. In her opinion, those who insisted on arriving late to scheduled appointments tended to fall into one of two categories: the passive-aggressive, who used their tardiness to exact a measure of revenge on others, and the utterly rude, who kept others waiting as an exhibition of personal power, a means of telling others, *I feel free to waste your time because I think mine is more important.*

She took a sip of tepid oolong tea with lemon and honeysuckle honey, brushed a lock of her curly chestnut hair from her eyes, and glanced at her wrist chrono. It counted down the final thirty seconds to 1600 local time, adjusted for the peculiar variances of chronometry on the Orion homeworld. *He'd better not be late.*

Twenty seconds before the hour, the person for whom she had been waiting stepped through the café's front door, took a cursory look around the room, and spotted her. Slim and blue-eyed, Data was a bit taller than the average human. His complexion was fair, and his head was crowned with a shaggy tousle of light brown hair parted on the right. He dressed in simple clothes—dark trousers and shoes, a cream-colored linen shirt, and a jacket of synthetic leather—and he moved with grace and confidence. Without a wave or any shift in his expression, he slalomed through the room of closely packed tables and back-to-back chairs filled by patrons of dozens of different species, working his way toward her with tireless resolve.

He reached her table and greeted her with one polite nod. "Is this seat taken?"

She responded with their prearranged challenge phrase. "I was saving it for my brother."

"All men are brothers—until the rent comes due." Tohm motioned for him to sit, and he settled into the chair across from her. "Thank you for seeing me on such short notice."

"No problem." She lowered her voice. "What name are you traveling under?"

Data leaned forward and whispered, "Daniel Soong." A one-shoulder shrug and a self-effacing half smile. "Call me sentimental." His mien shifted like mercury, at once sharp and businesslike. "I just want to say that I appreciate your discretion in this matter."

"And I just want to say that if certain notable persons hadn't vouched for you, we wouldn't be talking right now." Impatient, she stole a look at her chrono. "What do you need?"

The human-looking android reached inside his jacket, took out a translucent aqua-colored isolinear chip, and pushed it across the table to within a few centimeters of Tohm's hand. "A comprehensive search of the Orion banking system. The private databases and offline archives."

She extended one finger and sneaked the chip beneath her palm with a magician's sleight of hand. "What am I looking for?"

"Anything related to the finances of the persons and corporations identified on that chip." He cast furtive looks over his shoulders, as if he were concerned about mechanical surveillance or eavesdroppers on one of the most privacy-obsessed worlds in the quadrant. "The entities in question should already be known to your associates. Some of them have been flagged for investigation for more than a century, and all are currently on the SI watch list."

His demeanor was calm and professional, but the scope of what he'd requested put Tohm on edge. "This is quite a bit more than I was led to believe you'd need."

"What degree of aid had you anticipated?"

Studying his reaction, she said, "An address, perhaps. Maybe some comm records. Nothing quite this"—she tapped her finger on the isolinear chip— "incendiary."

The youthful android seemed unfazed by her admission. "Should I interpret your reticence to mean you cannot or will not assist me in this matter?"

"Not necessarily. But I'll need to know more about what I'm investigating."

Concern creased Data's brow, and a thin frown pursed his lips. "I am reluctant to say too much, for a number of reasons."

His evasiveness captured her interest. "What can you tell me?"

"The subject of my inquiry is an individual who has eluded Starfleet custody on at least two occasions, and who has traveled throughout the Federation and beyond under more than a hundred aliases. He possesses knowledge that I think might be vital to Federation security."

Tohm searched Data's face for any hint of mendacity, but his expression was all but inscrutable. "What makes you think the Orion banking industry has the intel you want?"

"As resourceful and independent as this person has proved to be, he still has occasional need of the Federation and its resources. But even if he did not, I believe he is unwilling to sever all ties with our culture. If he is to maintain such contact, however tangential, he must have some manner of financial identity we will recognize and accept. I have ruled out the Bank of Bolarus and the Ferenginar Credit Exchange as the havens for this identity. He would not entrust his fortune to depositories under the control of our rivals, and he cannot be using an account at an institution that reports its holdings to the Federation government. That leaves the Bank of Orion as the most likely shelter for his remaining financial personae."

I'll give him credit for this much: he's thorough.

She slid the chip off the table and tucked it into her pocket. "I'll see what I can do. But I have one more question." He cocked his head and affected a quizzical look, prompting her to ask, "You're not currently on active duty, so why are you *really* looking for this guy?"

Her query seemed to amuse Data, who suppressed a smile and looked at the table for a moment until he recovered his composure. "Let it suffice to say that it is . . . a family matter."

"All right, then." He appeared satisfied to let his answer stand, so she did the same. "I'll need a couple of days. How do I reach you?"

A tilt of his head in the general direction of downtown. "Contact me at the Royal Suite of the Imperial Star Resort, under the name Miller."

"The Imperial Star?" She was certain she must have misheard him. "The one inside the Nalori diplomatic compound?" He nodded. She was about to ask why he was using the *nom de voyage* Miller, then thought better of it. "Fine. I'll be in touch soon."

He stood. "I look forward to hearing from you." They shook hands, and Tohm was surprised to find Data's flesh warm to the touch, and his fingertips slightly callused. He smiled as he released her hand. "Good night."

Tohm watched Data weave his way out of the room, and then she slipped out of the café through its rear service door. For the briefest moment as she stood in the alleyway, she felt the dread of being watched—but when she turned to confront her stalker, she found only an empty lane, darkened windows, and the muffled drone of nighttime traffic in the Orion capital. *You're getting paranoid,* she teased herself. *Maybe you've been a spook for too long.*

Hands tucked into her pockets, she quickened her steps back toward the Federation Embassy. Because as certain as she was that no one was following her, she knew that in her line of work, sooner or later she would be wrong.

Radiant and prismatic, the gas giant's rings arced across the *Enterprise*'s main viewscreen. Picard gazed upon them in wonder, swelling with admiration for their ineffable beauty and harboring unspoken regret over the idea of tampering with such natural marvels.

Limned by the soft glow of bridge consoles, his crew attended to their duties with a minimum of conversation; semimusical response tones punctuated the white-noise hush of life-support systems and the low-frequency pulse of the impulse engines. Gathered around the aft bulkhead's master systems display were Lieutenant Dina Elfiki, the strikingly attractive young senior officer of the ship's sciences division, and two specialists from the astrometrics team: Lieutenant Corinne Clipet, a dark-haired and soft-spoken theoretical physicist from France, and Ensign th'Verroh, an astrophysicist who the year before had chosen to remain in Starfleet, even though it had meant being disowned by his family after Andoria's secession from the Federation. The trio of scientists had been charged with carrying out the principal tasks of the *Enterprise*'s current mission: infusing the rings of Azeban V with the same kind of regenerative metaphasic radiation that had made the Ba'ku planet inside the Briar Patch of such interest to Starfleet.

The trio's low murmuring, full of esoteric jargon and clipped reports, made poor fodder for eavesdropping, so Picard shifted his attention to the port-side station closest to his command chair. The ship's new chief of security, Lieutenant Aneta Šmrhová, was engaged in a hushed but tense exchange with the first officer, Commander Worf. The broad-shouldered Klingon loomed over the slender but athletic human woman, who'd recently had her raven hair shorn to a stylish and asymmetrical bob that swept forward on the right, beneath her jaw.

Šmrhová's struggle to preserve a façade of cool professionalism in the face of Worf's withering criticism was apparent, and Picard wondered—not for the first time in recent weeks—if his first officer was treating her unfairly. The young woman, a native of the Czech city of Ostrava, had served on the *Enterprise* for more than four years without drawing a single negative word from Worf, but since the first day that Picard had promoted her to fill the post left vacant by the death of Lieutenant Jasminder Choudhury, it had seemed as if Šmrhová could do nothing that met with Worf's approval. It felt uncharitable to ascribe Worf's hostility toward Šmrhová and his micromanagement of her job performance to his grief over the violent loss of his inamorata Choudhury, but Picard found himself at a loss for another plausible explanation for his first officer's behavior toward the new security chief. Compounding his concerns was the fact that Worf had pointedly declined several summons to meet with the ship's counseling staff, and after the senior counselor, Hegol Den, had made such a session mandatory, Worf had sat silently through two consecutive appointments. *If this situation doesn't resolve itself in the next day,* Picard decided, *I'll have no choice but to intervene.*

Worf stepped away from the security console and passed Picard as he returned to his seat on the captain's right. His mien was serious and alert. "Our activities continue to attract interest."

"The same ship again?" In the week since the *Enterprise*'s arrival at Azeban V, the crew had detected fleeting signs that they were being shadowed by a cloaked Romulan warbird.

The Klingon's aspect turned grave. "A new signal has been caught on sensors. Lieutenant Šmrhová and Ensign Rosado have reason to suspect our new observer is a Breen warship."

Picard frowned in concern. Just as they had been warned by Starfleet Command prior to starting their mission, they had become a locus for the Typhon Pact's attention. "What of the reports from the Beta Aurealis system? Have they been verified?"

A subtle nod. "A reconnaissance flight by the *U.S.S. Starling* confirmed the presence of a Tzenkethi mobile surveillance platform. It appears to have been deployed to monitor our operations here." He shot a disgruntled look at the rings on the viewscreen. "But if they learn how fruitless our efforts have been, they might soon lose interest."

"I suspect their interest will last as long as our attempts continue." He called up the most recent tactical scans on the command screen beside his chair. "Run three battle drills at random intervals over the next six shifts."

"Aye, sir."

Picard stood and walked aft to the master systems display, where he insinuated himself silently into Elfiki's work group.

As the other officers took note of his presence, their conversation tapered off, and the svelte Egyptian woman turned and graced Picard with a coy smile. "Captain."

"Lieutenant. Has your team made any progress since yesterday?"

Anxious, evasive looks traveled back and forth between Elfiki, Clipet, and th'Verroh. "That depends, sir," Elfiki said. "Do you consider documenting the myriad ways in which our first round of energizing pulses failed to produce anything remotely resembling metaphasic radiation to be evidence of progress?"

"Not as such, no."

She averted her eyes toward the deck to downplay her mild embarrassment. "Then I guess the answer would be no, we haven't made any significant progress. Sir."

"That's nothing to be ashamed of, Lieutenant. Setbacks and negative results are par for the course in scientific research." He gestured at the display. "How do you plan to proceed?"

Elfiki nodded at Clipet. "Corrine?"

The chestnut-haired Frenchwoman stepped up to the MSD and began keying in commands, triggering simulations on several screens. "We believe that part of the reason our first round of experiments yielded no change in the rings' energy output is that too many of the elements and compounds inside the rings are inert. However, there is a high concentration of kytherium in the rings' dust. I think that if we introduce a catalyst such as corvelite, we could break down the kytherium, releasing a number of highly reactive compounds that might respond to our efforts to initiate metaphasic conversion."

It was the most promising lead that Picard's crew had presented to him so far. "Very good. How long until we're ready to proceed?"

"Four days," Elfiki said. "We'll need to replicate a sufficient quantity of the catalyst to seed the rings, but we can't store that much at once, so we'll need to stock up to maximum capacity first, then continue production during the distribution phase."

Picard nodded. "Make it so."

Elfiki, Clipet, and th'Varroh replied in unison, "Aye, sir."

Picard returned to his chair. As he settled in, Worf leaned over and said in a low voice, "Do you think their plan will work?"

It was a legitimate question, but not one Picard knew how to answer. "It's hardly my area of expertise, Number One. But if I were to hazard a guess? I would say no."

Worf's glum mood deepened. "I do not understand why the *Enterprise* was chosen to carry out such an ill-planned experiment. Why not send a science vessel, instead?"

His question led Picard's eye back to the tactical report on his command screen, and the mounting evidence that the *Enterprise* appeared to have become the Typhon Pact's primary object of interest. "I suppose that depends on what, exactly, Starfleet hoped to accomplish by sending us here. If the goal was to replicate the rings of Ba'ku, then perhaps this was an error. But if the idea was to draw the attention of our rivals . . . then I'd have to say we've succeeded beyond their wildest expectations."

It was a slow day in the Happy Bottom Riding Club, the crew lounge of the *Enterprise*. Most of the tables were empty, and only a handful of officers and noncoms were scattered around the spacious compartment decorated in aeronautical memorabilia from twentieth-century Earth. Sal, the bartender, set down two glasses of real booze, one each before Geordi La Forge and Ravel Dygan, then stepped away to let the men contemplate the beverages they'd ordered on a mutual dare.

In front of La Forge was a squat tumbler of *kanar,* a syrupy alcoholic treat from Dygan's homeworld, Cardassia Prime. The chief engineer picked up the glass and rolled it in a slow circle, testing the viscosity of the fluid within; the *kanar* moved like industrial lubricant. He took a whiff of it and wrinkled his nose in confusion. Its sweeter notes seemed enticing, but it was laced with a pungent kick that threatened a less than benign drinking experience.

Wary of imbibing, La Forge said to Dygan, "You first."

The Cardassian operations officer, who was serving on the *Enterprise* courtesy of the Officer Exchange Program, seemed equally suspicious of his pale golden libation. He held it up to the light, sniffed it, then recoiled in fear and revulsion. "What did you say this was called?"

"Tequila." A mischievous grin lit up La Forge's face. "Be careful. It packs a wallop."

Dygan put down the glass. "Maybe this was a bad idea."

La Forge laughed. "Of course it is." He was still chuckling as he shook his head. "I haven't done something this dumb since I was at the Academy."

"My friends and I were much the same as cadets at the military academy on Kora II." The recollection turned his mood wistful. "It's hard to believe so many of them are gone now. Most of the people I knew back then died in the Dominion War." He wore a sympathetic expression as he added, "I'm sure that's a feeling you know all too well."

La Forge nodded. "Sorry to say, yes." He stared at the opaque surface of the *kanar* as he gathered his thoughts. "It's not that I can't make new friends, but it seems to get harder as I get older. And sometimes I just don't seem to get as close to new friends as I did to old ones."

"That's the way of things," Dygan said, staring through the amber lens of liquor in his hand. "We love best those we loved first." Then he took a maudlin turn. "Some things truly are irreplaceable." He banished his blue mood with an affected smile. "But sometimes they come back, eh? Your old friend Data, for instance."

"Yeah. . . . Data." Being reminded of his best friend's reincarnation left the normally gregarious La Forge momentarily speechless. More than four years after he had helped Data go to his doom aboard the *Scimitar* to save Captain Picard from the madman Shinzon and destroy a thalaron weapon that could exterminate entire worlds, La Forge had found himself assisting in his friend's return—inside the android body his creator, Noonien Soong, had made to enable himself to cheat death. All at once, four years of grief had been made moot; four years of loneliness and slow healing had been rendered meaningless. La Forge was overjoyed to have his friend back, but to his surprise, he had also discovered that he felt angry. He masked his unease with an awkward smile. "I still haven't really got my head around that."

Dygan struck an apologetic note. "I didn't mean to pry, or open old wounds."

"Don't worry about it." He dismissed the perceived offense with a wave of his hand. "As we say on Earth, water under the bridge."

After picking up and contemplating the tequila for a few seconds, Dygan set it back down with exaggerated caution. "I don't mean to make light of how confusing your situation must be, but I have to say . . . I envy you, just a little bit." He looked La Forge in the eye. "There are few things I wouldn't give to bring my best friend back from the grave."

The younger man's admission dredged up La Forge's submerged guilt. "I don't want to sound ungrateful, because I'm not. Having Data back is . . . amazing. If I could've done it myself, I would have. But the way it happened raises questions I don't know how to answer."

"Such as . . . ?"

At first, La Forge was reluctant to speak. Then he put aside his reticence and decided to confide in Dygan. "Well, for starters, on a purely semantic level, it's not really him but a *copy* of him. The original Data—body, mind, and soul—went up in flames with the *Scimitar*. This new Data has most of the original's memories . . . but not quite all of them. His memory of that life ends at the moment he uploaded his engrams into B-4's positronic matrix. But—and here's the part I can't quite get a handle on—except for a gap of about a day, he *remembers* being the Data I knew. And what are we, any of us, except the sum of our experiences? If he remembers the life he lived, how can I say he's not really him?"

Silent and pensive, Dygan ruminated on those points for a moment. He looked down at the glass in his hand. "Perhaps we should have saved this conversation for after the first round."

"You opened the floodgates," La Forge said.

"So I did." A far-off look in Dygan's eyes gave La Forge the impression he was thinking something profound. Then the Cardassian said, "I think that if he wasn't the man you knew, you'd have been able to tell when he was standing in front of you. Did he seem the same?"

La Forge thought back to the moment he saw Data sit up on the worktable inside the lab on Mangala, and the discussion they'd had before he departed the *Enterprise* in the *Archeus,* the ship the android had inherited from his father. "Yeah, he did. In every way. . . . It was him, I'd swear it."

"Then it was him."

Could it really be that simple? Was it possible that all the philosophical and ontological conundrums that seemed to accompany Data's resurrection were, in fact, irrelevant? La Forge wanted to think so; questioning his friend's return had felt like an act of denial, as if he were experiencing the stages of grieving in reverse—in effect, mourning his grief.

"I hope you're right," he said.

Dygan slapped a reassuring hand on La Forge's shoulder. "Trust me, sir." He lifted his glass, and La Forge did the same as the Cardassian added, "To old friends."

"To old friends," La Forge said.

He and Dygan downed their drinks in single pours—
then both men doubled over as they sprayed the deck
with spit-takes. La Forge gagged and smacked his
tongue against the roof of his mouth in a futile bid to rid
it of the sickening taste of *kanar,* and Dygan dropped
his glass as he coughed and gasped for air. From the
end of the bar and around the room came the knowing chortles of their shipmates. Pulling himself upright
against the bar, La Forge groaned. "An hour from now
I'm gonna be really sorry I did that."

"Then I envy you again," Dygan said with a grimace,
"because I'm sorry *now.*"

Joyful shrieks and squeals spilled into the corridor from
the *Enterprise*'s day-care nursery, and Doctor Beverly
Crusher felt her son René's pulse quicken as his excitement level surged in response to the sound of other
children playing. The toddler tried to sprint ahead of
her, only to be restrained by her gentle hold on his
wrist. "Calm down, René," Crusher said.

The nursery, located a couple of compartments away
from sickbay on Deck 7, was a bright and cheerful space
set up by the ship's Denobulan assistant chief medical
officer, Doctor Tropp. Its walls and carpeting had been
remodeled in soothing pastel hues, and it had been
stocked with a variety of toys—some educational, some
simply fun, all safe and hypoallergenic.

Crusher let go of René's hand as the door hushed
open ahead of them, and he scampered inside, his cherubic face bright with glee as he joined his friends, a
handful of young children of various humanoid species who ranged in age from eighteen months to three
and a half years. At two and a half, René was right in
the middle of the pack, but his friendly disposition and
gentleness of spirit enabled him to interact easily with

both the older and younger children. Seeing him hug his friends hello brought Crusher a feeling of contentment and an easy smile.

Looking up, she caught the eye of the nursery's principal adult supervisor and beckoned him with raised eyebrows and a small wave. Hailan Casmir was an Argelian teacher, musician, and puppeteer who appeared to be in his early thirties. He wore his blond hair in a loose mane that framed his lean, angular features, which were accentuated by his close-cropped, honey-hued beard. Casmir was married to one of the ship's engineers, a Bajoran woman named Lieutenant Taro Trinell, with whom he had fathered a daughter, Taro Katín, who was just a few months younger than René and had recently become one of the boy's favorite playmates.

Casmir shook Crusher's hand. "Doctor. A pleasure, as always."

"Likewise." She nodded at René. "I just want to let you know I plan on picking him up early today, around 1400, and he'll be out tomorrow."

Her news drew a frown of mild concern from Casmir. "Nothing's wrong, I hope."

"No, no. Just routine vaccinations, but he'll have to be isolated for twenty-four hours afterward, just to make sure he doesn't suffer any unexpected side effects." She crossed her arms and observed the children's playtime frenzy with a clinical eye. "How's everything going?"

"Splendidly," Casmir said. "Little René's become quite the ringleader around here. I don't know how much of that is natural charisma as opposed to the others' expectations of him as the captain's son, but he has a knack for setting the tone to suit his mood."

"Is that really a good thing?"

He shrugged. "It's neither good nor bad. He's got a

talent for imitating behaviors that he sees, and for persuading others to join him in doing things that he likes. On the other hand, he still has a bit to learn about sharing with others. But all of this is normal for a child his age."

She knew that Casmir was right. Her first son, Wesley, had gone through much the same process of socialization, though he had been less prone to taking the lead with his peers. Regardless, she harbored concerns. "Be that as it may, Hailan, try to encourage René to let someone else choose the games once in a while. I don't want the others to fall into a pattern of treating him differently because he's the captain's son."

"I'll do what I can."

His answer sounded agreeable enough, but Crusher sensed there was something he was holding back, something he was trying to avoid saying. "But . . ." she prompted.

"But . . . as he and his peers get older, if they remain on this ship, it won't be possible to separate their perception of his identity from his relationship to the captain. It's a natural part of informal socialization among most humanoids to develop layers of hierarchy. In earlier, less developed cultures, adolescent social groups often split along economic lines. These days, the divisions are usually based on achievements, in either academics or athletics. But on board a starship, where life is far more regimented, and a system of military rank defines the interactions of adults, children tend to model their relationships on those they see every day."

Crusher's first impulse was to debate Casmir's point, but she recalled having seen signs of exactly that kind of unconscious caste system aboard other starships on which she'd served, and it was consistent with accounts she'd heard from people who had grown up on starships or starbases. Children of officers tended to socialize with one another, as did the children of non-coms and enlisted personnel. Friendships that bridged those social divisions were common enough among younger children, but in adolescence, cliques tended to self-segregate based on any number of perceived criteria—including not just achievement but also popularity, species, and, yes, the ranks of their Starfleet parents.

Still, it was difficult for her to imagine her sweet, towheaded boy ever engaging in such superficial discrimination. "You raise some good points," she said to Casmir, "but I'm not sure it's as inevitable as you make it sound. After all, my first son, Wesley, was the child of two Starfleet officers, and he never treated others that way."

Casmir nodded. "You're right—the scenario I'm suggesting is far from preordained. Children's natural tendencies, the size of their social group, and how they're raised can all make a huge difference. Though I'd be willing to guess that in the case of your first son, he didn't start his socialization process as the son of the commanding officer."

"No, he didn't." She turned away from Casmir, hoping to call over René for a farewell hug and a kiss on the cheek before she left to start her shift in sickbay. Then she saw the boy deep in play with his peers, turning tight circles in eager, choppy steps, all of them laughing and whooping and making a happy noise that filled the room. All thought of interrupting him left her mind, and she let herself enjoy the sight of children at play . . . until she realized why their motions all looked so familiar. They all were chasing one another with arms outstretched, fists clenched, thumbs jabbed forward as they whooped at the tops of their lungs; they were pantomiming the firing of phasers, pretending to stun one another, collapsing atop one another in comical piles. And the last child standing was René, who opened his fist long enough to swat the left side of his chest, like a Starfleet officer tapping his combadge to open a channel.

Crusher turned back toward Casmir, who studied her reaction with a sympathetic expression. "So," he said, "I'll see you at 1400, then."

She pretended not to be discomfited by what she'd just seen, viewed now in the context of their conversation. "Yes. If that changes, I'll contact you." With a halfhearted smile, she backed out of the nursery and hurried back to sickbay, wondering as she walked whether it might be time to reconsider her family's future in Starfleet, after all.

2

Like everything else made under the official auspices of the Breen Confederacy, the laboratory code-named Korwat by the Special Research Division was drab, utilitarian, and utterly bereft of even the slightest hint of authentic cultural identity. Any detail, however minor, that might have betrayed the unique aesthetics that underpinned its functions had been stripped away long ago during the facility's design phase, leaving only the soulless practicality of cold machines.

Of all the places in which Thot Konar had hoped to make his mark and ensure his legacy, none had been so bleak or depressing as this. It was a far cry from the arid beauties of the Paclu homeworld inside the Breen Confederacy, his long-departed place of origin. Having since accustomed himself to the close-packed subterranean cities of worlds that dotted the Confederacy's border, or the cramped confines of the military vessels he had served on in his youth, he also found his current assignment disconcerting for its extreme isolation.

His only regular company for the last two hundred-odd days had been his subordinate, fellow SRD scientist Chot Hain. Though neither had spoken openly of anything other than their shared work—the revelation of personal details between colleagues was taboo within Breen culture and expressly prohibited by military regulations—a number of subtle nonverbal cues had led Konar to think Hain was female, though he remained unaware of her species. In truth, he wasn't entirely certain of Hain's gender, but unless and until new evidence contradicted his supposition, he resolved to think of the expert programmer as a female.

By the time he exited his private quarters, concealed head to foot in his people's mandated uniform—grayish green body armor and a roomy snout-shaped headpiece—Hain was already at her station in the main laboratory, at the end of the long passageway from their separate dormitories. She noted his arrival with a brief swivel of her chair in his direction, and her mechanically disguised voice issued from her suit's vocoder and was translated by a companion circuit inside his own helmet: "Sir."

"We have new orders." Konar saw no value to preamble or pleasantries, not when there was much to be done and little time in which to do it. "Command wants us to bring Operation Zelazo on line and deploy all assets immediately."

Hain ceased her labors and struck a confrontational pose as she turned toward Konar. "It's too soon to go operational. We haven't finished testing the control system, and I can't guarantee the synaptomimetic circuits will work as planned. I need more time."

"There is no more time. We have our orders. It's time to put our team in the field."

The junior scientist waved angrily at her screens of benchmark-test data, vital signs, and a thousand other metrics only she seemed to understand. "This is outrageous! Did you explain to Command what'll happen if we overload this system? Not only could we lose contact with our assets in the field, the entire system could crash beyond recovery. I mean, look at the size of that signal! It's not as if I can just run a backup on that, now can I?"

For all her passion and precision, she can be woe-fully impolitic, Konar lamented. "I've explained the dangers to our superiors, at length and in great detail. They've decided that recent developments merit such a steep calculated risk, and it's our duty to carry out their will."

Hearing the orders spelled out in stark and unforgiv-ing terms seemed to quash Hain's objections. "I under-stand." She turned toward her screens for a moment, then looked back at Konar. "Do we have any specific objectives beyond bringing our field team on line?"

"Yes. Download command protocol packet *Hai-rotekija.*"

Konar stood back and waited while Hain opened and reviewed their classified directive from SRD Command. He had already read it and knew how foolhardy it was. He was curious to see if his junior colleague could re-strain her righteous indignation long enough to obey orders. She spent twice as long poring over the file as he had; he wondered whether it was taking her lon-ger to parse their instructions or if she was using the time to collect herself before voicing a reaction. At last, she turned and regarded him with a casual lift of her snout, but her body language was tense and ill at ease. "It'll take two hours to initialize the transmitter," she said. "I'll have a steady uplink to our assets in the field within an hour after that. I need to request three hours of prep time for each agent, to make sure everyone is—"

"You can have one hour per agent, no more."

It was an unreasonable restriction, and they both knew it, but Konar had no choice. His agenda and timetable had been imposed on him by the head of the SRD himself, Thot Tran. He feared the possibility that Hain would choose this moment to make a stand that would bring them both an onslaught of undesirable attention from their betters.

Even concealed by the anonymizing armor of a Breen mask, her dudgeon was palpable. She answered with flat tones of acquiescence. "Very well. I'll limit the checks to vital systems only. Ready to commence Operation Zelazo on your order, sir."

"The order is given."

Without a word, Hain went to work, powering up every system in the lab and launching scores of new applications they hadn't yet started to debug, never mind test. In a matter of hours, their hastily convened operation would swing into action. Konar couldn't begin to estimate their odds of success, given the obstacles that lay ahead for them and those who were depending upon them. All he could do was hope that he and Hain hadn't just inaugurated a future disaster.

Not daring to expect the best but only to avoid the worst, he returned to his private quarters to inform his superiors that their mad scheme was at last under way.

Inside the antechamber, Thot Tran saw nothing at all, only darkness and silence. He knew he was being scanned by a variety of subtle instruments, checked for hidden weapons, discreet elements of potential compound explosives, or elevated vital signs that could suggest he harbored violent intent toward the Confederacy's head of state. Today, at least, he had borne none of those things to his meeting at the *Linnavhava*, the centuries-old official residence of the Breen leader.

Light assaulted him as the door to the domo's private office opened, liberating Tran from the security antechamber. He stepped forward without waiting for his eyes to adjust because he did not want to appear hesitant or timid. To be invited into the home of the domo was a rare event, even for someone of such elevated status as Tran, who served as the director of the Breen military's Special Research Division; it would not do for him to make a poor impression now.

At the end of the long room, seated behind a grand desk, wreathed in shadows broken only by the ambient glow of the holographically projected, gently curved screens that overlapped one another and surrounded him on three sides, was Domo Brex, the appointed leader of the Breen Confederacy. Like his predecessors, he had been elevated to his post by a vote of his peers inside the civil government, out of recognition for his years of service, his excellence as a manager and leader, and his ability to foster consensus on a variety of issues. His annual review had recently seen his tenure extended for another term, and he lorded over his personal sanctum with the relaxed composure of one who lived free of mundane worries.

Sighting his visitor, Brex banished his cocoon of holograms with one grand gesture, sweeping his hands outward in an arc from his chest. "Welcome, Thot Tran."

Tran approached to within a respectable distance of the desk and bowed his head. "I am honored to be received, Domo. How may I be of service?"

"My chief adviser informs me that your team at Korwat has begun their operation. Are the other elements of your initiative ready to move, as well?"

"Yes, my lord. I've seen personally to the details of every facet of this mission."

Brex stood and circled his desk in slow steps. "Good. But I need to impress upon you how vital this project is to the future of the Confederacy." Halting in front of Tran, the domo towered over him. His august presence projected power and menace. "We stand poised at a historic moment of opportunity, Tran. As I predicted, the Romulans' recent political overtures to the Federation have undermined their credibility with some of our more hard-line allies within the Pact. The Tholians' Ruling Conclave, in particular, has begun to lose faith in Praetor Kamemor's judgment, and I expect the Romulans' political capital with the Tzenkethi autarch has also been sharply reduced." All but touching the snout of his mask to Tran's, he asked, "You see the opportunity in this, yes?"

"If the Romulans are unwilling to lead the Pact, we will."

"Precisely." Brex stepped past Tran and kept walking. Intuiting the domo's desire, Tran fell into step behind him as he headed toward a sliding portal that led to a shielded promontory that overlooked the submerged capital city, which sprawled around the *Linnavhava*. Overhead, shafts of sunlight, broken by their passage through dozens of meters of arctic pack ice and a hundred meters of preternaturally clear seawater, danced through the city's great sectioned dome of transparent duranium and dappled the metropolis below. "Once we win the trust of the Tholians and the Tzenkethi, the Kinshaya will fall into line, and we will become the preeminent power within the Typhon Pact—and, by extension, all of local space."

Intrigued by the domo's curious omission, Tran asked, "What of the Gorn, my lord?"

"They have their role to play. As we all do." He rested his hands on a railing and leaned forward as he gazed out at the city. "But great victories, by definition, entail great risks, and this venture of ours is no different. If we want to take the future's reins, we'll need to make terrible sacrifices. Above all, each of our pawns must know as little as possible about their parts in this grand illusion we're about to conjure. The stakes this time are too dear for us to accept failure. We must have victory, at any cost." He looked down at Tran, the force of his personality too great to be contained by his plain disguise. "Do you understand what I'm telling you?"

Not wanting to presume to know the domo's mind, Tran replied, "Perhaps it would be best if you impressed it upon me in simple terms, my lord."

"If I tell you to burn an asset for the good of the mission, you burn it. If I tell you to give up a hundred secrets to protect the one that really matters, you obey without question. And if I need you and all those under your command to lay down your lives for the sake of victory—"

"It will be done without delay. Your word is law."

The domo clapped a massive, powerful gloved hand on Tran's shoulder. "Excellent. Victory is within our reach, Tran; it's time for us to seize it and take our rightful place." He turned Tran to face the city at his side. "Accomplish this task I've set before you, and for the next thousand years the galaxy will call the Breen its masters."

3

Matter and energy swirled in a shimmering tempest inside the replicator nook. Two plates, each adorned by a boneless chicken breast accompanied by sautéed asparagus and roasted parsnips sweetened with maple syrup, solidified with a musical hum from the whirling flurry. Crusher waited until the last glimmer of light and the last sonorous echo had faded before she reached in to retrieve that night's dinner for herself and Picard.

Her husband's voice, as deep as the night and as smooth as silk, carried from their son's adjacent room, where Picard sang a classic French lullaby:

> *"Frère Jacques, frère Jacques,*
> *Dormez-vous? Dormez-vous?*
> *Sonnez les matines! Sonnez les matines!*
> *Din, dan, don. Din, dan, don."*

Hearing the tenderness in his voice, she pictured him standing over René's bed, his gaze wistful as he tucked in his son for what they hoped would be an uninterrupted night of rest.

One of the advantages of the *Enterprise*'s current extended assignment to Azeban V was that Picard and the rest of the crew had been able to maintain regular schedules for nearly a month. There had been few surprises since their arrival, and Picard had taken advantage of their routine's sudden stability to spend more time helping with René. While Crusher prepared their dinner each night, he fed and bathed René, and then dressed the boy in pajamas and a night diaper—still a necessity, though René had coped well with toilet training over the past couple of months—before tucking him in for a few bedtime stories and a final lullaby to coax him to sleep.

Crusher had welcomed the extra help with René's daily routine, not only for the break it afforded her, but because she knew how much Picard cherished every moment with his son. Gone was the man who once had professed so ardently his dislike for and discomfort with children of any age. To see him now, lovingly attending his son, it amazed Crusher that it had taken Picard so long to start a family.

He emerged from René's room attired in loose-fitting civilian clothes and paused a moment to rub his eyes. His face brightened as he saw dinner ready on the table, and he crossed the room to join her and gave her a peck on the cheek. "Everything looks wonderful." They sat down and unfolded their napkins onto their laps, and he picked up the open bottle of wine from the center of the table. "Torrontes. An excellent choice." He half filled her glass, then his own.

"I'm glad you approve." She tasted the white wine, which was crisp and semidry, with pleasing tart notes and a hint of minerality. Its fruity bouquet mingled with the savory aromas of chicken and asparagus and the sweet fragrance of maple-roasted parsnips, and all the various notes complemented one another. Picard set down the bottle and dug into his dinner with a healthy appetite. Crusher took a bite of each item on her plate and followed it with a sip of wine. "Jean-Luc . . . I have an idea I'd like to run past you."

Picard looked up from his meal, at first *en garde* in the face of her verbal gambit, then he relaxed, swallowed, and gave a small nod. "Continue."

"After I dropped off René at the nursery today, I had an interesting conversation with Hailan. We talked about something that you and I haven't given much thought before this."

"Oh?" He set down his fork and gave her his full attention. "What, exactly?"

She chose her words with care. "We were discussing René's progress in socialization, and Hailan noted how well René got along with both older and younger children. I asked him to encourage René to let the other children choose the group's games or have first pick of toys once in a while, because I don't want him to grow up thinking he can behave selfishly just because he's the captain's son."

A sympathetic half nod. "I agree. What did Hailan think?"

"This is the part that troubles me. He thinks that as René gets older, if he remains with you on the *Enterprise* or some other ship, it'll become more and more difficult for him to separate his role within his peer group from his identity as 'the captain's son.' After I left the nursery, I looked into this myself, and it seems Hailan's right. There's no telling how René might deal with it. He might embrace it and become self-conscious, fearing to make a single mistake that might sully his—or your—reputation. Or he might rebel against it, and get into who knows what kind of mischief. But even if he manages not to let it affect him too much, he can't control how others are going to treat him. Some people will walk on eggshells around him because they're scared of drawing your wrath, and some will try to curry favor with him because they hope to use him to influence you. That's a lot of pressure for a young boy."

Her appraisal of the situation left Picard pensive. He removed his napkin from his lap and set it on the table next to his plate. "You're right. I hadn't given this much consideration. But it sounds as if Hailan raised some excellent points." He stroked his upper lip with his index finger for a second. "Do you have an opinion as to what we might do about this?"

She gathered her courage to make what she expected would be an unpopular suggestion. "I don't think it requires immediate action. All the reading I've done suggests that among very young children, the effects of such social connections are negligible. It won't really be an issue for another six or seven years. That being said . . . we might want to consider laying some ground-work for an eventual transfer away from starship duty."

"Hm." At first his reaction was inscrutable. Then he gave a slight nod. "Yes. That makes sense. I can ask my friend Louis on Earth to let me know of any opportunities that might arise in the private sector, and there's bound to be a university somewhere in the Federation that'll need a new professor of archaeology at some point in the next decade." He cracked a smile. "If worse comes to worst, we can always move back to the vine-yard in Labarre."

Unable to hide her incredulity, she arched one eyebrow at her husband. "You seem to be taking this in stride. To be honest, I expected you to put up more of a fight."

He picked up his wine, enjoyed a generous sip, then put down the glass. "Beverly . . . I've given more than six decades of my life to Starfleet. I don't think it's unreasonable to say that perhaps that's enough." He spread his napkin back across his lap and picked up his fork and knife. "In any event, as you said, it's not a decision to be made in haste. We have time."

Crusher was surprised to find her husband so receptive to the idea of returning to civilian life, and the ease with which he'd entertained the notion of casting aside his Starfleet career troubled her. As she watched him dig back into his dinner, she put a name to another feeling that was nagging at her: disappointment. The realization of her own hidden agenda gave her pause.

On some level, I was actually hoping he'd talk me out of it.

Before she could say anything to reopen the discussion, the overhead comm chirped and was followed by Worf's voice. *"Bridge to Captain Picard."*

The captain put down his utensils on his plate. "Picard here."

"Captain. You are needed on the bridge. We have new orders from Starfleet."

"On my way. Picard out." He pushed his chair back and leaned across the table's corner to kiss the top of Crusher's head. "Duty calls." As Crusher watched her husband hurry out, she found it impossible to imagine him being happy anywhere but on the *Enterprise*.

Looking out of place in gray trousers and a natural-linen shirt, Picard compensated by taking charge of the bridge with his voice as he emerged from the turbolift. "Number One: Report."

Worf stood from the center chair and turned to face Picard. "Federation Security has issued a full-sector alert. One of its patrol ships, a two-man vessel called the *Sirriam,* vanished without a trace two days ago in the Tirana system, two-point-two light-years from here." Picard settled into his command chair and called up the official orders from Starfleet Command. Worf sat down in his own chair and continued as Picard read. "Starfleet Command has instructed all vessels in this sector to aid the search. The *Enterprise* is the closest vessel to the *Sirriam*'s last known coordinates. Admiral T'Vos has ordered us to suspend our experiments and investigate."

Picard was alarmed to find Starfleet's official tactical report sparse on details. "Has there been any contact with suspected threat vessels in or around the Tirana system?"

"Negative." Perhaps anticipating Picard's next question, the Klingon added, "Glinn Dygan has completed an astrometric survey of the sector and found no anomalies that could account for the ship's disappearance. Lieutenant Šmrhová is monitoring known Typhon Pact frequencies, but we have detected no enemy signal traffic in the area."

It seemed to Picard that his first officer had matters well in hand. "What do we know about the Tirana system, Number One?"

"Not much." He swiveled his chair aft, toward Lieutenant T'Ryssa Chen, who was working at the master systems display.

The half-Vulcan, half-human contact specialist noted Worf's turn in her direction, and she stepped forward to address him and the captain. "Tirana's an A3 IV main sequence star. Seven planets: three rocky inner worlds, of which one is molten and the other two lack atmospheres, plus four gas giants. No indigenous life-forms, no known inhabitants."

"What would they have been doing there?" Picard wondered aloud.

Chen treated his rhetorical musing as a serious inquiry. "Their flight plan indicated it was a routine checkpoint on their assigned patrol route. They might have encountered smugglers, or detected a cloaked Typhon Pact ship, or tried to aid a civilian vessel in distress, or—"

"Thank you, Lieutenant," Worf cut in, silencing her torrent of hypotheses. He looked at Picard. "Until we have reason to believe otherwise, Captain, I recommend we treat this as a rescue operation—in which case, time will be of the essence."

As usual, Worf's reading of the circumstances agreed with Picard's. "Quite right, Number One." He raised his voice. "Helm, set course for the Tirana system, maximum warp. Engage."

"Aye, sir," Lieutenant Joanna Faur replied as she took the *Enterprise* to warp speed, filling the ship with the rising drone of its faster-than-light acceleration.

Glinn Dygan looked up from the ops console and seemed almost sad as he watched warp-stretched stars snap past on the main viewscreen. "A pity we didn't get to finish our experiments. It would have been a most remarkable thing to see." With a muted note of pessimism he added, "Assuming, of course, that it actually worked this time."

That might have been a bit much to hope for, Picard suspected. Something about the mission to Azeban V had never felt quite right to him. No matter how many times he'd reviewed the scientific briefs for the experiment, he had been unable to persuade himself that they were even remotely plausible. He was hardly an authority on subquantum chromodynamics and their applications to the spontaneous inception of metaphasic radiation, but he'd embraced the assignment with more than a small degree of doubt for its success. Now, the haste with which Starfleet had ordered such an involved experiment abandoned only compounded his suspicions.

He stood to head for the turbolift, then stopped beside Worf. "Have security and medical personnel prepared to initiate rescue protocols as soon as we reach the Tirana system. Make sure we have EVA suits ready, in case we need to send them into vacuum or a hostile environment. Also, have Commander La Forge prep engineering for a salvage operation."

"Aye, sir." Worf glanced toward Šmrhová, then back to the captain. "I recommend we also prepare tactical response plans—in case this turns out *not* to be a salvage-and-rescue."

It was a wise precaution that Picard himself had been about to order. "Make it so. You have the conn, Number One." Leaving Worf to ready the ship for whatever lay ahead, Picard walked back to the turbolift, determined to make the most of what might be his last quiet night alone with his wife and son before the vagaries of command tore him away once more.

4

Sequestered and shielded from accidental eavesdropping and curious eyes, Thot Konar powered up the subspace transmitter inside his quarters. He tuned its frequency with delicate nudges on its sensitive controls. Almost as an afterthought, he confirmed the encryption cipher was locked in, a safeguard upon which the mission and all their lives depended. The channel was open, but the response was slow. Konar feared he was transmitting in vain, that no one would answer, and he would be doomed to end his days entombed with Hain in this bunker.

Don't give in to paranoia. It was a simple mantra, but one he needed.

His encrypted hail was received, and in a fleeting crackle of static, his superior answered. Even though, in theory, only Thot Tran should have access to this comm channel, his challenge code appeared on the screen, affirming his identity and assuaging Konar's anxieties. *"Your transmission is late,"* said the director of the SRD. *"What is Korwat's mission status?"*

"All is proceeding on schedule." Konar relayed a data packet with the latest metrics from the base's internal monitors. "Units One through Four have been activated, and preliminary field tests have been promising. However, my operations manager insists we need at least another six hours to be certain that all systems will perform as intended in the field."

"Unacceptable. We have to compensate for a tactical error committed by the Spetzkar. In order to capitalize on our best opportunities, we need to proceed without delay."

Konar had suspected that the recent changes to the mission's timeline had been the consequence of a blunder by the Spetzkar, the elite special forces of the Breen military, with whose "assistance" the SRD had been saddled since the start of this hastily conceived operation. Now he knew for certain. "I am aware of the inflexibility of our schedule, sir. However, I concur with Chot Hain's assessment: If we spend the necessary minimum time in preparation now, we can avoid far costlier and less predictable delays that might arise later."

His argument was met by a long moment of silent contemplation from Tran. *"As you've said, Konar, our timetable is not flexible."*

"And what of our deployment plans? Are they also beyond discussion?" He called up several scenarios designed to govern the actions of assets in the field and patched them through to Tran on a split-screen feed. "I've reviewed these protocols and found them wanting."

His accusation was answered by defensive hostility. *"In what respects?"*

"They have no clear terms of engagement. Most of them have omitted several critical details of infrastructure or local geography. All but one lacks anything resembling a realistic exit strategy. Committing our agents on these terms will expose them to unnecessary risks."

"It is not for you to decide what risks are necessary. That choice belongs to the domo."

Tran's rebuttal left Konar floundering for a response. Until that moment, he had never heard the authority of the domo himself invoked in connection to Operation Zelazo. If the domo was involved in the planning of the mission, then any further objections Konar might make would only serve to blemish his military record beyond repair. "I didn't realize the domo was aware of our operational details, or that its sacrifices were intentional."

"In the future, you might find it beneficial to obey orders rather than debate them."

Konar bowed his head. "Understood, sir." Mustering what remained of his courage, he asked, "Can you clarify how Chot Hain and I are to execute these protocols? Our only desire is to carry out our orders and achieve our objectives, but we see no viable path to those goals."

His request was met by a disdainful downward dip of Tran's helmet. *"You disappoint me, Konar. We assigned you four of the BID's finest field operatives, agents renowned for their abilities at improvisation and adaptation. Do you really have so little faith in them?"*

The question was a rhetorical snare into which Konar refused to stumble. "It's for their sake alone that I ask these questions, sir. I don't want to squander such precious resources by relying upon faulty assumptions or outdated intelligence."

"Save your questions." Tran's patience had clearly expired. *"Bring your facility on line and deploy those assets. It's time to strike—before our enemies realize what we're really doing."*

When the hour came for Hilar Tohm's second meeting with Commander Data, she found herself in the position of being the latter to arrive. Nestled in one of the poorer quarters of Orion's capital city, the basement-level bar she'd selected for their rendezvous was dark and seedy but nowhere near as dangerous as it appeared. This late at night, however, it was packed with an odd mix of petty criminals and corrupt police, dabo hustlers and fleshmongers, out-of-work session musicians and fresh-from-work cooks and bussers from nearby restaurants, as well as a minor legion of alcoholics ranging from the highly functional to the barely conscious.

As agreed, Data was alone in the last booth at the end of the room, with his back to the wall and his eyes on Tohm from the moment she stepped through the front door. She sat on the banquette opposite his and folded her hands as she leaned forward. Heady fumes wafted up from his glass, and she wrinkled her nose at the potent perfume of alcohol. "What're you drinking?"

"Based on my oral analysis of the compound's ingredients, I have surmised this is the bartender's failed attempt to mix a Saurian Slammer. His ratio of Saurian brandy to Delovian nectar seems to have been inverted, and he failed to finish the recipe with the traditional dash of Arcturian bitters. If your question was a solicitation for a suggestion, I cannot recommend this."

"Noted." Her delicate fingers snaked up her jacket's sleeve and inside the fold of her shirt cuff, from which she retrieved an isolinear chip that she palmed and slid across the table to Data with expert sleight of hand. "The intel you wanted."

Data laid his hand over hers, as if they were intimates sharing a moment of comfort in contact. "Bless you." He let her slip her hand free, leaving the chip behind under his palm, and then he drew his hand back to his side and pocketed the chip. "Were there any complications?"

She shrugged off the question. "Nothing insurmountable." Watching his face for any sign of betrayed emotion, she added, "I have to admit, I was impressed by the sheer volume of raw data we found on this Vaslovik and his aliases. Who is he to you?"

"An acquaintance of interest."

His emotional control was absolute, showing not a hint of what might lurk beneath his surface. Tohm remained committed to drawing him out, somehow. "He's quite a peculiar fellow. I'm intrigued by some of the implications in his financial history. If I'm reading those reports correctly, he has to have been around for an unusually long time—centuries, at least. But his profile lists him as human. Did I miss something, or does that seem a bit strange?"

"I would be the first to admit that Mister Vaslovik is a *singular* subject."

The android's face gave away no secrets, but his evasiveness in the face of leading questions was telling, so Tohm pressed harder. "Even more remarkable is the fact that when I tried to run a cross-referenced search on Mister Vaslovik, there wasn't a shred of information about him or any of his aliases in Starfleet's databases. And that's odd, since almost every known person in recorded history has at least some kind of abridged biographical extract. But not your subject. He might as well be a figment of our imaginations for all Starfleet claims to know about him. . . . Which would make sense if his virtual history had been, shall we say, *expunged*."

"A fascinating hypothesis," Data said, artfully neither confirming nor denying any aspect of her supposition. "Not one I recommend you pursue, however."

"What aren't you telling me?"

Her accusatory question seemed to amuse him. "A great many things. For the most part, I am doing you a favor. The less you know about Vaslovik's life and work, the safer you will be."

"No doubt." He sounded sincere, but Tohm had met too many expert liars in her career to accept his assurances at face value. "Your concern for my safety is touching, Commander, but in my line of work, knowledge is power. I've taken some serious risks to get these records for you. A bit of quid pro quo doesn't seem like much to ask in return."

He frowned. "Things are not always what they seem." He shimmied out of the booth, stood, and offered her his hand. "Thank you for your help. I owe you a debt of gratitude."

It was time to concede rhetorical defeat. She shook his hand. "You're welcome."

"Good-bye." He let go of her hand and walked away down a dim, narrow hallway to the bar's rear exit. Tohm heard the door open, admitting the dull roar of the city night, and then it slammed shut, filling the hallway with echoes. *So much for getting a straight answer.*

An Orion waitress, barely out of her teens and so rail-thin that it made Tohm want to break the girl like a dry twig, shuffled in lazy steps to stand beside the booth. She looked down at Tohm, her eyes half-closed from either exhaustion or boredom. "What can I bring you?"

"Nothing. I was just leaving."

The green-skinned youth rolled her eyes, as if this were the greatest imposition she'd ever suffered, and then she slouched away to annoy some other customer. Tohm got up from the booth and left the bar by the front entrance, emerging onto a sidewalk bustling with pedestrian traffic, a dense mix of tourists and locals, Orions and offworlders, all jumbled together.

Swallowed up and made anonymous by the steady current of moving bodies, Tohm walked without fear down familiar streets, following a well-known route back to the Federation Embassy. Hands tucked into her pockets, head down, she felt all but invisible in the night . . . and yet, just as she had the last time she'd met with Data, she felt a sudden rush of paranoia, an inescapable sensation of being observed and tracked. Making use of reflections in vehicles' windshields and storefronts' windows, she searched for any sign of her shadow, only to once again find herself seeking after phantoms.

Her unease abated only slightly as she reached the embassy gate, flashed her identicard to the Starfleet sentries, and passed through to the secure diplomatic compound. Safe once more on friendly ground, she cast a final look back at the street, only to find her fears still at large.

Searching the night for a threat she couldn't name, she recalled a bit of advice she'd been given years earlier by one of her first mentors inside Starfleet Intelligence: *Never go looking for danger,* he'd told her. *It'll find you soon enough all on its own.*

5

Hours had passed since the *Enterprise*'s arrival in the Tirana system, and the crew had used every moment since then to execute their most intensive search patterns and thorough sensor sweeps, all to no avail. Worf stalked from one bridge station to the next, hoping at each stop to receive welcome if belated news of progress, but no one had anything positive to report.

Chen had reconfigured the bridge's aft consoles to search for subspace transmissions, distress signals on any and all known frequencies, any sign of artificial interference, and naturally occurring subspace radio "dead zones," but she had found the Tirana system quiet except for the constant scratch of cosmic background radiation. Šmrhová had found no evidence of wreckage, debris, or energy emissions consistent with beam weapons or high-yield detonations, such as plasma charges or photon torpedoes, and Dygan's meticulous survey of the surface of Tirana II, an airless world that had been deemed more habitable than Tirana I solely by virtue of the fact that its surface wasn't a molten hell, had yielded no sign of the missing Federation Security interceptor *Sirriam,* or its two patrol officers.

The turbolift door opened with a low hiss, and Captain Picard stepped out, this time attired in his standard duty uniform. He moved with a quick stride, his impulse to action clear in his bearing. "Any progress, Number One?"

"Not yet, sir." Worf met Picard in the center of the bridge. "We have detected no transmissions, found no evidence of battle, and no sign of the ship or its pilots." He nodded at the image of Tirana II on the main viewscreen. "Our initial sweep of the second planet's surface was negative, but we have begun a Level One search, starting from the polar latitudes."

Picard's concern manifested as a frown. "And what if the *Sirriam* is on the third planet?"

"I have ordered the *Roanoke* to conduct its own independent search. Lieutenant Commander Havers will command the runabout. She is gathering her flight team now."

"Very good." Speaking more confidentially, the captain asked, "Have we been able to acquire any reliable sensor readings of this system made during the time of the disappearance?"

Worf shook his head. "No, sir. The system is unpopulated and has few exploitable natural resources of any significance. Because it has no obvious tactical or strategic value, no long-range sensors monitor its activity, and it is rarely patrolled."

The captain stared at the screen, his brow creased in concentration. "If this system is so unremarkable, why was the *Sirriam* here?"

"Punishment detail," Worf said. Noting the captain's surprised reaction, he added, "Governor Nolon of Tyberius Prime took offense when the pilots arrested his son for a civil infraction." He shot a dour look at the screen. "What I want to know is, if the *Sirriam* was destroyed, who did it, and for what reason? And why is there no evidence of it?"

Picard met Worf's queries with a grim nod. "Excellent questions, Number One." He sighed. "For the moment, however, we need to confine our investigation to matters of a more timely nature." The captain stepped forward, closer to the ops and conn stations. "Glinn Dygan, how many terrestrial moons orbit this system's gas giant planets?"

The Cardassian checked his console. "Nineteen, Captain."

"Could the *Sirriam* have crash-landed on any of them?"

Dygan sorted through vast amounts of sensor data, winnowing his results with swift precision. "Yes, sir. The interceptor could, in theory, have survived an emergency landing on eleven of those moons. The others are too geologically active to make survival feasible."

"I want every shuttle we have prepped for a recon mission," Picard said. "We need close-range scans of every possible landing site for the *Sirriam* as soon as possible."

The ops officer struck a dubious note. "Does that not seem . . . *excessive,* sir?"

"Mister Dygan, if the *Sirriam* is intact and stranded on some solid body within this star system, then its pilots very likely have less than eight hours of air left to breathe. Whatever steps we take to locate and rescue them, it is imperative that we do so with great haste. Is that clear?"

Duly chastised, Dygan turned his gaze back toward his console. "Aye, sir. I will need two additional operations managers to coordinate that many simultaneous recon missions."

"Conscript whomever you need." Picard returned to his chair, and Worf stayed close at his side. After they sat down, the captain's demeanor became graver still. "Number One, has Lieutenant Šmrhová run any scans to check for cloaked ships in the system?"

"Yes, sir. She used the protocols we refined during the mission to Mangala."

As if Worf might be hiding something, Picard prompted him, "And . . . ?"

"She detected no cloaked vessels in the vicinity."

The captain appeared unconvinced. "Assume for a moment, lack of evidence notwithstanding, that the *Sirriam* was destroyed. If so, it must have been taken by surprise."

Worf nodded. "That stands to reason."

"Interceptors such as the *Sirriam* are fast and highly maneuverable, at both impulse and warp, and they have excellent sensors. The only way I can imagine that ship being attacked and unable to escape would be if it were ambushed—which suggests a cloaked adversary."

"Perhaps," Worf said. He did not want to contradict his captain without cause, but too much of Picard's hypothesis depended upon facts not in evidence. On the other hand, he had learned to trust Picard's instincts during their long years of shared service. The captain had more than earned the right to ask for Worf's support, even when all he had to go on was a hunch. For now, Worf decided, that was enough. "I will ask Šmrhová to run variations on the cloak-detection protocols. If there is a ship here using an updated cloaking device, we might be able to expose it by making unexpected random changes to our sensor frequencies."

"Make it so, Number One." The captain drew a deep breath and put on a brave face. "But for all our sakes, let's hope I'm wrong, and that we find the *Sirriam* before its time runs out."

"The *Enterprise* is continuing its orbit of the second planet. They don't appear to have detected us, but increased energy levels inside its shuttlebay suggest they are preparing to launch an unknown number of support craft."

Thot Raas, commander of the Breen cruiser *Mlotek,* acknowledged tactical officer Zadlo's report with a single nod and took a moment to consider the evidence in hand. As he'd feared, the disappearance of the Federation patrol ship several days earlier had triggered a swift response—and, as he'd warned his superiors would be the case after reviewing the latest reports of Starfleet's deployments in the sector, the *Enterprise* was the first starship sent to investigate.

We meet again, Raas brooded. *But this time the advantage is mine.* He took a perverse satisfaction in concealing his ship from the *Enterprise*'s sensors using the same methods the *Enterprise* had employed during its recent action against the factory he'd discovered on Skarbow III. Hidden within the polar magnetic field of Tirana IV, a massive gas giant, the *Mlotek* was operating at minimum power, a virtual ghost in the EM maelstrom.

Pazur, the first officer, ended her muted conversation with communications officer Vess and crossed the command deck to join Raas. "The *Enterprise* continues scanning all frequencies and transmitting hails to the missing patrol ship. It would appear they are proceeding on the assumption that this remains a rescue mission, or, at worst, a salvage operation."

"Good. Starfleet's search-and-rescue protocols are far more labor-intensive than their search-and-destroy patterns. That should buy us some time." He laid his hand on Zadlo's padded shoulder. "How long until the *Enterprise* is out of range, on the far side of the planet?"

Zadlo keyed several variables into his panel and studied the results on his screen. "Four minutes. They'll be in the sensor blind for just under two minutes."

Raas looked at Pazur. "Coordinate all stations. As soon as *Enterprise* enters the dead zone, we need to climb free of the magnetic field. Then we have to alert Thot Tran, before the *Enterprise* finds something it shouldn't. I'd prefer not to start a war by engaging them directly, but I will if necessary. I'm counting on you to make sure I don't have to."

"Sir, the difficulty in that scenario lies not in emerging to send the transmission, but in returning to cover afterward, before we're detected. If your objective is to avoid confrontation, it would make more sense to remain under cover and wait for the *Enterprise* to withdraw."

He wondered sometimes whether his second-in-command hoped to usurp his position by luring him into a clumsy error, or if she might in fact be guilty of harboring a negligent degree of naïveté. "Pazur, the *Enterprise* isn't going to withdraw until it finds what it came for, or until it's given a compelling reason to do so. We can satisfy neither of those needs, so we must seek aid from someone who can. As for the risk of breaking cover to send the alert, it can't be avoided. If we do nothing but wait and hope for the *Enterprise* crew to grow bored with their search, we'll all but guarantee our eventual discovery—and this entire mission will have been for nothing."

Pazur struck a defiant pose. "After the setback we suffered at Skarbow, I thought you'd welcome a chance to settle accounts with the *Enterprise* and its captain."

"If you ever hope to command a ship of your own, you'll need to learn how to separate the personal from the professional. Knowing one's opponents—understanding their strengths and shortcomings, their tendencies and passions—is not about developing vendettas. Grudges are nothing but dead weight, Pazur. Never forget that."

"What, precisely, should our message to Thot Tran say?"

Raas pondered that. He had to at least consider the possibility that the *Enterprise* or some other ship or entity might intercept the message in transit and eventually decode it. Prudence demanded he take steps to guard against such a breach. "Set encryption mode *zagadka*, idiomatic cipher *klamac*. Message to read as follows: 'At sunset, the weevil digs in the grain. Raptors circle the hollow. The steed stands in the forest. The farmer must ring the bell before dark.' Message ends. Make certain it is marked for Thot Tran's eyes only."

"Understood, sir." Pazur walked back to Vess to see the message prepared, and then she continued her circuit of the command deck, preparing each station for the intricate choreography Raas expected of them in just a few minutes' time. On the main screen, the Starfleet cruiser slipped out of view beyond the curve of the second planet's northern hemisphere. As the last trace of it vanished from sight, Pazur posted a countdown on the viewscreen. "Thirty seconds until they enter the blind spot. All stations, stand by." Seconds ticked away, a steady erosion of moments, and when the timer on-screen ran out, it switched to a new, two-minute countdown. "Helm, z plus thirty thousand, full thrust. Comms, stand by to transmit on my mark. Tactical, stand ready to engage cloaking device."

Helm officer Tren replied, "Clearing the magnetic

DAVID MACK

field in nine seconds. Eight. Seven." The scant moments stretched out as he counted down the seconds, as if tempting fate to expose the *Mlotek* to discovery, until finally he declared, "We're clear."

"Transmitting now," Vess said. "Initiating signal, waiting for confirmation."

"There's no time," Raas insisted. "Send the burst now."

Pazur put herself between Raas and Vess. "Sir, that's a clear contravention of protocol."

He was in no mood to argue with her. "We have seconds in which to act, Pazur. If we—"

"Confirmation received," Vess said, obviating the brewing debate. "Burst packet away."

Fortune favors us for a change. Relieved beyond words, Raas decided not to test his luck. "Helm, z minus thirty thousand, full thrust. Comm systems back to standby."

Tren guided the ship on its vertical drop back into the shelter of Tirana IV's magnetic field. "Z minus thirty thousand, sir. Now answering all-stop, holding at station."

The timer on the main screen ticked down through its final seconds, and a few moments later, the *Enterprise* reappeared from behind the thumbnail curve of Tirana II.

"Good work, everyone," Raas said. "The delicate part is done. Next comes the hard part. Now . . . we wait."

6

The chronometer on the bridge of the *U.S.S. Atlas* flipped from 0759 to 0800, and first officer Commander Sophie Fawkes swiveled the center seat toward the turbolift, which opened as if on cue. As reliable as a quantum clock, Captain Morgan Bateson emerged and greeted his XO with a polite but taut smile behind his dark brown beard. "Good morning, Fawkes."

"Good morning, Captain." She picked up the padd at her side, stood, and handed the device to Bateson. "No news from the planet, and all decks answer sitrep normal."

Bateson reviewed the shift report. "I'd hardly call our current status normal, would you?" He handed back the padd and shook his head. "It feels like a ghost ship, it's so damned empty. What operational genius thought a skeleton crew could run a *Sovereign*-class starship?"

She wrapped the bad news in an awkward smile. "Um, I believe that would be you, sir."

"Blast it to hell, don't remind me." He settled into his chair, and Fawkes remained on her feet beside him. A quizzical look scrunched his brow. "When you say 'no news from the planet,' does that include the shore patrol?" She tried to hide a frown, only to wince instead. Bateson sighed. "It's all right, Sophie, I'm sitting down now. Just tell me what happened."

To refresh her memory, she called up the arrest reports on her padd. "The consensus appears to be that some kind of a brawl started at an . . . *adult* entertainment center, sometime around 0320. About two dozen of our personnel were involved, and witnesses claim one of our officers assaulted and incapacitated five members of the local police force."

The captain pinched the bridge of his nose. "Please tell me it wasn't Or-Tal."

"I would, but that would be a lie, sir. He's being held pending bail."

Bateson winced. "Doesn't *that* set a fine example for the crew. Our second officer gets himself arrested fighting with police. I can hardly wait to explain *this* to Starfleet Command. Contact the Federation Embassy on the surface and have him bailed out, please."

"Aye, sir." Fawkes chose not to add insult to injury by pointing out the irony that Or-Tal was also the ship's chief of security. She reasoned the irascible Miradorn would catch enough hell as it was when he finally made it back to the ship. *No need to throw fuel on the fire.* "What about the rest of our people who got nicked last night?"

She recognized the conflict raging behind Bateson's glower. The disciplinarian in him clearly wanted to let his rambunctious junior personnel suffer for their mistakes, but his sense of duty to his crew made the notion of leaving them in foreign custody unacceptable. "Add their names to the bail bond and have Ambassador Císol expedite it. I want those people back here by 1400 and scrubbing out the heads on the rec deck by 1405." He looked past Fawkes at the image of Orion on the main viewscreen and rubbed his thumb against his fist. "To hell with this 'extended shore leave' charade. Junior personnel can stay on the surface for now, but I want all senior officers and bridge officers recalled, on the double."

"Are you sure that's necessary, sir? I think this is the first shore leave Doctor Kitto's taken since she came aboard three years ago, and I hear Mister Tzasiz is on a winning streak in one of the casinos."

Her appeal garnered no sympathy from Bateson. "You can offer them my apologies once they're back on board, but I don't want to risk our CMO and chief engineer winding up on the next arrest report from the shore patrol. Rescind their leaves with immediate effect."

"Yes, sir." Fawkes worried that, in contrast to the quiet mood that reigned aboard the *Atlas,* her captain seemed extraordinarily on edge. She knew why, of course, but it troubled her.

Before she could think of a politic way to raise the topic with him, an alert warbled from the security console, turning both their heads toward Lieutenant Karithal, a slender Thallonian woman with a ponytail of jet hair and a deep scarlet complexion, who served as the *Atlas's* deputy chief of security. She silenced the alert and reported in a calm and softly lilting voice, "An attempted security breach has been reported at the meeting site's perimeter."

The news brought Bateson to his feet. "Who tried to breach the site?"

Karithal looked for an answer, then shook her head. "It doesn't say, sir."

He became more agitated. "Is there damage? Was anyone hurt?"

Once again, the deputy chief was at a loss. "I've read you the entire message, sir. I've sent a request for more details, but it hasn't been acknowledged."

The captain paced toward Karithal, then back toward Fawkes, then toward his chair, his hands moving erratically, as if he were desperate to hit something or choke someone. "It might be hours before someone gives us a straight answer, if then." He was like a wild thing suddenly caged, and it was obvious that it rankled him. "To hell with this," he muttered. He raised his voice as he quick-stepped toward the turbolift. "I'm going down there to find out what the hell just happened. Karithal, sound Yellow Alert and have an armed security team meet me in Transporter Room One. Fawkes, you have the conn." He strode inside the waiting turbolift and snapped, "Deck Two!" Then the doors closed, leaving Fawkes once again in command—but no closer to having the slightest idea what the hell was happening on the Orion homeworld below.

For a few blissful moments, Captain Morgan Bateson was aware of nothing except the placid haze of the transporter beam, the ineffable sense of being outside himself, a consciousness in fleeting transition, free of its prison of flesh, however briefly.

Then came the tingling embrace of the annular confinement beam, the subtle galvanic sting of rematerialization, and the fading mellisonance of the beam underscored by a low rush of displaced air. A busy street in Orion's capital took shape around him, and it was pandemonium: shouting voices, soldiers and police running every which way, the distant bleating of alarms. It was an hour before dawn, but where Bateson expected to see a black sky filled with stars, he saw only a salmon-hued glow, the product of urban light pollution run amok.

As the confinement beam released him from its protective grip, Bateson turned to look behind him. He stood outside the main gates of the Bank of Orion, a magnificent corkscrew skyscraper in the heart of the eclectic metropolis. Built not to resemble a fortress but to serve as one, the financial institution's headquarters projected an aura of majesty and invulnerability. *Exactly what one would want in a bank,* Bateson realized. The enormous building loomed large in the capital's skyline, and it was ringed entirely by a twenty-meter-tall fence of tritanium bars topped with barbed wire and backed by an invisible force field and a fifty-meter-deep drop that Bateson was surprised hadn't been filled in with murky water and underfed aquatic predators.

The only street-level route across the chasm was the walled bridge on the other side of the main gates, and sentry houses at either end of the bridge were equipped with military-grade antivehicular and antipersonnel weapons, which were manned by a well-armed and expertly trained private security force. There were secret underground passages that led in and out of the bank, but those were even more fiercely defended than the main entrance.

Caught in the crisscrossing foot traffic outside the gate, Bateson stumbled as someone much larger than him shouldered him out of the way. He turned, ready to fire off a scathing stream of invective, but held his tongue as he saw who had jostled him: a hulking Gorn archosaur carrying a battle rifle. Gorn troops were all around him, intermingled with security personnel from the *Atlas*—some of them in uniform, some undercover in civilian garb—and what looked like a battalion of Orion riot police, decked out in body armor and black-visored helmets, and carrying transparent-aluminum shields and a variety of nonlethal weapons. Bateson bladed through the Brownian chaos of dodging bodies toward the closest member of his crew, a Selay lieutenant from the security division. "Zsestoz!"

The lanky reptilian turned and snapped to attention, apparently surprised to see Bateson on the planet's surface. "*Ssssir!*" His enunciation of the *s* sound was exaggerated when it came at the start of a word, a biological affectation he couldn't help.

"What the hell happened? We can't get a straight answer through the regular channels."

Zsestoz flicked his tongue and hissed. "The local police and bank *sss*ecurity haven't told us anything, *sss*ir. All we've heard was the *sss*ame alert that was *sss*ent to the ship."

"Find the Orions in charge, from the police and the bank, and bring them here. *Now.*"

"Aye, *sss*ir."

The lieutenant stepped away and was swallowed by the swarming mass of aimless activity that surrounded the bank. Bateson had just started pondering worst-case scenarios when he heard a deep, rasping growl behind him. Mastering his natural instinct to cringe or flee, he put on a blank mask of disinterest and turned to confront his opposite number in this incipient fiasco, the captain of the Gorn battle cruiser *Hastur-zolis*. "Commander Tezog. A pleasure."

The archosaur bared his prodigious fangs. "What are your people hiding from us?"

"With all respect, Commander, I think you'll find it's the Orions who are hiding something from both of us." Out of the corner of his eye, he saw Zsestoz waving him over to a pair of Orions—one in a uniform festooned with insignia, the other in a smartly tailored suit. Bateson directed the Gorn commander's attention toward the pair. "But if you'd care to join me, I think that together, we might finally get some answers."

Tezog lumbered past Bateson without acknowledging the diplomatic gesture, and the captain followed him. One advantage of letting Tezog take the lead became readily apparent: people were much faster to make a path for him than they had been for Bateson. He stayed close behind the Gorn, then stepped forward alongside him as they reached the Orions.

The police official was a paunchy man of middling years; his dark jade scalp was partly visible through his thinning hair, and his thick mustache was the most memorable feature on his otherwise bland face. Representing the Bank of Orion was a tall and athletic woman in her prime, with a dense mane of natural curls the hue of dark copper framing her elegant features and emerald-colored eyes. Zsestoz gestured at the policeman first, then the woman. "Captain Bateson, this is Commandant Keilo Essan of the Orion Colonial Police, and Akili Kamar, Director of Security at the Bank of Orion."

Bateson greeted the Orions in turn. "Commandant Essan. Director Kamar. This is Commander Tezog of the *Hastur-zolis*." He waited until they'd offered their unanswered smiles to the Gorn, then he continued. "As I'm sure you can understand, we'd both like an explanation."

"For what?" Kamar's deflection was cold and smooth.

Tezog took half a step and invaded the woman's personal space, but she held her ground as he said through gritted fangs, "Your people reported an attempted security breach."

Essan held up a hand to Tezog. "That's still under investigation." He signaled with a gesture for the Gorn to back up from Kamar. After a long, low snarl, Tezog complied.

"I'm sure your inquiry is top-notch," Bateson said to

the Orions, "but I need to insist that my security team be involved. We have sensor technology that—"

"That won't be necessary," Kamar said.

The Gorn commander inched forward again. "We *insist*."

"Be that as it may, the bank's regulations don't permit it, and Orion law recognizes our jurisdiction over criminal acts that transpire on our property. I assure you both, it's not personal." Kamar tilted her head toward Essan. "Part of my role here is to make sure the commandant doesn't overstep *his* bounds, either." She regarded the milling packs of military personnel with open disdain. "Now, please remove your troops from our property with all due haste—before I'm forced to file formal charges against them for trespassing." She turned and walked to the main gates, which were opened ahead of her and closed behind her.

Essan clapped his hands and rubbed them together. "If there's nothing else, then?"

Bateson had little patience for bureaucrats on his best days, and this day was already shaping up to be far worse than merely mediocre. "On the contrary, Commandant. I can't help but notice that even though Director Kamar insists her people have jurisdiction, your people seem to be doing all the detective work outside the perimeter. And since the message I and Commander Tezog received described this incident as an *attempted* breach, I suspect whatever evidence there is to be found here is *outside* the bank—under *your* jurisdiction."

The commandant grew increasingly nervous. "Actually, Captain, the bank's property line extends more than thirty meters beyond the perimeter fence. We're still inside their jurisdiction."

Tezog edged forward beside Bateson, adding his own

brand of hulking menace to the conversation. "But *your* people are the ones in possession of the evidence."

"Captain . . . Commander . . . please. You're putting me in a most untenable position."

His protests only fanned Bateson's ire. "You do understand what's at stake here, yes? Under the circumstances, do you really think that either Tezog or I will settle for anything less than your complete cooperation?"

The Gorn commander added, "I warn you, Commandant: *Yes* is the wrong answer."

The Orion shot fearful glances at Tezog and Bateson, then held up a hand in surrender. In his other hand, he slowly lifted a small communicator and spoke into it.

"Essan to Major Jarek."

A man answered over the comm. *"Jarek here, sir."*

"Please meet me near the main gate at once. Essan out." He put away the device and cracked a meek and worried smile at the starship commanders. "He'll be just a moment."

The three of them waited without speaking for close to a minute until another Orion police official arrived, snapped to attention in front of Essan, and saluted. "Sir."

The commandant returned the salute and spoke quickly. "Do you have all the scans we've taken so far?"

"Yes, sir," Jarek replied.

"Good," Essan said. "Transmit them all to the *Atlas* and the *Hastur-zolis*." At Jarek's first sign of hesitation, he added, "*Now,* Major. That's an order."

Jarek lifted a tricorder-like device from a holster on his hip. "Yes, sir." He keyed in commands while Essan, Tezog, and Bateson watched. Several seconds later, he switched off the device. "Done."

"Thank you, Major. You're dismissed." The commandant shooed his subordinate with frantic gestures, then he turned back to the starship commanders. "Are we quite finished now?"

Tezog activated his wrist-mounted communicator. "In a moment." He spoke a long string of hisses, rasps, growls, and clicks into the device, then listened to a similar string of noise in reply. He turned off the comm. "Now we're done." He bowed his head slightly at Bateson. "Captain." And on that note, he turned and stalked away, marshaling his soldiers behind him.

Essan didn't wait for Bateson's permission to depart. He hurried away, back into the relative safety of a clutch of Orion police, leaving Bateson to mop up his share of the mess. The captain tapped his combadge. "Bateson to *Atlas*."

Fawkes answered, *"Atlas here. Go ahead, sir."*

"Beam up all our security teams from the bank's perimeter. It seems we've stumbled into the middle of a jurisdictional pissing match down here."

"Understood. I'm alerting all transporter stations now." In the background of the comm channel, Bateson heard muffled voices, and Fawkes replying under her breath. Then she was back, sounding anxious as hell. *"Sir, we've started analyzing the scans the Orions just sent up."*

He was certain he heard a warning of bad news in her tone. "And . . . ?"

"I'd rather not say on an open channel, sir."

That was all he'd needed to hear to know the situation was worse than he'd feared. "Hold that thought, Fawkes—and have me beamed up on the double."

Two hours, one troubling meeting, and four cups of coffee later, Bateson was seated at the desk inside his ready room on the *Atlas*, facing the image of Admiral

Marta Batanides. She wore her bone-white hair pulled back into a knot at the back of her head, but a few wild wisps framed her lean features, which even now retained much of the angular beauty of her youth. Her steel-blue eyes widened at the news Bateson had just shared. *"Would you repeat that, Captain?"*

"Energy readings detected by the Orions during the failed incursion were one hundred percent consistent with those generated by a Soong-type android."

Batanides reclined and pressed her fingertips together in front of her lips, as if she were praying. Given the gravity of the Orions' discovery, Bateson wouldn't have blamed her if she were. After collecting her thoughts, she asked, *"Are you and your crew absolutely certain?"*

"As certain as we can be, working from someone else's scans."

She took another moment to think, then she nodded. *"All right. The good news is that the Orions probably won't recognize those energy signatures for what they are. It's possible the Gorn might not know what they mean, either—but once they share that intel with their Typhon Pact allies, the Romulans and the Breen will both know what they're looking at. Which means we don't have much time to contain this."* She picked up a padd and keyed in some commands. *"According to the daily logs from our embassy there, the SI section chief, Commander Hilar Tohm, had two meetings with the Soong-made android known as Data over the past two days."*

The mention of the android's name stoked Bateson's interest. "Data? From the *Enterprise*? But . . . I thought he was dead!"

"It's a long story, Captain, and a few notches above your clearance level. For now, let it suffice to say, he was dead, *but he got better."*

One of the drawbacks of answering to an admiral with oversight responsibilities for Starfleet Intelligence, in Bateson's opinion, was that she had a knack for reminding him just how far out of the loop he was most of the time. For now, he would have to content himself with answers to lesser queries. "Do we know why he met with Tohm? Or why he's on Orion?"

"Not yet. The duty logs only noted that the meetings occurred. To find out the substance of her interactions with Data, we'll have to debrief her and check her private files."

Having dealt more than once with Starfleet Intelligence, he feared he was about to be left in the dark again. "By 'we,' I presume you mean your people in SI."

"Correct. But you're not being sidelined, Morgan, I promise. In fact, there's something equally important that I need you and your crew to handle."

"And that would be . . . ?"

There was a new edge in her voice. *"You need to track down Lieutenant Commander Data and take him into custody. If he was involved with the attempted breach at the bank, he'll be on his guard, which means he'll be exceptionally dangerous."*

She sent over a data packet, and a Starfleet Intelligence dossier about Data opened on one side of Bateson's monitor. The principal image of Data closely resembled the android he remembered meeting years earlier, but with one key difference: he now looked fully human.

"We have it on good authority that Data has become quite expert at disguising himself," Batanides continued, *"and that he can even fool biometric sensors into thinking he's any of a number of species. We know he can mimic voices; we also have unverified reports that he might have learned to spoof retinal pat-*

terns. *Tell your people to approach him with extreme caution."*

"Understood."

"One more thing, Morgan, and this is vital: Make sure no one—especially not Data—contacts the Enter-prise crew. The last thing anyone needs at this stage is Picard and his ship racing to Orion and attracting the Typhon Pact's attention to us in the process." She sighed and shook her head in quiet frustration. *"We've come too far to let this fall apart. We're counting on you to hold it together."*

"I will, Admiral."

An encouraging half smile. *"Good hunting, Captain. Batanides out."*

She closed the channel, and Bateson's screen went dark. He exhaled and felt his strength falter under the weight of responsibility. *This was not how this was supposed to go.* He drew a deep breath, hardened him-self for what had to be done, and got up from his chair.

Time to start a manhunt.

Keeping pace with the headlong floodcrush of people moving through the starport in Orion's capital made Data imagine himself being swept away by a mighty river, a slave to the current. It was an imperfect analogy, he knew, but his new brain and programming tended to make strange connections and draw peculiar asso-ciations. *Perhaps that was an essential ingredient of my father's genius,* he speculated. *The ability to imagine seemingly unrelated ideas in fusion.*

Thinking of his father filled him with melancholy. It seemed odd to him that he should miss Noonien so deeply when he possessed all of the man's memories—his entire lifetime of experience, all his skills, all his vast knowledge. But knowing every detail of the life

Soong had lived was not the same as having him there in the flesh. It was not the same as being able to share a moment with him, or the singular experience of knowing one was being seen through a parent's all-forgiving eyes. Knowing all that his father had ever said was not the same as hearing what he would say now if he were alive. Memories were no substitute for the man himself.

Lost in this wilderness of maudlin reminiscence, Data was three-tenths of a second slower than normal to realize that he was being followed. It wasn't the first time he'd had this feeling since arriving on Orion. It had happened on the night he'd arrived, and shortly before both his meetings with Hilar Tohm. Unable to corroborate his suspicions, he had tried to dismiss them as mere paranoia, the product of an emotional misfire in his positronic matrix. Now it haunted him again—the sensation of being watched. Of being hunted.

He quickened his pace, hoping that if he could get off the main thoroughfare and into the service corridors, he could either confront his pursuer or evade him long enough to beam back to the *Archeus* and get off the surface. Once out of orbit he would be free to engage his ship's cloaking device and resume his hunt for the Immortal once known as Emil Vaslovik.

The crowd ahead of him thinned as he turned a corner. At first it felt like an opportunity: open ground, free of obstacles. Then he saw it for what it was: a danger zone. An area devoid of camouflage or cover. The nearest escape points ahead of him would be too far to reach in time if his pursuer had a beam weapon. At the risk of hastening the confrontation, he chose to stop and double back into a more densely trafficked part of the starport. He flipped up his collar and lowered the brim of his hat to hide his face, then tucked his hands into his pockets and lowered his chin as he rounded the corner, returning the way he'd come.

As soon as he made the turn, he heard the bark of an angry masculine voice.

"Commander Data! Drop to your knees and place your hands on your head!"

A dozen Starfleet personnel in black commando uniforms had emerged from concealed positions along the corridor, and ten more looked down from the level above. They all aimed their combat rifles at Data, and a clatter of running footsteps behind his back told him that he was surrounded. Civilians scattered, screaming in panic, as the Starfleet security force advanced on Data, slowly shrinking their perimeter around him. A male Bajoran seemed to be the one in charge. Data froze as the man shouted, "Commander! This is your final warning! Drop to your knees and place your palms on your head!"

With careful, slow movements, Data lowered himself first to one knee, then he tucked the other knee under himself. Before removing his hands from his pockets, he clutched the quantum transmitter he'd concealed in his pocket, and which held a prerecorded message he'd saved in its transmission queue as a hedge against an unforeseen emergency. A single tap on the finger-sized metallic cylinder sent the SOS to the one person Data knew he could trust to answer it. Then he took his hands from his pockets and placed them atop his head.

"Hold your fire," he said. "I surrender."

7

The door signal was so understated that it barely rose above the ambient background hum inside Picard's ready room. The captain closed the crew evaluations he'd been reviewing to fill the time between Worf's increasingly bleak reports on the search for the *Sirriam*. "Come."

With a faint hiss, the door to the bridge slid open. Chief engineer La Forge entered holding a small metallic cylinder the size of his finger. Worf was close behind him. Both men wore stern expressions. Holding up the device, La Forge said, "Captain, you need to hear this."

Picard stood and stepped around his desk to meet his two most senior officers. In addition to serving as the ship's chief engineer, La Forge had accepted a promotion several months earlier and was now the ship's second officer, third in command of the *Enterprise*. It had been a long overdue recognition, in Picard's opinion. Not only had La Forge served with distinction at his side for many years, it was a sensible precaution to have a senior member of the ship's chain of command serving somewhere other than on the bridge, and main engineering was the only location other than auxiliary control from which one could have full command of the ship.

"What's this about?"

La Forge held up the device. "I just got a message from Data, on this quantum transmitter he gave me before he left the ship a couple of months ago. Listen."

He pressed one of the cylinder's controls, and Data's voice filled the room as if he were there with them. *"Geordi, this is Data. I am on the Orion homeworld. I need your help. Please come at once."*

"That's the entire message," La Forge said. "I've tried hailing him. He doesn't answer."

Picard was troubled by the brevity of the message. "You're certain it's genuine?"

"Data has the only quantum device linked to mine." La Forge frowned. "If he sent that, he's in trouble. And if someone else sent it posing as him, then he's in even *more* trouble."

It was a reasonable argument, and Picard shared La Forge's sense of obligation to their old friend, but he didn't have the luxury of simply defying orders and abandoning his mission. He looked at Worf. "Number One? Where do we stand with the search for the *Sirriam*?"

The Klingon wore his disappointment like a crown of shame. "So far, we have no leads. The *Roanoke* has detected no sign of a crash site on the third planet, and none of our shuttles have found any sign of the interceptor on the gas giants' moons. If the pilots did survive a crash landing in this system . . . they likely ran out of air more than two hours ago."

"Then, even in our most optimistic scenario . . . those men are dead."

Worf breathed an angry sigh. "Yes, sir."

He shared his first officer's frustration. As remote

as the likelihood of a successful rescue had seemed, Picard had dared to hope they might save the lost agents and bring them home to their friends and families. But if there was no way the men could be saved, if the *Enterprise*'s mission to the Tirana system was now little more than a glorified salvage effort, then he had to place the needs of the living ahead of the needs of the dead, regardless of what his superiors might have to say on the matter. Still, he knew it would be wise to make certain he and his crew had at least a modicum of legal cover for their actions.

"Number One . . . based on your reading of Starfleet's general rules and regulations . . . would you classify Mister Data's message to Commander La Forge as a distress signal?"

A smirk indicated that Worf understood Picard's implicit suggestion. "Yes. I would."

"Then our course of action seems clear." Picard stepped back behind his desk. "Number One, recall our search teams and have Lieutenant Faur plot a course to Orion. Mister La Forge, when Commander Worf gives the order, we need to be ready for maximum warp. Understood?"

La Forge smiled. "Yes, sir."

A devious gleam shone in Worf's eyes. "Will you be informing Starfleet Command of our change in plans, sir?"

Picard sat down. "I shall. Though I *have* been rather absent-minded of late, Number One. If I haven't contacted Starfleet by the time we reach Orion, please remind me to do so."

"Understood, sir."

"Dismissed." Worf and La Forge turned to leave. The door slid open ahead of them, but they halted at its threshold when Picard called after them. "Gentlemen?" He waited for them to turn around, then he continued. "As far as the rest of the crew is concerned, treat the reason for our change in plans as need-to-know information."

Both men nodded, then continued on their way. The door closed after them, leaving Picard once again sequestered with his thoughts. For a moment, he considered contacting his superiors and apprising them of Data's call for help and the *Enterprise*'s response, but years of experience with Starfleet's endless layers of bureaucracy had taught him the inestimable value of discretion; if one never asked permission, one could never be refused.

He made his decision and resolved to stand by it. If, after all was said and done, apologies needed to be made, there would be time for that later.

We've only just welcomed Data back from the dead, he reminded himself, *and I quite literally owe the man my life. . . . If he needs our help, he'll have it—no matter what.*

Data sat in silence at the minimalist monotanium table inside the claustrophobic interrogation room, waiting to see who next would walk through its lone door. The gray thermocrete walls were bare, and feeble light came from a naked fixture high overhead. No surveillance devices were visible, but Data was sure they were there, and that he was being observed. He was shackled at his wrists and ankles with magnetic manacles. The chair beneath him—also monotanium—was bolted to the floor. It would take only a token effort for him to rip it free, and he knew at least three ways to use his internal circuits and power supply to deactivate and remove his restraints, but he knew such actions would only worsen his already poor situation.

Though he had been moved around via transporter beams a few times in the hours since his arrest, he had noted enough details on signage and accoutrements in the institutional-looking corridor outside the interrogation room to deduce that he was being held inside the Federation Embassy. *Most likely I am on one of its secure underground levels, from which I cannot be rescued by a transporter beam.* According to his memory of the layout for this embassy—one of many seemingly trivial facts he had accumulated during his decades of Starfleet service—there were many layers of armed Starfleet security between him and the closest exit, and multiple redundant safeguards to prevent him from getting there.

The door slid open. In shuffled a lumbering, bovine-featured hulk of a humanoid, a Grazerite. He wore a Starfleet uniform accented with the burgundy turtle-neck of a command officer and carried a thin briefcase of brushed nickel-aluminum alloy. As the door closed, the Grazerite set his case atop the table, pulled back the chair opposite Data's, and sat down.

"Good morning, Mister Data."

"Good morning. Who are you?"

"Lieutenant Commander Peshtal-Azda." He extended a beefy hand, then retracted it when he realized Data was in no position to accept the friendly gesture. "I'm your attorney."

Data eyed him with dubious curiosity. "I do not recall asking for legal counsel."

"The Starfleet JAG office sent me. But don't let that fool you—I'm actually competent." He opened his case and took out a padd. "So, let's see, here." Scrolling through the files stored on the device, he subvocalized a number of worrisome murmurs. He looked up and squinted. "I want to make sure there's been no mistake—you are Lieutenant Commander Data, yes?"

What an odd question. "Yes."

Peshtal-Azda held the padd at arm's length while

squinting even harder. "No offense, but you look a bit different than your service record photo."

Data cracked a sly smile. "I had some work done."

"Apparently." He tapped at the padd. "Has anyone told you why you're here?"

"Not yet." He leaned forward, hoping for a look at the padd's screen, but the Grazerite kept it tilted just out of view. "Am I correct in assuming I am inside the Federation Embassy?"

The lawyer nodded. "For now. Starfleet asked the local police to pick you up, but they refused because no one can produce any evidence against you."

Lifting his shackles as high as he could, Data replied, "Yet I am in custody."

"Well, that's because the evidentiary standard for a military tribunal is significantly lower than for a civilian criminal trial." Data started to voice an objection, but Peshtal-Azda cut him off with a raised hand. "I know you think you're a private citizen, but Starfleet considers you an officer on reserve status, which means you remain subject to its authority."

Starfleet's regulations were vague with regard to the status of officers who were returned to life after being declared dead, but Data had no difficulty believing someone had persuaded the admiralty to reactivate his commission without his knowledge or consent. He let out a low, bitter chuckle and shook his head. "Would it be too late for me to resign?"

A sour look telegraphed the lawyer's reply. "A bit."

"With what crime, exactly, have I been charged?"

"So far? Attempted breaking and entering, and criminal trespass. But there are more charges under investigation, and if the JAG office gets its way, you'll be facing all of them." Peshtal-Azda picked up the padd and navigated its contents with a distracted air. "My job is to defend you, here and in court. But I can't do that unless you trust me." He leaned forward. "Let's start by having you answer a few questions to set up your alibi. Why are you here on Orion?"

Data had been afraid this line of questioning was coming. "I cannot say."

Peshtal-Azda scowled at him. "Commander, I'm your lawyer. Anything you tell me is protected by attorney-client privilege. And don't worry about the surveillance systems in the room—by law they have to be deactivated whenever a defense counselor is meeting with a client. Now, let's try that question again—and answer truthfully. Why are you on Orion?"

"I am here because of a private family matter."

His answer was met by narrowed eyes and a glum frown. "Can you be more specific?"

"I can. I choose not to be."

The lawyer tapped a fat index finger on the table-top. "Data, you're in serious legal trouble, and it's only going to get worse if you don't cooperate with me. The JAG office tells me you met with Starfleet Intelligence section chief Hilar Tohm twice during your stay on Orion, and that she helped you acquire copies of top-secret files from the Bank of Orion. Is this true?"

"It is."

"What was in the files she obtained for you?"

He knew his next answer would not be well received, but that could not be helped. "I am sorry, counselor, but I believe you lack the requisite security clearance for that information."

The Grazerite made a fist, closed his eyes, took a deep breath. Then he stared at Data. "Commander, we don't have time for this. Tell me what was in those files."

"I will not. Perhaps you can ask Commander Tohm to share that information with you."

"Excuse me?"

He wondered why his lawyer hadn't already pursued this line of inquiry. "If you doubt my description of my business on Orion, speak with Commander Tohm. She can corroborate my explanation, and attest to the personal nature of the intelligence she shared with me."

Peshtal-Azda regarded Data with a long, silent glare. "Commander Tohm is dead."

In just four words, the true scope of Data's legal predicament began to come into focus. He hoped his initial assumption was wrong, but he needed to be sure. "How did she die?"

"She was murdered in her apartment, here inside the embassy compound. Medical scans have confirmed her time of death was between five and six hours before your arrest."

"Does the JAG office currently consider me a suspect in her murder?"

"Let's just say you're definitely a 'person of interest.' Especially since, roughly two hours before your arrest, the energy signature of a Soong-type android was detected trying to break into the Bank of Orion." He raised one bushy eyebrow with accusatory flair. "Do you happen to have a ready explanation for *that*, Commander?"

"No." The first sickening sensation of fear twisted in Data's gut and filled his mind with panicked loops of questions. "I have no explanation for that whatsoever."

"I was afraid you'd say that." The lawyer put away his padd, closed his case, and stood up. "I know you could escape. Don't. Stay here, and don't talk to anyone except me, about anything." He knocked on the door. A guard on the other side unlocked and opened it. Peshtal-Azda grumbled under his breath as he left. "Why must I get all the *interesting* cases?"

8

From across the lab, Konar took note of Hain's hunched posture over her console, her defensive, pulled-in body language. Her head was down, and though she must have heard his steps as he approached, she didn't turn to observe him as she normally did. Even when she was engrossed in her work, she rarely exhibited a focus this intense. It boded ill.

He stopped behind her shoulder. "I need a progress report on the Orion operation."

She cringed, then looked back over her shoulder. "It wasn't my fault."

The update was off to an even worse start than Konar had feared. He'd already been forced to contend with unrealistic schedules, unrelenting superiors, and untested technology; now he could add a paranoid colleague to his legion of impediments. "What happened?"

"The break-in at the bank failed." Hain called up multiple screens of synchronized data set for accelerated playback. "This was recorded during the mission. We followed the plan the Spetzkar sent us, to the last detail." She pointed at a map of the street grid in the Orion capital. "The team approached through the underground passage, as directed. They cut through the outer barrier, and everything seemed to be on schedule. Then Dolon hit some kind of energy field here, just inside the bank's sublevel." One of her screens became a jumble of code and static. "He took some heavy damage from a feedback pulse inside the field. Half his body's motivators are fried, and there's damage in his sensory hardware."

Konar studied the mission logs and was impressed by their tremendous clarity and the wealth of raw information the team had been able to relay back to the lab, even from such a great distance. "What happened next?"

Hain skipped ahead in the data playback. "The team withdrew and used preplanned escape route six. One hour and nine minutes later, they returned to the safehouse."

"With Dolon?" Konar asked. Hain nodded. "Is the damage reparable?"

"No, not with the limited resources they have." She looked up at him, and the pitch of her voice climbed, her anxiety detectable even in the garbled noise from her vocoder. "It wasn't my fault, sir. The mission protocols from the Spetzkar expressly forbade me from modifying the plan in any way. I couldn't add precautions or countermand questionable tactics. All I could do was walk them into a trap. I didn't even have the option of aborting the mission."

She was so excitable. *If only she could master her passions,* Konar thought, *she could go far. But she suffers from the curse of short-term thinking.* "No one will hold you accountable for the mission's outcome. I assure you, the Spetzkar design these operations with great care and attention to detail. As long as you followed the protocol, you have no cause for concern."

"That's what I'm trying to tell you, sir: there is cause

for concern." She summoned another screen of technical data. "Dolon's sensor-blocking circuit shorted out on contact with the energy field. Before his power cell failed, he was exposed to the bank's sensors for several seconds. During that time, he would have emitted an energy signature unique to Soong-type androids." Her hands moved with frantic grace across her console, calling up more and more information from various sources. "The Orion police don't seem to know what the readings mean, but they shared them with the Gorn and Starfleet ships in orbit. I don't know if the Gorn have accurate intel on the androids, but Starfleet is almost certain to recognize it."

Konar saw her point. "You're right, they will. And if we can't repair Dolon, we can't risk bringing him back on line. The moment he powers up, he'd lead Starfleet straight to the other three androids. Have the rest of the team dismantle him and melt him down."

"Destroy him? But that'll leave only three to complete the rest of the mission."

"I'm aware of that. But under the circumstances, we have no choice. At best, he's dead weight; at worst, he's a liability that could expose the rest of the team."

Hain regarded her wall of screens with a posture that conveyed despair. "How are we supposed to rewrite the rest of the mission profile to work with only three androids?"

"That's not our concern. I'll file my report with Command and let them deal with the loss of Dolon. As soon as they send back a revised mission plan, we'll proceed."

Even translated, Hain's reply was rife with bitterness. "Let's hope their next plan proves more successful than the last one."

He couldn't tell her that the last plan had been

more successful than it had appeared, and that it had achieved every one of its true objectives—none of which had been known to Hain. Instead, he told her the only thing that he could: "Begin preparations for Phase Two." He walked toward the long corridor that led from the lab to his quarters, but before he started down the passageway, he turned back. "Hain." She turned to look at him, and he saluted her with a subtle lift of his mask's snout. "Good work." She accepted the compliment without a word and acknowledged his praise by returning to her labors.

There was still much to be done on Orion, Konar knew. Before it was over, he and Hain would be called upon to accomplish a feat without precedent in local history, one that would send political aftershocks throughout all of known space. And despite the enormity of what they had been asked to do, he knew that if the mission went as intended, their true roles would not be remembered by history. In the annals of the galaxy, the two of them would not merit so much as a footnote. Despite the river of blood they would be compelled to shed, they would die forgotten.

But the Breen Confederacy would live on. It would be remembered forever.

From her first step inside the uplink center, Hain felt the intense, dry heat that filled the dim room. The culprit was the transmitter, a bizarre construction of black crystal infused with indigo fires unlike anything else Hain had ever seen. In addition to making possible the control of their androids across vast distances, it bled heat like a dying star.

Arrayed at ninety-degree intervals around the transmitter were four uplink pods, bulky cylinders more than two meters long that extended from the transmitter like spokes on a wheel. Each gray cocoon was barnacled with subsystems—heat exchangers, power regulators, feedback buffers, and dozens more. Hain moved from one pod to the next, checking to make sure they were functioning correctly and that their signal outputs were correct and within tolerances.

At the foot of each pod was a primary control panel. Hain activated the panels on Pods One, Two, and Three as she walked the perimeter of the circular room, stopping to verify that the return signals from the androids all were being received and processed with total fidelity.

Visual and auditory signals were the easiest to confirm. Observing the team members through one another's points of view, she could see that none of them had any obvious cosmetic damage. They all appeared to be perfectly normal humanoids—a male Orion, a female human, and a male Trill. By contrast, the team's tactile, olfactory, and gustatory senses were harder for her to quantify remotely. The best Hain could do was confirm that the signals were transiting the pods' preprocessors and emerging unchanged. *So far, so good.*

She averted her eyes as she passed the dark and deactivated Pod Four.

Her uniform's thermal regulator activated, and she felt a soothing rush of coolness circulate through its sleeves and pants, into her gloves and boots, and best of all inside her helmet. Although she wasn't nearly as sensitive to heat as the Amoniri, she disliked perspiring inside the armor she was required to wear at all times, except when she was alone in her quarters. Her pulse slowed as her body temperature cooled, and she relaxed herself with a deep breath.

On the far side of the room from its airlock, which protected its entrance, was an operator's master console with a chair. Hain settled into the seat, made a final check of the uplink's nodes, and opened a channel to her agents. "Berro. Olar. Sair. Do you all copy?"

The team's lone remaining female answered first. *"Sair here."*

"This is Olar. I read you."

"Berro, affirmative."

They sounded in good spirits. That was encouraging. "All your numbers check out at this end. How do you three feel? Any anomalies after that run-in at the bank?"

"Negative," Sair said. *"Self-diagnostics came up clean. But we can't wake up Dolon."*

It was time to break the bad news to the team. "Dolon's gone. He took too much damage from the energy field, and the feedback pulse cooked his brain."

Berro asked, *"So, what now?"*

"Disassemble his body into as many parts as possible, and use the molecular acid packs in his field kit to melt him down. We can't let his body be found, and we can't risk you slowing down by taking it with you. It's dead weight now. Get rid of it."

Her order met with skepticism from Olar. *"What about his parts that won't melt down?"*

"Break them down with the sonic drill and dump them in a river. Or a sewer. But get rid of them, and make certain they won't be found. Understood?" The operatives acknowledged the order. "All right. After you finish that, I should have new orders for you. Signing off."

She terminated her link to the trio and observed for a few minutes until they began breaking down Dolon's now useless body and preparing it for dissolution. It was going to be a slow and tedious process, and Hain had no desire to keep watching. Satisfied that the team was on mission and still fully operational despite the setback at the bank, she reset the master panel and uplink pods' monitors to standby and headed for the exit.

Inside the airlock, the plunge in temperature sent a chill down her back. Her uniform's regulator, as usual, was slow to adapt to such a rapid change in environment. She shivered as she tapped her security code into the airlock's keypad, opening the door that led back to the main area of the lab. *Why can't the SRD task a few scientists with improving these uniforms?*

It was a rhetorical question, but as she glanced at her regular duty station, she was sure she saw the answer. Visual feeds from Berro, Olar, and Sair showed three overlapping perspectives on the coldhearted dismemberment of their comrade. Dolon's body had represented a significant investment in terms of materials, labor, and research, and now it was being tossed away as garbage. How many other technologies could have been developed for what that had cost? How many more people throughout the Confederacy could have been fed?

Hain would never speak such subversive questions aloud, of course. She knew better than that, and had even seen with her own eyes what became of those who failed to heed history's bitter lessons. In the end, a bit of sweat, a cold shiver, and a pang of conscience felt like small prices to pay for the privilege of staying alive.

9

Starlight that had been stretched into passing streaks contracted to points on the main viewscreen as the *Enterprise* dropped out of warp eight million kilometers from Orion. Picard noted the crescent shadow darkening the tiny blue-green orb of the Orions' homeworld, the edge of night creeping in its petty pace through its endless cycle.

Lieutenant Joanna Faur called out her report without looking up from the helm. "We've secured from warp and are on orbital approach at full impulse. ETA, two minutes."

"Thank you, Lieutenant." Picard glanced at Worf. "Contact the Federation Embassy on the surface. We might need their help locating Mister Data."

The Klingon nodded. "Aye, sir." He got up and walked starboard to one of the auxiliary consoles, from which he could send a secure transmission to the embassy.

An urgent tone warbled from the security console, and Lieutenant Šmrhová muted it as she assessed its cause. "Captain, there's another Starfleet vessel in orbit—the *Atlas*."

Hearing the ship's name jogged Picard's memory.

"That's Morgan Bateson's command." He peered at the viewscreen, on which a tiny gleaming speck betrayed the first sign of the other *Sovereign*-class starship. Perplexed, he muttered, "What would *he* be doing *here*?"

"Whatever their business, they're hailing us, sir."

Picard was intrigued and concerned in equal measure. "On-screen, Lieutenant."

The image on the forward viewer changed from the slowly growing sphere of Orion to the bearded, balding head of Captain Morgan Bateson. He looked a bit grayer in the temples than he had the first time Picard had seen him, when Bateson and his previous command, the *U.S.S. Bozeman,* had emerged from a temporal loop in which they'd been snared for nearly ninety years. In the sixteen years since that incident, Bateson and much of the rest of his twenty-third-century crew had acclimated well to the twenty-fourth century—Bateson himself best of all. Not only had he briefly commanded the *Sovereign*-class *Enterprise* during its 2372 shakedown cruise, his leadership in the battle against the Borg a few years earlier had earned him accolades in the civilian press as "the hero of Vulcan" and "the right captain in the right time."

For all his fortune and fame, however, Bateson was in a foul mood, nearly red in the face with anger. *"Picard! What in blazes are you doing here?"*

Picard stood and tugged his tunic smooth. "Good to see you again, as well, Captain."

"Just answer the question," Bateson snapped. *"You're supposed to be at Azeban."*

It struck Picard as odd that Bateson would be so well acquainted with the *Enterprise*'s deployment orders, but then he remembered how high-profile the mission had been and chalked it up to the burdens of celebrity. Nonetheless, discretion still seemed to be in order. "We were. An alert diverted to us to the Tirana system, and then a distress signal brought us here."

Bateson mustered an insincere smile. *"We're not aware of any distress signal originating from within this system, Captain. I'm afraid you must be mistaken."*

"I assure you, we're not." Keen to test Bateson's reaction, he added, "We received it on a dedicated channel from our former shipmate, Lieutenant Commander Data." The other captain's mask of composure faltered. *He's not much of a poker player,* Picard mused.

Almost as swiftly as Bateson's façade had faltered, it recovered. *"I'm afraid you've been misled, Captain Picard. Now, as much as I hate to pull rank, I need you and your ship to reverse course and leave this system, immediately."*

"Pull rank? We both wear four pips on our collars."

Moment by moment, Bateson's glare grew colder. Beneath his graying beard, his facial muscles bulged as he clenched his jaw. *"Check your recent orders from Starfleet. I have full authority over operations in this sector."*

Glinn Dygan pulled up a screen of data on the operations console, checked it, then nodded over his shoulder at Picard. "Confirmed, sir."

Knowing that Bateson's authority and orders were genuine only deepened Picard's sense that something was amiss. "Morgan. What exactly is going on here?"

"You're in no position to ask questions, Picard, so—"

"I'm asking them anyway," Picard said, stepping forward to emphasize his point as he challenged Bateson to explain himself. "This is damned irregular, Morgan, and you know it. I have it on good authority that one of my men, a Starfleet officer to whom I owe my life, is in danger on the planet's surface—and I'm not leaving until I know he's safe."

Šmrhová looked up from the security console, eyes wide and voice raised in alarm. "Captain, there's a Gorn battleship in orbit. Its energy signature matches the *Hastur-zolis*."

Dygan swiveled his chair around to face Picard, and he dropped his voice to a whisper. "Sir, I'm reading a number of coded transmissions between the *Atlas* and the *Hastur-zolis*."

Bateson teetered on the verge of fury. *"Damn you, Picard! Your presence is jeopardizing my mission. You need to leave orbit. Right now."*

Picard stared at Bateson, trying to read the truth in the man's baleful stare. Behind his red masque of anger was . . . fear. "What mission?"

"I'm giving you twenty seconds to reverse course."

Before Picard could respond, a small icon in the corner of the screen cued him that the channel had been muted. He turned to see Worf step briskly to his side. The first officer turned away from the viewscreen and spoke in a confidential hush. "While communicating with the embassy, I detected a coded transmission between the *Atlas* and a transceiver inside the Bank of Orion. The encryption frequency was November-bravo-seven-nine-white."

Picard froze. The frequency Worf had identified was one of the most carefully regulated cipher codes in the Federation. To the best of his knowledge, it was used by Starfleet for only one purpose: top-secret communication with the Protection Detail, a special elite division of the civilian-run Federation Security Agency. He looked at his XO. "You're certain, Number One?"

"Positive." He grimaced. "If they are here, that can mean only one thing."

A grim nod of comprehension. "President Bacco is on Orion."

* * *

"We won't make unilateral concessions here," President Nanietta Bacco insisted. "If you want our help with this, we won't settle for a simple nonaggression pact. We'll need to negotiate a real partnership—a binding treaty of alliance."

Sozzerozs, the Gorn imperator, tasted the air with his tongue and hissed. "That is too great a risk. The other nations of the Typhon Pact would seek revenge for our betrayal."

"Not necessarily," interjected Safranski, the Federation's secretary of the exterior, and a senior member of Bacco's cabinet. "The Hegemony's withdrawal from the Pact would weaken them substantially in several sectors, and an alliance with the Federation would make any reprisal against your people tantamount to an act of war against us." The slim Rigellian shifted his posture to better address the rest of the Gorn delegation. "I don't think the other Pact nations are ready to risk open warfare just yet—and certainly not under those conditions."

Wazir Togor, the imperator's top adviser, hissed. "We do not share your optimism."

"Well, then," Bacco said, feeling all her hopes for progress wither. She drummed her fingers once on the tabletop. "It appears we're at an impasse. . . . Again."

Seated with Safranski and Bacco on one side of the conference table were Esperanza Piñiero, Bacco's chief of staff and senior political adviser, and Cort Enaren, the Federation Councillor from Betazed. Facing them from the other side were their opposite numbers from the Gorn Hegemony: Imperator Sozzerozs; *Wazir* Togor; *Nizor* Szamra, a key member of the Gorn *Nizora,* or senate; and *Zulta-osol* Azarog, whose title Bacco had been told meant "foreign minister." Thanks to Bacco's years spent living on and serving as governor of Cestus III, she'd had a fair deal of experience with the Gorn, and normally she could tell one individual from another. However, she suspected these four members of the Gorn's elite ruling caste must have been close cousins, because she would have been hard-pressed to tell them apart if not for the colors of their tunics: crimson for Sozzerozs; turquoise for Togor; gold for Szamra; and immaculate white for Azarog.

They all had been sequestered for the past few days—far too long, by any measure, in Bacco's opinion—in the luxurious but windowless secure underground chambers of the Bank of Orion, one of the more defensible locations in known space, and one of the most discreet. The vault-like space in which Bacco and Sozzerozs had agreed to hold this top-secret summit had no surveillance systems, was shielded against transporter beams, energy weapons, and intruders, and—most important of all—was situated on neutral ground for both sides. The nonaligned Orion Colonies often were a source of trouble because of their tendency to turn a blind eye to acts of piracy launched from within their territory against targets outside of it, but in this instance, their longstanding political neutrality had made possible a meeting that otherwise might have been scuttled preemptively by arguments over something as simple as the venue.

Piñiero hunched forward a bit, bowed her head, and slowly turned her hands palms-up and spread them slightly apart, a conciliatory gesture that had been found to have a slight calming effect on the Gorn when discussions became tense or heated. "Your Majesty." She pivoted to offer the show of respect to the others, as well. "Venerable elders. While I understand that the risks for your people are significant, I think we need to keep in mind the many well-considered reasons you cited when you asked for this summit. Azarog told us that you and your court feel marginalized in the decision-making process of the Pact; Togor confided that your people feel overshadowed by the military strength and prowess of the Romulans and the Tzenkethi, and that your scientists worry their efforts are being co-opted and eclipsed by those of the Breen. These are all issues you can address by allying yourselves with the Federation. You would recover full political autonomy, and, as a formal ally, you would benefit from a mutual-defense treaty and access to a wide range of our ongoing research."

Her upbeat attempt to start the talks over from scratch drew low snarls of contempt from the Gorn. Szamra challenged Piñiero with an unblinking stare, a contest from which the chief of staff wisely demurred by deferentially averting her gaze. "You make it sound so simple," said the *nizor*. "But you continue to ignore the political realities of our situation. Withdrawing from the Pact will be a very unpopular decision within the Hegemony. A majority of the *Nizora* supports continued membership, as does a slim plurality of our people."

Enaren harrumphed. "So what?" The elderly Betazoid crossed his arms and shot a sour look at Szamra. "It's not as if you let your people vote. So who cares if they don't approve?"

Togor replied, "Spoken like someone who's never lived in fear of a popular rebellion."

"People don't rebel when they're happy and treated fairly," Enaren shot back.

Not again, Bacco lamented. She had chosen to bring Councillor Enaren to the talks as the sole representative of the Federation Council because he was influential and popular, and because if the summit led to a treaty negotiation she would need someone on the Council who was knowledgeable about its myriad issues. Unfortunately, Enaren had demonstrated a rare talent for annoying the Gorn. For a politician, he was one of the least politic people Bacco had ever met. *If only Andor hadn't seceded from the Federation, I could've brought zh'Faila.*

"Silence," rasped Sozzerozs. "Realigning ourselves with the Federation would carry a steep political price. While many of our people have no desire for war with the Federation, neither do we desire to make its way of life our own."

"There are other factors," Togor added. "Our economy has thrived because of trade with our Typhon Pact partners. The Romulans have become our most important export market. If we leave the Pact, they will likely close their borders to us. Losing that market would devastate us."

Safranski was eager to respond. "The Federation's a huge market, Togor—one that continues to accept your products, despite your membership in the Pact. We can elevate your trade status to that of a 'most favored nation.' It would reduce import tariffs on your goods and improve your currency exchange rates against the Federation credit."

"As promising as that sounds," Azarog cut in, "it fails to address the single most pressing obstacle to a formal alliance between us: the Klingon Empire." He directed his next remarks directly to Bacco. "While it might be possible for us to make peace with the Federation and convince our people to respect that choice, our history with the Klingons is much longer and far bloodier. They have threatened us many times, and only our membership in the Pact has halted their incessant raids along our border. If we leave the Pact, they will see us as a weak target, ripe for conquest. Is your Starfleet prepared to stand against the Klingons in *our* name? And if the Klingons push us to war, and both sides call to you for aid, who will you answer? Or would you just fall silent, profess neutrality, and let your greater ally have its way with us?"

Bacco sighed. "I admit, that's a difficult question. To be honest, it's not one I'm prepared to answer at this stage. There are too many legal, political, and practical issues to consider first."

Piñiero looked away from the table and took on a distracted air. It was an affectation Bacco recognized from experience: her chief of staff's attention had been captured by something being communicated via her in-ear transceiver. Then the dark-haired, olive-complexioned woman turned back to the table. "Perhaps now would be a good time for a break."

"Very well." Togor rose from his *glenget,* a Chelon-made piece of furniture designed to suit species that were more comfortable kneeling than sitting. "Let us reconvene in two hours."

"Agreed," Bacco said. She and Sozzerozs stood, and their delegations did the same. Wary but polite nods were exchanged as the two groups filed out of the room by separate entrances. Once they were out of the room and moving down the corridor to their suites, Bacco fell into step beside Piñiero and asked softly, "What was that about?"

"We have a situation brewing in orbit. The *Atlas* is in a standoff with the *Enterprise.*"

That was not the bad news Bacco had expected. "What's the *Enterprise* doing here?"

"I was saving this for later," Piñiero said with a frown. "Last night's attempted break-in? Bateson's crew says the sensor readings show a Soong-type android was involved, and they arrested Lieutenant Commander

Data this morning at the starport, less than ten kilometers from here. He's being held at the embassy in connection with the breach, as well as last night's murder of the Starfleet Intelligence section chief for Orion."

The president shook her head. "And somehow Picard found out about it and brought one of the most closely watched ships in the fleet right to our summit."

"That's not all. He's on his way down. He wants to talk with you, in person."

A disgruntled sigh barely scratched the surface of Bacco's irritation.

"So much for keeping a low profile."

Lean, silent, and serious, the pair of Protection Detail agents met Picard outside the main gate of the Bank of Orion. One was a human man in his thirties, with dark blond hair, prominent ears, and a strong jawline. The other was an Andorian *thaan* whose chiseled, glacier-blue cheekbones were framed by shock-cut white hair. They wore identical dark suits, slate-gray shirts, and black ties, and their eyes were concealed by matching black wraparound glasses that Picard suspected were equipped with full-spectrum light-enhancing technology. He didn't see any weapons on them, but he couldn't say if that was because their sidearms were so well concealed, or because they had been required to forgo them while on Orion soil.

The Andorian moved forward as Picard stepped free of the transporter beam. "Captain. I'm Agent th'Neyloh. This is Agent Sinkonnen. Please raise your arms."

Picard let th'Neyloh frisk him as Sinkonnen took a slender, compact scanner from an inside pocket of his suit coat. The rectangular device was barely large enough to fill his palm. As the Andorian backed away from Picard, Sinkonnen put away the scanner. "He's clean."

"Follow us, Captain," th'Neyloh said. The gates behind him opened inward, toward the bank, and the protection agents led Picard past armed Orion soldiers and across the low-walled bridge. Picard stole glances to either side, but he couldn't get an angle that would let him see the bottom of the man-made chasm that ringed Orion's fortified financial headquarters. As soon as the trio was clear of the entrance, the gates swung closed behind them.

Heavy doors awaited the trio at the far end of the bridge. The portals opened with a great clanging of retracted bolts and bars, and their inward swing was ponderous. As the doors parted, Picard saw they were more than a meter thick and sheathed entirely in durable-looking metal. He wished he could ask someone more about them, but he doubted any of the bank's personnel would be forthcoming with specifics regarding its security technology.

The skyscraper's interior was opulent to the point of being breathtaking. High overhead, the ceiling of its cavernous lobby and first floor was decorated with gold-bordered, intricate murals inspired by ancient Orion myths. Picard beheld his reflection, moving under his feet across the polished marble floors. Priceless paintings and illustrations from across the galaxy adorned the walls, and elegant sculptures stood on white pedestals beneath artful illumination. Great curving staircases, mirror images of each other, dominated either side of the yawning space and led to what appeared to be an even more sumptuous mezzanine.

To Picard's disappointment, the agents led him past the stairs, into a lower-ceilinged area beneath the mezzanine, and around a corner to a long passageway barred by a manned gate. An Orion inside an armored guard station pressed a button and released the lock on the gate as they drew near. Sinkonnen moved ahead and opened the gate, while th'Neyloh trailed Picard through the checkpoint and closed the gate behind them. During that momentary pause, Picard noted the force field emitters subtly recessed into the walls, floor, and ceiling just past the barrier.

They continued to the end of the interminably long hallway and into a waiting elevator. Sinkonnen keyed in a multicharacter security code, then stared into a retinal scanner to start the lift's descent. Just as Picard had come to expect of starship turbolifts, the elevator conveyed no sense of movement. The hum of magnetic coils and the faint buzzing of the overhead light were the only sounds inside the car. Then the doors opened, and th'Neyloh led him out into a sublevel with carpeted floors, elegant furniture that would have looked at home in an Earth palace of centuries past, and dozens of pieces of art hailing from cultures spanning known space and eras stretching back more than two millennia. It was as ostentatious a display as any Picard had ever seen promulgated by the Ferengi, but its sense of style was far more subdued and refined.

Sinkonnen stopped at a door, opened it, and ushered Picard through. "In here, sir."

Picard walked through the doorway to find President Bacco and her chief of staff waiting on the other side. Bacco, a proud, white-haired woman in her eighties, sat in a high-backed, leather-upholstered chair behind a gorgeous desk of carved mahogany. Esperanza Piñiero, an olive-skinned, dark-haired woman in her late fifties, stood to the right of the desk, facing Picard. Out of the corner of his eye, he noted another figure in the room and glanced sideways to see another protection agent dressed in black and gray—a short but powerfully built human man in his forties, with dark hair and a

Van Dyke beard. Unlike his colleagues, he wasn't wearing the wraparound sunglasses. Putting the man out of his thoughts, Picard turned his attention back to his commander-in-chief. "Madam President. Thank you for seeing me."

"Well, it's not as if you gave me much choice, did you, Captain?" She waved to the guest chairs in front of her desk. "Sit down."

He picked the chair on the left and sat down. "I've been informed by the Federation Embassy that Lieutenant Commander Data is being held there in Starfleet custody."

Bacco nodded. "That's my understanding, as well."

"What happened?"

With one glance, the president deflected the query to Piñiero. "We're still looking into that," said the chief of staff. "He was arrested sometime this morning. We learned of it only an hour ago, but Ambassador Císol assures me that all proper protocols are being observed."

He wasn't sure he liked the sound of that. "What does that mean, exactly?"

Piñiero met his accusatory stare with cool equanimity. "The Starfleet JAG office has provided him with legal representation, and its Criminal Investigation Division is checking his alibis and comparing them to the limited evidence in hand."

"Ambassador Císol suggested that Data might be facing murder charges."

Anxious looks passed between the two politicos. Piñiero remained on point. "Yes."

"I refuse to believe him capable of such a heinous crime."

The president's aspect was grave, her voice empathetic. "This news came as a shock to me, as well, Captain. I'd also like to think it's not true. But a Starfleet officer is dead, and the evidence in hand suggests a Soong-type android tried to breach the perimeter of this bank in the midst of our summit meeting. What's more, before Commander Tohm was murdered, she had accessed restricted files regarding this bank and had passed them to Commander Data, only hours before the attempted incursion and her own murder. He's not being held on a whim."

"If the charges against Mister Data are as serious as you say, he's entitled to the best possible defense. I'd like to ask that the *Enterprise* and her crew be tasked to the investigation."

His plea provoked a cold glare from the president. "To be frank, Captain, I'd prefer you and your ship weren't here at all. There was a reason I had Leonard"—she paused at a cautionary cough by Piñiero, then corrected herself—"Chief Admiral Akaar send your ship to Azeban. But now that you're here, the damage is done." A sigh of resignation. "I'll ask Captain Bateson to share all sensor data from the break-in with your crew. Though I doubt you'll find anything his people haven't—the *Enterprise* doesn't have a monopoly on talented officers."

"I would never suggest that it did, Madam President." Sensing that his welcome was rapidly expiring, he pressed on to the final item of his agenda. "I'd like to ask your permission for myself and my two senior officers to meet with Commander Data."

Piñiero asked with cynical suspicion, "And why would we allow that?"

"It's my understanding that Commander Data has been less than forthcoming, even in confidence to his own defense counsel. Perhaps I or one of my officers could be of assistance. We've served with Data for many years. He might be willing to confide in us." Bacco and

Piñiero looked unmoved. "We would, of course, share any actionable intelligence."

Piñiero glanced at the president, seeking guidance, and was answered with a grudging nod. She looked back at Picard. "We'll see what we can do."

"Most kind, thank you." Picard got up and offered his hand to Piñiero, who shook it not with any sign of cordiality but a dry air of requirement. Then he dipped his chin toward Bacco, an old-fashioned gesture of deference. "Madam President."

She answered him with an impatient lift of one gray eyebrow. "Captain." Then she looked across the room at her personal protection agent. "Steven, show the captain out."

"Yes, Madam President." The agent stepped smartly to the door, which opened as soon as he moved within range of its automated sensor. He fixed his stare on Picard, a hard-eyed look whose silent message would be clear in any language: *Get out.*

Picard made his exit in silence, his face a mask of confidence, even as he wondered what manner of disaster he'd involved himself in this time.

10

Another day of clueless shareholders and useless subordinates was at long last finished, and Siro Kinshal was glad to be free of them. Free of the meddling inquiries of the board of directors, the banal dilemmas of those who feared to show enough initiative to solve their own problems, and the petty complaints of those who felt their own meager contributions weren't being hailed with drunken fervor. Kinshal was fed up with the lot of them.

Loosening the collar of his dress shirt, he breathed freely. Coming home was more than a mere temporal milestone in his endless march of days. It was an act of self-liberation, a casting off of oppressive fashion and a reclamation of the man he'd once been but often felt as if he'd forgotten: the artist, the poet, the tender soul who'd chafed at the suggestion of a career in high finance, a life predicated on greed and selfishness. Everything had seemed so easy when he'd been young. All his arguments had felt so pure, so untainted. He missed that sense of sanctity, that great righteousness, the belief that his soul was so pure that it could change the galaxy.

But that had all been nonsense. He saw that now. No

one ever changed the galaxy, the world, society. It was all too big, too powerful, too uncaring to bend to the passions of one soul. It was the crucible that broke people down, reduced them to their basest elements, and remade them in its own callous image: the hard and the soulless, the empty and the heartless, the selfish and the cruel. Those were all that ever emerged whole from the fires of the modern world. Everything good, everything noble, everything kind was burned away, turned to slag or smoke, consumed and forgotten. This was the ugly truth of life, of the universe: There was nothing but the now, and you either ruled the now or it ruled you. There was no middle ground.

He stepped through his front door, turned off his apartment's security alarm, and dropped his briefcase on the floor just past the threshold. That was where he left it each night when he came home. Why bring it an inch farther inside than it needed to be? He never opened it once he was here. Its contents were part of that rotten, merciless, corporate hell he'd left behind on the other side of the city. Why would he ever let that evil contaminate his last refuge? This was his place; work had no dominion here. *Damn them,* he raged. *They steal enough of my life as it is.*

Plodding in heavy steps across his living room, he kicked off his shoes one at a time, shed his suit coat, and discarded his necktie with a lazy toss onto the back of the sofa. The maid would police them up and wash them all tomorrow while he was away. He unbuckled his belt and stepped out of his trousers on his way into the kitchen.

Kinshal arrived at his replicator nook wearing only his undershirt, his shorts, and his socks. Resting his forehead against the cool blue tiles above the machine, he mumbled through lips numbed by alcohol, *"Orroyo."*

The replicator whirred into action, spinning energy and raw mass into a plate of sticky, boiled grains topped with a fatty seafood stew, a traditional Orion favorite. He was especially partial to his machine's version of the dish, which had been patterned from an original recipe prepared years earlier by his mother. This was as close as replicated fare came to perfection.

Inside a storm of glowing particles, heralded by a musical wash of noise, the delicacy took shape, and he reached for it, eager to recapture a moment of his squandered youth in a mouthful of salty, savory decadence.

A cold wire looped around his throat and sliced into his flesh with brutal force.

Gasping for air he couldn't find, fighting to scream through his severed larynx, Kinshal clawed at his maimed throat, tried to pull the garrote from his neck. Its wire sliced off his fingertips, which tumbled to the floor between his feet, into the spreading pool of his blood.

He flailed his arms, threw wild backward jabs with his elbows, but found only air.

Vital warmth sheeted down the front of his undershirt as his sight grew dim and his head swam. Afloat in the last wave of his own consciousness, he cast about for answers, for a reason, but found nothing. Nothing but darkness and silence.

Nothing.

Hain watched the Orion man's body on the lab's main screen. When the corpse ceased twitching, she opened a channel to her team in the field. "Berro, he's dead. You can let go now."

"I wanted to sever his spinal cord to make sure," Berro replied over the comm.

"You've succeeded. Put him down." She checked the feed from the other android deployed to Kinshal's residence. "Sair, get the retinal pattern."

Sair's visual feed showed her moving into position above Kinshal's still-warm body. The android's face pressed to within inches of the dead Orion's, and Hain saw its fingers pry open Kinshal's eyelids as wide as they would go. Then the high-resolution receptors in Sair's ocular sensors scanned Kinshal's retinas and transmitted their patterns back to the lab. Hain put the scan through a filter to make sure it was clear enough for their purposes. "That looks good, Sair. You're clear. Berro, get rid of that body, and make sure you leave his apartment spotless. Our profile on Mister Kinshal says he has a maid who cleans his residence daily. I don't want her calling the local authorities because she found bloodstains in the lavatory."

"Understood." The android agents set to work, moving with tireless efficiency as they removed all traces of their presence from the premises. Berro cooked the man's corpse into sludge with a few packets of concentrated bioreactive acid and flushed the watery sludge down the shower drain. Sair sprayed the apartment with an aerosol of nanites that would break down any incriminating fibers, and then dissociate themselves into innocuous carbon atoms. Within minutes of the murder of Kinshal, there was no evidence that the crime had ever occurred.

Hain added the retinal scans to her biometric profile of Kinshal, a file that encompassed everything from his DNA and his body-mass distribution to his voiceprint and now his retinal patterns. Those had been the last pieces of the puzzle, ones whose acquisition had been postponed until the latest possible moment. But with the SRD pressuring Operation Zelazo into premature action, the timetable for Kinshal's demise had been accelerated. The next day of operations would determine the mission's outcome—and Hain knew that failure was not an outcome her superiors would be willing to accept.

Satisfied her profile on Kinshal was complete, she reopened the channel to her agents. "Wrap it up and get out of there. As soon as the new template's ready, we'll begin Phase Two."

11

Had he not seen it with his own eyes, Worf would not have believed such a facility was part of a Federation embassy. The secure sublevel of the diplomatic headquarters on Orion was as bleak and austere a place as he had ever visited. Its sublevel was defined by bare walls and floors of thermocrete, as well as hardened portals that seemed better suited to a Klingon maximum security prison. Of course, that's what this rarely mentioned area of the embassy was: a prison.

Armed Starfleet officers assigned to the embassy guarded the door to the interrogation room in which Data was being held. As the human ensign entered a code to unlock and open the door, the Bolian lieutenant supervising him warned the trio from the *Enterprise,* "Be careful. The prisoner's restraints have been removed. If he gives you any trouble, we'll be right outside."

Worf suppressed his impulse to gut the Bolian. "We will *not* need you."

The door opened. Picard entered first, and Worf followed him inside, trailed closely by La Forge. As soon as all three of them were inside the cramped room, the guards closed and locked the door behind them.

Data—whose human appearance and civilian clothes

still caused Worf a moment of cognitive dissonance—grinned at the sight of his former shipmates. "Captain! Worf! Geordi!" He got up from his chair, shook the captain's hand, clasped Worf's forearm and slapped his shoulder, then hugged La Forge. "It is good to see all of you. Thank you for coming."

"Nothing could have kept us away," Picard said. His smile faded as the reason for the visit weighed upon him. "Data, we don't have much time. Are you aware of all that's happened pertaining to your arrest?"

The android nodded. "Yes, sir. It seems I am considered a suspect in the murder of the SI section chief, Commander Tohm. As I lack a clear alibi for the period in question, I am unsure how I will verify my innocence in this matter."

La Forge raised a hand to interject, "One thing at a time, Data. What're you doing here?"

"I have been looking for clues that will lead me to Emil Vaslovik. Commander Tohm helped me access the records of the Bank of Orion to verify some of my suspicions."

The captain looked confused. "Was that why you tried to gain access to the bank?"

"I did no such thing, sir."

His assertion sparked worried glances among the three *Enterprise* officers. Worf decided to cut to the heart of the matter. "If it was not you who tried to enter the bank . . . could it have been another Soong-type android?"

"That would seem to be the most reasonable conclusion," Data said. "Are Captain Bateson and his crew aware of the android factory we discovered sixty-eight days ago?"

"Not yet," Worf said. "That incident was classified as top secret by Starfleet Command."

The news did not seem to trouble Data. "Still, when it is made available to the JAG office, that should make it possible to secure my release."

Picard's mien turned grim. "I wouldn't be so sure, Mister Data. We still lack evidence that any of those androids are present on Orion. And there is the additional complication of the severity of the breach at the bank." Noting Data's lack of understanding, the captain continued. "The reason Starfleet is involved in the investigation is that President Bacco is conducting a private summit inside that institution."

Data nodded at a curious angle. "That would account for their exaggerated response."

La Forge stepped around Worf to clear his line of sight to Data. "Is it possible the Breen have figured out how to program some of the androids they removed from the factory?"

"I do not think that is likely." Data wore a look of stern thought. "None of the software they had at the factory would have enabled them to activate and program a positronic brain." Looking up at Picard, he added, "They were not even close, sir."

More pragmatic concerns nagged at Worf. "However they have been activated, we need to track them down. Is there any way we can find them before they act again?"

"Its energy emissions seemed to have been camouflaged," La Forge said. "I'd guess they probably have access to sensor-spoofing hardware and software, which would mean they could make these things show up to sensors as whatever they want—or as nothing at all."

The speculation seemed to give Data an idea. "You might be able to detect short-range fluctuations in electron potentials caused by the androids' positronic brains."

La Forge shrugged. "If their sensor blinds are good enough, we might not even be able to read that. But it's still worth a try." He looked at Picard. "I'll have Taurik work something up."

"Very good." The captain fixed his worried stare on Data. "What concerns me, Mister Data, is your legal predicament. Have you provided your defense counsel with any account of your whereabouts during the hours in which Commander Tohm was murdered?"

Data nodded. "Yes, sir. Unfortunately, the dearth of public surveillance technology on Orion has made it all but impossible to confirm my alibi."

Picard frowned. "I admit that in principle I find their devotion to individual privacy commendable. The notion of a state monitoring its people's every action troubles me. Unfortunately, in this instance, audiovisual records of the public transit system, or of routine electronic commercial transactions, might save you from a lifetime in prison."

"The irony of my situation is not lost on me, sir."

The captain laid his hand on Data's shoulder. "Don't worry, Data. I give you my word: the *Enterprise* and its crew will not rest until you are free." He looked at Worf. "Number One: Do whatever it takes to confirm Mister Data's alibi. That's an order."

It was a directive Worf was eager to carry out. "Aye, sir."

Basking in dry heat and feasting on raw meat, for the moment Imperator Sozzerozs had no cause for complaint. *Say what you will about the Orions, they understand hospitality.*

He and his retinue lounged in the private suite the bank's staff had prepared for them. To accommodate the particular needs and preferences of Gorn physiology, all of the suites' regular furnishings and embellishments had been replaced with appointments suited to the archosaurs. Its walls had been removed, creating an open floor plan that satisfied the Gorn's preference for clear lines of sight. Organically curved slabs of volcanic rock were spread out, giving Sozzerozs and each member of his delegation his own territory in which to repose beneath the ruddy glow of heat lamps that simulated the radiation of their native star. Steam baths were never more than a few strides away, and even the artwork had been tailored to their aesthetics. The spacious chamber was decorated with sculptures carved from a type of obsidian that remained cold even when exposed to extreme temperatures, and to which had been applied electrically conductive filaments that created bright thermal patterns visible to the Gorn's infrared visual receptors.

The only part of the suite that wasn't bathed in magnificent warmth was the buffet, which had been larded with the most remarkable assortment of raw meats Sozzerozs had ever seen. Mammalian meats, poultry, fish, Chelonian delicacies, even a smorgasbord of small live prey—it was a banquet that made clear the Orions took the time to learn about their guests and spared no expense to please them and make them comfortable.

Which meant, naturally, that his chief adviser Togor had to find some way to spoil it.

"I have the full report of this morning's disturbance, Majesty."

Bowing to the demands of his office, Sozzerozs put aside his Sybaritic indulgences and gave his attention to the *wazir*. "What happened?"

"A failed attempt to breach the secure perimeter. Four persons appear to have been involved, but the Orions are unable to specify the perpetrators' species or genders." He held out a glossy black data tablet for Sozzerozs to look at. "The first one to strike the bank's force field was incapacitated. His accomplices carried him away during their retreat."

Sozzerozs slid off his basking rock. "And this matters to us because . . . ?" He plodded across the rough sandstone floor to the buffet. Togor followed him.

"The bank's sensors detected strange energy readings when the first intruder hit the force field. We've not yet identified those readings, but since this morning, the Starfleet personnel on the planet have maintained a state of high alert. They also executed a rapid deployment into the capital's starport this morning. Witnesses to the incident say a human man was arrested, but the Orions and the Federation refuse to identify him, or reveal their charges against him."

The imperator loomed over the buffet table, savoring the wide selection of raw victuals. His adviser remained half a step behind him, watching his every movement with intense focus. "Why should we be concerned about what appears to be a strictly internal Federation matter?"

"Because, within hours of the man's arrest, the Federation vessel *Enterprise* arrived in orbit, and its captain has been granted a private audience with President Bacco."

The bad news whipped the imperator about-face. "The *Enterprise* is here?"

"Yes, Majesty."

Anxiety drove Sozzerozs to grind his fangs. "Could their arrival cause Bacco to cancel the summit? The Federation has tried to avoid attracting the attention of the rest of the Pact."

Togor reacted with a pensive tilt of his long head. "They might withdraw, but I doubt it. Their efforts to shift the Pact's focus away from Orion has been done at our request. Most likely, they will seek to gauge our reaction to the *Enterprise*'s presence, and then act accordingly."

"Good." Sozzerozs speared a handful of bright red meat on his talons, shoved it into his maw, and chomped hungrily. Bits and flecks of half-masticated flesh leaped from his gullet, peppering the gritty floor and Togor's silken tunic. "When they sound us out, make sure they know we remain committed to the summit. And just to maintain appearances, make some kind of formal objection to the presence of the *Enterprise*. We can't let on that it doesn't matter."

Togor raked up a shredded mess of raw fish on his own jet claws. "I understand, sire." He shoveled the delicate fillets into his mouth, where they all but disintegrated as soon as he started to chew. "What shall I tell Thot Tran when Domo Brex demands an update?"

"Tell the Breen nothing more than you absolutely have to. It's bad enough that we let them bully us into this scheme of theirs. I won't have us leaping to do their bidding every time they deign to ring some metaphorical chime."

"As you command, Majesty." He picked idly at the glistening cuts of poultry. "Should I ask for an estimate of how much longer we are expected to prolong this charade?"

Sozzerozs swallowed a deep growl of irritation. "A waste of time."

The *wazir* bowed his head and backed away. "Understood, Majesty."

Alone again, Sozzerozs chose to relish the moment while he could. He stepped down into one of the steam baths and submerged up to his neck. The flow of hot vapor under and around his scales was deeply soothing, a desperately needed relief. There had been as much truth as falsehood in the stories he and his courtiers had spun for Bacco and her aides, but the one great omission was the only fact that really mattered: the summit was just for show.

Neither he nor his advisers knew the true ultimate objective of the Breen. All that Brex and Thot Tran had shared was that these talks were a key element in a cooperative intelligence mission that would benefit all members of the Pact, and the Gorn's only directives were to make the secret conference drag on for as long as possible, and to ensure the Federation did everything in its power to "distract" the Typhon Pact, for the safety of the Gorn, out of deference to "the dire political risk" they claimed to be taking by engaging in such negotiations. Meanwhile, in star systems scattered across the quadrant, the Breen and Tzenkethi would play their parts, pretending to be ensorcelled by Starfleet's comical attempts at misdirection.

The imperator suspected the Breen were overreaching in a futile effort to prove themselves the Romulans' equals in the arts of subterfuge, but that wasn't what vexed him. The itch beneath his scales was the fact that he was now playing a starring role in this farce—and he had no idea how it was supposed to end.

Dodging and shouldering through a crowded sidewalk in Kinarvon, one of Orion's major cities, the *Enterprise*'s chief of security looked grouchy and uncomfortable in civilian garb. "This is ridiculous," Šmrhová said. "I feel like a character in a holodeck program."

La Forge felt bad for her; he was enjoying his break from the constraints of the uniform. "Lighten up, Aneta. We're supposed to be incognito."

"Sure we are. Two humans on Orion, and one of us has cybernetic eyes."

He shot an offended glare her way. "What? I'm wearing dark glasses."

"Yeah, at night." She rolled her eyes. "That's not suspicious. No, sir."

Noting the street sign overhead, he nudged her to the right. "Turn here." They rounded the corner onto an avenue busy with road traffic and pedestrians, and blazing with neon light from store signs whose reflections shimmered across wet pavement. La Forge plucked a miniaturized padd from his overcoat pocket and stole a look at its screen. He tilted his chin up toward their destination. "That's the place up there, on the left." He spotted a break in the traffic and darted across the street with Šmrhová right alongside him. They slowed when they reached the far sidewalk and stopped to size up the shop they'd come to find. He peeked through the front window and saw shelves and display cases packed with high-tech gadgets, spare parts, and precision tools of various origins—Federation, Klingon, Romulan, Ferengi, and many more. The engineer smiled. "Yeah, this looks like the kind of place Data would shop."

"Great. Let's hope its owner is more helpful than the transit workers we questioned." She lifted her hands as he stink-eyed her. "I'm just saying, we've retraced every step Data said he made last night, and so far no one remembers seeing him."

La Forge sighed in exasperation. "What did you expect? We're dealing with Orions."

"That's my point. It's like these people have a genetic predisposition not to remember anything—conversations, romantic trysts, contracts, murders. How can the whole damned species have amnesia, Geordi?" She plunged her hands inside her trench coat's pockets and stewed beneath a few stray locks of her sable hair. "We're trying to save a man's life, and all these people care about is not getting involved. They make me sick."

She wasn't wrong, and he knew it. Persuading Orions to meddle in one another's affairs, or to involve themselves in the troubles of offworlders, was one of the most difficult tasks known to social engineering. But for Data's sake, they had to find a way.

He sidled up to her. "Look, this is the last place on Data's list. We didn't come this far just to quit. Whatever happens, let's just go in there and get this over with."

"Fine." She turned and led him through the shop's front door. Inside, they tried to act casual, as if they were just random customers browsing the store's wares, but the sinewy, bald Orion man behind the counter challenged them in an angry, nasal voice. "What do *you* want?"

Hoping to disarm him with kindness, La Forge grinned. "Hi, there."

"Don't 'hi' me. You want something or not?"

Šmrhová posed herself seductively against the sales counter and gave the owner a come-hither stare and a salacious but coy half smile. "No need to be so rude, Mister . . . ?"

He tried to hold on to his blustering bad mood, but it melted away as he looked into the comely brunette's dark brown eyes. ". . . Jasser."

She batted her eyelashes and bit her pouting lower lip. "Well, Mister *Jasser,* there is something we want." She took her own micropadd from her pocket and held it toward Jasser. On the device's screen was an image of Data as he currently appeared. "This man says he was here for over an hour last night, buying a number of computer parts. My friend here has the list."

Taking his cue, La Forge held out his micropadd,

on which was displayed a list Data had compiled from memory, detailing every item he had purchased at the shop, how much he had paid for each one, and how long he had been there.

Šmrhová waited for Jasser to take note of the list, then she continued. "We're trying to help him verify his story, and we'd be very grateful if you could check your records and confirm these purchases, and the time they occurred."

Jasser looked away from her, shook his head, and backed up half a step. "No, sorry. I don't remember anyone like that."

La Forge pointed at the interface panel for a retail-service computer. "Could you just check? If he was here when he said he was, it'd be a big—"

"No, no. I'd remember a big sale like that. You must have the wrong place."

"I'm quite sure we don't," La Forge said. On a hunch, he glanced up and around, using his eyes' full-spectrum sensitivity to look for telltale energy flow patterns and electromagnetic disturbances. He found them: in the corners, behind the counter, and overhead in the center of the shop. Pointing at the hot spots he knew had been camouflaged with decorative mirrors—or, in the case of the one directly overhead, disguised as a smoke and fire detector—he said to Jasser, "You have this whole place wired for surveillance. To prevent shoplifters, right?"

The Orion stammered. "I . . . I don't know what . . . what you're—"

"Spare me," La Forge said. "I know that recording your customers is considered a major breach of privacy. Not quite illegal, but definitely unpopular, am I right? If anyone ever found out about those six little cameras . . ." He let the implied threat linger between them.

"Please! You wouldn't!" The man turned his imploring gaze from La Forge to Šmrhová and back again. "Don't do this, I beg of you. My reputation would be ruined."

An evil smile possessed Šmrhová's face. "No one ever needs to know, Mister Jasser. All we want is a copy of the sales receipt, and the vid footage that proves our friend was here."

Jasser looked as if they were prodding him with a firebrand. "You don't know what you ask! The moment they get used as evidence in any court on Orion, I'll be blacklisted!"

"They'll never be seen by another Orion," La Forge said. "This isn't for a local criminal matter, it's for a Starfleet military tribunal."

A weight of concern was lifted from Jasser's shoulders, and his face brightened. "Starfleet? A military hearing?"

Šmrhová nodded. "That's right. Completely confidential, and not subject to review by the Orion authorities. Plus, if your security records show our friend was here, you'll help prove him innocent of a serious crime, and scuttle a major military investigation."

Now the man beamed with delight. "Well, why didn't you say so in the first place?" He clapped his hands and rubbed them together. "I will sell you a copy of my security video for one hundred thousand Federation credits."

La Forge tried not to act flabbergasted, but his jaw fell open. "Excuse me?"

Jasser rolled his shoulders in an exaggerated shrug. "A man has to make a living."

"Are you sure you're not part Ferengi?"

The security chief was back to simmering. "A hundred's a bit rich for our blood. We'll give you twenty-five."

The Orion pounced on the opportunity to haggle. "Ninety."

Though he had no idea where he and Šmrhová would get this kind of credit, La Forge joined in the process. "Thirty-five."

"Eighty-five."

"Fifty," Šmrhová said.

A faux frown and a shake of his bald green head. "Eighty."

La Forge was tired of the back-and-forth. "Sixty. That's our final offer."

The Orion folded his arms and put on a defiant air. "Seventy-five. Not a credit less."

Šmrhová drew a compact hand phaser from her coat pocket and pressed its emitter crystal to Jasser's temple. "How about this? My friend copies it and your sales records from last night for *free,* and I don't blast your head into dust." She added in a menacing whisper, "After all, who're you gonna tell? You can't exactly call the cops and admit we took something you don't want anyone to know you have, now can you?" She motioned La Forge behind the counter with a tilt of her head. "Get the copies, and remember to erase the record of our visit."

"On it," La Forge said, vaulting over the counter and setting himself to work retrieving the information from the shop's computer. In less than a minute, thanks to a few passwords coerced from Jasser's memory by Šmrhová's vivid descriptions of a phaser's destructive potential, La Forge held up an isolinear chip. "Got it. We're good to go."

Šmrhová waited for him to get back over the counter, and she backed out behind him, keeping her phaser tucked against her hip but trained on Jasser's center of mass every step of the way. Stepping through the doorway, she pocketed the weapon and blew the Orion a kiss.

"Pleasure doing business with you."

Hurrying down the street into the cover of night, La Forge shook from the adrenaline rush. He was still winded as they slowed down. "That wasn't exactly by the book, Lieutenant."

"Neither was paying a bribe we can't afford." She caught his warning glare. "Sir."

"Point taken." He handed her the isolinear chip. "This proves Data was on the far side of the planet when Hilar Tohm was murdered. Send a copy of it to Data's lawyer. Once that's done, we can move on to our next problem."

"Which is?"

"Now that we can show Data didn't kill Hilar Tohm, we need to prove another android tried to break into the bank."

"Do you think the two crimes are connected?"

"Only one way to find out," La Forge said. "Let's go have a look at her apartment."

12

Breathing a contented sigh, Bacco put down her fork and picked up her wine. "That was amazing," she said to Piñiero, "but I can't eat another bite. I just want to take a nap."

In the four-and-a-half years since Nanietta Bacco was first elected president of the United Federation of Planets, she had consumed many a late dinner with only her chief of staff for company. Most of those working meals had been taken at Bacco's desk inside her office on the fifteenth floor of the Palais de la Concorde in Paris, and had consisted of something whipped up on short notice. The food, after all, was never the point of those ad hoc repasts; it was just something to keep her and her advisers from starving while they debated points of policy or the consequences of *realpolitik* in an increasingly volatile galaxy. They rarely made time for anything beyond essential sustenance; their schedules just didn't permit such luxuries.

Tonight, their table for two had been a study in culinary extravagance. The bank's executive chef had treated them to a splendid five-course meal—soup, appetizer, entrée, salad, and dessert—accompanied by a flight of wines that far surpassed any she had ever imbibed before. Every dish had been a marvel of presentation and substance, the portions perfect in size to leave them satisfied but not overburdened. However, for Bacco the best part of the meal had been the company. She had known Piñiero for decades, since the younger woman had been a child, and she had come to think of her as a trusted friend as well as her chief of staff. In the past several years they had weathered a tumultuous first term in office, and now they were plotting strategy for next year's reelection campaign, which already promised to be fiercely contested. Bacco's connection with Piñiero had deepened to a level she had come to think of as kinship. She was a part of Bacco's family.

Piñiero dabbed the corners of her mouth with her napkin, then set it down beside her plate. "Please tell me I can skip the reception tonight. I'm begging you."

"If I have to go, so do you. This is what I pay you for."

"I thought you kept me around for my scintillating wit and brilliant intellect."

"Nope, just a pity date for official state functions." She savored a tiny sip of Sancerre, reveled in its floral nose and honeyed flavors. "All kidding aside, we need this to go well tonight. Today's talks felt like a setback."

The younger woman didn't mask her disappointment. "They were. Every time we started to make progress, the same issues tripped us up. It's like the agenda's booby-trapped."

Bacco suspected there was more than a seed of truth in the complaint. "Do you think they're doing it on purpose? Maybe trying to wring bigger concessions out of us?"

"Who knows?" She sipped her Jack Daniel's neat. "I'm meeting Safranski tomorrow for breakfast, to see if we can defuse a few of those traps before they come up."

"Good. We could use a break in there. And not *just* in there. Lately, it seems like the Typhon Pact's breathing down our necks everywhere we go—the slipstream fracas, that fiasco with the Tzenkethi's artificial wormhole, not to mention losing Deep Space 9." She felt torn between hope and surrender. "It feels like every time we have another showdown, it ends with them gaining the advantage. Swinging the Gorn back to our side would be a big win for us. This summit's a major opportunity, and we can't afford to waste it. . . . We need this."

"I know." Piñiero's somber mien reflected the gravity of Bacco's point. "Which is why we might need to accept that we can't accomplish everything at this one meeting. Maybe the best plan for now would be to use these talks to lay the groundwork for a second meeting, a tripartite discussion involving Chancellor Martok and maybe even Emperor Kahless."

"First, we'd have to meet separately with Ambassador K'mtok, and then with Martok."

Piñiero continued the thought as if it had been her own. "We'll bring the Klingons on board first before we put them in a room with the Gorn. Makes sense. But I wonder how much both sides will try to get from us in exchange for burying the *bat'leth,* if you know what I mean."

"That's a good point. We can't go overboard with promises unless we want to be the only ones making sacrifices for the sake of peace. At the same time, we can't be cheap about this. Effecting this big a shift in the balance of power might be worth rebuilding a few worlds for them, or ceding colonization rights in some of the outer sectors, to get them both to the table."

They sat back, both of them pondering that scenario, turning it over in their imaginations. Before they resumed the discussion, the door signal chimed softly. Bacco turned toward the doorway as she called out, "Come in."

It slid open, and the bank's chairman, a trim and dapper Orion man named Siro Kinshal, stepped inside, shadowed by Bacco's personal protection agent, Steven Wexler. The executive stepped up to the women's table sporting the gracious smile of a head waiter. "Madam President. I hope your dinner was satisfactory."

"Everything was wonderful, thank you."

Kinshal looked at Piñiero. "Our pastry chef wants to know if you enjoyed dessert."

"Very much. Send her my compliments."

"It will be my honor, Madam Piñiero."

Bacco smiled as she observed Kinshal's demeanor toward her friend. *If I didn't know better, I'd say he's hitting on her. I'd better jump in and save her.* "Is the rooftop arboretum ready for tonight's reception?"

"Almost, Madam President. Your protection detail is still securing the venue."

"I see. I just want to let you know I've added a few more names to the guest list."

Unfazed, Kinshal nodded toward Wexler. "Your agent has the particulars?"

"He will. We're finalizing the list now."

"Very good. I'll see him tonight during the final security check. Might I recommend you both take advantage of the interim to freshen up, and perhaps steal a few moments of rest?"

Piñiero mirrored Bacco's amused expression. "You read our minds, Mister Kinshal."

"In that case, I shall take my leave. With your permission, Madam President."

"Granted. We'll look forward to seeing you tonight."

Kinshal bowed slightly. "Until then." He backed

away five steps, turned, and made a prompt exit that managed not to look the least bit rushed.

As soon as the door closed, Bacco smirked. "I think he likes you."

Piñiero raised an eyebrow and glanced at Wexler. "Agent, if that man tries to touch any part of me other than my hand, *shoot him*."

"Yes, ma'am."

Standing in the center of the Bank of Orion's lush and exquisitely manicured rooftop arboretum, awash in the fragrance of citrus flowers and freshly turned earth, Agent Steven Wexler saw potential security risks everywhere he looked. He pointed at the glass-paneled dome overhead and asked the bank's director of security, "Are there any buildings in the capital tall enough to have a direct line of sight into this space?"

"None." Akili Kamar, the tall, copper-haired, and enticingly athletic Orion woman spoke with calm confidence. "This is the tallest structure in the city. Air traffic has been rerouted and our airspace marked as restricted for the duration of tonight's event." She looked up but kept her hands folded behind her back. "As fragile as the dome appears, it is quite resilient. Those panels are transparent duranium, and they are protected from the outside by a shaped force field, and reinforced by another inside. Nothing short of a full-scale bombardment, or an impact by something larger than a commercial passenger ship, can breach it."

Hazizaar, the *sikta* for Imperator Sozzerozs—a title that Wexler had learned meant "captain of the Gorn leader's personal guard company"—pivoted slowly and hissed as he studied the perimeter. "There are too many points of ingress and egress."

Kamar took a moment to study the room's layout.

"Most of those doors will be sealed before the reception begins. Only three will be active tonight." She pointed at the two exits that opened into short hallways that led to two dedicated elevators programmed for access to the delegations' respective residential suites. "One each will be reserved for the use of your leaders and their escorts." Then she turned toward the room's main entry, three sets of Brobdingnagian double doors side by side. "That will be the primary entry point for guests and bank security personnel. I trust the sensor arches we've provided meet with your approval?"

"Yes," Hazizaar said. "But I want guards on all the other doors."

Before she could object, Wexler added, "So do I. And I'll go a step further. I want one of my people and one of Hazizaar's on opposite sides of each sealed door."

Their unified request ruffled the ostensibly unflappable Orion. "Such measures are not an efficient use of your limited personnel. If you are adamant regarding that deployment pattern, the bank's security contingent can . . . ." Her voice trailed off in the face of unwavering stares from Wexler and Hazizaar. "Very well. I'll leave it to the two of you to assign your people as you see fit, and mine will patrol the main room, disguised as catering staff."

"That works for me," Wexler said. He nodded at the replicator nooks behind the wet bars and buffet tables. "How certain are we that no one can tamper with those?"

"Positive." Kamar oozed smug surety. "Not that it matters. We won't be using replicated food or beverages at tonight's event. Everything is being prepared fresh by our chefs, and all drinks will be mixed to order from real spirits."

Wexler cleared his throat. "Nothing consumable enters this room until it's been scanned by trained medical personnel from both my team and Hazizaar's."

"Naturally. I assure you, Agent, we haven't forgotten the protocols your service shared with us prior to your visit. We're well aware of the precautions that must be observed."

The snap of fast-approaching footsteps turned Wexler's head. Siro Kinshal, the bank's fastidious and ever-smiling chairman, approached with the genial affect of a man who had spent his career solving the problems of others. "Good evening. Is everything ready for tonight?"

"Just sorting out a few last-minute details," Kamar said.

Kinshal looked at Wexler. "Nothing serious, I hope?"

"No, sir. Nothing we can't fix."

"Very well. Do you have President Bacco's final guest list?" Wexler handed a data chip to the chairman, who tucked it inside his jacket but maintained steady eye contact with him. "Splendid." Something about Kinshal's stare made Wexler uncomfortable. It might have been its unusual duration, its unblinking ferocity, or the way the middle-aged Orion seemed to gaze straight through Wexler's eyes. By instinct, Wexler rarely shied from a challenge, but this time he felt compelled to look away from the man and try to direct him toward the inscrutable archosaur. "Hazizaar? Anything else you want to bring up?"

The Gorn took one more look around. "No."

Kamar smiled. "Excellent." She nodded at Kinshal. "I'm sure you have other matters to attend, sir. Please be assured, the reception will start on time, and security will be ready."

"Carry on, then." The executive walked away, one hand in his pocket, as if he had not a care in the world. To be so nonchalant in the midst of such an affair, he was either the most confident man Wexler had ever seen, or an idiot without peer in the known galaxy.

Wexler wanted to write the man off as a fool, but the way Kinshal had stared at him, looking him right in the eye without fear or self-consciousness . . . that troubled him. Not that it was the sort of thing he'd have any idea how to document in his daily activity log. *Got eyeballed by a strange middle-aged Orion man* was more likely to end up as poker-night joke fodder for his smart-ass friends than as actionable intelligence for the agency.

"Let's finish our tour of this floor and the one below," Kamar prompted him and Hazizaar. "The sooner we work out the details, the sooner this party can get started."

Hazizaar and Wexler signaled their agreement. They followed the Orion security specialist out of the arboretum, continuing their efforts to anticipate and prevent every possible disaster that might befall their heads of state. Wexler knew that no defense was ever perfect. Mistakes could be made. Enemies could divine weaknesses heretofore unknown. Every day that he reported for duty, he knew that might be the day he finally failed.

All he could do was strive with every ounce of vigor and every spark of thought to make certain today would not be that day.

Parading around in another person's identity, Olar felt exposed, obvious, even ridiculous. He was certain someone would see through his traveling deception, his shadowplay of another man's life, but to his amazement, no one did. Impersonating the bank's chairman, Siro Kinshal, he had come to understand that the man must have been terribly isolated and desperately lonely. None of his peers or subordinates, it seemed, knew him well enough to realize that Olar was little more than a smiling doppelgänger, an unctuous replicant of the man they'd pretended to know.

They either feared him or had no care for him at all, Olar realized. *I walk around in his likeness, and no one knows the difference.* For a Breen accustomed to living behind a mask, it felt strangely natural once he'd realized the parallel. *His aloofness was his mask. The peoples of the outerworlds are just as anonymous as any of us. Their disguises are simply less obvious.*

He passed Kinshal's tall and elegant female executive assistant on the way into his corner office and issued orders without slowing his hurried pace. "No calls, no visitors."

"Yes, sir," the young Trill woman said, half risen from her chair, as if expecting to be summoned for dictation or maybe some salacious purpose behind closed doors.

Disappointment dimmed her hopeful expression as Olar added, "Thank you, Idina."

The door closed behind him, and he forced himself not to gape at the cityscape that wrapped around him on two sides, a sparkling wonder beyond floor-to-ceiling plates of glass. Instead he turned his back on the jeweled beauties of night on Orion and sat down at Kinshal's broad, uncluttered desk. *How marvelous it must be to delegate every bit of tedium from one's life,* he thought. *And how worrisome to think that every outsourced duty is being mishandled.*

He closed his eyes and opened his mind, seeking out the soothing pulse of light and color that he had come to associate with his handler, Hain. *Are you there?*

Her patient voice echoed inside his mind as if it were his own thought. *<Affirmative. Did you get the retinal scan as requested?>*

I did. Using techniques he had practiced before the mission, he accessed the stored data and let it pass through him and over the river of light to Hain. *Did you monitor the encounter?*

Hain's reply was slow in coming. <*Affirmative. We noted a few variances from the metrics on file. I'm amending the matrix now.*>

He imagined the risks that Sair would be facing, and he grew concerned. *Do you need me to be there? I know the layout of the garden. I could help.*

<*That won't be necessary.*> Her thoughtcolors were agitated. <*Stay out of sight and be ready to handle damage control.*> A gray pause. <*Starfleet's poking around. They don't seem to be onto you, but just in case, do you have an exit strategy?*>

He swiveled his chair to gaze longingly out the windows at the urban sprawl stretching away beneath him. *Several, as instructed. How long until Sair is transfigured?*

<*We're finalizing the template now. The new build should be ready for deployment shortly. Can you be at the rear service entrance in exactly twenty-nine minutes?*>

Olar checked the chrono on his desk and considered how long it would take to traverse the building's locked-down floors without attracting the attention of the Orions' security forces, the Gorn's imperial guards, or the Federation's presidential protection agents. *No problem.*

<*Good. It's crucial Sair be inserted before they leave the sublevel. Can you do that?*>

Already visualizing the means to his end, he replied, *Yes. I'm ready.*

Hain's hues of approval and confidence tinted their shared thoughtwave. <*Excellent. You're a hero, Olar, but don't be a martyr. Once you bring Sair inside, get clear. Even if everything goes as planned, this will all be far from over, and we're going to need you.>*

I understand.

Calming shades and dulcet tones preceded her reply. *<Thank you, Olar.>*

The connection between them receded into the background of his consciousness, but he knew his every action was being monitored and observed, recorded for posterity and analysis. Knowing he was under her watchful protection was a comfort; to be alone, to live without a witness, was the only notion that truly frightened Olar to his core.

He checked the chrono. Twenty-eight minutes to the rendezvous. In nine minutes, he would leave the office and follow a circuitous route to the service level.

Within forty-five minutes, Sair would be in position, and Berro would be clear.

In an hour's time, the fate of the galaxy would be sealed, and this day would become a turning point in history, a hinge on which would turn the fortunes of countless lives extant and to come. Everything—even the shape of the future itself—depended upon what Olar did next.

It was almost enough to give him an inflated sense of self-importance, save for the one bitter irony that he had accepted as the price of his greatness.

After the deed is done . . . I will be forgotten.

Success would bring no accolades, no veneration, no statues—no reward except a fleeting moment of satisfaction. For Olar, that would be enough. He was a patriot. But if this really was his hour to die, he had come prepared.

Because he had no intention of dying alone.

13

Nothing had been touched or moved. Sealed behind a Starfleet Security emblem hastily affixed to the door, Hilar Tohm's apartment was exactly as it had been when her body was found. Her furniture was spare and simple. Few mementos adorned her shelves: a bright orange miniature conch shell, a vintage twenty-third-century Starfleet communicator, and a short row of hardcover books bound in black leather: the collected works of William Shakespeare, the horror fiction of Edgar Allan Poe, and several volumes of Trill folk tales and poetry spanning four centuries.

La Forge faced Šmrhová across the center of the living room. In the Dixon Hill pulp detective stories favored by Captain Picard, La Forge would have expected to find a silhouette of chalk lines, a negative-space caricature of Tohm's demise. Instead there was a tiny flag on a slender metal pin, and on that flag an evidence-reference number and an embedded nanochip on which had been recorded a copy of the scans taken before the body's removal.

Šmrhová finished downloading the chip's data to her tricorder. "According to this, her neck was snapped." A detail raised her dark eyebrows. "Whoever did it was strong enough—and brutal enough—to splinter her third and fourth cervical vertebrae."

Picturing the moment sickened La Forge. Despite his years of service in Starfleet, including combat experience in two wars, he had never been able to inure himself to violence. No matter how many times someone told him it was necessary and righteous, he had never been able to divorce himself from the ugliness of sentient pain and the finality of death. *Maybe I just have too much empathy,* he speculated. Then he wondered whether that could ever really be considered a bad thing. Why would it be wrong to have compassion for others?

Snapping fingers broke his spell of distraction. He blinked and saw Šmrhová staring at him. She sounded impatient. "I said, I'll check the bedroom. Can you give the kitchen a look?"

"Sure." They split up, both of them straining to pierce the veil of the mundane and seize upon some clue that the embassy's Starfleet Security detachment might have missed. La Forge tried not to feel self-conscious about the fact that he hadn't known Tohm personally. How would he tell the difference between what was typical in her home, and what wasn't? He searched the kitchen but couldn't have said for what, exactly. Nothing struck him as odd. There were no strange residues, no inexplicable foreign objects, no signs of a struggle. Just as the original report had indicated, there were no fingerprints or DNA traces present except Tohm's.

He turned off his tricorder, disgruntled at the lack of progress, and returned to the living room as Šmrhová walked out of the bedroom. He shot her a hopeful look. "Anything?"

She shook her head. "No signs of struggle, no DNA, no prints. You?"

"The same." La Forge frowned. "This is ridiculous. She didn't snap her own neck."

"That much we know." Šmrhová took another look at her tricorder's screen. "There were ligature marks on her throat consistent with a large humanoid hand. Someone else was here—someone who left no biological traces."

The ominous tone with which she'd added that last detail made her implication clear, and La Forge didn't like it. "I know the absence of evidence doesn't help Data's case, but it can't be used against him, either. We just . . ." He lost track of his sentence as a new thought occurred to him. "You said the marks on Tohm's throat were consistent with a humanoid hand. Can we use them to estimate the size of the hand that killed her?"

"Only within a range of probability. There was so much bruising and torn skin that the variance is fairly wide. Unfortunately, Data's hand size is just within the possible range."

La Forge hid his disappointment as another exculpatory opportunity slipped away. "That figures. If it wasn't, his lawyer would have pounced on that already."

"It's a good bet." Šmrhová turned off her tricorder and holstered it under her jacket. "There's nothing new here. It's just as much a dead end as the security report says." She nodded toward the door. "Ready to head outside?"

He put away his tricorder. "Might as well."

They resealed the room behind them, then took the lift down to the ground floor. Neither of them spoke as they passed through the residential building's small foyer. Its double doors parted ahead of them, and they strode side by side into the night. It welcomed them with a wash of sultry heat, a humid gust perfumed with tropical scents and the ozone bite of air pollution. La Forge wrinkled his nose and grimaced as the late-night swelter leached sweat from his pores.

The campus of the Federation Embassy Compound was quiet except for the faraway roar of the city, a deep and coursing wash of noise that reminded La Forge of crashing surf.

Beside him, Šmrhová pointed upward at a number of not so artfully concealed surveillance devices. "No wonder the killer managed not to get caught on vid. Even a Pakled would be smart enough to steer clear of those."

He was skeptical. "Knowing the cameras are there doesn't make them easy to avoid. The coverage of the compound was pretty tight, and there's no record of anyone entering or leaving the residential building." He nodded toward the main gate. "And unless it was an inside job, it's unlikely the killer walked in or out through the front gate."

"All embassy personnel had alibis that checked out. All the Starfleet personnel were accounted for, and so were the civilian staff and the SI operatives. The only random variable in the equation is our killer—and the only motive on the table is Data's."

"Sorry, I just don't buy it."

They waved to the armed Starfleet guards manning the gatehouse, and the five-meter-tall, solid front portals swung inward. The avenue outside was quiet. La Forge led Šmrhová outside, and they began a slow stroll around the compound's perimeter. A high wall encircled the embassy grounds, and it was topped at regular intervals with surveillance cameras—all of them angled inward, at the diplomatic campus. "So much for getting any footage of pedestrians in the area on the night of the murder," Šmrhová said.

"Looks that way." La Forge pulled out his tricorder and began scanning the sidewalk as they continued their perambulation. It glistened underfoot, shimmering from recent rains, giving him little reason to hope he might find even a hint of trace evidence.

Šmrhová peeked over his shoulder at the device's display. "What're you looking for?"

"Anything that might lead back to Tohm's apartment. If we can find a clue that suggests how the killer got out, or what direction he went, that would be more than we have now."

With needling humor, she replied, "I like how you just assume the killer is male."

"First, how many females, of any species, have hands big enough to have made the marks found on Tohm's throat? Second, it's just a quirk of speech for grammatical convenience."

"If you say so."

He was on the verge of thinking up something clever to say when he heard the hum of a hovercar's motor behind him, and then came a flash of green lights and the single whoop of a siren. A man's voice amplified by a loudspeaker barked, *"Halt."*

La Forge and Šmrhová turned to watch the police hovercar land a few meters behind them. Its gull-wing doors lifted open, and two civilian law-enforcement officers—one male, one female—stepped out of the vehicle. The male officer kept his hand on his sidearm as he and his partner approached the duo.

Šmrhová feigned confused innocence. "Is something wrong, officers?"

"Hand over your scanning devices, please," the male officer said. As if in punctuation to his order, his partner set her hand on the grip of her sidearm.

Offering up his tricorder with slow caution, La Forge

wondered whether the shop owner whom Šmrhová had held at phaser-point had filed a complaint, after all. "Is there a problem?"

The female Orion snatched the tricorder from La Forge's hand, and the male officer took the tricorder from Šmrhová. The man tinkered with one device's settings while his partner held the other and kept her eyes on the two humans. "The use of scanning devices in public spaces without a warrant is illegal on this planet," she said.

Her partner turned off the first tricorder. "This one's wiped. Give me the other one."

They traded devices, then she continued talking to Šmrhová and La Forge. "Normally, this would get you a few weeks in jail. But seeing as this is your first offense, we're letting you go with a warning." She handed back the first tricorder to La Forge.

Apparently unwilling to take good luck at face value, Šmrhová asked, "How do you know this is our first offense?"

The male Orion looked up from his work to glare at her. "You think we don't know who you two are? You're from the *Enterprise*." He tossed the second tricorder to her. "Your scanning devices have been blanked. If we catch you using them outside your embassy again, they'll be destroyed, and you'll face criminal charges." With a mocking tip of his hat, he added, "This little chat's been a diplomatic courtesy. You two have a good night, and stay out of trouble."

The two Orions walked back to their vehicle and climbed inside. Its gull-wing doors lowered shut as the hovercar ascended into the hazy pink glow of the metropolitan night, and then the sleek aircar sped away and blended back into distant streams of traffic.

Šmrhová looked at the memory-wiped device in her

hands. "Well, that's just great." She jammed it back into its holster on her hip. "No wonder this place is called a criminals' paradise."

As they started walking back to the embassy's gate, La Forge played devil's advocate. "On the other hand, you have to give them credit for their commitment to personal privacy."

Her gaze was a poisoned arrow of scorn. "Yeah. . . . I'll bet that's a real comfort to Commander Tohm."

It would be so much easier to explain if only I could tell him why.

Separated from his subordinate by light-years of distance, the buffer of the subspace channel, and the anonymity of their nearly identical uniforms, Thot Tran struggled to convey the urgency of his directive without exposing its true strategic rationale. "You already have your assets in place, Konar. Why can't you complete Phase Two?"

"First, because this updated mission profile has no exit strategy."

"Why should that be of concern?"

Konar leaned forward, snout down, clearly treating the conversation as a confrontation. *"Sir, this operation represents a massive investment by the SRD, as do each of our active assets. We've already lost one. Can we really afford to squander another so carelessly?"*

It was a problem of definitions, Tran realized. That, at least, could be easily remedied. "I do not consider the sacrifice of an asset, no matter how costly it might be, to be a waste when it happens in pursuit of victory. Even our most optimistic scenarios carry a high risk of losing any asset committed to this type of operation."

The discouraged scientist averted his eyeline, and his shoulders slumped. *"I'm not suggesting a major delay. At most, it would take an additional hour to devise an extraction strategy to recover our asset once its mission is accomplished."*

"Adding an extraction to the timeline increases the duration of the asset's engagement, elevating the risk that it will be damaged or incapacitated, leading to its premature capture and analysis. Forcing our targets into action without a retreat scenario has a high probability of ending in the complete disintegration of the asset, which will preserve operational security."

"You want the asset destroyed?"

Why did he sound so shocked? Was it so hard to imagine? "Not if it can be avoided without altering our timetable. But if the alternative is that the enemy acquires it intact for analysis before we've prepared it for them, then yes, I would prefer it be destroyed."

"I find your conclusion extreme, but so be it. However, that brings us to my second concern. Taking action now presents serious tactical hazards."

"I wasn't aware that you were a master tactician as well as a scientist."

Konar tensed at the implied slight but struggled to conceal his reaction. *"The scenario as written poses a threat to our allies, and it risks inflicting significant collateral damage—the one thing we've been expressly ordered to avoid, for fear of alienating our neutral hosts."*

"That's not your problem."

"So you say now. But if this operation goes wrong, where will the blame be laid?"

Tran wondered if the scientist was being deliberately obtuse. "Konar, you're in the midst of executing one of the most important covert operations on foreign soil in the history of the Confederacy. I should think you would have hundreds of concerns more pressing than worrying about something as inconsequential as blame."

"Spoken like someone immune from the consequences of his actions."

"Hardly, I assure you." He uploaded a new data packet and transferred it to Konar on the data subchannel. "Here's something new to occupy your thoughts: We've been ordered by the domo to commence full operational status, effective immediately. You and your associate need to have all assets on line in the next twelve hours."

Konar flinched. *"That's insane! How are we supposed to go fully operational while coordinating tonight's already rushed mission?"*

"Calm down. The remaining assets don't need to be deployed, just activated."

The clarification only added to Konar's befuddlement. *"What purpose will that serve?"*

Researchers, unlike soldiers, could be so very exasperating. "It isn't necessary for you to understand the rationale behind my every command. What matters is that you follow orders."

"Without question? Even if I have reason to believe the orders you've given jeopardize the effectiveness, secrecy, and security of this operation?"

"Even then."

After a moment of quiet seething, Konar asked, *"What if I were to decide that you and the domo have both gone mad, and I refused to follow these reckless orders?"*

"Then you would be single-handedly responsible for sabotaging one of the most vital strategic operations in the history of the Confederacy, I would charge you with treason, and the domo would send a company of Spetzkar to storm your laboratory and kill you." A mocking tilt of his head underscored his low-key affect of menace. "Any further questions?"

Konar straightened his back, aware that his attempt to take a stand had backfired in the worst possible way. *"No, sir. We'll proceed with tonight's operation as ordered, and we'll have the remaining assets activated by morning."*

"Good." He leaned forward, toward the comm's vid sensor, for dramatic effect. "Have a little faith, Konar. I give you my word: Even if your entire operation seems to be in disarray, everything will unfold exactly as I intend. This is chaos by design, a choreographed mayhem years in the making. Don't screw it up by trying to fix what needs to be broken."

Like a shadow at sunset, Konar's dark mood stretched ahead of him and preceded him inside the lab. Hain felt her supervisor's aura of angry resignation before she turned to look at him. Something had shaken him. His footsteps were slower than normal, his bearing was robbed of confidence, and in spite of the sanitized quality of communication through Breen vocoders, as he spoke she sensed that his voice lacked its usual conviction.

"We've been ordered to move ahead and complete Phase Two," he said. "Tonight."

A sick dread turned inside her. *"Tonight?* Are they out of their minds? Don't they realize how many noncombatants will be there? We could be talking collateral damage in the dozens. Maybe more—a lot more, if this thing goes wrong."

He shook his head. "They don't care. We've been ordered to proceed."

The single-mindedness of the directive felt surreal to her. "Didn't you explain that—"

"That we have no exit strategy? That friendlies could get caught in the crossfire? That it would take only a few hours to prep an extraction scenario? Yes. Thot Tran doesn't care."

It made no sense. "Did he say why we need to move tonight?"

"No, and I'm learning it's unwise to ask for explanations." He handed her a data rod. "He also sent new orders, to be carried out in parallel to our current assignment."

She took the slender cylinder of data crystal from him and plugged it into an input on her console. "Like it's not hard enough running a high-risk op on an accelerated schedule, now he wants us to—" She lost her train of thought as the new orders scrolled across her center screen. "What is this? Tell me they're not serious." She looked back at Konar, who avoided her gaze. "Konar! Have you seen these orders? Do you know what they want us to do?"

"We don't have any choice." He had the stooped comportment of a beaten man.

Angry heat warmed her face, and she felt her pulse quicken. "No, no, *no*. They can't do this to us. They obviously have no idea what they're asking for, or they wouldn't be doing this."

"I am assured by Thot Tran that he and the domo understand the situation perfectly, and that we are the ones who lack perspective." She interpreted a crackling of static from Konar's vocoder as a heavy sigh. "At any rate, we have our orders."

Hain turned back to her screens of data and absorbed the scope of what was being set in motion. "I don't understand. This plan ends at asset activation."

"I know." Konar sounded tired, implying he'd already had this conversation with Tran.

"But what's the point? Why power them up without programming? Without guidance?"

– 140 –

Konar stared at the screens. "I don't know. I asked, but they refused to explain. It seems we're expected to comply based on nothing more than our trust in the domo's wisdom."

"But without programming, we can't operate the sensor screens. They'll be radiating all sorts of high-energy particles within minutes of start-up. How are we supposed to mask that?"

"They didn't say."

Quaking with frustration, she balled her hands into fists. "This is ridiculous! If we do this, we'll breach our own security! Starfleet isn't stupid. They'll detect these emissions, and they'll know what they mean." Her rage intensified as Konar half turned away, ignoring her rant. "We've spent *years* on this project, Konar! No one else understands how much research, how much work went into all of this! We're on the cusp of some major discoveries, and they're asking us to throw it all away! For what? What's so important that it's worth this?"

He held up a hand to forestall further discussion. "We have our orders. They're not open to debate. And Thot Tran assures me that actions which look like mistakes are anything but. So unless you want to end up in a labor camp somewhere, I suggest you obey."

"This isn't right." She started keying in sequences to carry out Thot Tran's second directive. "How am I supposed to do this and run the current op?"

"Let me worry about our team on Orion," Konar said. "I can coordinate now that Sair's in position." He took a seat beside Hain and recomposed his panel's interface into a configuration he found convenient and comfortable. "And, even though Thot Tran doesn't care, I have an exit plan that can get Sair out of the crossfire once the main objective is completed."

The situation remained less than ideal, but Hain

knew she was in no position to contest the orders of a *thot,* especially not one so politically savvy and connected as Tran. What could be so important that it would be worth scuttling one of the SRD's most cutting-edge projects? After all the years and resources that had been plowed into the study of cybernetics, artificial intelligence, and robotics, why risk exposing the entire program now, after the incorporation of foreign technologies had finally made its most recent discovery viable? She was certain she would never understand the whims of executive power or the moral calculus of the privileged.

There was nothing more for her to do but carry out her orders.

The first part would be simple. A broadcast command on the passive-receiver frequency would trigger the startup circuits on all the remaining assets. Hain keyed up the pulse, checked the channel assignment, then sent it. Moments later, her status screens flooded with pingbacks from worlds throughout the sector as the embedded assets were awakened from their dormant states, empty vessels hungry for a purpose she could not yet provide. At a glance, they all seemed to have activated as planned. Now would come the tedium; one by one, she would have to access their systems and confirm that each one was fully operational—except, of course, for the lack of a mind or any sort of functional programming. She could only assume those things would come later, as they had for the Orion assets.

"All the units are on line," she told Konar. "Starting benchmark tests."

He remained intent on the tasks in front of him. "Tell me if you find any anomalies."

She stole a look at his screens and glimpsed the

improvised exit strategy he was writing for Sair. "Do you really think that'll work?"

"As long as Olar can hold up his end, we can bring them both out in one piece."

She wasn't sure she shared his faith in Olar. "And if he can't?"

"Then Berro will have to make sure no one finds any trace of them in the bank's wreckage."

14

La Forge gazed up at a stern visage, a face that looked as if it had been chiseled from dark malachite and cast in a permanent glower of intimidation. Next to it was another much like it, only far less welcoming. "We don't care if you've been sent by the Great Bird of the Galaxy itself," said Tall-Green-and-Ugly. "You don't have permission to enter the bank."

He and Šmrhová held up their Starfleet photo ID cards—documents for which they had rarely had any use, on or off the ship—as if presenting the Orions with proof of their affiliation would change their answer. "We're from the *Enterprise*," La Forge said. "We've been tasked with investigating the attempted break-in, and—"

"We don't care," said Taller-Greener-and-Uglier. "You have no jurisdiction on the surface of our planet, and even less inside the walls of this bank."

Their refusals spun up Šmrhová's temper. "This is a matter of Federation security."

"No, it's a matter of bank security, and we'll conduct our own investigation—without your help." They pointed away from the main gate, into the sprawl of the capital. "Why don't you two go back to your embassy, or your ship, or anyplace other than here?"

The jade goliaths turned and walked away, crossing the bridge to the bank as the gates swung closed in front of La Forge and Šmrhová. La Forge sprang forward, hoping to pursue them onto the bridge, only to be hurled backward when he slammed into an invisible force field. He hit the ground hard, landing flat on his back. The impact knocked the air from his lungs, but it hurt far less than the wound to his pride. When the chartreuse spots faded from his vision, he saw Šmrhová's hand extended to him. He grasped it, and she helped him up. "Thanks."

"You're welcome." She shot a look at the dark-suited Orion security guards, who climbed the bank's front staircase and vanished through its main entrance, then she turned back to face La Forge. "That could have gone better. What's Plan B?"

He rubbed the ache from the back of his head. "I didn't know we'd need one."

"What made you think they'd let us in?"

A shrug. "I don't know. Their cops had no problem sharing the sensor data from the break-in, so I didn't think they'd object to letting us inspect the crime scene."

She reacted with cynical incredulity. "Did you look at the sensor data yourself? It was fairly low-res, and more than a bit limited in bandwidth. It was designed to pick up a narrow range of energy signatures and avoid any details that could be used against the bank."

"Such as internal structures, or other security features."

Šmrhová nodded. "Exactly. The thought of us down there with state-of-the-art Starfleet sensor equipment, taking sensor readings of their bank's secure sublevels, must give them fits. We're probably lucky they didn't shoot us just for suggesting it."

The duo started walking, paralleling the imposing tritanium barricade that ringed the pit surrounding the bank like an empty moat. Eyeing the grand skyscraper beyond the barrier, La Forge couldn't help but wonder what dark secrets it hid. "So, we're not getting inside without a good reason or a printed invitation from the president. Where does that leave us?"

"Walking in circles," she said as they turned the corner.

The night was young but the street was nearly deserted, a fact La Forge found peculiar. Then he noticed a lone figure on the sidewalk ahead of him and Šmrhová—a person with a wiry frame and a hunched posture who walked with the stiff gait of age. Within moments, it was clear the other pedestrian was trying to intercept them rather than pass by.

Before they met, the stranger stopped shy of the closest streetlamp's pool of light, as if fearing to be exposed, but still he waved to La Forge and Šmrhová. "You're from Starfleet."

The two officers stopped, and Šmrhová took the lead. "That's right."

"I tried talking to the bank's security people, but they won't listen."

La Forge adjusted the settings on his cybernetic eyes, enhancing his night-spectrum vision and compensating for the streetlamp's salmon-hued glow. At once, the man's face was clearly visible. He was an elderly Orion. His pale green face and pate were leathery and lined with fine wrinkles. Unkempt tufts of ashen hair above his ears matched his bushy white eyebrows, and his eyes were a sallow yellow, almost to the point of being colorless. Lowering his voice, La Forge asked, "What's your name?"

"Pollus." He glanced at the skyscraper. "Kal Pollus. I'm a custodian at the bank."

Šmrhová inched toward the man, but he backed away, so she stopped and tried to infuse her voice with a soothing tone. "What did you try to tell the bank's security people?"

"You understand, I could lose my job for talking to you."

Trying to assuage the man's fear, La Forge said, "We can treat this as an anonymous tip. But first we have to know what we're dealing with. Now, Mister Pollus . . . what did you see?"

"A perimeter breach. On the service level." He looked over his shoulders, as if fearing the sudden appearance of an eavesdropper. "The boss."

A bemused glance passed between La Forge and Šmrhová; clearly, neither knew what to make of the man's cryptic allegation. Once again, La Forge let the security chief lead the investigation. She asked, "What 'boss' are you referring to, sir?"

"The chairman!" he snapped, as if it were obvious. "He turned off the alarms and opened the door for someone, let them in. Then he went one way and they went the other."

Alarmed and intrigued, La Forge asked, "Chairman Kinshal? Did you see who he let inside? Could you identify that person?"

Pollus shook his head. "Wore a hood. Didn't see the face." He shot a desperate, imploring look at Šmrhová. "Told them, but they wouldn't listen! Said I should mind my own business—pay more attention to my work and less to the boss." He looked back and cupped one hand over a white-knuckled fist. "Then my foreman said I was done for the night. Sent me home, told me he'd dock my pay if I kept making trouble."

DAVID MACK

"And you're positive it was the bank's chairman?"

The Orion nodded. "Yes. It was definitely Boss Kinshal. I'm sure of it."

It was too soon for La Forge to say exactly what Pollus had witnessed, but from what the man had described, it had the hallmarks of a conspiracy in the making. One look at Šmrhová's anxious eyes made it clear to him that she'd arrived at the same conclusion.

She put an edge of command in her tone. "Go home, Mister Pollus. We'll handle this from here. But for your own safety, forget what you saw, and forget you ever talked to us."

He signaled his understanding with a curt nod, then he shuffled away with awkward steps, retreating into the night. La Forge and Šmrhová turned back to face the way they'd come, both of them knowing what had to happen next, and how precarious that was going to be.

"Even if we get Bacco's protection detail to let us in," Šmrhová noted, "the bank's security force won't be happy about us barging into Kinshal's office."

"I'm more concerned that without a sensor lock on the guy, he could get away from us. If he slips out of the building when we're not looking, we might never see him again."

Šmrhová frowned. "Only one thing to do, then." She pulled open her jacket to expose the concealed combadge pinned to her shirt. "Time to call in the cavalry."

Few indignities Worf had ever suffered compared to the imposition of being ordered to don his Starfleet dress uniform. He had no idea who or what would be flattered by the awkward cut of the off-white jacket with broad gold trim, but he suspected the snug blue-gray vest had been designed to kill by slow suffocation. Even the trousers, which except for gold stripes down the legs had seemed identical to those he wore with his regular duty uniform, felt stiff. He found it impossible to move freely in the clothes without rending them at the seams.

Whoever designed this should be shot, he decided.

To his chagrin, the dress uniform had been designated as mandatory for all officers attending the president's reception on Orion that evening—and Captain Picard had made clear that attendance, too, was compulsory. As much as Worf would have preferred to remain on the bridge of the *Enterprise* in the captain's absence, that had never been an option.

Hoping for even a momentary respite from his uniform's choke-hold fit, he sneaked his index finger under his jacket's collar and gave it a gingerly tug away from his throat.

A friendly slap on his back startled him, and he jerked his hand back to his side. Then he saw Glinn Dygan sidle up beside him. The youthful Cardassian beamed with excitement. "What a party! This is really something, isn't it, Commander?"

Worf glumly scanned the domed rooftop arboretum. Its pathways were dotted with government officials from the Federation and the Gorn Hegemony. At various key junctures stood either tuxedoed-and-eyeshaded protection agents from Federation Security, or members of the Gorn Imperial Guard dressed in silver armor draped with purple silk. "It is . . . *something.*"

"If someone had told me just a few years ago that one day I'd be attending a reception with the president of the Federation and the Gorn imperator, I'd never have believed them." Dygan did a double take at Worf. "But look who I'm talking to. You killed one Klingon chancellor and all but appointed his successor. This must seem routine to someone like you."

Many terms less flattering than *routine* occurred to Worf. He frowned. "No."

As a young Orion woman passed by carrying a tray of drinks in slender crystal flutes, Dygan snagged two of them with nimble hands and a quick smile. He extended his arm and offered one of the beverages to Worf. "Sir?"

"I am not in the mood."

Dygan spread his arms in an expansive gesture. "But it's a *party*."

"It is a formal event, and we are here as both Starfleet officers and guests of the president. We cannot afford to impair our judgment."

His rebuke left the Cardassian looking troubled and confused. After a few moments of awkward deliberation, Dygan put down both drinks on an empty cocktail table behind them. Then he turned to stand beside Worf, facing in the same direction with his hands clasped behind his back. "So . . . if we're not here to enjoy ourselves . . . why *are* we here, sir?"

"You can enjoy yourself. Just not too much." Hoping to end the conversation, he walked away toward one of the buffet tables. Dygan, however, trailed behind him, as if they were bound together on a chain gang. Worf turned and faced him. "What are you doing?"

The younger man blinked and was flummoxed. "Following you."

"Why?"

"Well, it's just . . . you seem to know what you're doing, sir."

Worf was speechless. He couldn't contradict Dygan's answer without denigrating himself, and he couldn't concur without appearing conceited. Instead, he breathed a low sigh, turned, and continued to the buffet table, where he grabbed a plate and started choosing morsels from the gourmet smorgasbord that had been laid out for the event. As before, Dygan was a step behind him, loading up his own plate and apparently using Worf's to gauge the proper quantities. Confronted by the Klingon's glare, he simply smiled.

As they reached the end of the table, Worf turned and blundered into the middle of a conversation between a pair of clean-cut young men in bespoke suits. The taller of the two was fair-haired and clean-shaven, and to Worf he looked (and smelled) human; the other man wore a mullet of dark hair and a black handlebar mustache in the style long favored by the Efrosians. Both spoke in the rapid style of politicos accustomed to jockeying for verbal dominance.

"I'm not saying it's likely," argued the Efrosian, "just possible."

"If it were possible, we'd already be doing it."

Worf tried to slip past them. "Excuse me." His bid for escape was thwarted; the two men were nose to nose and refused to budge. He tried to turn back, only to find Dygan on his heels.

The Efrosian made large gestures as he spoke, as if pantomiming his point made it more persuasive. "But if we can lure the Gorn out of the Pact—"

"A fool's errand," the human said, rolling his eyes, "but go on."

"—then we could focus on supporting the dissidents inside the Breen Confederacy, and lay the foundation for a future peace. In a decade or two we—"

Anger drove Worf to interrupt, "If you think you can make deals with the Breen, then you are a fool." He thrust his plate into Dygan's free hand, slopping some of his appetizers onto the man's polished dress armor, then he poked his finger against the shocked Efrosian's chest. "The Breen have no use for diplomacy, and they are not to be trusted."

The human tried to interpose himself between his friend and Worf, but he failed. "I know the Breen aren't receptive to diplomacy now, but if Bodell's right, and the dissidents are able to supplant the current regime—"

"That will *not* happen," Worf warned. "If there are Breen dissidents, the best they can hope for is escape. If they oppose the domo's forces, they will be cut down like *taHqeqpu'*."

The Efrosian stammered, "But—but if we support them, then they—"

"Then they will pull us into a civil war," Worf said. "More of our people will be slaughtered by the Breen, and once again we will gain nothing."

Perplexed, the human and Efrosian wrinkled their brows at each other. Then the human cast a quizzical look at Worf. "*Once again?* I'm sorry, but we don't know what incident you're referring to. Could you enlighten us?"

Only then did Worf realize he had alluded to Jasminder Choudhury's murder.

Fury and shame warmed his face, and he shouldered his way free of the two politicos, eager to be anywhere else, doing anything else, with anyone else. As he expected, Dygan hurried after him, portering both their plates like a dutiful squire chasing his knight. When they stopped near the far side of the arboretum, he held Worf's plate out to him. "Sir?"

"Throw it away." He turned and stared out the towering windows at the sparkling midnight jewel of Orion's capital. "I am not hungry."

"This is absurd," Picard said. "Why have a political reception if the guests won't talk to one another?"

Bacco sipped champagne through a sardonic smile. "Welcome to my world, Captain."

Her chief of staff risked a furtive glance over her shoulder. "No one wants to make the first move." She finished off her own drink in a quick tilt. "Or start an interstellar incident."

Picard stood with Doctor Crusher in a closed circle that included Bacco, Piñiero, and Captain Bateson and Commander Fawkes from the *Atlas*. On the far side of the arboretum, gathered in their own closed ring, were Imperator Sozzerozs and the elite members of his retinue. It reminded Picard of the way teenagers tended to divide themselves into cliques, discrete sets that rarely if ever overlapped. "There must be some topic of interest that's free of controversy."

His assertion met with stares that ranged from incredulous to weary. Bateson cocked an eyebrow. "You think so? Name one."

"The weather is usually a reliable source of small talk."

The president grimaced. "The Gorn have done nothing but complain about how cold Orion is, and at least once in every meeting they remind us of the huge favor they're doing us by suffering what they consider to be freezing temperatures for our comfort. So, as you might imagine, the subject of weather has become rather a bone of contention around here."

"I see." Undeterred, he offered another idea. "What about sports? Or games of chance?"

Piñiero made a sound that was equal parts grunt, snort, and chortle. "The Gorn have never really seen the point of competitive sports that don't involve mortal combat. As for gambling, Togor has insisted since the first day of the summit that he was cheated by a rigged table in one of the capital's swankier casinos."

All at once, Picard was on the spot, and he saw Crusher fighting an urge to laugh out loud. "I had no idea there were quite so many impediments to social integration with the Gorn." He stole a look at Sozzerozs and his entourage; the archosaurs were making a blood-soaked, flesh-spattered mess out of a corner buffet that had been stocked with assorted raw meats to meet their nutritional requirements. "I presume food and wine hold little promise as ice-breakers."

"Good guess," Fawkes said under her breath.

From the far side of the roof, Picard thought he heard the sound of Worf raising his voice, but he couldn't make out what his first officer was saying. The Klingon was engaged in some kind of intense discussion with two men, junior aides attached to Bacco's delegation, an Efrosian and a human. For the moment, the situation seemed under control if a bit tense, so Picard returned his attention to the matter of inspiring his wallflowers to cross the room.

"What about art?" When no one pounced to tear down his idea, he elaborated. "It's my understanding that the Gorn have a highly refined aesthetic sense, and that they have a long tradition of thermal sculpture, which appeals to their ability to see heat signatures."

Bacco nodded. "I've been to some of those exhibits. I had to use special glasses to see something that approximates what the Gorn perceive, but it was quite lovely."

Fawkes interjected, "They also have a fascinating musical tradition. They use focused sonic pulses the way Terran music uses bass frequencies. A Gorn symphony can leave you feeling like you've been pummeled by a prizefighter."

"Well," Crusher said, bright with optimism, "it sounds like there's plenty to talk about with the Gorn. Plus, inviting them to tell us about their culture not only helps us understand them, it might make them feel more at ease—and make the next round of negotiations a bit less tense. Which I thought was the entire reason to hold an event such as this."

"Yes and no," Bacco said. Her mask of propriety faltered, and she turned a sheepish look at Picard. "The fact is, I understand the Gorn far too well. I dealt with them for years when I ran Cestus III, more than enough to know they're dragging these talks out, though I don't know why. But if you want to know the real reason I'm in no hurry to go chat with them, it's that we've been talking to these annoying lizards for almost a week now. We're running out of things to say. And if I can be completely honest, I'm getting sick of looking at them across the table."

Bateson raised his glass to her. "Seconded, Madam President." To Picard, he added, "Try spending a week maintaining an antipodal orbit from a Gorn battleship that changes velocity without warning, forcing you into a never-ending game of 'your side, my side.' Trust me, Jean-Luc, it gets old very quickly."

Disappointed but not yet resigned, Picard summoned his courage. "Times like this are when we most need diplomacy, Madam President. It's when our rivals and our enemies least want to talk that we should seek understanding. It's when we most desperately yearn to give in to the temptation of isolationism that we must reach out." He glanced toward the Gorn, then smiled at Bacco. "Even when we know it will leave us *bored beyond belief.*"

Bacco chuckled and shook her head. "All right, Captain. You win." She started the long walk across the room, with Piñiero at her side and the four Starfleet officers close behind her. Over her shoulder, she added softly, "But I'm warning you right now: if this works,

I just might name you ambassador to the Gorn Hegemony."

Crusher grinned at the president's good-natured threat, and so did Picard.

"Madam President," he said, "that's a risk I'll simply have to take."

They were waiting in the executive floor's lobby as La Forge and Šmrhová stepped out of the lift: an archosaur from the Gorn Imperial Guard and a black-suited Vulcan from the Protection Detail, both armed and deadly serious. The duo from the *Enterprise* was barely clear of the lift when the Vulcan fell into step with them. "Why did you demand our presence here?"

La Forge said, "We have a credible witness who says the bank's chairman, Siro Kinshal, facilitated a security breach, and the bank's security division failed to investigate it."

They moved with purpose toward the entrance to the executive suites beyond the lobby. As they and their Gorn counterpart approached the door, the Orion receptionist sprang from her chair to block their path. "This is a restricted floor! You can't go in—"

A shoulder-check by the Gorn knocked the young woman from his path, and she tumbled wildly backward across the polished marble floor. Unlike the sliding portals that were endemic to modern buildings and ships throughout local space, the door to the bank's private suite of senior executive offices was made of an intricately textured wood, stained a deep reddish brown and embellished with ornate carved designs. Šmrhová reached the door first, gripped its golden knob, and found it locked. She glared at the receptionist. "Open this door. Right now."

The undernourished-looking young woman had tears

in her eyes as she reached under her desk. "I'm calling security! You have no right—" Her rant was interrupted by a deafening slam and the splintering of wood
as the Gorn punched the elegant wooden door clean off
its hinges. The fractured wooden slab struck the floor
with a resounding boom, and then he stomped over it
on his way toward the chairman's office. Šmrhová and
the Vulcan followed him inside.

La Forge paused in the doorway just long enough
to flash a sarcastic smile at the sprawled receptionist.
"That's okay—we'll just let ourselves in."

The quartet's passage through the broad, artfully
appointed hallways was met by shrieks of alarm and
a steady stream of calls to the bank's security center.
Doors slammed shut and executive assistants scattered
ahead of them. In less than a minute they were only a
few meters away from the chairman's closed door, and
the rumble of running footsteps echoed from every corridor behind them, drawing closer by the moment.

Guarding the door to Siro Kinshal's office was a tall
and elegant Trill woman who wore her black hair in
a stylish crown atop her head. She stood with arms
crossed over her white blouse, her left leg straight
beneath her and the right extended, revealing one
long and shapely thigh from under her knee-length
gray skirt. "And just *where* do all of you think you're
going?"

Two teams of Orion security personnel in black-on-
black faille suits converged with weapons drawn on the
foursome outside Kinshal's office. The Vulcan and the
Gorn each faced off toward a different group of Orions,
their own military-grade sidearms at the ready.

La Forge and Šmrhová dared to step forward, and
the Trill woman advanced to meet them. The engineer
held up his empty hands. "Let's all calm down here"—

he glanced at the nameplate on her desk—"Idina. We need to speak to Chairman Kinshal immediately."

Idina looked down her elegant nose at La Forge with unbridled hauteur and defiance. "Do you have an appointment?"

He heard the smack of contact and the crack of breaking cartilage before he realized that Šmrhová had cold-cocked the woman with a blindingly fast jab. The Trill collapsed to the floor, her once-perfect nose broken and bleeding, consciousness wrenched from her grasp. Šmrhová stepped over her, all business. "Appointment, my ass."

She tried the knob on Kinshal's door, then shook her head at La Forge. "Locked."

He lifted his foot, and she stepped aside as he kicked the door open.

Half a second later he barely dodged clear of the disruptor blast from inside the office.

The beam slammed into the Gorn's flank and blasted away a chunk of his torso. Šmrhová and La Forge dove to the floor as the Vulcan protection agent somersaulted to cover behind the receptionist's desk, rolled into a squat, and returned fire.

A searing flash and a peal of thunder were followed by pitch-black darkness and the delicate music of shattering glass swallowed by a roaring wind. La Forge set his eyes to night-vision mode, transforming the darkness into frost-blue twilight. Looking up, he saw that the floor-to-ceiling wraparound windows of the chairman's office had been blasted out, likely by shaped charges, exposing the corner space to open air more than four hundred meters aboveground.

Then Chairman Kinshal emerged from cover beneath his huge, heavy desk. He looked straight at La Forge, who clearly observed that the chairman's left hand had been stripped of flesh by the explosion—revealing the distinctly Soong-type android mechanisms underneath. Then Kinshal turned and ran—and leaped out into the night, falling like a stone.

La Forge sprang to his feet and dashed inside the smoke-filled office, and Šmrhová followed him. At the edge of the now open floor, he grasped one of the bent structural beams to anchor himself. He looked down, expecting to see Kinshal's body strewn across the avenue far below. Instead, he saw the fleeing executive on the rooftop of the slightly shorter building across the avenue from the bank—scrambling to his feet and looking for his next route of escape.

He reached under his jacket and tapped his combadge. "La Forge to *Enterprise!*" Then he nudged Šmrhová. "Your tricorder! Get line-of-sight coordinates to that roof."

As the security chief powered up her tricorder, Lieutenant T'Ryssa Chen's voice replied over the comm, "*Enterprise. Go ahead, Commander.*"

"We're in pursuit of a suspect. We need site-to-site transport, ASAP."

Šmrhová pressed the tricorder's transmit pad. "Coordinates sent!"

"*Received,*" Chen said. "*Stand by for transport.*"

The duo tensed in anticipation of the transporter's embrace. Šmrhová kept her tricorder powered up and in hand. "Ready for this?"

Pride demanded he not speak the truth, but honor prevented him from lying. That left evasion. "Are you?"

"Let's get the bastard," she said with a fierce look.

Then the world turned white and filled with a euphonic hum as the transporter beam took hold—and flung them headlong into the chase.

"Red Alert!" Snapping out orders like a drill chief had never been T'Ryssa Chen's style, but circumstances demanded it, and by a quirk of fate, scheduling, and Picardian whimsy, she was the one occupying the center seat while the ship's five most senior officers were on the planet's surface. "Weinrib, get us into a geostationary orbit, directly above the capital! Balidemaj, get a lock on the suspect in case they lose visual contact."

Ensign Jill Rosado responded to multiple alerts on the ops console. "Site-to-site transport complete. Transporter Rooms Two through Eight standing by for new coordinates."

La Forge's voice squawked from the overhead speaker, *"He jumped again!"*

An urgent, rapid beeping shrilled from the ops panel, signaling the receipt of new coordinates from Šmrhová. "Target locked," Rosado said. "Transporter Room Two has the ball."

The alert Klaxon whooped and red situation lights flashed on the bulkheads as Lieutenant Abby Balidemaj reported from the security station, "I can't get a lock on their suspect. He's using a sensor blind." She keyed in new commands. "Switching to visual tracking."

"We're splitting up to cut him off," Šmrhová said via the comm. She sounded breathless, and her normally satin-smooth voice quaked while she ran. *"Get ready for new coordinates!"*

Chen spun her chair around to face the master systems display. "Elfiki?"

The ship's senior science officer looked overwhelmed by the task of coordinating the *Enterprise* crew's actions with those of the *Atlas* crew, the Federation Security agents and Orion police, and to the limited degree that it was permitted, the Gorn. She composed herself and looked back toward the command chair. "The *Atlas* is maneuvering to a complementary angle for visual tracking. Federation Security is locking down the bank, and the Orion police are threatening to arrest everyone." She shifted her gaze toward the viewscreen. "And the Gorn have left their orbital position and are accelerating into our hemisphere."

Oh, great. The last thing Chen wanted to deal with right now was a combat scenario.

More strident tones emanated from the ops console. Rosado quelled them with a few fast taps. "Target locked. Transporter Room Three has the ball."

"Visual tracking's up." Balidemaj relayed the sensors' data stream to the main viewer. It was a vertiginous view of the Orions' capital city, less than a degree shy of a perfectly vertical angle on the close-packed rooftops of the metropolis. The deputy chief of security made some adjustments. "Magnifying." A small quadrant of the image on the screen swelled to fill the rectangular frame, and all its details resolved into hyper-real sharpness.

A lone figure leaped across the chasm between two skyscrapers, landed hard on the far rooftop, and tumbled. Seconds behind him, two figures met at the first building's edge. Then came the warbling from ops, and Rosado reacted with speed and precision. "Locked! Transporter Room Four has the ball. Transporter Room One reports ready and standing by."

"Automatic tracking engaged," Balidemaj reported. "As long as we maintain visual contact, we—" Her voice trailed off as the image on-screen shifted to a rooftop veiled in mist.

Propelled by anxiety, Chen sprang from the command chair. "Reduce magnification!"

Balidemaj scrambled to reacquire visual contact as La Forge's angry voice resounded from the overhead speaker. *"Enterprise! We've lost visual contact! Please advise!"*

Elfiki called out, "Stand by, sir!" She spun back toward the master systems display and started reconfiguring one of the sensor stations.

Chen moved quickly to her friend's side and lowered her voice to a discreet hush. "What's the plan, Dina?"

"I'm resetting the sensors to look for changes in the mist cloud on that roof that aren't consistent with standard models of Brownian motion. It should just take a few more . . . got it!" Working with grace and speed, she transmitted her data to Šmrhová's tricorder and patched into the comm channel. "Commander! Target is bearing two-five-one from your position and descending. I think he found a staircase access! Routing civilian police to your location!"

A few seconds later, La Forge hollered back, *"Found it! Heading inside!"*

"Nice work, Dina," Chen said, then she hurried back to the command chair. "Rosado, have a security team beamed down to cover that building's street-level exits, and ask the *Atlas* to do the same. Balidemaj, I need an update on that Gorn battleship. What's it doing?"

"Holding station at two hundred thousand kilometers, sir."

Until that moment, Chen had been under the impression they were acting in cooperation with the Gorn, but the *Hastur-zolis*'s sudden shift in posture worried her. "Energize shields, but don't raise them. Then charge all weapons to ready standby, but don't lock any targets."

The other bridge officers looked up from their posts at Chen, as if she had just issued General Order 24 or something. For a moment, she felt horribly self-conscious, as if by arming the ship's defensive systems she had just committed some grievous faux pas. Then she imagined what Captain Picard would do if his crew ever reacted this way to one of his commands. She aimed an unforgiving stare at Balidemaj and marshaled her best impression of a confident captain. "That is an *order*, Lieutenant."

To her relief, it worked. Balidemaj returned her attention to her console. "Aye, sir."

As the shields and weapons charged, the rest of the bridge crew resumed their duties. For a moment, Chen almost felt entitled to gloat a little bit.

Then she heard La Forge's worried voice over the comm.

"Enterprise? I think we have a problem."

After chasing the preternaturally fast bank chairman down several flights of stairs and losing ground to him in a long service corridor, the last thing La Forge had expected to find on the other side of the door at its end was a bustling multilevel galleria packed with civilians.

"We're in a shopping mall," he said for the *Enterprise* crew's benefit as he and Šmrhová waded into the crowd. "And I don't see the suspect anywhere."

All he did see was moving bodies and bobbing heads, a sea of green skin into which the fleeing chairman had vanished. Kinshal could be anywhere in the dense knots of people milling about on the promenade that ringed a huge rectangular atrium, in the center of which was suspended a holographic projector filling the air at ninety-degree intervals with four identical audiovisual promotions. Unabashedly cliché and mawkishly sentimental images were paired with earworm jingles, all enticing consumers to spend their hard-earned salaries on all manner of luxuries they couldn't possibly need. *Never mind a criminals' paradise,* La Forge thought. *From where I'm standing, this looks like Ferengi heaven.*

"I have an idea," Šmrhová said as she stepped away from him.

He reached out and caught her arm. "You know you can't just start shooting in here."

"Trust me." She tugged her arm free and slipped out of the flow of foot traffic, and he dodged through the moving maze of bodies to join her. Facing the wall, she pulled her tricorder free from its holster under her coat and fiddled with its settings. "That holographic projector up there? It's Bolian-made. Most of the time it runs a loop from its built-in memory. It's usually hard-wired into a control system, but if memory serves . . ." She smiled. "It also has a wireless option." Her good mood turned devilish. "And the mall's marketing team never changed its default password." She called up a file from the tricorder's memory and routed it to the control screen for the projector. "Watch the crowd for anyone who starts running."

Moments later, the titanic saccharine advertisements playing in the center of the mall changed to an image of Siro Kinshal, accompanied by text in several major languages of local space, all of which cited his name and the phrase Wanted by Orion Colonial Police.

Half the crowd ignored it, and the other half received it with guarded anticipation, as if it were merely the setup for some kind of avant-garde promotion. Then, two levels below La Forge and Šmrhová, a woman's shout rose up from sonic fog of crowd noise: "Hey! That's him!"

A disruption in the river of window-shoppers rippled outward as people fell against one another, shoved and jostled by the frantic fugitive as he sprinted toward a descending escalator.

"Got him," La Forge said. "He's heading for street level, east exit!"

"Acknowledged," Chen replied from the *Enterprise.* *"A team from the* Atlas *is there."*

Below, Kinshal lunged through the mall's east exit into the street. Šmrhová put away her tricorder and drew her phaser as she stepped to La Forge's side. "We need to be there. *Enterprise,* beam us to the east exit."

"*Transporter Room Five has the ball,*" Rosado said over the open channel.

The beam took hold of them, and the interior of the mall vanished in a swirl of prismatic particles and a rush of white noise. When it faded, and the beam's protective hold abated, La Forge and Šmrhová were on the street outside the mall.

Starfleet security officers lay in the street. Some were stunned and groaning; a few had been slain by brute force, their skulls pummeled or their heads torqued until their necks snapped. Civilians fled in every direction, screaming over the wails of approaching sirens, and sounds of phaser fire echoed from the alleyway across the street. Šmrhová pointed and ran. "This way!"

La Forge struggled to keep up with her, but she was more than twenty years his junior and, he was embarrassed to admit, in far superior physical condition for a prolonged chase. As she disappeared into the alley's misty shadows, he stumbled to a halt and struggled for breath. "*Enterprise,* do you have a visual on the suspect?"

"*Negative,*" Chen said. "*Something's obscuring our view of the alley.*"

"La Forge to Šmrhová. Do you see him?"

She replied with bitter dudgeon, "*I can't see a thing in this fog.*"

He studied the roiling vapors with his eyes' infrared filter. "Actually, I think it's steam."

"*I don't give a damn if it's the mists of Avalon. I'm running blind here.*"

The prospect of failure led La Forge to grind his

teeth. He took out his tricorder and started a sweep using ultrasonic echo-location. *"Enterprise, do you have anything? Maybe signs of movement in the steam? Or a signal from the chairman's personal comm?"*

"Sorry, sir," Chen said. *"We're coming up empty."*

He shut off his tricorder and slapped it shut. "That makes both of us." He tucked the device back under his coat and walked back toward the street. "Šmrhová, meet me back at the mall's east entrance. Chen, we need a medical team at those coordinates, on the double."

"Acknowledged. Medical teams are beaming down now."

"One more thing," La Forge said. "Have the police issue a warrant for the chairman's arrest—and inform Data's lawyer there's at least one other android in town."

In the past seven minutes, Picard had learned more than he'd ever wanted know about the history of Gorn thermal-contrast sculpture. What he'd hoped would be a simple conversation-starter had turned out to be a personal hobby of Azarog, the Gorn *zulta-osol*, who had seized the chance to regale them all with tales of his long-nurtured dream of leaving politics to become an artist.

Making a show of noticing his empty glass, Picard tried to back out of the conversation circle. "If you'll excuse me, I—" Bacco cut him off with the slightest grasp of his arm.

"Oh, you can't leave *now*, Captain." The president fixed him in place with a threatening stare above a mirthless smile. "Not when Azarog is just getting to the best part of his story."

Bateson piled on to the verbal assault. "Indeed, Captain. Given your deep appreciation for the arts, I have to believe you'd never forgive yourself if you missed a moment of this."

Deprived of a graceful exit, Picard mustered his most genial demeanor. "Of course." He bowed his head slightly to Azarog. "My apologies, *Zulta-osol*. Please continue."

"As I was saying," the archosaur said, resuming his anecdote, "it was on my first journey outside the Hegemony, during a visit to Trill, that I first encountered the cold springs beneath that planet's arctic volcano. The interplay of temperatures there inspired me to experiment with the notion of thermally inverted sculpture, layering materials of decreasing conductivity to create a heart of fire in a metaphorical sea of darkness."

Togor, the imperator's *wazir*, hissed. "Do you expect us to believe that *you* invented the *Koziol-zellos* school of thermal sculpture?"

Azarog straightened his posture and rose to his full height. "I was an early pioneer of it."

Nizor Szamra bared his fangs. "I say this with the greatest respect, old friend: that is the most ridiculous lie I have *ever* heard—and I have spent half my life in *politics*."

From Picard's combadge came a single beep, followed by an incoming signal. *"La Forge to Captain Picard, Priority One."*

This time no one tried to stop Picard as he backed away from the group to continue the conversation at a discreet remove. "Picard here. Go ahead, Geordi."

"Captain, the bank's chairman, Siro Kinshal, is an android infiltrator."

"You're certain of this?"

"Positive. We tried to arrest him, but he got away. But the witness who led us to him said he helped someone else breach the bank's secure perimeter to enter the bank."

Picard's pulse quickened. "An accomplice. Do we know who it is?"

"Not yet. But if these androids can impersonate someone like Kinshal, they could be just about anyone. Captain, I think the president's life might be in danger."

"Acknowledged." He turned and saw that all the Federation Security protection agents in the room seemed to be reacting to news delivered via their in-ear subvocal transceivers. "Keep looking for the chairman. I'll alert Starfleet Command as soon as the president's secured."

"Yes, sir. La Forge out."

Filled with a sudden paranoia that anyone in the room other than himself, his wife, or the president might be an assassin in disguise, he hurried back down a path bordered by looming fronds to rejoin the two heads of state and their VIP guests. As he shouldered his way back into the group, he noticed Bacco's senior protection agent, Steven Wexler, moving in their direction at a quick step. "Madam President, Your Imperial Majesty," Picard said, "forgive the interruption, but I have reason to believe the bank's security has been compromised. I strongly advise you all to return to your secure suites in the sublevel immediately."

To his surprise, no one voiced a word of protest. Bacco nodded to Sozzerozs. "Lord Imperator, I think we should say good night. Be well and safe, and we'll meet again tomorrow."

"Most sensible, Madam President," the imperator said. "May fortune keep you from harm until we meet again. Ms. Piñiero, Captains, Commander, Doctor— good night."

The Gorn moved with dispatch toward their designated private exit. Bateson and Fawkes stepped away as the *Atlas*'s first officer tapped her combadge and hailed her ship. Picard gently took hold of Crusher's elbow, and then he turned to confer with Bacco's protection agent.

Wexler charged at Picard with manic eyes and a drawn phaser. "DOWN!"

For a tiny fraction of a second, Picard froze. Everything happened so fast, but his fear-fueled rush of adrenaline made it feel as if time had slowed down.

He and Crusher turned their heads to look over their shoulders. Esperanza Piñiero was drawing a compact phaser from under her shirt and raising her arm. Whoever her target was, Picard realized, whether it was President Bacco, Imperator Sozzerozs, or anyone else at the reception, he and Beverly were standing in her line of fire.

The other protection agents were swarming toward Piñiero, most of them reaching to draw concealed weapons, and the troops from the Gorn Imperial Guard were belatedly snapping into action and converging to surround their imperator.

Piñiero's thumb tensed over the phaser's firing stud.

Bacco stared at her chief of staff, frozen in place by terror and shock.

There was no time to think, so Picard acted by instinct, and did what had to be done.

He pulled Beverly to the floor and draped himself over her as a living shield.

Angry screeches of weapons fire filled the rooftop garden. Grunts and groans followed as the wounded and dying fell all around Picard, who didn't dare to look up. An ear-splitting detonation left him dazed and squinting in pain, and then his nostrils filled with the searing bite of tear gas. As the shrieks and ricochets of small arms receded, he opened his eyes, only to wince as his tears flowed but failed to salve the burning pain

caused by the smoke. From the far side of the rooftop
he heard another explosion, followed by the brittle
melody of shattered transparent duranium. Through the
kaleidoscope lens of his tortured eyes, he saw Wexler
crouched in a defensive pose over the prone form of
the president, his weapon drawn. Then fiery pain in
Picard's chest wracked him with agonizing coughs until
he freckled his hands with bloody spittle.

His grip on consciousness weakened, and as it
slipped away all he could do was hope that his snap
decision hadn't just cost the Federation one of the finest
presidents in its history.

No matter what direction T'Ryssa Chen turned, she was
met by the shrill warbling of alerts from every console
on the *Enterprise*'s bridge.

Balidemaj's face blanched as she reported, "The
Hastur-zolis just raised shields! It's going weapons-hot
and coming about in a combat posture, bearing one-
nine-one mark four!"

"Somebody get me an update from the surface,"
Chen ordered. "Helm, hard about. Ops, cancel the manhunt and give me targeting sensors."

The signal traffic on the master systems display,
which Elfiki had retasked into a mission-coordination
center, redoubled into a flood of raw intel. The brown-
eyed Egyptian science officer trembled with frustration
as she fought to keep up with it. "All channels from the
surface are going haywire! Local police, Federation Security, the Gorn Imperial Guard—there's so much chatter I can't tell what's going on."

"Contact the captain," Chen said. "I want locations
and status for all personnel on the surface. Find out if
they're in trouble."

Elfiki nodded. "I'm on it."

"Sir," Balidemaj called out, "the Gorn are locking weapons on us and the *Atlas*!"

Chen felt like a wind-up toy torqued to its breaking point. "Hail them!"

The security officer sent the hail, then frowned. "No response." Then she creased her brow in alarm. "Sir, the *Atlas* has raised shields and is locking weapons onto the Gorn ship."

One hand on her hip, the other massaging the pounding ache from her temples, Chen wondered how much worse this situation could get. "Hail the *Atlas*."

Plagued by the fear that everything was spiraling out of control, Chen forced herself to take a deep breath, but her mind refused to be calmed; it just kept on spinning in ever-tighter circles, a drill of fear inside her psyche. *Five minutes ago we were running a manhunt; now we're one bad temper away from starting a war. What the hell just happened down there?*

The screen switched from the tableau of the *Atlas* and the *Hastur-zolis* squared off for battle to an image of the officer currently in command of the other *Sovereign*-class ship. To Chen's profound dismay, the human-looking man wore the pips of a lieutenant commander; he outranked her. That would make her next task all the more difficult.

Hoping he hadn't been as quick to note her rank, she made a subtle pivot to angle her insignia away from the vid sensor, then adopted a most imperious attitude. "This is T'Ryssa Chen, commanding the *Starship Enterprise*. Identify yourself!"

He seemed taken aback by the force of Chen's demand. *"Lieutenant Commander Boaden Ackles, second officer. Why are you hailing us?"*

"Are you trying to start a war? Release your weapons lock and stand down!" Chen knew she didn't have the advantage of rank, the privilege of commanding a superior vessel, or the primacy of involvement; that left her with only one option—bluffing.

Ackles bristled at her command. *"Are you out of your mind? They locked weapons on us! They're moving into an attack posture!"*

"We'll deal with the Gorn, Commander. But if you turn this into a shooting match, it'll mean war. Release your weapons lock, beam up your officers from the surface, and break orbit." She studied his reaction. He didn't react right away; he was thinking too much, and that would only lead to questions Chen wasn't equipped to deal with. Once again doing her best imitation of Captain Picard, she snapped at Ackles, "That's an order, Commander! I won't tell you again!"

The force of her voice broke the man's concentration and impelled him to action. *"Acknowledged, Enterprise."* He nodded to someone off-screen. *"We're beaming up our people now. You're on your own from here. Good luck. Atlas out."*

In a blink the viewscreen reverted to an image of Orion from low orbit. The *Atlas* pivoted away from the *Hastur-zolis* and accelerated away, leaving only the *Enterprise* to face the angry Gorn. Chen returned to the command chair, determined to make the second half of her ruse as successful as the first. "Dina, hail the Gorn again. Abby, keep our shields up, but take our weapons down to standby. Gary, adjust our orbit: keep us between the Gorn and the *Atlas*."

Tense seconds ticked away as Chen wondered how she was going to avert a calamitous showdown with the Gorn ship. She was still at a loss for a plan when Elfiki announced, "I have contact with the Gorn ship. Channel ready."

"On-screen." Every stray fact Chen had ever learned

about the Gorn raced through her thoughts as the view-screen changed to an image of the command deck of the *Hastur-zolis*. Dominating the frame was an extreme close-up of a Gorn's face, its nostrils flaring and fangs bared, its topaz-colored eyes fixed on Chen. She confronted the intimidating archosaur with all the calm and confidence she could fake. "This is T'Ryssa Chen, commanding the *Starship Enterprise*. To whom am I speaking?" *Please let this trick work twice.*

"I am Gith Saroz, commanding the Hastur-zolis. *Surrender and prepare to be boarded."*

Chen considered his demand for all of one-third of a second. "No."

"You have twenty seconds to—"

"I said, *no*."

The Gorn's nostrils flared. *"You are in no position—"*

"Stand down," Chen said, matching the archosaur's unblinking stare.

Saroz bellowed, *"After one of your delegation tried to assassinate our imperator?"*

"You can prove that?" Challenging him was a calculated risk; if it backfired, their already ugly situation was going to get much, much worse.

To her relief, Saroz hesitated—not long, but long enough to confirm her suspicion that there was reason to doubt the Gorn's one-sided version of events. *"The Imperial Guard informs us a member of the Federation delegation used a concealed weapon to attack our imperator."*

Elfiki hurried to Chen's side. "Federation Security says Bacco's chief of staff opened fire with a phaser at the reception. But the president's protection agents say Piñiero's target was unclear—she also opened fire on President Bacco and Starfleet officers."

"I see." Armed with the new information, which she knew Saroz had heard over the open channel, Chen faced the Gorn with new resolve. "It sounds as if the situation's not as clear as you made it out to be, Gith Saroz. I recommend we both stand down and return to our assigned orbits while our people on the surface investigate the attack. I, for one, would rather not start a war based on faulty intelligence. Wouldn't you agree?"

The Gorn exhaled loudly, flaring his nostrils. A low growl rattled in his throat. Then he answered in a dry rasping voice, *"Agreed. We will return to our orbital sector. But be warned,* Enterprise—*we will be watching you, and your people on the planet."*

"We'll be keeping our eyes on you, too. *Enterprise* out." She looked at Balidemaj and slashed her thumb across her throat. Balidemaj cut the channel before Saroz could ruin the fragile détente. Chen sighed with relief as she turned back toward Elfiki. "Damn, that was close."

"Closer than you think." Elfiki lowered her voice. "What I didn't mention was that one of Piñiero's shots killed Szamra, the Gorn legislator—and that she escaped from the bank."

"What about the president?"

The science officer frowned. "She's all right, just really shaken up. But once the details start coming out, this'll turn into a bona fide mess. And now that the *Atlas* is warping out of the system, it'll be up to us to keep the civilian news media from finding out about it."

Chen shook her head. "And just like that, I already miss talking with the Gorn."

15

Tattered veils of smoke lingered between smoldering trees, masking the full extent of the damage to the once-verdant rooftop arboretum. Beverly Crusher strode along the main path, stepping over branches blasted loose from the trees, weaving around debris scattered in the pandemonium that had followed the shooting, and checking on the dozens of medics tending to the wounded and the dead. Nine agents from Bacco's protection detail had been hit—five fatally—in the wild crossfire during Piñiero's escape. Four soldiers from the Gorn Imperial Guard had been killed, and seven others had been seriously hurt.

Now the rooftop was swarming with armed security and medical personnel from the *Enterprise* and the *Hastur-zolis,* as well as investigators from both ships and the Orions' civilian police force. President Bacco and Imperator Sozzerozs, along with the surviving members of their respective retinues, had been spirited away to the relative safety of their private suites on the bank's secured sublevels. The most prominent casualty, unfortunately, was Szamra, whom everyone had been counting on to sway key opinions in the Gorn Imperial Senate. The venerated *nizor* lay beneath a tablecloth liberated in haste from a nearby buffet table.

Picard stood near the main entrance to the arboretum, answering questions from and offering advice to the bank's executives and its security director, Akili Kamar. Crusher watched her husband for a moment, torn between gratitude and resentment. *If he hadn't tackled me,* she reminded herself, *I'd probably have been Piñiero's first victim.* But as much as she wanted to see him as a hero for saving her life, she couldn't forget that he had chosen to shield her rather than act to stop Piñiero. More damningly, he had saved her instead of protecting the president.

She knew she could rationalize away his actions, if she wanted to. Technically, as Starfleet officers they were sworn to obey the civilian government and uphold its laws, but the life and person of the president were the responsibility of the Protection Detail. It might even be legally proper to argue that Picard's responsibility as Crusher's commanding officer was to protect her life and vouchsafe the *Enterprise* and its crew. But legalisms and sophistry were no longer any comfort to Crusher. There was no undoing what had been done, and even though Picard had made no error and committed no offense against Federation law or his Starfleet oath, he still had shattered her conception of who he was. Instead of a hero . . . she had a husband.

A feather-light touch on her arm made her turn to see the *Enterprise*'s assistant chief medical officer, Doctor Tropp. The grouchy, middle-aged Denobulan regarded her with the bleary gaze of someone roused from a deep sleep. "We're done with triage. The ones that are safe to be transported are being moved up to the ships, since we can't send anyone to the local hospitals without raising red flags for the media."

"I understand. How many are we still trying to stabilize?"

"Two of Bacco's agents, and one of the Gorn." He nodded in the general direction of a team of surgeons, nurses, and technicians from the *Enterprise* who were huddled over the two critically injured Federation protection agents. "I'd put their odds at about fifty-fifty. Might be a bit higher if you could lend a hand."

Crusher nodded. "I'll be there in a minute. Go back and keep things moving."

"Understood." Tropp shuffled away, obviously exhausted but soldiering on.

She walked in the other direction, toward the arboretum's entrance. Picard finished his conversation with the bank's security chief, who stepped away as Crusher joined her husband. "We're starting to beam up the casualties," she said. "But the last few aren't stable enough yet."

Picard squeezed Crusher's shoulder. "If things are under control here, it might be best if you returned to the *Enterprise* now."

"Not until I make sure the last two wounded agents are out of danger."

Doubt darkened his expression. "Surely, Doctor Tropp can handle—"

"Jean-Luc—are you trying to get rid of me?"

Her accusation left him taken aback. "Not at all. But in light of recent events, a greater emphasis on security seems warranted, don't you think?"

She didn't know whether to take his explanation at face value or to plumb for a hidden agenda. Before she could decide, La Forge and Šmrhová arrived and headed directly to the captain. "Sir," La Forge said, "we got here as soon as we could. Is everyone all right?"

"No one from the *Enterprise* was hurt," Picard said.

"Unfortunately, several members of the president's protection detail have been killed, as have a number of Gorn imperial guards. Do we have any leads on the bank's chairman?"

Šmrhová shook her head. "No, sir. And it sounds like your shooter got away, too."

"Regrettably, yes." He pointed around the arboretum. "Somehow, she planted a handful of explosive devices after the area was secured. Most of them were tear gas intended to cover her escape, but a high explosive near one of the far exits enabled her to slip past security."

Worf and Dygan emerged from the bustle of activity filling the smoky rooftop and joined their shipmates. The first officer appeared agitated. "Sir," he said, "Glinn Dygan and I have made a thorough analysis of the shooter's escape."

While Worf drew a breath, Dygan jumped in to continue. "During the firefight and then her escape into the service stairwells and elevator shafts, the shooter engaged in several bouts of hand-to-hand combat, against both Federation personnel and Gorn soldiers."

"Piñiero served in Starfleet before she worked for President Bacco," Worf said, reclaiming control of the briefing. "She was a highly trained officer, but nothing in her record suggests she is capable of besting a Gorn in hand-to-hand combat."

Dygan cut in, "Even stranger, sir, she left behind no genetic material on her victims. Considering how much force she applied, she should have left traces of dermis and blood on each of the personnel she assaulted. However, one of the Gorn reported striking her with a bladed weapon. When we scanned it, we found trace particles of bioplast sheeting."

The news drew a grim nod from La Forge, who

looked at Šmrhová and explained, "The same material used to create the skin of Soong-type androids."

As ever, Picard reacted to the worsening crisis with calm decisiveness. "If Ms. Piñiero *has* been replaced by an android, we need to prove that fact as quickly as possible—not only to clear her name, but to preserve the peace. Number One, share this with Data's defense counsel, but make sure he understands this information is top secret. Geordi, I want you and Lieutenant Šmrhová to return to the *Enterprise*; keep looking for evidence to clear Mister Data. Doctor Crusher and I will stay here to direct the investigation and keep an eye on the president." Picard's already dour mood turned grave. "One last thing: do not share this information with the Gorn until we have a better understanding of their true role in this debacle." He fixed his visage into a mask of hard resolve. "Work quickly, and exercise extreme caution. . . . Dismissed."

Nanietta Bacco couldn't stop herself from shaking, yet she felt numb, inside and out. Cloistered in her private suite, all she could think about was her friend's inexplicable betrayal. Nothing had seemed amiss before the shooting started. Piñiero might have been a bit less talkative than usual, but that wasn't uncommon when they were in social settings; whenever they were out and about, Piñiero had always been careful not to upstage her president. Before every meeting or event, she had entrusted to Bacco all her best talking points, all her best jokes, and—when necessary—a selection of scathing retorts to keep her critics in line.

So how did she end up pointing a phaser at me? What went wrong?

Her bitter ruminations were interrupted by the chiming of the visitor signal.

She wanted to shout *Go away!* but knew that wasn't an option. Shirking the burdens of her office would be unpresidential. She tried to compose herself into a semblance of dignity as she called out, "Who is it?" The confrontational edge in her own voice startled her.

A man's voice replied through the comm, *"Madam President? It's Cort Enaren. May I come in?"* Did he sounded worried or condolent? It was hard for her to tell without seeing him.

Torn between an urge for isolation and a yearning to fill the sudden void in her life, she opted for the latter. "Come in, Cort."

Heavy clacks and low hums resounded from the door as the protection agents outside unlocked it to admit Enaren. As the elderly Betazoid councillor entered, he was trailed closely by Agent Wexler, who no longer wore a jacket and had moved his sidearm holster from under his arm to his right hip. Stern and watchful, he kept his hand on his phaser and his eyes on Enaren.

"Steven," Bacco scolded, "is that really necessary?"

Wexler continued to observe Enaren as he answered. "Yes, ma'am, it is. After what happened at the reception, I'm not taking any chances."

She traded a look of quiet exasperation with her visitor. "Well, I certainly can't fault him for being thorough." Then she narrowed her eyes at Wexler. "Tell me, Steven: if you're protecting me from Councillor Enaren, who's to protect me from you?"

Her mocking question made the agent think. He lifted his free hand and spoke into his cuff. "Kistler, get in here." His attention never wavered from Enaren—not even as the door opened and Alan Kistler, another agent from Bacco's personal protection team, stepped inside.

Kistler was a few centimeters taller than Wexler but

nearly two decades younger. His combination of Peruvian and Irish ancestry had given him fair skin and a thick head of wiry hair, handsomely cherubic features, and dark brown eyes. Like his fellow agent, he had doffed his suit jacket and now wore his phaser on his hip. In a glance he sized up the situation inside the room, then he looked to Wexler for direction. "Sir?"

"Alan, if I do anything that even remotely *looks* like a threat to the president or the councillor, shoot me."

The second agent set his hand on his phaser. "Yes, sir."

Bacco didn't know whether to be amused, horrified, or reassured. Enaren drank in the moment with the aplomb of one who has grown too old to be shocked by life's oddities, then he noted with a droll deadpan, "We seem cursed to live in interesting times, Madam President."

"Don't we always?" She led Enaren to a pair of facing armchairs and motioned for him to sit down as she did likewise. "What can I do for you, Councillor?"

He folded his hands on his lap. "Actually, I came to see how I could be of help to you." More quietly, he continued, "I know how you feel right now, Madam President."

"I appreciate your sympathy, Cort, but I doubt you could understand exactly what—"

"I wasn't speaking figuratively, Madam President. I'm a Betazoid. I *know* how you feel."

His explanation left Bacco feeling even more vulnerable than she had before his visit. "No offense, Cort, but that's just creepy."

He turned his palms outward. "Forgive me. I didn't mean to alarm you. Please believe me when I promise I'm not poking around inside your mind. Most of the time I shield myself from other people's thoughts, as much out of respect for their privacy as for the sake of my own sanity. But the emotional storm you've got brewing . . . well, it's too powerful to ignore."

"I think that's to be expected, don't you?" To his credit, he didn't respond right away. Apparently, his gifts enabled him to sense that she was merely pausing to compose herself. "Esperanza was more to me than my chief of staff, Cort. Even more than just a friend. I'd known her almost her entire life. . . . She was family, as close to me as my own flesh and blood."

Enaren became briefly pensive. "Are you certain it was her in the arboretum?"

Something about the way he'd asked the question led her to wonder if he knew more about the situation than he was saying. "Who else would it have been?"

"Officers from the *Enterprise* found evidence in the arboretum to suggest that the shooter wasn't really Esperanza, but an android replicant of her."

She leaned forward, her attention fully engaged. "Why haven't I heard about this?"

The white-haired Betazoid frowned. "I think they're keeping certain details a secret while they continue their investigation. Possibly to prevent a panic, and maybe to avoid tipping off the enemy to the extent of their knowledge."

His explanation sounded reasonable, but another question bothered her. "How did *you* find out about this?" Rather than answer, he looked at the floor. Bacco began to intuit the truth. "You'd left the arboretum by the time the science teams arrived, so you couldn't have overheard Picard and his officers talking." She hardened her gaze into an accusatory glare. "I thought you shielded yourself from other people's thoughts— 'out of respect for their privacy.'"

"Most of the time, I do." A sheepish smile and a

small shrug. "In times of emergency or a direct threat to my president, I make exceptions."

"I knew there was a reason I liked you." Feeling a bit more relaxed, she leaned back and sank into her chair. "If that was an android masquerading as Esperanza, then she might still be alive somewhere, if we can find her soon enough."

He was slow to mirror her optimism. "Yes, perhaps."

"But you don't think it's likely. Do you?"

She could see him wrestling with his conscience, and she wondered whether he would think it better to lie for the sake of her morale, or to tell her the cold truth. The regret in his eyes telegraphed his decision. "I don't think it's likely, Madam President. In most cases of infiltration by impersonation, the doubled individual is eliminated to reduce the risk of detection."

Despite knowing it had been coming, it had been a painful thing to hear. Bacco bit back on her surge of grief and nodded. "Thank you for telling me the truth, Cort. But until we find proof that she's gone, I have to hang on to hope."

In his green eyes she caught a faint glimmer of admiration, and he mustered a wan smile. "I would expect nothing less, Madam President."

"We can't know for certain that the attack was part of the Breen's operation," Azarog said. His head was the only part of him not submerged in the bubbling sludge of the Gorn suites' warm mud bath. "Piñiero's actions might have been a coincidence."

"Don't be an idiot." Sozzerozs paced and let the hot, arid climate inside his suite ease his aching muscles and rejuvenate his senses. "Events of this magnitude rarely occur by chance."

Wazir Togor perched atop an ersatz rock ledge and

basked beside one of the suite's primary heating elements. "What would the Breen gain from killing Szamra?"

Sozzerozs stopped pacing and looked down his snout at his adviser. "Now I know you're being obtuse. You watched the same security recordings I did—she was aiming at Bacco. Szamra was collateral damage—and I would have been, too, if not for Bacco's bodyguard."

"You assume Piñiero was aiming at Bacco," said Azarog, with barely half his snout sticking out of the mud. "Based on what I saw in those recordings, we could make a solid argument that she was aiming at you."

Togor added quickly, "A fact we can turn to our advantage when talks resume." He stretched his long sinewy body across the faux-rock slab. "Let me leverage a scandal like that, Majesty, and we'll be able to wring any favor we want from the Federation."

Azarog sat up out of the mud, which clung to him like a new hide. "We're not supposed to gain the upper hand, just keep them at the table. Using this incident to force them into concessions might jeopardize our primary mission by bringing the summit to a close."

The imperator resumed his languid trudging back and forth between Azarog and Togor. "I have begun to doubt the value of our so-called mission. I agreed to waylay the Federation president and play the part of a distraction. I did *not* agree to act as live bait for an assassin." He stopped midway between the *wazir* and the *zulta-osol*. "There is much the Breen aren't telling us. If that really was Bacco's chief of staff who went on that rampage, how did Thot Tran and his Spetzkar induce her to violence? If it was an impostor, how did they substitute her for the real Piñiero without being detected? And what if she had succeeded? What if she had killed Bacco and me before that bodyguard shot her and forced her to retreat?"

Uneasy looks traveled between Togor and Azarog. The *zulta-osol* asked, "Was that a rhetorical question, my lord?"

"It was not. Had the assassin succeeded, what do you think would have been the result?"

Togor rose to the challenge. "The crew of the *Hastur-zolis* would have interpreted your murder as an act of war and opened fire on the two Starfleet vessels."

"Who would have overpowered it," Sozzerozs pointed out.

Azarog added, "Giving your son no choice but to name himself imperator and declare war on the Federation." He let out a long, low hiss. "Which would be most calamitous."

"In less than a day," Sozzerozs said, "our reserve forces in the adjacent sectors would attack all Federation targets within range. Based on wargame scenarios I have reviewed with our fleet commanders, the response from the Federation and the Klingon Empire would be swift and decisive. And under the terms of our mutual defense treaties with the other members of the Pact, the entire quadrant would be plunged into war in a matter of weeks."

It was a chilling prospect, and it left the three of them hushed for a moment. When Togor broke the silence, he sounded baffled. "Why would the Breen risk that? Just as important, why would they risk *your* life, Majesty?"

"Forget about bullying the Federation," Azarog said. "We should use this to force favors from the Breen. We honored our pledge to aid them in matters of mutual defense, and they have repaid us with treachery."

"We don't *know* that," Togor warned. "We only *suspect* it. Unless we find evidence that proves this to be the work of the Breen, we can't risk alienating them with baseless accusations." He looked at Sozzerozs. "We can further both our agendas by directing your Imperial Guard to cooperate with Starfleet, by helping it investigate the attack. By presenting ourselves to the Federation as partners in the pursuit of justice, we can gain access to their findings about the incident. If they find evidence that implicates the Breen, they will have reason to share it, because doing so will exonerate them of responsibility. And that evidence will enable us to confront Thot Tran, and make him pay for his betrayal."

Azarog was skeptical. "And if the investigation finds no such evidence?"

"Then at least we will have prolonged our interaction with the Federation delegation, thereby accomplishing our original mission of attracting the attention of their government, military, and intelligence agencies." He lifted his snout with a hint of pride as he looked at Sozzerozs. "Honor will be served—and justice will be given its chance, as well."

It was a sound plan—conservative, proportional, and strategically balanced. Advice such as this was why Sozzerozs had trusted Togor as his *wazir* for most of the past decade.

"Togor, order Hazizaar and his men to assist the Starfleet investigation in all ways possible. Azarog, I want you to make sure Szamra's death isn't used to fan political fires back on the homeworld." The imperator straightened to his full height and imagined the day when he would make Thot Tran pay for treating him as if he were expendable. "I'll make sure the summit continues. But mark my words: if we find proof that Thot Tran tried to have me killed, our proposal to forsake the Pact and forge a new alliance with the Federation will cease to be a ruse."

16

The last time La Forge had used a holodeck to investigate a mystery, he had been dressed as Doctor John Watson and Data had been playing the role of Sherlock Holmes. Together, they had explored multiple interactive variants of all the stories from Sir Arthur Conan Doyle's canonical tales of the great detective. Although he'd usually followed Data's lead, in accordance with the stories' designs, he had often found it hard to hold his tongue when he found the clues first.

However, standing with Šmrhová inside a holodeck simulation of Hilar Tohm's apartment, complete with a detailed reproduction of the woman's battered corpse, he had trouble finding anything to say. The two of them had paced around the body for close to an hour, and he had listened with muted revulsion as Šmrhová rattled off picayune observations about the abrasions on Tohm's neck, the angles at which her cervical vertebrae had sheared, or what the blood traces scattered about the room suggested about the progress of her fight against her killer.

The security chief kneeled once again beside Tohm and leaned close to examine her. Like a child who had found a dead animal, she poked it with seemingly morbid curiosity. "Okay, so we've fixed the time of death based on the body's internal temperature, the postmortem buildup of lactic acid in the muscle tissue, and overall rates of cellular breakdown in her brain tissue. But I think her attacker tortured her first."

"Based on what?" Her hypothesis troubled him, but he was obligated to seek details.

She pointed at Thom's head. "Look at all the bruising and blunt-force trauma. Not much of it looks as if it was meant to be fatal. I think whoever killed her was trying to beat something out of her. Her killer wanted something. Given her line of work, I'd guess information."

Drawn in by her speculation, he kneeled on the other side of the body. "Are you sure? What if those were defensive wounds? You said yourself the place shows signs of a struggle."

"True. But look at her left hand. The knuckles of her index, middle, and ring fingers are all broken, but she didn't do that by punching someone. They were bent backwards."

He inhaled sharply through his teeth, reacting to the imagined pain of such an injury. "Ouch." In his thoughts, he could almost hear the sound of the knuckles breaking; it was a grotesque notion—and then he realized this was the first he'd heard of it in connection to Tohm's murder. "Why wasn't that in the original crime-scene report?"

Šmrhová shook her head. "I don't know. Maybe they missed it."

"Or maybe someone covered it up." He could see from Šmrhová's raised eyebrows that she thought he was inventing bogeymen. "I'm not saying it's some grand conspiracy. But think about where she worked. What if Starfleet Intelligence realizes she was interrogated by force? They might want to avoid a lot of difficult questions—for instance, the kind that might lead to people without the right clearance levels digging through all of Tohm's active projects."

"There's another possibility." She stood up, and La Forge did the same. They looked down at the body as Šmrhová continued. "Tohm kept her superiors and Starfleet informed of what she was working on—that's how they knew to pick up Data so quickly. Well, if they know what kind of intel she was digging up for him, they might already have a suspect in her murder—one they aren't telling us about."

La Forge's thoughts turned to Data's search for the Immortal known as Emil Vaslovik—or Flint, or Akharin, or any of a hundred other identities. The Immortal's existence had been a subject of vital interest to Starfleet and Federation Security ever since the discovery a decade earlier that he had a number of foolproof shortcuts around their computer security protocols.

If she asked one too many questions, or maybe the wrong questions, about Vaslovik, there's no telling who might have taken notice, he realized. Although the Immortal had tried to present himself as a benign figure during his last known encounter with Starfleet, his previous interactions had been confrontational and violent. La Forge had no doubt such a man was capable of committing murder to safeguard his privacy. By the same token, he could imagine a wide variety of parties who would kill to track down the Immortal and steal his secrets.

Šmrhová noted the faraway look in La Forge's eyes and snapped her fingers in front of his face. "Hey! You still with me, sir?"

"Hm? Yeah, sorry about that. I was just thinking."

"About . . . ?"

He knew he couldn't explain the Vaslovik situation to her. Even though she was now the *Enterprise*'s chief of security, she lacked the necessary clearance to be told about the Immortal, his connection to Data and Noonien Soong, and why such knowledge would be worth killing for. He flashed his most disarming smile. "Nothing. Just got distracted, that's all."

A comm tone interrupted their simulation, and it was followed by a deep voice. *"Lieutenant Commander Peshtal-Azda to Lieutenant Šmrhová."*

The security chief replied, "Šmrhová here. Go ahead."

"Hello, Lieutenant! I'm the JAG defense counsel for Lieutenant Commander Data."

"Yes," she said, masking her impatience, "I know who you are."

"Oh! Splendid. Well, I've been informed you're heading up the Enterprise*'s independent investigation into the murder of Commander Tohm, so I wanted you to be the first to hear the good news: I've secured Mister Data's release from custody, effective tomorrow at 0900."*

La Forge and Šmrhová faced each other, both wide-eyed with shock.

"Excuse me, this is Commander Geordi La Forge. How did you get Data released?"

"Thanks to the evidence you and Commander Worf provided, I was able to demonstrate to the presiding JAG officer that Data has an alibi, and that there is at least one other Soong-type android on Orion who has infiltrated the bank with obviously hostile intentions. In legal parlance, that provided Data the benefit of something we like to call 'reasonable doubt.'"

La Forge laughed with joy and relief. "That's fantastic!"

"I can hardly believe it myself," Šmrhová said. "No offense, counselor."

"Oh, that's all right," Peshtal-Azda said. *"I understand completely. It's easy to forget that sometimes our legal system actually works."*

It had been more than an hour since Picard and Commander Tezog of the *Hastur-zolis* had convened inside a secure conference room within the Bank of Orion, and the room—which under any other circumstances would have felt spacious to Picard—had begun to feel not unlike a jail cell. Adding to his discomfort was the Gorn's insistence on keeping the room's thermostat set above thirty-three degrees Celsius. While that created a cozy environment for Tezog, Picard had long since become soaked from head to toes in perspiration.

Tezog flicked his forked tongue and pushed a padd across the broad, lacquered wood conference table to Picard. "The report from Kinshal's home."

A glance at the padd made it seem clear why Tezog had called his attention to it. "No body, no signs of struggle. And not one fingerprint or trace of genetic material from Kinshal."

"Almost as if it had been wiped clean on purpose." A low growl churned deep inside the archosaur's chest. "Which suggests Kinshal was murdered, and his apartment sanitized."

Picard nodded. "Precisely." He skipped ahead in the report. "The Orion Colonial Police seem to share our suspicions. They've listed Chairman Kinshal's disappearance as suspicious, and as a likely homicide."

"Likely? How much more proof do they need?"

The captain's face slackened to a weary grimace. "Unfortunately, the law on Orion prohibits filing a charge of murder in the absence of a corpse or other incontrovertible evidence of foul play, such as an audio-visual record."

The Gorn unleashed an angry hiss through his fangs. "Ridiculous! There are hundreds of ways to dispose of bodies without leaving a trace." He pounded the side of one scaly fist on the tabletop. "This planet makes a mockery of the law!"

Commandant Keilo Essan of the OCP replied as he entered the room, "We prefer to think of our world as a bastion of individual liberty, unfettered by the controlling hand of the state."

"You mean a free-for-all," Tezog said through a snarl.

"Please," Picard interrupted, "we're all working toward the same goal." Hoping to prevent the situation from spiraling out of control, he continued. "Commandant, is it safe to assume you're here because your people found something?"

The middle-aged Orion wiped a fresh sheen of sweat from his balding pate. "Yes, in fact. We've found your would-be assassin, Ms. Piñiero."

Both the starship commanders moved to the end of the table to flank Essan. Tezog reached him first and loomed over him. "Where is she?"

"We have her in our care. She's being transferred to the Sieelek Medical Center."

Picard kept his tone civil despite its urgency. "What is her condition?"

Essan seemed surprised by the question. "She's *dead*, Captain."

"*Merde.*" *So much for questioning her,* he lamented. "How did it happen?"

The commandant removed a palm-sized data device from an inside pocket of his jacket, activated it with a gentle tap, and checked it. "According to the first officers on the scene, she appeared to have been strangled."

"How convenient," Tezog replied, his suspicions of the Orions clearly intensifying.

"I assure you, Commander," Picard said, his voice sharp, "Ms. Piñiero's demise is anything but convenient." He turned his ire back toward Essan. "Who knows about this?"

"The three of us," Essan said, thinking as he spoke. "The half-dozen police and medical personnel who found the body and are transporting it to Sieelek. And after the body reaches the medical center, the coroner and probably at least one assistant."

"Unacceptable," Picard snapped. "This information needs to be contained before it goes any further. We need to have the body beamed up to the *Enterprise* at once."

His demand rankled Tezog. "Why? So your people can whitewash the autopsy and force-feed us a report that miraculously exonerates your failed assassin?"

"Don't be absurd." Picard stepped past Essan to confront Tezog, nose to snout. "What would you have us do? Beam her to your ship for examination?"

A wider baring of fangs. "It *was* our imperator she tried to murder."

Picard stood firm against the foul stench of Tezog's breath, a hot gust that reeked of rotting flesh. "From where I stood, she seemed to be aiming at our president."

Essan pushed his way between the two starship captains. "Enough of this! The crime was committed in our jurisdiction, and her body was recovered there, as well. What the two of you want is irrelevant. The coroner at Sieelek will perform the autopsy."

The commanders backed away from each other. Picard reluctantly broke eye contact with Tezog to confront Essan. "Commandant, you must understand what a volatile situation this is."

"I never would have guessed."

Picard ignored the Orion's sarcasm. "The outcome of this investigation could be the spark that ignites a war. Surely, you must see that every detail needs to be treated with the utmost care. We can't afford to let history's course be dictated by a misunderstanding."

Essan scowled. "It might shock you to learn, Captain, that we practice advanced medicine and investigation on Orion, just as you do in the Federation. But even if we had nothing but dull knives and candlelight, the fact would remain that while you and your people are on the surface of our planet, you're subject to our laws. The autopsy happens here."

"You're suggesting that I stand by and let you autopsy a senior member of the Federation government, the president's appointed chief—"

"Yes, I am. Right here, right now, as far as we're concerned, she's nothing more than a common criminal—one who broke our laws on our soil. This is nonnegotiable."

Tezog edged closer to Essan, who backpedaled himself against the wall. The hulking Gorn stared down at the Orion as if sizing him up for an appetizer. "Why should the Hegemony trust an unverified report?" He let Essan squirm a moment. "Out of respect for your national sovereignty, I consent to your coroner performing the postmortem examination. But in the interests of transparency and political goodwill, I strongly suggest you invite medical doctors, one from each of our ships, to observe the procedure and advise your coroner as they see fit."

Caught between Picard and Tezog, the commandant shed his imperious attitude. "A most sensible compromise, Commander Tezog. I'll see to it that your ships' physicians are welcomed at the medical center, and that the examination is held until they both arrive." He leaned his head toward the door. "By your leave?"

Picard stood aside and let the commandant exit. After the Orion was gone, Picard shot a conspiratorial glance at Tezog. "How did you know I was pressuring him to release the body merely as a prelude to asking for joint supervision of the postmortem?"

The archosaur gave his raptor-like head a rakish tilt. "It's what I would have done."

An octagonal bank of color-corrected lamps above the examination table snapped on and flooded the room with blinding white light. Beverly Crusher lifted an arm to shield her eyes, and beside her the chief medical officer from the *Hastur-zolis,* Doctor Oszor, shut his eyes and growled.

"Sorry," the coroner said from the other side of the table.

Doctor Ramil Landar was a boyish Orion man—not least because he had barely passed the threshold of adulthood by most humanoid standards. He seemed flippant, unserious, and disorganized. His hair was a wild, uncombed mess, and the lower half of his green face was darkened by a swath of rough stubble. He reached up, dimmed the lights a bit, and adjusted their focus to dispel the harsh shadows on the body.

Lying on a sheet of grated steel above a drainage well, atop a broad pedestal that hid the examination table's extensive plumbing, was the corpse of Esperanza Piñiero.

As the light diffused and diminished in brightness, Crusher's eyes adjusted, and she studied the naked cadaver's copious injuries. "Can you open her eyes for me, please?"

Landar gently pried open the lids, giving Crusher

and Oszor a look at the bloodshot corneas underneath. "Severe petechial hemorrhaging," Oszor noted.

"And ligature marks around the throat," Crusher said. "Can we have a scan of the trachea, please?"

The Orion powered up the table's built-in imaging sensors, which superimposed a holographic model of Piñiero's corpse over the real thing. Manipulating the hologram with balletic waves of his hands, Landar lifted the detailed imagery of her throat and neck into midair between himself and Crusher and Oszor. Spreading his hands, he enlarged the three-dimensional graphic. "It's been crushed." He pointed at the spinal column. "Whoever choked her applied enough pressure to snap C3 and C4."

Oszor leaned close and studied the rest of the corpse. "I see no other signs of trauma." He looked up at Landar. "Any internal injuries within the torso?"

Landar generated another scan and raised it up for study. Rolling the hologram over and turning it around, he made a swift review of Piñiero's vital anatomy. "No ruptured tissue, no broken bones. No sign of blunt-force trauma." He shrugged at Crusher and Oszor. "So far, I'd say cause of death looks like asphyxiation due to strangulation."

"Did you run a tox screen?" Crusher asked.

He scratched the back of his neck. "Yeah, but we didn't get much. Traces of moderate alcohol consumption, standard beta blockers, and cholesterol-reduction meds."

The Gorn physician tenderly lifted Piñiero's right arm, studied its underside, then laid it back down before repeating the process with the left arm. "No defensive wounds on the arms. Her attacker had a grip on her throat before she knew what was happening."

Crusher bent down and eyed the dead woman's

hands. "Doctor Landar, did you take any scrapings from under her fingernails?"

"Not yet." He handed her a slender, delicate-looking tool with a round-edged spoon tip. "Be my guest." Crusher took the implement and smiled at the young man.

Working with slow precision and a feather touch, Crusher retrieved several bits of soft matter from beneath each of Piñiero's fingernails. Each small mass was catalogued separately, along with a notation designating from which finger it had been recovered.

When she had finished, she handed the tray of sealed samples to Landar. "How soon can we have these analyzed?"

"A few seconds." He pointed over his shoulder. "The electron chromatograph's right over there. Hang on while I put these through." The coroner stepped away.

Oszor asked Crusher in a low rasp, "What do you expect to find?"

She couldn't tell him that she expected to find trace particles of bioplast sheeting because the *Enterprise* crew suspected a Soong-type android had been involved in the attack at the arboretum, or that the fugitive chairman was very likely also an android.

"I don't know," she lied. "Maybe skin or blood residue if she was able to scratch her attacker before she died. All it would take is a few cells to point us at a suspect."

The Gorn didn't respond to that speculation. Instead, he accessed the exam table's systems and ran some new tests, studying everything from the breakdown of brain cells and muscle tissues to the body's general lividity and the progress of rigor mortis.

Landar returned, holding an Orion data device similar to a padd. "All right, sorry to be the bearer of weird news, but your gal here didn't have any biological residue under those nails except her own. What she did have was trace particles of bioplast sheeting." He handed the tablet to Crusher. "I guess your prime suspect's a mannequin."

Oszor stared up at his test results, and his irises dilated. "This woman did not perpetrate the attack on the rooftop." He highlighted several lines of data. "The levels of lactic acid present in her muscle tissues are inconsistent with the general rate of observed cell breakdown. Also, two of the medications in her system were administered by a timed-release implant. Those drugs continue absorbing into tissues postmortem, but based on the timing of her implant, too much of the drug has been absorbed." He looked at Crusher. "This woman has been dead for at least six hours, well before the incident on the rooftop. But someone placed her in stasis to fool us into thinking she had been dead for less than two hours." To the Orion coroner, he added, "I think Esperanza Piñiero was murdered so that she could be framed for the assassination."

The accusation made Landar back up half a step and raise his hands. "Hey, sure. You'll get no argument from me. But if I could make one little suggestion?" He waited until Oszor and Crusher both motioned for him to go on. "Before you go and start spinning conspiracy theories, you might want to have an answer to this question: *Framed by who?*"

That, Crusher had to admit, was indeed the question.

17

Misery was everywhere, cloaked in stench. Šmrhová materialized from the transporter beam in the heart of a slum district inside Orion's capital, drew her first breath of local air, and gagged on it. The street was an open sewer, a fetid river of urine and waste water littered with garbage. Decaying buildings, some without doors on their entryways, squatted on either side of the narrow road, packed together like filthy giants crouching shoulder to shoulder in the dark.

No matter how many times Šmrhová witnessed the reality of poverty, she remained boggled by the fact of its continued existence in cultures that possessed the ability to eradicate it—but not the will. The Orions, it seemed, were one such culture. Opportunistic and cutthroat, they had little compassion for those of their kind who failed to thrive, no matter the reason. Born into disadvantage and squalor? *Too bad*, said the plutocrats who controlled the levers of government and the engines of industry. Though the practice of sentient trafficking had moved largely underground, it was an open secret that the Orions remained involved in the slave trade, not only of aliens but their own kind, as well. To them, it was merely a fact of life, as routine as smuggling, black market weapons, and fraud.

Or, as the Orions like to call it, personal liberty. Šmrhová tried to mask her contempt; after all, tolerance of alien viewpoints was one of the cherished values of the Federation. But confronted by an ethos that glorified individual selfishness at the expense of society, which let a select few reign as oligarchs over a permanent underclass that was brainwashed to adore them for it, she was tempted to rebel against Starfleet's open-minded policy of noninterference and start leveling the Orions' economic playing fields, one dead robber baron at a time.

A man called out, "In here, Lieutenant." She turned to see an Orion police officer in the doorway at the top of a short flight of steps. He beckoned her. "Your shipmates are inside."

She climbed the stairs and sidestepped past the cop. "Where's your vehicle?"

"On the roof. It's not safe to leave them unattended in the street."

"Yeah, *that's* encouraging." She followed him through the demolished interior of what appeared to have been, in better times, a multi-unit apartment building. Walls had collapsed or been smashed down, there were holes in the rotted floors, and exposed plumbing and wiring were visible everywhere. Odors of stale urine and a skunk-like funk that she had learned to associate with smoked narcotics permeated every room; it was the stink of failure.

The cop led her to an open door and a staircase leading down to the basement. "They're down there with our lab techs and a few of the Gorn."

"Thanks." She passed him and descended the rickety, creaking stairs. Harsh white light flooded the basement, but judging from the dank and moldy quality of the air, Šmrhová guessed the underground space spent most of its time shrouded in darkness. Moisture obviously had sneaked in through prominent cracks in the concrete walls and floor, and cobwebs stretched like cloud cover between the half-rotted wooden joists close overhead.

Worf and La Forge stood in the center of the long room. Opposite them were two Gorn from the Imperial Guard. The four of them seemed to be the only ones actually doing anything useful. The half-dozen Orion police milling about all sported the same weary look that made Šmrhová suspect they had long since stopped even pretending to give a damn about their jobs.

Joining her shipmates, she looked down at the empty space on the floor between them and the Gorn. "I presume this is where Piñiero's body was found."

"Correct," Worf said.

She looked up and around, squinting against the glare from the portable floodlights. "No windows. Only one way down, with not much reason to come here. And I don't mean to speak ill of Orion's Finest over there, but . . . I get the impression they don't patrol this neighborhood very often. So how, exactly, did they find Piñiero's body all the way down here?"

"Anonymous tip," La Forge said. "Or so they say."

The security chief folded her arms and pondered the alleged sequence of events. "Who would come down here? Thieves? There's nothing here worth taking. Someone looking to get rid of a body of their own? Why would they call in a tip to the police?" Unanswered questions and improbable scenarios nagged at her. "This isn't adding up for me."

"Maybe this'll change the equation a bit." La Forge showed her the readout of his tricorder. "We're picking up fresh traces of thorium. They make a path through the building." The engineer nodded toward Worf, then the Gorn. "We found the first traces down here. Hazizaar confirmed the reading and followed the trail to the roof."

Šmrhová took hold of the tricorder and paged through the scans La Forge had made. "So, you're thinking whoever dumped Piñiero's body tracked it in."

"Exactly." He shrugged. "I know it's not much, but it's the best lead we have."

Worf added, "It is the *only* lead we have. But we mean to make the most of it." He tapped his combadge. "Worf to *Enterprise*."

Chen answered, *"Enterprise. Go ahead, Commander."*

"Have you found any leads on the source of the thorium we detected?"

"We've been comparing sensor data with the Hastur-zolis. *I think they've got something, on the far side of the planet: an abandoned thorium breeder reactor. Signature impurities in the samples you sent are a perfect match for the isotopes at the reactor plant."*

Šmrhová interjected, "We need to secure that power plant."

"Already done, sir." Chen sounded pleased with herself. *"Armed security forces from the* Enterprise *and the* Hastur-zolis *have taken control of the plant pending formal action by the Orion Colonial Police."* Her good mood faded abruptly. *"Unfortunately, we found no one there, and no sign that it's been used as any kind of a base of operations."*

La Forge, who had been listening intently, spoke up. "Chen, we need you to make a full sensor sweep of the planet's surface, looking for any other traces of that same isotope."

"Ahead of you again, sir. Elfiki's running the sweep

now, and the Hastur-zolis *is scanning the opposite hemisphere to save us time. We've ruled out a number—Hang on.*" The comm channel went quiet for a few seconds, then Chen returned, her voice aquiver with nervous excitement. "*Sirs? Are you all ready for transport?*"

Worf's brow furrowed. "Why?"

"*Because we have a lock on a thorium trace inside the capital—and it's moving. At the risk of sounding presumptuous, I think we've found our suspect.*"

Without delay, Worf snapped, "Three to transport! Energize!"

It was a wall of bodies, a slow and shuffling mass of humanoids twenty people wide stretching for blocks, and no matter how aggressively La Forge shouldered through them, he felt as if he were pushing against the ocean, struggling to get ahead of the current.

He thought he heard Worf's voice over his combadge, but the street noise was overwhelming. Hovercar traffic zoomed past high overhead, the humming of their magnetic drives rising and falling, working definitions of the Doppler effect. Advertisements in the garish, neon-lit storefront windows of the capital's Center City district blared trite slogans and music that was blatantly manipulative and designed to haunt the memory. La Forge cringed and fought to ignore them—which only made him all the more aware of them, and drove the infectious melodies into his brain. Thousands of walking feet would have filled the night with the close thunder of footfalls under the best of conditions, but on the rain-slicked pavement, each step resounded with a wet slap of contact, so that the throng carried the patter of rain with them.

Chen's voice squawked from his combadge and

pierced the gray noise of the street. *"Enterprise to La Forge! Do you see the suspect?"*

"Not yet." He adjusted his cybernetic eyes' sensitivity to alpha-particle emissions specific to the wavelength of thorium-229. His ability to perceive the telltale isotope had been Worf's reason for putting him on point as they sought to identify and capture the suspect. But either by chance or by design, their quarry had taken refuge among the masses, using their sheer numbers as a shield. He grew frustrated. *"Enterprise, how close am I?"*

The first reply was lost in the clamor of voices and a banshee wail set to power chords promoting some new holosuite thriller program. La Forge covered his right ear and shouted, "Say again, *Enterprise!*" He listened closely, his uncovered left ear turned toward his combadge.

"About five-point-one meters, bearing zero-zero-six off your present heading."

Eyes locked in the direction Chen had indicated, La Forge slalomed through the crowd, mumbling "sorry" and "excuse me" over and over as he hip-checked one person after another out of his path. Two huge aliens of a species he had never seen before refused to be parted, forcing him to detour wide around them. As he cut in front of the pair, he collided with another person.

She looked up at him from within the deep cowl that had hidden her face.

It was the doppelgänger of Esperanza Piñiero. The duplicate of the dead chief of staff was perfect in every detail save the cosmetic damage wrought by Wexler's phaser to the bioplast sheeting on her throat. La Forge looked her over in a glance and saw thorium-229 alpha particles escaping from radioactive smears on her shoes.

Then he saw red, a split second before he doubled

over from the pain of being punched in the face, gut, and groin, all in the span of a second. Winded and nauseated, he swatted his combadge. "La Forge to away team! She's running! And she still looks like Piñiero!"

Rapid chatter filled the channel, but over the shouts and alarums spreading through the crowd, La Forge couldn't tell what any of his shipmates was saying. He forced himself into motion, following the path of least resistance—the swath the escaping android had cut through the knots of aimlessly drifting pedestrians moving between the theater district and the row of tourist hotels lining the city's central traffic artery.

In the spreading tumult, he heard disruptor fire, followed by screaming. Moments later he hurdled over fallen civilians, some wounded, some dead, all unlucky enough to get caught in the crossfire between the android and the Gorn imperial guard she had killed.

More noise from his combadge. He caught only the end of Chen's update. *"—bearing zero-seven-two off your current heading!"* Turning to his right, he saw the main entrance to a towering, ultramodern tourist hotel, the Sahalax Grand Oasis. More than a dozen people had been knocked to the ground near the fountain in front of the luxury tower, and the hotel's doormen and bellhops were scrambling to provide assistance. *Looks like our suspect's handiwork.*

Disregarding propriety or risk, La Forge barreled through the gawkers and rubberneckers between himself and the hotel's entrance. He looked left and right, then struggled to see through the dark smoked-glass windows into the lobby. *"Enterprise, is she in the hotel? I don't see her."*

"Same bearing, but range is opening fast. She's gaining altitude!"

Altitude? La Forge looked up.

Built into the glass-paneled façade of the hotel were a half-dozen glass-walled elevator pods, conveyances for those who loved scenic views of the capital's stunning cityscape. Two were stationary, two were descending, and two were ascending. He focused on the closer of the two climbing pods and increased his eyes' magnification to five times normal.

The doppelgänger was inside the pod. She looked down at him, teased him with a smirk, and waved with a coy waggling of her fingers.

La Forge drew his phaser from under his jacket, aimed, and fired.

His weapon's brilliant vermillion beam struck the bottom of the elevator pod. A fiery blast erupted from the point of impact, and the lower half of the pod disintegrated.

The android started to fall, then she caught a handrail inside the lift pod.

He fired again, and this time the beam slammed into the android's gut. Light flared as she was knocked loose, and then she fell, tumbling out of control as she plummeted to the street.

Civilians screamed and scattered as the android's body fell. Several dozen meters above the ground, she bounced off a protruding portion of the hotel's sign. Her scorched, limp form cartwheeled erratically into the fountain outside the hotel's entrance. The water in the fountain was far too shallow to offer any kind of cushion, and the body landed with a loud splash, a sickening thud, and an ear-splitting crack.

La Forge saw that he had become the focal point for a couple of hundred bystanders, all of whom watched fearfully to see what he would do next. He tucked his phaser under his jacket and hurried to check on the fallen android. As he leaned over the edge of the fountain to get a better look at the body, a crimson flash of light behind its eyes was accompanied by a muffled pop of detonation. Then black wisps of smoke snaked out of the stricken android's ears, nostrils, and slack mouth. He frowned; he recognized when someone was covering their tracks.

He heard Worf before he saw him. "Excuse me. Stand aside. *Move.*" The Klingon shouldered his way out of the crowd, and Šmrhová was close behind him. They jogged to La Forge's side and eyed the sparking, smoldering synthetic corpse in the water. Worf put away his phaser and looked at La Forge. "Nice shot."

"Thanks." Sirens wailed in the night, distant but swiftly getting closer. "Now what?"

Worf stepped over the fountain's outer wall and waded out to the body. He waved for Šmrhová and La Forge to join him. "Quickly!" They did as he said, and plodded shin-deep through the ice-cold chlorinated water. When they had surrounded the android, the first officer tapped his combadge. "Worf to *Enterprise.* Four to beam up. Energize when ready."

"Acknowledged," Chen replied. *"Stand by, sir."*

Šmrhová shot a surprised look at Worf. "Removing evidence from a crime scene? I don't think the Orions are gonna like that, do you?"

The air filled with the musical hum of an imminent transporter effect, and Worf shot a devious look at the security chief. "It is easier to obtain forgiveness than permission."

18

Bleary and rubbing the sleep from her eyes, Nanietta Bacco sat down at the desk in her bedroom and activated the comm display. A vivid image of Captain Picard appeared, and the venerated starship captain greeted her with a polite smile and a curt nod. *"Madam President."*

"I was told this is urgent, Captain. Urgent enough to merit waking me up?"

Picard's mien turned serious. *"Yes, I believe so. I wanted to inform you of several important developments in our investigation of the attack in the arboretum."* Icons on the screen indicated that he had transferred data files to her. *"The body of Esperanza Piñiero was discovered a few hours ago, in an abandoned building within one of the capital's less wholesome districts. An autopsy supervised by my chief medical officer, and verified by the chief surgeon of the Hasturzolis and the Orion medical examiner, has proved that Ms. Piñiero was murdered prior to the attack. Her body was held in stasis and then planted for us to find. In short, she was framed, Madam President, and now we know how."*

Speaking succinctly and directly, Picard summarized how his crew had come to suspect the shooter in the arboretum was an android, and the process by which their investigation had led to the discovery of Piñiero's android impostor.

"Has that android been captured, Captain?"

"Yes, she has, by my chief engineer, Commander La Forge. Thanks to my first officer, the body is now on board the Enterprise, *where it is undergoing extensive study. However, we seem to have aggrieved the local police by removing it from the planet's surface."*

Knowing the defensive tendencies and volatile tempers of the Orions, Bacco imagined Picard must be grossly understating the matter. "Don't worry about that, Captain. I'll have Ambassador Císol explain to them that it's a matter of Federation national security."

"I've also been told that the Sahalax Grand Oasis hotel is quite irate about some damage that Commander La Forge caused in the course of capturing the android."

"Screw 'em. They can bill me."

Her answer seemed to put the captain at ease. *"Thank you, Madam President."*

"Do you and your crew have any theories about the origin of that android?"

"Our current theory is that it was sent by the Breen. We know they had unfettered access for an unspecified length of time to the factory the Borg had built for Lore, when he'd promised to lead them to a fully synthetic existence. However, our colleague Mister Data assures us the Breen lack the programming and engineering knowledge to create working positronic brains. Which leaves us searching for clues to explain how this impostor, and the one who impersonated Chairman Kin-

shal, could have acquired them—or functioned without them."

She nodded and stifled a yawn. "Keep me informed of your findings, Captain."

"*We will.*"

Her mind turned naturally to political concerns. "I've also been given to understand that the crew of the *Hastur-zolis* has been working with your people on the investigation. How has that been? Do you get the sense their efforts are genuine?"

The captain sat back a bit and considered the question. "*To my surprise, yes. My officers tell me that the Gorn have been unusually forthcoming with information and quick to support our actions when we've met with opposition from the Orions. To be truthful, they've comported themselves more like our allies than like members of a rival power.*" He leaned forward, his eyes bright with curiosity. "*Do you think that might bode well for the outcome of your summit?*"

"I don't know. I hope so." A heavy sigh left her feeling drained, but for the first time since the attack, she felt as if a weight had been lifted from her, and she realized it was because she had been freed from the crushing guilt of doubting her lifelong friend. "Captain, I want to thank you and your crew for all you've done since you arrived. I know that I came down on you pretty hard when you got here, maybe harder than I should have. But thanks to you, I know that my friend didn't betray my trust. I don't have to wonder what happened; I know."

"*All part of the service, Madam President.*"

"No, it was much more than that." As much as she wanted to shed tears of sorrow and relief, she refused to let them fall. In her mind, she could almost hear Piñiero chiding her, *It wouldn't be presidential.* "I want you to know that I feel as if I owe you a personal debt of gratitude. You gave Esperanza back to me. Thanks to you . . . now I can grieve."

Picard struggled to keep his eyes open as he plodded into his quarters. His every step felt leaden, his shoulders ached, and a crick in his neck felt as if it had worsened into a pinched nerve. The day had seemed interminable, one calamity and setback after another. He was relieved to see its end. *One can only hope that tomorrow improves our fortunes,* he mused.

Starlight was the only illumination in the main room. The quarters he shared with Beverly and René were located on the starboard side of the *Enterprise*'s elliptical saucer, which meant they usually faced away from whatever planet the ship might orbit. Now that the ship was holding in a geostationary orbit above the planet's capital, it shared the city's schedule of night and day. In just less than ninety minutes, when the planet's surface and the *Enterprise* once again faced Pi^3 Orionis, the photosensitive coating on the ship's thousands of transparent aluminum windows would automatically darken to protect the ship's personnel from being blinded.

Here's hoping I've long since drifted off to sleep by then.

His first visit was to René's room. He leaned in the open doorway and filled with an ineffable bliss as he watched the boy sleep. Nothing in life gave him greater comfort than seeing his son safe and at rest in his own bed. He had come to view these moments as fleeting instants when, no matter what else had gone wrong in the universe, this much remained right.

For the sake of stealth, he reached down and slipped off his shoes. Then he padded across the room, his sock feet silent on the carpeted floor, to stand beside René's bed. The boy's breathing was slow, deep, and regular, and beneath closed lids his eyes darted to and fro. *When I was his age, I dreamed of the stars—or so my father always said. But I've already given René the stars.* He gazed with wonder at his son. *What could he be dreaming of?*

It was a question only René might be able to answer, but Picard wasn't selfish enough to wake the boy just for that. He reached down and gently stroked René's fine, almost silken hair. Then he gave the boy a whisper of a kiss on the top of his head before he stole away, sneaking from the room with a light step and bated breath.

His plan to skulk into his own bed without waking Beverly was dashed when he slipped through the open doorway to see her lying awake, staring at the overhead. She turned on her bedside lamp and acknowledged him with tired eyes. "Thought I heard you come in."

"I stopped to check on René."

She stretched and yawned. "I figured."

He removed his uniform jacket and tossed it into the corner. "Trouble sleeping?"

"Some." She watched him sit on the bed and pull off his pants. Her poker face was impenetrable. "I've been thinking about you."

A kick sent his trousers into the corner atop his jacket. "What about me?"

"What you did at the reception. Saving my life." Her features scrunched with disapproval. "What the hell were you thinking, Jean-Luc?"

He paused with his undershirt half-off, still wrapped around his arms. "Excuse me?"

"You heard me." There was real anger in her voice; it was quiet and deeply buried, but its presence was unmistakable. "I was standing right next to you. I saw everything you did."

Curious but alarmed, he pitched his undershirt into the corner, then turned to face his wife. "And what, precisely, did you see?"

Crusher's blue eyes bored into him. "You were standing in front of an armed assassin, almost close enough to touch her. And with the lives of two heads of state hanging in the balance, you pulled *me* to the floor. You shielded *me*."

Her ire had taken him by surprise. "Would you have preferred I let her shoot you?"

"What I would have preferred was for you to defend the president."

Despite his sincere wish to remain calm, he felt himself growing defensive. "That's why she has the Protection Detail, Beverly. Defending her is *their* job, not mine."

"Funny, I don't recall Captain Kirk making that distinction when he saved President Ra-ghoratreii from a sniper at the Khitomer Conference."

Stung, he recoiled and stood. "That's the most absurd thing I've—"

"You swore an oath!"

"To defend the Federation, and obey the lawful orders of my superior officers and our elected leaders. I'm a Starfleet officer, not a palace guard." He softened the edge in his voice and tried a different tack. "If I'd tried to intervene, I might have gotten in the agents' way and actually prevented them from doing their jobs."

She crossed her arms and stared at the ceiling, pointedly avoiding looking at him. "I didn't think this was the sort of man you were when I married you."

Unwilling to suffer her harangue at point-blank range, Picard moved to the end of the bed, desperate for some literal and figurative space in which to regroup. "Maybe I wasn't."

Combing her fingers through her sleep-tangled red hair, Crusher spent a few seconds with her eyes shut. When she opened them, she eyed Picard as if he'd betrayed her. "What are you saying, Jean-Luc? That three years ago you would've leaped to her defense?" Dismay and disappointment darkened her angular features. "Has becoming a father changed you that much?"

"I think it has." He looked at Beverly but remained silent until she met his gaze and with a subtle easing of her brow signaled that she would let him have his say. "I admit that I chose kin over country. But I think that decision was not only right but logical."

He saw that she harbored doubts, but he pressed on. "If Nanietta Bacco had been killed last night, the Federation Council would appoint a president pro tem and schedule a special election. In six weeks or so, a new president would be elected and sworn in. In the interim it would be a tragedy and a political mess of epic proportions, but our system of government is designed to cope with such things. It would go on."

Picard edged his way back along the bed, gradually closing the distance between them. "The same would be true if the assassin had killed Imperator Sozzerozs. In the short term, we and the president would have had our hands full preventing it from leading to war, but within days Sozzerozs would be succeeded by his son. From a grand-scale political standpoint, the death of one head of state is little more than a footnote in the history of a civilization."

He sat down on the bed beside her and lowered his voice. "But if I had lost you, there would be no replacing you in my life—or in René's. The same would be true if I'd been killed. Or worse yet, both of us. . . .

Beverly, I waited a long time to start a family, perhaps too long. But now that I have one, nothing in the universe matters more to me. Not my president, not my oath of service, nothing. If that diminishes me in your eyes . . . so be it."

Crusher spent the next minute deep in thought, mulling all that he had said. He sat beside her, quiet and patient, waiting to see if his confession had made matters better or worse. Then she rolled over, turning her back on him, and tugged the bedsheets up over her shoulder.

"Beverly . . . ?"

"Go to sleep, Jean-Luc." She reached out and turned off her bedside lamp. "I get the feeling tomorrow's going to be another very long day."

19

Twisted, shattered, bent, and burned, it remained a marvel of engineering. No matter how much damage it had suffered in the course of its capture the previous night, La Forge reminded himself, it was still a Soong-type android. *Well, ninety percent of it, anyway.*

Ensconced inside the largest and most extensively equipped research laboratory aboard the *Enterprise*, the captured android body had been under the strictest guard possible. Armed security officers had been stationed inside and outside the lab, and a transporter-scrambling field had been projected around it since the body's arrival. La Forge had intended to get some rest and start his tests at 0900, but after lying awake for three hours as the victim of an adrenaline rush, he'd given up trying to sleep and arrived at the lab just before 0800, coffee in hand.

The sensor array above the workbench was just finishing its first series of detailed scans of the body when the lab door swished open, and Data walked in.

La Forge put down his padd and stylus, and rushed to meet his friend with a smile on his face. "Data!" The bemused android stuck out his hand for a shake and got a bear hug instead. The engineer gave Data a fraternal slap on the back. "Man, is it great to see you!"

"It is good to be seen," Data said, returning the back-slapping embrace. They parted, and he nodded toward the body on the workbench. "I was told you captured one of the androids."

"Sure did!" He led Data to the table. "I just took a peek at its insides. It's definitely one of the androids from the factory we found on Mangala, but it's been heavily modified."

Data looked down at the battered duplicate of Esperanza Piñiero. "I can see that."

"Yeah, they've been upgraded to look fully human—or Orion, or whatever humanoid they want, apparently. But it's not as sophisticated as the chameleon tech in your body. This one swaps out modular parts to change things like height, body mass, and retinal patterns." He pulled back a phaser-blackened, scorched-smelling flap of artificial skin from the abdomen and pointed at a device inside the torso. "They've also got sensor-feedback systems, so they give off life signs and bioelectrical signatures that make them scan like whatever they want."

As he studied the modified android, Data's eyes widened. "Intriguing." A birdlike tilt of his head preceded a wry smile. "But not very efficient. Whoever made these changes was likely a skilled roboticist"—he shot a meaningful look at La Forge—"but a mediocre cyberneticist." He straightened his posture and circled the table to view the body from the other side. "I find it hard to believe that the same entity responsible for such crude modifications to the body could be capable of successfully activating, stabilizing, and programming a positronic brain."

"And you'd be right, Data." He pointed at the head.

"Ready for a surprise?" Data nodded, so La Forge carefully detached the exterior cranial plates from the defunct android, exposing the interior of its head. Where he had expected to find a dead positronic matrix from which he might suss raw intel or at least valuable clues, there were only broken, splintered hunks of partially melted black glass. He looked expectantly at Data. "Any idea what *that* is?"

Data was perplexed. "It appears to be volcanic glass."

"That's *exactly* what it is. More to the point, that's all it is." La Forge crossed his arms and frowned at the mystery lying on his workbench. "How could this thing function with a chunk of glass for a brain? I mean, that's almost like saying it literally had rocks in its head."

Poking at the cracked obsidian glob, Data creased his brow. "These fractures and deformations are recent. Could this damage have occurred during the battle for its capture?"

"I think it happened after it hit the ground. Just as I reached the body, I saw a flash of light behind its eyes, and then smoke came out of the ears. I figured it was a self-destruct thermal charge, but I also assumed it was torching a positronic brain, not a glass brick."

Data plucked a needlelike fragment of black glass from inside the head and held it up to the light. "I think it is safe to assume that when this unit was functional, this brain was intact. Whatever was done to it has been very effective at preventing us from reverse-engineering it."

"You're telling me." He sighed. "I have a dozen more tests to run on the body, but I doubt we'll find much we don't already know. The real key to this thing is that jumble of crap it used to call a brain. Problem is, I have no idea how to start deconstructing this mess."

His complaint seemed to spark an idea in Data. "In

that case, Geordi, we need to find someone on the ship who can. Who else has clearance to study this body?"

La Forge shrugged. "No one except you, me, Doctor Crusher, and Lieutenant Šmrhová."

"Then we need to speak to Captain Picard, and ask him to declassify this technology for study, or elevate the security clearances of all *Enterprise* science and engineering personnel to whatever level is necessary to permit their assistance. I think our analysis will benefit from a synthesis of opinions by experts in a variety of scientific and engineering disciplines."

The suggestion made La Forge want to laugh; it sounded simple, yet he knew that it would likely be a nightmare once Starfleet Command's bureaucracy got involved. "Just one problem with that plan, Data: the admiralty will never approve it. It makes too much sense."

Data seemed undeterred. "True. Fortunately, I believe we are currently in the president's good graces—and the last time I checked, she outranked the admiralty."

"I didn't remember you being this devious." He grinned and slapped Data's shoulder. "I like it." With a sideways nod toward the door, he added, "All right. Let's go talk to the captain."

Morning arrived in Ki Baratan, the capital of Romulus, with red skies and sultry heat. A thick haze blanketed the city, shielding it from the blazing eye of the sun even as it smothered the people with its muggy embrace. Pedestrians and venders had begun to pack the streets, and great crowds had already thronged the city's ocean beaches, eager to take advantage of high tide.

Looking down upon the teeming masses from her

private office atop the Hall of State, Praetor Gell Kamemor wished she could lose herself among them. *If only it were so simple.* She pivoted away from the window to face her visitor, Chairwoman Tesitera Levat of the Tal Shiar, whose news had filled her heart with icy wrath. "Do we know who was behind the attack?"

"Not yet, Praetor." Levat was decades younger than Kamemor, but one would not have thought so, seeing them together. Whereas the praetor still had a proud countenance, a lean physique, and lustrous raven hair untouched by time's graying hand, the new leader of the state's intelligence apparatus looked ravaged: thick around the middle, her face creased with worry lines, and her close-cropped, ash-gray hair frosted with white above her ears.

Kamemor looked out the window, but her thoughts were even further away. "Why is Sozzerozs meeting with Bacco in the first place? Do we know the meeting's agenda?"

Levat folded her hands behind her back. "It's not yet clear. We learned of the summit only a few hours ago, and the reports have been . . . contradictory. Our source on Earth says the Gorn approached the Federation to talk rapprochement; our source on Gornar says the summit's a sham, but to what end remains currently unknown."

"Feints and deceptions aren't the Gorn's style. Could they be in league with someone?"

The intelligence chief nodded. "Possibly."

"This couldn't have happened at a worse time, Tes. After all we've done to achieve détente with the Federation, something like this could put us on a path to war."

"It's fortunate, then, that the shooter missed her targets."

That choice of words turned Kamemor's head. "Targets? Plural?"

A cautious half nod. "So it seems. Our source says the assassin could've been aiming at either Bacco or Sozzerozs—or maybe both of them."

The more she learned, the less she understood what had happened. "Who stands to gain from their murders? More important, how did they turn Bacco's own chief of staff against her?"

Levat grimaced with uncertainty. "Who benefits? Hard to say. As to how she was turned, I'm trying to verify a report that suggests Piñiero was framed." She cleared her throat. "There are unconfirmed accounts that an android replicant of Piñiero was captured by Starfleet."

"An android?" The news from Orion strained credulity more with each new revelation. Kamemor walked to her desk. "Who's capable of fielding that kind of technology?"

Levat approached the desk as Kamemor sat down. "To be honest, no one we know of. But the two powers that are closest would be the Federation and the Breen Confederacy."

"The Federation I can understand. They backed Soong's early work, and they had that android in Starfleet for all those years. But how do the Breen figure into this?"

The Tal Shiar chairwoman gestured at Kamemor's desktop computer interface. "We found new intelligence that suggests the Breen have ramped up their research into cybernetics." She waited until Kamemor called up the file and then recounted its highlights as the praetor skimmed its details. "They've been sourcing components on the black market, and there's chatter on the back channels about Starfleet destroying a factory the Borg built for mass-producing Soong-type androids, on a planet near Breen space. If that's true, and the Breen found it first, they might have acquired any number of prototypes, and done who knows what with them."

Kamemor reclined and steepled her fingers. "Assume the rumors from Orion are true. Further assume that the Breen built the android replicant of Piñiero. What are they up to?"

Levat pressed the side of her fist against her upper lip while she considered her answer. "They might have used the Gorn as bait to lure the Federation to the table, so that they could make an attempt on Bacco's life in a setting of their choosing."

"Using the Gorn would make sense," Kamemor said, "given the past goodwill between them and the Federation."

A nod. "It also explains why Starfleet made a point of drawing our attention to the *Enterprise*'s activities in the Azeban system: they hoped to distract us from the Orion summit."

"I still don't see why the Breen would go to this much effort to assassinate Bacco—or Sozzerozs, for that matter. If they'd killed the president, we'd have had no choice but to disavow them to avoid being dragged into their war. I imagine the Tholians and the Tzenkethi would support them, but I doubt the Kinshaya would. As for the Gorn, they might sit it out just to prove themselves innocent of the whole mess. They're brutes, but they have a semblance of honor, and I doubt they'd appreciate being tarred as liars just to protect the Breen."

The chairwoman looked worried. "An all too plausible scenario, Praetor—one that could have shattered the Pact. Had the shooter killed the imperator, the Gorn might well have declared war—though upon whom, it's difficult to say. If they knew in advance of the assassination plot, they'd blame the Breen. If they didn't, they'd almost certainly blame the Federation—after which point they'd refuse to consider any evidence to the contrary." Her anxious frown became a blank stare of shock. "It seems we have providence alone to thank for the fact that we didn't awaken this morning to find ourselves at war."

"A less than comforting thought." Kamemor sat forward, propped her elbows on the desktop, and folded her left hand over the right. "The question, then, is what to do next."

"Our options are limited," Levat said. "Although we suspect the Breen are manipulating events on Orion, we have no proof of that. Even if we did, it would be politically dangerous to meddle in their foreign affairs. If, as you said, we need to be able to disavow them in a worst-case scenario, it's to our advantage to keep our distance, literally and figuratively."

It was cautious, sensible advice. *Perhaps too cautious.* "What if we acquired proof?"

Taken aback, she asked, "Are you directing me to obtain such proof?"

"I'm asking you to evaluate how such evidence would affect our options."

Levat had the wary affect of one who suspected she was being led into a trap. "My advice would remain the same: stay out of the fray."

"Very well. For the time being, we shall." A deep breath became a sigh of frustration. "But if the Breen force me to choose between endorsing their crimes and salvaging the goodwill I've earned from the Federation, then Domo Brex is going to be *very* disappointed."

Thot Tran listened as a midnight wind howled outside the triple-layered windows of the circular audience chamber, obscuring Breen's glaciated landscape with the winter storm's relentless onslaught. Hail pounded the chamber's reinforced dome with a constant but irregular percussion.

He reveled in nature's furious voice, all but unknown to the masses populating the Breen capital of Ansirranana. The common folk lived their lives deep beneath the arctic sea, sheltered from the harsh touch of the elements and the prying eyes of outworlders. Relatively few ever qualified for starship service; fewer still ascended high enough in the ranks of the Breen armed or civil services to merit a visit to this chamber for an audience with the domo.

Tonight, Tran had been granted the privilege of standing at the right hand of Domo Brex while he heard the protests of the senior *thotaru*, who had united in opposition to Tran's bold move to secure the Confederacy's future. *I can't blame them for being afraid,* he decided. *Most of them have held the rank of* thot *far longer than I have. And now I'm poised to surpass them all and pave the way for my future as the next domo.*

The room's guest entrance opened, revealing a curved turbolift car spacious enough to hold up to ten persons at a time. Tonight it held only four—the highest-ranking officers of the Breen military, the elder warlords of the *thotaru*: Thot Vog, commander of the fleet; Thot Saav, commander of all terrestrial forces; Thot Naaz, who had been Tran's predecessor in charge of the Special Research Division before he was promoted to take command of the recently militarized Breen Intelligence Directorate; and Thot Pran, the supreme commander of the Breen military, second in authority only to the domo himself. The quartet strode out of the lift two by two, with Pran and Naaz in front, Vog and Saav behind. They marched in formation across the great inlaid emblem of the Confederacy to stand at attention before Brex, who stood behind a lectern on a tiered podium that occupied a quarter of the chamber's floor.

"Welcome," Brex said. The four *thots* answered him with wordless salutes. "Speak."

Invoking the perquisite of rank, Pran was first. He stepped forward and pointed at Tran. "This one has overstepped his bounds, Domo. He has arrogated power he hasn't earned, and dared to command forces not under his authority."

"I gave him that authority." Brex pointed at Naaz. "You."

Pran stepped back as the commander of the intelligence services stepped forward. "Thot Tran's mission profile was poorly considered, Domo. If it is allowed to proceed, it will squander precious intelligence assets that have taken years to develop."

The domo gestured at Tran but kept his snout pointed at Naaz. "Tran apprised me of the costs before he began. I weighed them against the potential rewards and judged the risk worthwhile. Do you believe my decision to have been made in error?"

Naaz bowed his head. "With the greatest respect and deference, Domo . . . yes. Even if Tran's mission unfolds precisely as intended, and all his objectives are achieved, it will come at the cost of a major Intelligence Directorate program on which we've spent more than three years and one-point-eight billion *sakto*. By any reasonable measure, even his victory will be a failure."

Brex looked at Tran, then back at Naaz. "I'm prepared to answer to the Congress for my decision to authorize his operation. In my estimation, the sacrifice of a purely experimental program within our foreign intelligence service is more than offset by the long-term strategic gains we stand to enjoy. So, while I acknowledge your protest, I overrule it." He waved Naaz back into the ranks and pointed at Vog. "You."

The fleet commander sidestepped clear of Pran, then stepped forward to address Brex. "Domo, my arm of the military stands to gain the most from Thot Tran's mission, but after reviewing its particulars, I must concur with my peers. The scale of Tran's scheme alone is the single best argument against it. Based on intelligence reports from Thot Naaz, there's no indication the Federation is even aware of the breach—which means there is no call for such an urgent and costly action to exploit it. I respect Thot Tran's objective, but in this case, I think a more patient approach to the matter would lead to success at a far lesser cost."

The domo leaned forward, a posture of clear menace. "If we had the luxury of time, I might be inclined to agree with you, Vog. But circumstances have weighed against us. The loss of the slipstream prototype at Salavat, and the corruption of our archived backups of the drive schematics, left us at a tactical disadvantage versus the Federation. Their fleet was diminished by the Borg invasion, but they're rebuilding quickly, and launching a new slipstream-capable ship every month. We need something to level the playing field, a technology to keep them in check." He dismissed Vog by pointing at Saav. "Speak."

Saav stepped around Naaz and snapped back to attention. "Domo, let me affirm my support for all that my peers have said regarding Operation Zelazo. All I have to add is this: speaking as the one whose forces are most directly at risk executing this ill-conceived plan on foreign soil, I respectfully ask that you abort the mission before it goes any further."

"It's too late for that," Brex said. The sudden shifts in the quartet's postures betrayed their surprise and dismay—and filled Tran with profound satisfaction at their expense. The domo continued, "On my orders, the recovery ship has been deployed to the primary target, and it's past the point of no return. The assets are in position, and our forces are committed. All that remains now is to give the Federation exactly what it wants—and then we'll take what's ours."

20

Two hours earlier, La Forge had thought of the *Enterprise*'s main science laboratory as spacious. Now, packed with most of the ship's science specialists and a handful of engineers whose areas of expertise included computers, software, robotics, or cybernetics, the lab felt cramped and crowded. Excited voices talked over one another as geologists traded theories with computer scientists, xenologists compared notes with theoretical physicists, and Lieutenant Dina Elfiki moved through the room like a whirling dervish, trying to wrangle the chaos into order.

La Forge and Data stood back near the room's entrance and observed. The engineer leaned against a bulkhead, arms folded across his chest, legs crossed at the ankles. Data, who had always seemed so stiff when he tried to act nonchalant, now stood next to La Forge with his hands tucked casually into his pants pockets, his head at an angle, and a wry smile on his face. He nudged La Forge with his elbow. "Told you it would work."

"Let's not go counting our chickens, Data. It hasn't worked yet."

"Give it time." He pulled his right hand free and encompassed the room with a sweeping gesture. "This is the way to solve problems, Geordi. Let brilliant minds come at it from every angle, with no rules and nothing too strange to be considered."

The offbeat statement compelled La Forge to shoot a dubious look at his best friend. "That sounds like something your father would've said."

Data thought it over, and conceded the point with a shrug-nod. "I suppose it does. In many ways, I feel closer to my father now than I ever did in my first life. Perhaps the fact that I now carry his memories inside me leads me to emulate his attitudes and echo his sentiments."

Ignoring the hubbub in the room, La Forge gave all his attention to Data. "Is that how you're drawing the line between who you were and who you are? 'First life' and 'second life'?"

"It seems appropriate," Data said. "Because my prior self was destroyed, his original continuity of consciousness ceased to exist. Mine is therefore unique and separate, and by virtue of sequentiality, *second*. As distinctions go, this one seems far from trivial."

Debating philosophy, ontology, or semantics with Data inevitably gave La Forge either a headache or a prolonged bout of depression, but he pressed on. "Okay. So, what if sometime in the future, you decide to upgrade to another body? One with better programming, engineering, materials, whatever. Would you have to think of that as your third life?"

"Not necessarily. Now that I understand the process, I believe that I could, if I wished, transfer my consciousness into a new body without an interruption of awareness. My mind would travel between forms while remaining sensate. In such an event, the move to a new body would be merely an event within the continuity of my second life, not a new existence."

There were half a dozen follow-up questions La Forge wanted to ask, but he was interrupted by Elfiki's manic exclamation from across the lab: "I think we've got something!"

La Forge pointed at Data. "To be continued." Then he and Data started dodging through the cluster of personnel on their way to Elfiki. The scientists and engineers backed up to make room for them as they joined the lieutenant at the workbench, upon which lay the partially disassembled android. "All right, Dina. Talk to me."

The lithe Egyptian woman brushed a lock of her dark brown hair behind one ear, and she gestured around the room at other officers as she named them. "Lieutenant Newitz found that the composition of the glass inside the android's head was an exact match for the synthetic obsidian Tholians manufacture for their starships. Lieutenant Anders from Xenology pointed out that the specific density of the glass matches that used in the Tholians' thoughtwave transmitters." She picked up a padd and used it to call up scans and simulation graphics on the large display screen behind her. "In some of the glass samples, Lieutenant Talenda detected an unusual fluctuation in the subquantum membrane, suggesting a possible quantum entanglement, which Anders says is consistent with current theories regarding the operational principle behind thoughtwave transmission. But what's really fascinating is the relay that connected the obsidian to the body's control circuits. According to Ensign Lamar, it bridges three distinct technologies. At one end it communicates with the obsidian transceiver, so that interface is Tholian. The core of the relay consists of Romulan components. And the other end has been reverse-engineered to pass buffered signals to and from a Soong-type android's proprioceptive controls and sensory matrix."

Data regarded the brain with a new appreciation. "Most remarkable."

La Forge studied the enlarged schematic of the signal relays. "Why is the relay core using Romulan parts? Why not translate directly from the obsidian transceiver to the body?"

Elfiki split the screen to add a new set of data, a dense jumble of raw code. "Because the relay started out as Romulan technology. It was developed as part of a telepresence research program back in the twenty-second century."

"I remember reading about that," La Forge said, his memory jogged. "They were using a tiny ethnic subgroup of telepathically gifted Andorians—"

"The Aenar," Elfiki cut in.

"Right. They used them to remote-pilot drone starships across interstellar distances. But the program fell apart once it was exposed and they lost access to the Aenar." He shifted a piece of the ruined obsidian transceiver to get a better look at the mostly slagged relay underneath. "So, we have a Tholian transceiver with a Romulan telepresence interface inside an android body that we know was stolen by the Breen. The Typhon Pact's learning to pool their resources."

Data stared at the screen full of code, then he looked at Elfiki. "Lieutenant, would it be possible to use the information we have to block the thoughtwave frequency being used to control these androids? Or to track them, identifying both receiver and source?"

She looked over her shoulder at Anders and Lamar. "Guys?"

Anders, a tall woman with dark hair and an aquiline visage, nodded. "In theory? Sure. But the odds of deducing the frequency from this bunch of shards aren't good."

Lamar, whose long blond hair, square jaw, and athletic build had led some of the crew to nickname him Thor, added, "It'd be a big help if we could capture one of these things intact. Then we'd have a real shot at finding out what makes it tick."

"Sounds like a plan," La Forge said. With a nod he signaled Data to follow him as he moved for the door. "Let's go tell Worf we have a new mission objective."

The empty chair and *glenget* that only a day earlier had been occupied by Esperanza Piñiero and *Nizor* Szamra felt to Imperator Sozzerozs like open wounds.

He was flanked on his left by Togor and on his right by Azarog. Staring back at him from the other side of the table was President Bacco. Seated to her right was the frost-haired Councillor Enaren, and on her left was the Federation's secretary of the exterior, Safranski, who had been introduced as a Rigellian, looked like a Vulcan, and was alternately as taciturn as a rock and as verbally aggressive as a Ferengi. No one had spoken of the previous night's bloodshed, but it continued to cast a shadow over the summit, making the Federation's insistence that it continue seem more like a symptom of denial than an act of hope.

Perhaps I could cling to some shred of optimism if I didn't know we brought them here on a lie. Dwelling on that shameful truth filled Sozzerozs with bitter resentment toward the Breen.

"I'd like to begin this morning by thanking you all for agreeing to resume our talks," Bacco said. She emulated the salutary spread-hands gesture that the late Piñiero had mastered with such grace. "It would be easy to abandon diplomacy in the wake of tragedy. Our hope is that your willingness to continue the summit indicates you share our commitment to a successful outcome, one that will benefit both our peoples."

As rehearsed, Togor answered on behalf of the Hegemony. "Thank you, Madam President. We, too, are encouraged by your desire to resume our conversation. The only tragedy greater than yesterday's deaths of our trusted colleagues and sworn defenders would be if we permitted their lives to be lost in vain. To honor the blood they have shed for us, we will continue to work toward the goals that first brought us here."

Sozzerozs's leathery visage betrayed no sign of his cynical brooding. *Why do such noble sentiments so often come cloaked in lies?*

Cort Enaren, Betazed's elderly but still commanding representative on the Federation Council, pressed on to keep the meeting going. "At the risk of trying your patience, venerable elders, I would like to suggest we start fresh. We expect the shift in circumstances has led to changes in expectations and estimations on a number of points. So, rather than attempt point-by-point revisions of our earlier agendas, we suggest that it might be more efficient to draft new language that reflects our situation as it is, rather than as it was."

Azarog let out a low, soft hiss of approval. "This seems wise. Recent events have given us reason to expect violent reactions by other powers—perhaps those of the Typhon Pact, or another local power that prefers not to see the Hegemony and the Federation in alliance."

Safranski nodded. "Understandable. Shall we discuss strategic matters first, then?"

The imperator rasped, "What would be the point?" All eyes in the room fixed upon him. Gorn and humanoids alike regarded him in shock—and, in the case of his countrymen, with anger. Officially, under the terms of their membership in the Pact and their specific agreement with the Breen Confederacy, they remained engaged in a campaign of deception, with instructions to drag out the summit until cued to terminate their efforts. Sozzerozs, however, was weary of the ruse. "We have been here for days that never seem to end, talking in circles around issues that refuse to be resolved. You ask us for concessions we cannot afford to make. We ask you to guarantee outcomes that are beyond your control. You insist we risk the wrath of five major powers to side with your Federation—but when we demand you intercede to spare us from the wrath of your blood-bond ally the Klingon Empire, you mew that you can't interfere in their politics." A long, slow-rolling growl resonated inside his chest. "This is all a waste of time."

A tense and awkward silence settled over the room.

Then, in a voice that was calm but also brooked no argument, President Bacco declared, "Everyone, please give me and Imperator Sozzerozs the room."

Her subordinates Enaren and Safranski stood without hesitation and moved toward their exit. Togor and Azarog looked to the imperator for instruction, and he nodded his concurrence. The *wazir* and *zulta-osol* rose from their *glengets* and lumbered out of the meeting room. As they exited, Bacco pointed first at her personal defender, Wexler, and then at Hazizaar, the *sikta* of Sozzerozs's Imperial Guard corps. "That includes the two of you. Out."

Wexler bristled at the impetuous dismissal. "Madam President, I—"

"Out, Steven. That's an order."

The agent looked at Hazizaar, who looked at Sozzerozs, who nodded his permission. Eyes locked on each other, alert to the tiniest sign of betrayal, the two elite defenders slipped reluctantly from the room. Doors clicked shut after them, and then the two heads of state faced each other across the table with no witnesses, no advisers, no intermediaries.

"Let's cut the bullshit," Bacco said, her veneer of genteel civility shed like a worn-out skin. "This whole summit's been a waste of time, hasn't it? You've been running us in circles, forcing us to make the same arguments over and over, asking for promises you know we can't make. If you really came here to make a deal, we'd be making one—wouldn't we?"

He appreciated her lack of guile, and the unblinking ferocity of her eye contact. "You are quite the scholar of the political game, Madam President. I salute you."

"Save the salutes. Just tell me the truth. Hell, at this point, I'll settle for *part* of it."

As much as he admired Bacco's forthright quality, he knew that to admit too much too soon might doom any hope of real progress. But to squander the opportunity this moment represented would constitute a political and strategic failure of an even greater magnitude. "Our demands have been as unreasonable as they are intransigent. And I confess that you are correct: this has been entirely by design. I regret that I cannot explain in greater detail."

The human woman took a moment to think about his response. It was a trait that he found commendable. Too many persons he had encountered in the political arena spoke solely for the pleasure of hearing their own voices, and a frightening number sought to fill every silence even when their minds were so evidently devoid of original thought. But not Bacco . . . she could think and speak at the same time when necessary, but she was a thinker first.

She leaned forward and narrowed her eyes as if to pierce his rhetorical defenses with visual acuity. "You were pressured to come here by another member of the Pact, weren't you?"

The galaxy could use a few more leaders like her, Sozzerozs lamented.

"For the sake of discussion, let us assume—in a purely hypothetical sense—that what you say is true. Further assume that the same party that compelled us to this summit did not see fit to explicate its motives for doing so—but has made clear what the price of betrayal would be."

Bacco's countenance grew stern. "Would this hypothetical external political actor be one that's known to have a cultural affinity for masks?"

He was impressed that she—and likely, by extension, Starfleet and the Federation government—had been so quick to connect the Breen to the previous night's attack. "It might."

"And how might that external power react to a political realignment that sides the Hegemony with the Federation?"

He no longer saw any purpose to prevarication or procrastination. It was time to tell her the truth. "If such a realignment occurred, I would be assassinated without delay, as would my sons and brothers. Then a noble sympathetic to the killers' agenda would be backed with a covert infusion of wealth and external political support, ensuring his ascension to the imperatorship. Within a few years, the Hegemony would be mobilized against the Federation as a proxy fighter—a mercenary too stupid to realize it's been bought and sold as a slave."

Her gaze remained as hard and cold as steel, but when Sozzerozs tasted the air with his tongue, he caught the metallic tang of her fear. *She understands the true stakes now. Good.*

Once again, she didn't rush to reply. She was somber and pensive. As she considered the matter, the scent of her fear swiftly dissipated—and as it faded, his respect for her increased.

She folded her hands on the tabletop. "The rise of a new imperator whose principal loyalty lies outside the Hegemony would not be in the best interests of your people. And if the Hegemony were transformed into a client state, that could severely destabilize the balance of power within the Typhon Pact." A sly look. "I don't think that would please Praetor Kamemor."

"No, it would not." He fought the urge to grin in response to her implied proposition.

A hint of a smirk gave the president a mischievous quality. "Perhaps, before we worry about brokering a truce with the Klingon Empire, we should focus on strengthening the Hegemony's bonds of friendship with a nation it already counts as an ally: the Romulan Star Empire. Considering the efforts the praetor has made to normalize diplomatic relations with the Federation, that would be an easy negotiation for us to mediate on your behalf."

He grasped her reasoning. If the Romulans were sincere in their desire for détente, then a stronger relationship between the Hegemony and the Star Empire would serve two purposes at once: it would bring the Gorn under the wing of a larger power with the technological prowess and military strength to persuade the Breen not to meddle in the Hegemony's affairs, and it would give the Gorn a chance to steer the Romulan government toward a lasting peace—and maybe even, in a generation or two, a formal alliance. "That would be a worthwhile outcome for the summit, Madam President—provided it can be accomplished with discretion."

The human smiled. "Trust me, Imperator—discretion is what we do best."

Surrounded by a labyrinth of rusted pipes, ruptured conduits, and derelict reactor housings, Šmrhová was plagued by the suspicion that she was being deceived. Acting on a request from Commander La Forge and Mister Data, she and Worf, along with a security detail and science specialists from the *Enterprise,* had beamed down to the last site the defunct android was known to have visited before its capture: the abandoned power plant. Now the security chief stood in the shadow of the main reactor under a patch of open sky—a luxury made possible by the long-ago collapse of the main building's enormous roof—and she felt . . . *manipulated.*

A huddle of officers outside the entrance to the reactor's control center split up, and from its nucleus emerged Commander Worf. The Klingon looked as irritated as Šmrhová felt, and he walked toward her with long and purposeful strides. As he approached conversational range, he said in his bold baritone, "Our teams have found nothing."

"I didn't think they would," Šmrhová grumbled.

Worf met her mild complaint with a severe glare. "Explain."

"Are you kidding me?" She waved her arms at the cavernous corroded facility. "Look at this place, Commander! No power, no comm lines, no access to the city's infrastructure—at least, none that we've found so far. What were we supposed to find here? A hideout?"

He refused to blink or back down. "A clue, Lieutenant."

"Well, I think we've already found it, sir." She nodded toward the vast, murky pool of contaminated water that, thanks to evaporation, only half covered the dormant heat exchangers. "As far as I can tell, the thorium traces are the only thing to find here. What's more, I think we were supposed to find them—and the android copy of Bacco's chief of staff."

The first officer scrunched his brow with a doubtful frown. "I do not see what an enemy would gain by exposing its own assets in that manner. Especially not one so valuable."

"Neither do I, but think about how we got here." She held up fingers one at a time to keep count as she continued. "One, Geordi and I acted on an unsolicited tip that led us to expose Chairman Kinshal at the bank. Two, the Piñiero impersonator, despite having an almost perfect shot at any target she wants, missed the president and the imperator, then escaped. Three, we get an anonymous tip that leads us to the real Piñiero's body. Four, we find thorium traces that lead us here, to the power plant, and that leads us straight to the Piñiero look-alike."

Worf shook his head, refusing to accept her conspiracy theory at face value. "The shooter missed because the president's protection agent shot her first. And the anonymous tip could have come from a citizen who saw suspicious activity and reported it."

"Have you dealt with the Orions, Worf? They're not the type to tip off law enforcement."

With smug assurance, he replied, "Then why did the bank's custodian warn you and Commander La Forge about the chairman's breach of security?"

"I asked myself the same question. Unfortunately, I didn't ask it until an hour ago. I just heard back from the bank's personnel director. They have no employment record for anyone named Kal Pollus. Or any name remotely similar, for that matter."

That news sparked his interest. "Then who was it who gave you the tip?"

She shrugged. "No idea. I had Balidemaj run a check against the Orions' public databases and census information to see if we could find him, but the only match for that name is a man who died ninety-two years ago."

"Naturally." The first officer's imagination was clearly engaged. "Could your informant have also been an android? An accomplice of the infiltrators?"

"I don't know. Considering that they know how to spoof our sensors, I don't see why it couldn't have been. Of course, it could just as easily have been some random low-life paid off to bring us the information and give us a fake name."

Worf crossed his arms, and his body language became tighter and more closed-off as his gaze became a thousand-meter stare, fixed on some unseen idea in his mind's eye. "Whether he was another android, a biological accomplice, or a paid cutout is irrelevant. No matter how he learned of the plan to infiltrate the bank to assassinate the president and the imperator, the more important question is this: Why would someone who possessed that information choose to share it with us? And was it given to us by the conspirators themselves—or by someone seeking to sabotage them?"

"All excellent questions," Šmrhová said. "Unfortunately, I don't have answers for any of them—yet." She looked around at the roving teams of investigative scientists. "So, what do we do next? Because honestly, I don't think this is a productive use of our time."

He frowned, then sighed. "Very well. Order all teams to finish their current tests and return to the *Enterprise*. Then join me and Commander La Forge outside the plant's main gate." He started walking away, his mind focused on whatever plan he was concocting.

Šmrhová called out, "What's our next move, sir?"

He stopped and looked back. "We tell the Orions we are halting our investigation and preparing to leave the planet." His eyes brightened with a gleam of diabolical amusement. "If I am right, someone is about to make certain we have a very good reason to stay."

21

Berro squatted down, took Olar's hand, and helped his comrade sit up in the open transmogrifier pod, from which climbed clouds of noxious vapor. Freshly re-shaped from his previous identity as Siro Kinshal into a nondescript young male Vulcan, Olar seemed woozy and bewildered. Steadying the other agent with a hand on his shoulder, Berro asked, "How do you feel?"

"I've been better." Olar blinked his eyes hard, then drew a deep breath. "Was it my imagination, or was the turnaround on that really fast?"

"It wasn't your imagination." He pulled Olar to his feet.

After a few seconds, Olar regained his balance. He nodded. "I'm okay." He let go of Berro's hand and pressed his fingertips to his remodeled face. "How did it turn out?"

"Better than mine." Even though it was just a temporary visage on a distant avatar, Berro still felt mildly self-conscious about the aesthetic shortcomings of his android's latest template. He imagined his new form—bald with a bulbous nose and bulging eyes beneath wild graying eyebrows—must have been modeled on the ugliest human male in existence. "Run your diagnostic.

I'll ping the lab coats and see if we have new orders yet."

Olar turned away as he submerged into a full-system diagnostic scan, and Berro faced in the other direction as he accessed the circuit for the direct comm line to their handlers at Korwat. The hailing prompt buzzed only once before Hain replied, her voice like a disembodied presence inside Berro's mind. *<This is Control. What's your status, Berro?>*

He concentrated on sending his response mentally rather than speaking aloud. *All objectives completed. We've made the switch to our new identities. Olar's running a system check, but I don't expect any complications. We're ready to receive the extraction plan.*

An apologetic note in Hain's voice heralded bad news. *<Change of plans. Extraction's been postponed. Konar has new orders from the head of SRD.>* A tiny jolt, like a nervous twitch inside Berro's brain, accompanied the upload of a data file into his body's storage buffer. The embedded application self-launched, and in a matter of seconds his field of vision filled with written mission briefs and tactical maps detailing the engagement strategy. *<It's a direct assault. Note that the principal targets are the same as during Sair's deployment, but the operational objective has been changed, as have the parameters for engagement.>*

The more Berro read of the mission plan, the more certain he became that someone had drafted it in error. Losing his focus, he muttered, "Control, this can't be right."

It was Konar's brusque voice that replied, *<What's the problem, Berro?>*

Olar finished his self-analysis and turned to face him, signaling that he was joining the conversation. Berro acknowledged him with a look as he replied to

Konar. *Our tactical profile up to this point has been built around infiltration. This isn't what we were trained for.*

Konar was dismissive. <*Ridiculous. You have combat training.*>

Close-quarters combat, yes. But this combines urban guerrilla combat with commando tactics. Did he truly not understand the problem? Or was he merely being obtuse in order to stifle discussion? *Sir, this is a mission for the Spetzkar, not us.*

<*If we could send in the Spetzkar, or get permission to train some of them to control these avatars of yours without surrendering the entire project to their control, we would.*> Konar reined in his temper and tried to affect a conciliatory note. <*I know we're asking a lot of you two, and some of it is outside your normal expertise, but this is what has to be done.*>

Olar looked stunned as he pored over the plans. "Sir, do you have any idea what kind of collateral damage this plan will cause?"

<*Yes, we do. It can't be helped.*>

Maintaining a cool demeanor was taxing Berro's patience. *Our original mission profile expressly forbade excessive collateral damage. We were told that neither the Orions nor the Gorn would tolerate any fatalities among their people. Has that changed?*

The supervisor's tone became strained. <*Assume that it has. From now until the end of the operation, all restrictions on the use of deadly and overwhelming force are rescinded.*>

Berro was prepared to accept the conversation as concluded until Olar silently pointed out a series of fine-print details in the mission profile. Once more incensed at the illogic of the SRD's orders, he fumed, *What about the endgame scenario you've sent?*

Resentful and obviously weary of the argument, Konar replied, *<What of it?>*

Olar snapped, "Sir, did you even *read* it? Most of the expected outcomes involve our destruction. Even the most optimistic projection results in our avatars being damaged beyond repair. Never mind the potential risks to us, what about the sheer waste of resources?"

Konar's response was infused with a low-key, barely contained rage. *<Your role in this undertaking is not to second-guess your betters, Olar. It's to obey and carry out your confirmed orders, and accomplish the objectives we set for you, whether you agree with them or not, and regardless of whether you understand the rationales behind them. Do you understand?>*

"Yes, sir." The two field agents exchanged worried glances. It was obvious now to both of them that despite all the time and resources the SRD had invested in the program, it was being treated as if it were worthless, just some expendable resource to be spent at will.

<You have your orders. Make sure you follow them precisely. The timing of events has been planned in great detail, and it's vital that the enemy continues to act on our schedule.>

Understood, Berro projected back along the thought-wave. *We'll need a half hour to prep. We'll be in attack position in precisely forty minutes.*

<Good. But remember to think before you act. Everything depends on the final result. Control out.> Konar's voice departed from their thoughts, but Berro and Olar both knew that the supervisor and Hain were watching their every movement and listening to their every word. That was the worst part of this mission, in Berro's opinion. Even when he seemed to be isolated, he was never truly alone. Few notions terrified him more deeply. His only solace growing up in the masked anonymity of

Breen society had been the sanctity of his privacy, its inviolability. Now he lived a life on display, hidden behind nothing more than the faces of strangers.

He let go of his petty grievances and kneeled to open the munitions crate. "I'll prep the charges," he said to Olar. "Make sure the rifles and sidearms are charged."

The other agent shook his head and opened the wardrobe in which they kept their small arms. "I really hoped it wouldn't come down to this."

"So did I." A rueful grimace broke through Berro's stoic façade. "But I kind of figured it would." He lifted a shaped demolition charge from the crate. As he studied the blue-gray cone, he felt the strange calm that comes from facing the inevitable. "So it goes. Let's get to work."

A gentle warbling of the door chime prompted Picard to bark, "Come!" The portal to the bridge slid open with a soft *whish,* and the captain trained scathing looks on his senior officers as they filed in by rank: first Worf, then La Forge, followed by Šmrhová. The last person to enter was Data, still garbed in civilian clothing. *What a difference context makes,* Picard thought with a hint of bitter reminiscence. *If these same officers marched in here of their own accord instead of in response to my summons, I might expect them to announce a mutiny.*

The door closed, affording them a measure of privacy. The three officers and Data lined up in front of Picard, who fixed his reproachful glare upon Worf. "Number One, did you inform the Orion Colonial Police and the Federation embassy that our departure was imminent?"

The first officer kept his chin raised and his bearing proud. "Yes, sir."

Picard stood and circled around his desk in slow

steps. "You are aware that the decision to leave orbit is a prerogative reserved for a starship's *commanding* officer, are you not?"

"I am." For one who had just committed a grave breach of protocol, he was quite calm.

Moving down the line, Picard stopped to confront Šmrhová. "It's my understanding that you informed President Bacco's protection detail of our decision to leave Orion."

"Aye, sir," the security chief replied, her manner cool and matter-of-fact.

Quick looks at La Forge and Data gained the captain no insight into their reactions, just a reminder of how solid their poker faces were. "Commander La Forge. Mister Data. Did either of you know about this sudden change in our plans?"

They overlapped each other's replies, leaving Data's dry "No, sir" buried beneath La Forge's emphatic "First I'm hearing of it, Captain."

That brought Picard back to his first officer. "Mister Worf . . . I trust you can explain?"

"I can." He seemed content to stand on his terse reply until Picard shot him a look that made clear his query hadn't been rhetorical. "Lieutenant Šmrhová showed me that all the clues we have followed in our search for the androids seem to have been fed to us on purpose, by someone with access to the details of their mission."

Šmrhová added, "In each case, sir, the leads came from either an anonymous source or one whose identity was later found to be an alias. Commander Worf and I believe that we're being manipulated, steered to find what someone else wants us to see, when they want it seen."

Worf affirmed Šmrhová's account with a nod, leading Picard to ask, "To what end?"

"We don't know yet," she said. "But whatever they're up to, it seems really important to them that we keep playing along. Our hope is that by creating the impression the *Enterprise* is leaving orbit, we can force the enemy into action while they're still off balance."

The reasoning behind Worf and Šmrhová's plan came into focus for Picard. "And since we don't know which institutions have been compromised by the enemy, there was no choice but to misinform our embassy and the president's detail, in addition to the Orions."

"Correct," Worf said.

Picard accepted the explanation with a slow, sage nod as he walked back behind his desk. "Very well." He sat down and looked up at the Klingon. "In the future, Number One, I would appreciate being read into these plans before you carry them out."

"Understood."

Satisfied that he had made his point, he turned his attention to La Forge and Data. "Have we made any more progress in our study of the android's transceiver system?"

"Not a lot," La Forge said. "We've been narrowing down the possible range of subspace frequencies and harmonic subfrequencies it might use, but without a working transceiver, we have no way of knowing if we're even close."

"Keep working on it." To Šmrhová he added, "Remind your security teams that capturing any hostile androids intact will be of paramount importance should we confront more of them."

She nodded. "I will, sir." Then her optimism dimmed. "Unfortunately, I can't say the same for the Gorn or the Orions. Depending on what their part in all this has been, if they get to the androids first, they might frag them just to keep them out of our hands. If it comes to that, I'm not sure I can stop them without causing at least one interstellar incident, maybe two."

"Then it's all the more imperative that we find the androids first, Lieutenant." He looked at Worf. "That will be all for now, Number One, but I'll expect regular updates as soon as—"

"Bridge to Captain Picard," Chen interrupted over the comm. *"We're receiving an urgent message from the Orion Colonial Police."*

He sprang to his feet. "On my way."

His officers and Data fell in behind him as he left the ready room and crossed at a quick step to his command chair. Noting the captain's approach, Chen vacated the center seat and moved aft to the master systems display. As Picard sat down, Worf took his seat beside him, and Šmrhová relieved Balidemaj at the security console. Data, meanwhile, did his best to remain inconspicuous, standing near an unmanned console along the starboard bulkhead. Once everyone was in position, Picard pointed forward. "On-screen, Lieutenant."

The curve of Orion was replaced by Commandant Essan. *"Captain! Thank the spirits you haven't left orbit yet! We think we've found the lair used by the assassin and her conspirators."*

"That's excellent news, Commandant." He shot a furtive glance at Worf and caught the faintest inkling of a self-satisfied smirk on the first officer's face. Looking back at Essan, he resisted the urge to color his words with sarcasm. "How did you uncover its location?"

Essan hunched his shoulders. *"I'm told it was an anonymous tip. Luckily for us, it's panned out."* It was a struggle for Picard not to wince when he heard Essan utter the words *anonymous tip.* Through will alone he kept a straight face as the Orion continued. *"We've al-*

ready alerted the Gorn, who are sending more of those Imperial Guard brutes. I thought you'd want your people to have a chance to examine it before the lizards stomp all over it."

"Most considerate, Commandant. Thank you. Please transmit the coordinates, and I'll have a team there in two minutes. *Enterprise* out."

Šmrhová closed the channel, restoring the image of Orion's northern hemisphere to the viewscreen. Worf swiveled his chair toward Picard. "Orders, Captain?"

"Take an evidence collection team and an armed security detail to this alleged lair. Have Lieutenant Šmrhová, Commander La Forge, and Mister Data join you."

"Are you sure that is wise, sir? This could be a trap."

Picard shook his head. "I doubt that, Number One. As you suggested, I suspect this is merely the latest in a long trail of bread crumbs, meant to lead us to another dead end. Look past *what* our enemies want us to see . . . and find out *why* they want us to see it."

Long banks of computers, rows of compact replicators, and a staggering variety of precision tools filled the spacious loft, making passage through the converted industrial space tedious. Blacked-out windows added to its claustrophobic atmosphere. Worf stood near the room's center so he could observe all the members of the investigation team while they worked.

A few meters away, Data sat in front of a workstation into which he had linked himself with an optronic cable. A green blur of alien numerals and symbols scrolled sideways across the black screen of the terminal in front of him. On the other side of the low wall of computers, La Forge examined the meticulously arranged tools with his tricorder. Behind him, Šmrhová conferred in discreet whispers with Lieutenant Ilana Reichert, the team's munitions specialist.

Two security officers from the *Enterprise* guarded the loft's entrance, outside which a handful of Orion police paced while muttering angrily about "jurisdiction" and "sovereignty." Worf understood the Orions' hostility to the Starfleet team's presence, but he did not care how they felt. *They have no one to blame but themselves. They are corrupt and unreliable. If they could be trusted to investigate competently and impartially, we would not have to be here.*

La Forge held up a fragile-looking metallic spike that resembled a surgical implement. "This is some high-tech equipment. Some of it's Romulan; I'm guessing the implements made from obsidian are of Tholian design." He eyed the assorted tools. "There's almost enough here to build a new android from scratch—assuming we knew how." Data shot a look of mild offense at the engineer, who added with a chastised frown, "Present company excluded."

The android accepted the apology with a jog of his chin and returned his attention to the lateral stream of symbols coursing over his monitor. Loath as Worf was to interrupt Data in the middle of what might be a complex task, he asked him, "Have you found anything in their files?"

Data's focus didn't waver from the screen. "I have not. These drives were subjected to a secure-erasure protocol. None of their data remains, though I have found fragments of the original system software. It appears to be of Breen origin."

"That's consistent with our theory of where the androids came from," La Forge said.

Their impromptu conference was interrupted by

the arrival of Essan and Hazizaar. The Orion police commandant followed the Gorn imperial guard, who slalomed through the room's myriad obstacles with a speed and dexterity Worf did not expect. As they met in the middle of the room, Hazizaar seemed to make a special effort to intrude upon Worf's personal space. "We have completed our search of the rest of the building," the archosaur said. "None of the other floors are occupied or show any sign of recent visitation." He hissed as he looked around at the busy swarm of Starfleet scientists. "What have you found up here?"

Worf inched forward, in an implicit challenge to the Gorn. "Not much," he lied. Then he turned his glare upon the commandant. "Thank you for your assistance." Meeting the Gorn's stare, he added, "Both of you."

Essan blinked as if Worf had spat in his face, and Hazizaar asked with uncamouflaged umbrage, "Are you dismissing us, Commander Worf?"

He yielded nothing to the rhetorical challenge. "Yes, I am."

The archosaur and the Orion seethed, but as Worf had suspected, neither was prepared to argue without their own forces inside the room. Essan turned and beckoned Hazizaar with a tilt of his head. "The room is rather crowded, *Sikta*. Perhaps we should let them—"

Hazizaar poked a scaly, clawed digit against Worf's chest. "This is a mistake, Klingon. We are on the same side here. We both want the same thing."

Worf snarled. "We will see."

The commandant used both hands to steer Hazizaar away from Worf. "We should go." At first Essan's effort to prod the Gorn seemed futile; then Hazizaar turned away from Worf and followed the Orion out of the room.

Šmrhová wended around the makeshift lab's obstacles and sidled up to Worf. "Anonymous tips and dead-end clues. It would almost be funny if it weren't so aggravating."

"Indeed. Has your team found anything?"

"Chemical traces, all over the place. Based on the compounds and residues we found on the workbenches, it looks like they were putting together some heavy-duty explosives."

Alarmed, La Forge put down the tools he had been studying. "What kind?"

"Thermokinetic charges with tricobalt cores. Old-school, but they'll pack a punch."

Dismayed frowns passed between La Forge and Worf, who both knew enough about military munitions to grasp the threat such weapons posed. Augmented by modern detonators and catalysts, a charge small enough to fit in one's hand could unleash a nightmarish blast. Worf asked Šmrhová, "Do we know how many they might have?"

"No idea. But we have to assume they're armed with at least one." She gestured toward a wardrobe that stood in the corner, its doors open to reveal a single rifle and a pair of pistols. "We also found power cells for four different types of Romulan disruptors, but only two types of weapon. Which suggests the missing small arms are with the androids."

La Forge grew anxious. "Explosives, combat weapons . . . Sounds like they're geared up for a major attack." He directed a meaningful look at Worf. "Is it possible that the reason for giving up their lair would be to draw our focus here while they take another shot at—"

Picard's voice blared from Worf's combadge: "Enter-prise *to Commander Worf! Stand by for immediate site-to-site transport!*"

Data and La Forge scrambled to stand with Šmrhová and Worf as he replied, "This is Worf. What is happen-ing?"

"*The Bank of Orion is under attack!*"

22

Through the fading shimmer of the transporter beam, La Forge beheld a scene of fiery bedlam. Moments later he was free of the transporter's hold, and he sprang forward, waving his arms to part the curtains of black smoke that surrounded and suffocated him.

Wreckage and bodies littered the street. Most of the dead were Orions—some in the tailored suits favored by the bank's employees and executives, some in the paramilitary garb of its armed security personnel. A twist of smoldering metallic debris was all that remained of a crashed hovercar, and as La Forge neared the bank's towering main gates, he was startled to find them missing. They had been blasted inward, torn apart and ripped from their mighty hinges.

Moving ahead on either side of him were Worf and Šmrhová, who advanced toward the breached gateway with their phasers drawn. Several meters behind them, La Forge heard another rush of transporter noise and deduced that reinforcements had arrived to secure the perimeter.

Then he heard Data call out, "Commander Worf! Stop!" The first officer and Šmrhová turned around as Data emerged from the black fog. "The bank's force field is still active. Two more steps, and you both will suffer a potentially fatal electrical shock."

La Forge cycled through his eyes' various wavelength sensitivities until he saw the radiant shell of energy surrounding the bank. "Good catch, Data!" After a few more adjustments, he found a wavelength that let him peer through the veil of smoke. Looking ahead, he saw the force field was only the first of their problems. "Guys, the bridge is gone."

Šmrhová sounded as if she hoped he'd misspoken. "You mean it's retracted?"

"No, I mean it was extended, and someone blew up the middle of it. It's *gone*."

The first officer tapped his combadge. "Worf to *Enterprise*!"

Picard answered, *"Go ahead, Number One."*

"Captain, the androids have entered the bank. We are unable to pursue. Can you beam up the president and her delegation?"

"Negative. We can't transport through the bank's scrambling field."

Šmrhová clasped Worf's arm. "Sir, if the bank's been breached, the Protection Detail will move the president to the secure sublevels. Even if we bring down the force field, the *Enterprise* won't be able to beam her out of there." She winced as smoke wafted into her eyes.

Explosions inside the bank blew out all the windows on the east side of the first floor, scouring the street with a storm of splintered glass. Everyone but Data reflexively turned away, ducked, and covered their faces as the blast stung them with its needle wind.

The delicate music of fine debris raining onto pavement was lost in the thunder of the detonation, which echoed and reechoed off the majestic steel-and-glass façades of the capital's financial sector. La Forge's ears rang and throbbed. He lifted his hands from his face and saw that Worf and Šmrhová were down, stunned from their wounds. Then he realized he was bleeding from hundreds of minuscule wounds all over his body—and so was everyone else in the street.

Everyone, again, except Data. The android's synthetic skin was flayed and torn, revealing bits of the machinery underneath, but he seemed oblivious of his cosmetic damage. He stepped briskly to La Forge's side. "Geordi, are you all right?"

"I'm okay, Data. . . . Mostly."

"Please give me your phaser."

Dumbfounded, La Forge stared at his best friend. "Why?"

"I need it to stop the assassins." He looked toward the bank. "Please, Geordi. We do not have much time. Trust me."

He handed his weapon to Data. "How're you getting in?"

Data checked the phaser's settings. "My new positronic matrix has a low-power subspace transceiver similar to that used in tricorders. Using my native ability to perceive the force field's specific frequency, I will interplex the subspace transceiver with my—"

"Never mind. Just go."

Data smiled, nodded once, then turned and hurried toward the gateway.

As La Forge watched his friend jog toward danger, he braced himself to see the worst, to witness Data being violently repelled by the field or, worse, fried to pieces inside it.

Instead, he saw a shimmer of distortion envelop Data just before he reached the field—and then Data passed through the barrier, causing only the faintest ripple of disturbance as he went. Once through, he accelerated to a full run, moving faster than La Forge had thought possible for a biped, and then he launched himself from the edge of the sabotaged bridge. He soared across the gap as if weightless and landed on the far side without missing a step. Then he ascended the majestic marble staircase and was inside the bank, beyond La Forge's sight.

After a decades-long career spent avoiding notice and evading confrontation, Berro had to admit he found a certain perverse catharsis in being ordered to unleash a truly manic rampage.

He moved through the bank's corridors with Olar at his back, guarding their rear from pursuing bank security personnel, while he himself cleared the path ahead in an orgy of mayhem and bloodshed. His disruptor rifle screeched like a Berengarian raptor as he peppered the offices along his route with suppressing fire. Screams of terror and howls of agony came back to him like a chorus serenading his march to almost certain self-annihilation.

Behind themselves they had left a clearly marked trail of carnage. *Not that it matters,* Berro reminded himself. *With the security center blown to bits, there's no way they'll get the force field down in time to keep us from getting to our target.* He wasn't worried about the bank's pathetic security forces. They might be sufficient to stop a flesh-and-blood intruder who felt pain or gave a damn whether he lived or died. Against Berro and Olar, they were nothing more than targets of opportunity.

Their next task lay just ahead, at the end of the corridor: the elevator to the bank's secure sublevels. Predictably, as they neared to within half a dozen steps of the elevator's control panel, two bank guards in riot gear charged out from ambush positions, their weapons blazing. Searing bolts of energy cooked off another layer of Berro's bioplast skin and armored undercoat, and he actually lost half a step of momentum before he steadied his aim, killed the guard on his right, then stopped in a blink, pirouetted like a dancer, and snapped off a second shot, killing the guard on his left. He was back in motion toward his objective before the second body hit the floor.

Olar was firing a steady barrage back the way they'd come, and stray shots from their pursuers slammed into the walls above and beside them. Berro ignored the fusillade and focused on patching himself into the elevator's control panel with an optronic cable. The connection was verified in seconds, and he triggered the program stored in his body's memory storage core. A virtual display was superimposed over his visual field, apprising him of the application's progress. Another lucky shot by some underpaid Orion slammed into Berro's back, momentarily jolting his system with static. To his relief, the program continued, unaffected.

It finished with an abrupt burst of data transfer, and the maintenance controls for the elevator unlocked. "We're in," he said as he keyed in the command to open the doors—and overrode the blast-proof barriers that were supposed to snap into place and obstruct the elevator shaft in the event of an unauthorized access. The doors cracked open, then parted fully to reveal the pitch-dark abyss beyond. He poked his head in and looked up to make sure the lift car wasn't overhead, primed to be dropped on him. "Clear above." Then he looked down and saw the top of the car far below. "Locked down at the bottom, just like we figured."

Olar looked back over his shoulder into the shaft. "Think we could jump it?"

Not liking their chances, he goaded Olar, "You first."

"No thanks. Start climbing."

Berro slung his rifle and clambered inside the shaft, feeling for one of the built-in ladders recessed into the wall on either side of the doors. His hands found purchase, and once he had footholds, he started his descent.

Olar scurried into the shaft seconds later. "Fire in the hole!" He raced to catch up to Berro, but he was still a few rungs behind as a massive detonation shook the entire building, and a wall of orange fire jetted through the open doors above.

Flames engulfed them, setting them ablaze. Berro blocked out all sensations from his olfactory receptors. *Our hair might be synthetic, but it still stinks when it burns.*

Dust rained down from above, and then the lights inside the shaft went out. It took a second for Berro to shift his eyes into night-vision mode. As soon as he did, the first things he saw in the cool-green twilight were his own hands, reduced to skeletal frameworks with barely enough bioplast on the palms and fingertips to grip the rungs or wield a weapon. He glanced at Olar, whose entire body now resembled an animated skeleton with glowing eyes.

"For the record," he said as they continued their descent, "you look terrible."

Olar looked back at him. "You're no great beauty, either." Despite clearly having no lungs, he breathed a tired sigh. "So much for job security."

"Madam President, there's no time! Move!"

It had been a long time since anyone had dared to bark orders at Nanietta Bacco, and it didn't much matter that the shouting was coming from her senior protection agent. She still didn't like it. "Dammit, Steven, I will not be locked in a vault like a piece of property!"

Agent Wexler had the intense demeanor of a man who knew he was about to wade into battle. "Ma'am, it's the most secure space on this level, and that's where you need to be!"

Through the open door of her private suite, she saw over his shoulder the other members of her elite protection team suiting up with body armor and charging phaser rifles. There was a scent of panic in the air, something she had never seen afflict them before.

"Steven, what's going on?"

"The elevator shaft's been breached. We have less than two minutes to get you to the safe room." He pushed open her door and took her by the arm. "We need to go!"

On any other day, she would have demanded he take his hands off her, but the hardness in his eyes made it clear this was not the time or place to argue about protocol. She let him pull her into motion without a word of protest. As they jogged down the hallway toward the safe room, five more of her agents fell into formation around her, a moving wall of defenders.

They turned the corner at a run, sprinting the final meters to the safe room. Its circular, meter-thick duranium door stood open, primed for her arrival. Inside the safe room, Councillor Enaren and Secretary Safranski stood shoulder to shoulder with Imperator Sozzerozs, *Wazir* Togor, and *Zulta-osol* Azarog.

Agent Kistler stood inside the room, waving for them to hurry. "Come on!" He motioned for Bacco to continue past him, and she moved to the back of the room with the others. When she turned and looked back, she saw Wexler and Kistler standing with two of the Gorn imperial guards, all of them facing the closing safe room door. The massive portal shut with a resounding clang and a heavy boom. Then deep thrumming noises signaled the engagement of the door's vault-grade magnetic locks.

Wexler and his counterpart from the Imperial Guard acknowledged each other with slow nods. Then the agent faced the door and said with deadly calm, "If anything comes through that door that isn't one of ours, we kill it first—and ask questions later."

The Gorn beside him hissed. "Agreed."

Wounded and terrorized civilians flooded the bank's corridors, a raging current of bodies in desperate retreat. Data knifed through the crowd, following the assassins' trail of destruction.

From beyond a corner ahead of him, a cacophony of disruptor fire split the air. Stray shots and ricochets leaped from the passageway. He steeled himself for a headlong charge into the barrage. Suddenly free of fleeing civilians, he broke into an all-out run and turned the corner.

An intense flash of light nearly overloaded his visual receptors. Three-thousandths of a second later, a ground-shaking boom was followed by a shock front of displaced air that launched him backward and slammed him through a wall, into a long office space packed with hastily vacated cubicles. Propelled by the blast wave, he smashed through partitions and office furniture for several seconds before a jumbled mound of debris collapsed on top of him.

Punching and twisting, he fought his way free in a matter of seconds. All around him, the bank's offices were on fire. Bundles of charred wiring drooped from the now-exposed ceiling infrastructure, spitting sparks and filling the air with the hot snaps of wild electricity. He spent 108 milliseconds running a self-diagnostic and determined he had suffered only cosmetic harm.

Looking ahead toward the origin of the blast, he saw only a wall of twisted steel and broken concrete, the aftermath of a major collapse triggered by the explosion.

So much for following the trail.

His built-in subspace transceiver picked up a flurry of panicked chatter on the frequency reserved for use by the president's protection agents. One voice declared, *"The elevator shaft's been breached!"* Another replied, *"Condor, stand by to move Renaissance. Falcon, move Traveler and Chalice to the Grotto. We'll meet you there."*

Data spotted a door to an emergency exit stairwell, ran to it, and nearly knocked it off its hinges as he bashed through it at full speed. To his relief, the stairwell, which had been reinforced against such disasters as fires and explosions, was unobstructed and brightly lit. There was no route down into the sublevels, which left him only one way to go. Taking the stairs three at a time, he raced up three floors to get above the damage from the blast.

Arriving at the fourth floor, he saw that its reinforced metal fire door had no handle and was marked in several languages with the advisory No Re-Entry on This Floor.

He lifted his right leg and kicked it with enough force to bend it in half. Then he ripped it off its hinges and flung it down the stairs behind him. Nervous-looking Orions in fancy suits scrambled out of his way as he charged into the hallway and rounded the corner at a mad run for the elevator at the far end. The low rhythmic buzzing of building alarms filled the air, their pitch rising and falling as he passed each office with an open door.

A trio of Orion guards in body armor and visored

helmets charged into his path at the end of the hallway, converging between him and the elevator's control panel. None of them bothered to issue a challenge
as they brought their rifles to bear. Data snapped off
three shots in under half a second. Each maximum-stun
phaser shot struck one of the guards in the head.

They fell like dead weight, and he hurdled over
them without breaking stride.

Four steps later he arrived at the elevator's control
panel, ready to hack its systems. Instead, he found the
panel dark and unresponsive. *The intruders must have
overridden the system.* He tucked his phaser inside one
of his jacket pockets, wedged his fingers into the sliver-
thin gap between the elevator doors, and pried them
open with one steady effort.

The shaft beyond was dark and reeked of burnt hair
and scorched metal. A mournful groaning of metal
echoed from the bottom of the shaft, and Data spied a
flash of ruddy light briefly obscured by moving shadows. He adjusted his eyes' magnification setting and
shifted to an ultraviolet night-vision mode. The scene
below snapped into focus in time for him to see two
android endoskeletons, denuded of all but remnants of
their fleshly guises, scrambling through the forced-open
emergency hatch of the lift car parked far below.

In just under three picoseconds, he considered his
choices.

*It will take me two minutes and twenty-nine seconds
to climb down. In that time, the attackers could reach
the president and kill her.*

*I could jump, but from this height there is an eighty-
six-point-four percent chance the trauma of impact will
inflict sufficient damage as to render me inoperable.*

*Rappelling is the best choice under the circum-
stances, as long as it is feasible.*

He turned and evaluated the structural integrity of the office architecture behind him. Switching to an infrared mode, he saw the support beams inside the walls. Most of them were insufficiently anchored for his needs. *I will have to make my own anchor.* He drew his phaser, adjusted its settings to a drilling mode, and fired a snap shot at an angle through the wall above the elevator's control panel. As he'd planned, the beam bored clean through the thermocrete, making a fist-sized gap ideal for his purposes.

He put away his phaser and pulled open his shirt, snapping off the buttons, which skittered across the floor. A mental command unlocked an access panel on the front of his torso, and he pushed it in and aside with a gentle nudge. Then he reached inside his abdominal core and found the spool of duranium microfilament wire that his father, Noonien Soong, had built into this new-and-improved body years earlier. *Lucky for me Dad was a planner.*

Attached to the end of the wire was a carabiner similar to those used by mountaineers but far more resilient. He unspooled a few meters of wire, passed the end of it through the hole he'd shot through the wall, and secured the carabiner around the wire in front of the hole. A hard tug satisfied him that the lock was secure and the wall was strong enough to bear his weight.

Then, before his emotions could cloud his resolve with doubt and fear, he jumped into the shaft and plummeted into free fall. Inside his torso the spindle whirred like a revving engine, filling the shaft with a crisp buzzing as it fed out slack without resistance. He drifted toward the wall and pushed off with a gingerly press of his toes. Noting the rapidly decreasing distance to the top of the parked elevator car, he engaged the braking mechanism on the spindle, which whined in protest even as it slowed his descent and then arrested it at the exact moment his feet touched down atop the elevator. He locked down the spindle, reached inside himself, and, in a coordinated action, retracted its anchoring pins with his mind and pulled it free with his hand.

Liberated from his body, the spool—which still had more than a hundred meters of wire on it—dangled from its slack. As Data lowered himself through the elevator car's open top hatch, he made a mental note to retrieve the spool later.

Assuming I survive.

Banishing pessimism from his thoughts, he drew his phaser and pressed onward, hoping for the president's sake that he could reach her in time.

Worse than the anticipation of what might be coming, Bacco decided, was the simple fact of not knowing what was happening. Chatter over her agents' in-ear transceivers was barely audible, and the safe room was completely insulated from everything outside, including sound. She considered asking Wexler for an update, but he and Kistler seemed intently focused on monitoring the actions of their comrades outside the safe room.

Sozzerozs startled her with a whisper so close she felt his warm breath on her ear. "Perhaps we should have retreated rather than fortified."

"If that was an option, we'd have done it," she said in the same hushed tone. "As fast as these intruders are moving, they'd almost certainly have caught us in transit."

Wexler held up his hand and shushed them. "Something's happened." He pressed his hand to his ear. "Falcon, this is Eagle. Do you copy? . . . All units, this is Eagle. Respond."

Beside him, the senior Gorn imperial guard muttered a string of untranslated guttural commands into his wrist comm. He, too, received no reply. He looked at his peer, and the two archosaurs lifted their weapons and braced them against their bare, scaly shoulders. The ranking guard looked back at Sozzerozs, Togor, and Azarog. "I recommend you get down, my lords."

The imperator did as advised, pressing into a corner of the safe room's rear wall and crouching low. Togor and Azarog moved with him but remained standing to shield him.

Sonorous vibrations coursed through the floor, and within seconds Bacco realized that the source of the tremors was the room's ponderous metal door—its magnetic locks were being released and its bolts retracted. Her two protection agents traded grave looks, then lifted their own rifles and set themselves into combat postures. Over his shoulder, Wexler said, "Madam President, you might want to follow the imperator's lead."

There was no time to argue, no time to think—the door was starting to open. Bacco, Enaren, and Safranski retreated to the back of the room and huddled into the opposite corner from the Gorn. Further emulating their partners in distress, Enaren and Safranski did their best to position themselves between Bacco and whatever was about to come through the door.

Smoke billowed into the safe room as the door opened wide enough for air to move past it. The imperial guards and protection agents took that as their cue to start firing through the widening gap. Bacco covered her ears to block out the piercing shrieks of energy weapons. They continued firing as the door swung away, until at last it was fully open, and the four of them seemed to fill the narrow passageway outside the safe room with a wall of fire.

Two bolts of blue-white energy flew in from a low angle and felled the pair of Gorn. As the archosaurs collapsed, their chests hollowed and scorched, their limbs twitching, another blue-white salvo slammed into Kistler and Wexler. Both men were hurled backward and struck the steel floor with their eyes open but lifeless, and their rifles clattered away, just out of reach.

Then came footsteps unlike any Bacco had ever heard: hard and metallic, uneven and scraping. Two monstrous shapes, walking skeletons with eyes of fire, limped down the hallway, silhouetted by firelight as they lurched forward through smoke and shadow.

Togor sprang forward to seize a rifle from one of the imperator's fallen defenders. Safranski tensed, as if to make a leaping bid for Wexler's weapon.

One of the skeletons raised a pistol and snapped off a shot with casual ease, and the top half of Togor's head vanished in a flash of light and heat, followed by a sickening stench. Safranski backed down, apparently not willing to test his luck or his reflexes against such odds.

The killers emerged from the smoke. It was clear the androids had suffered horrendous damage—they were dented and scorched, one of them was missing a foot, and the other had lost its lower jaw—but they remained intimidating enough that no one in the room dared to move as the duo crossed the threshold into the safe room.

For a moment the androids stood, disruptor pistols in hand, studying the room. Bacco wondered if they were deliberating whether they needed to kill everyone, or just the heads of state. Then she stood, determined not to meet her end on her knees, cowering like a child.

Sozzerozs also rose up to his full height, as if daring the androids to execute him.

One-Foot took aim at the imperator, and No-Jaw pointed his weapon at Bacco.

Waiting for the end to come, she realized she was more angry than afraid.

Shots were fired, and the safe room filled with blinding light.

No-Jaw sank to its knees, its guts smoldering with reddish fire, its eyes dark and lifeless.

One-Foot spun to return fire at someone behind it. A man sprang from the smoky darkness and slapped the weapon from the android's skeletal hand. The weapon clattered across the floor as the skeleton grappled with its attacker, landing blows that Bacco thought would be fatal—but her rescuer fought on, hammering the android with brutal punches and elbow strikes. Then he snared the mechanical terror in a jujitsu-style hold, twisting its body and tackling it to the floor. He jabbed his hand through a recessed panel beneath the android's metallic ribcage, thrust his fingers sharply upward—and the android went limp. Its eyes dimmed and went dark.

The hero of the hour stood and turned toward Bacco and Sozzerozs—revealing the exposed mechanical parts of his own ravaged face and head. Despite herself, Bacco recoiled, and Sozzerozs hissed with alarm. Holding up his empty hands, the last android standing spoke with an almost comical degree of formality. "Madam President, Lord Imperator: There is no cause for alarm." He lowered his hands. "I am Lieutenant Commander Data, *U.S.S. Enterprise.*"

23

It felt strange to see fellow Breen without their armor and masks, but Thot Konar knew these were special circumstances whose importance outweighed the Breen's greatest cultural taboo. He stood between the last two functioning uplink pods as their lids lifted open like a beetle's wings, hinged at the end nearest the obsidian uplink transmitter, whose violet inner fires baked the isolated chamber with a steady dry heat.

Berro, a golden-furred Fenrisal, sat up inside Uplink Pod One, his tongue dangling beneath his snout, his nostrils flaring with each labored breath. "I need a drink." His paw-like hands gripped the sides of his gray cocoon, in which he'd dwelled for the last hundred-odd days.

Ninety degrees around the transmitter, in Uplink Pod Two, sat Olar. The burly, broad-shouldered Paclu palmed a heavy sheen of perspiration from his bald, four-lobed, pale blue head. "And I thought it was hot when you stuck us into these things." He groaned and rubbed his neck.

"Welcome back," Konar said. "You've both performed magnificently."

His compliment drew a homicidal glare from Berro. "No thanks to you." He continued through bared fangs.

"We could've finished it, you know. We had every advantage."

"Be grateful. If I hadn't intervened, you'd have ruined everything."

The confrontation put Olar on his guard. "Berro? What happened?"

"After you went down, I still had a shot. And I'd have taken it—but my hand froze." Hate blazed in his eyes as he glared at Konar. "I couldn't fire. Then something forced me to go to close quarters against the Starfleet android. Even then, I still might've had a chance, if my proprioceptors hadn't been cut."

Konar said nothing; he hadn't come to argue.

"Don't jump to conclusions," Olar said. "We'd taken a lot of damage."

Berro's ears flattened against his head, a sign of anger. "No. I know exactly what my operational status was. I was banged up but battle-ready. The only explanation for what happened is that someone here cut my connection before I could finish my mission."

"You accomplished your mission the moment you entered the safe room."

Olar seemed almost ashamed to speak up. "Negative, sir. My avatar was terminated before I could fire, and it sounds like Berro was—"

"What did you two think your mission was?"

The two agents stole wary glances at each other. It was clear they sensed they had been challenged with a trick question. Berro answered, "You ordered us to enter the Bank of Orion by force and assassinate the Federation president and the Gorn imperator."

"Had that been your true objective, you'd both be eternal heroes of the Confederacy." Konar spread his arms in salute. "Instead, you've made possible an even greater victory."

A pall descended as the two agents began to grasp the implications of Konar's praise. Olar's face remained blank as he swallowed, betraying his alarm. "If our real objective wasn't to assassinate the two leaders . . . what was it?"

"Unfortunately, the two of you aren't cleared for that information."

Berro sniffed, apparently having caught a scent in the air. He leaned to his right to look past Konar, through the open airlock and down the long corridor beyond—at the end of which lay Hain's corpse, most of her back reduced to a concave disruptor scorch. Olar followed his partner's gaze and noted the dead body with a stare of cold, stupid terror.

Konar shrugged. "All part of the plan, I'm afraid. As for you two . . ." He stepped back and aimed his disruptor at the naked agents. "Let's just say we have one more job for you."

Only under the rarest and most dire of circumstances could the Imperial Guard take action without regard for the wishes of their imperator, but an ages-old decree by the *Nizora* had imbued them with the authority to act preemptively to defend the life of their leader, even when he did not wish to be saved. So it had been this day, when Hazizaar, returning too late to defend Sozzerozs from the androids' pell-mell assault, had exercised his right to spirit the imperator clear of further peril for the good of the Hegemony.

Sozzerozs had protested, of course. He had demanded to remain, insisting, "My mission here is not yet finished!" None of that had mattered to Hazizaar. The only relevant fact now, he'd said, was that the attack the imperator had miraculously survived had also proved beyond any reasonable doubt that the Bank of

Orion was nowhere near so defensible nor impregnable as its executives had led the Imperial Guard to believe. If the location was not secure, then as far as Hazizaar was concerned, the summit was over. He was taking the imperator home.

Within minutes of their rescue by the Starfleet android Data, Imperator Sozzerozs and *Zulta-osol* Azarog had been beamed back aboard the battleship *Hasturzolis*, along with the body of Togor. Less than a minute later, the Gorn warship had left orbit of the Orion homeworld and jumped to warp speed.

The first thing Sozzerozs did was power up his encrypted subspace transmitter and send a priority signal to Domo Brex of the Breen Confederacy. *It is time he and I spoke in person.*

Simmering with rage, Sozzerozs waited more than a minute to see some confirmation that his signal had been received and acknowledged. Every moment's delay only added to his wrath. At last, he saw the emblem of the Breen Confederacy: a crimson eye with slim daggerlike triangles above and below, and two pairs of curving tusk-like shapes on either side of the eye, one swooping upward, the other downward.

It blinked away, revealing a figure cloaked in the traditional anonymizing armor of the Breen. At once he knew it was not Brex, whose armor and mask were singularly distinctive, gold with red and black accents. This individual was dressed in gray-green armor, and his matching mask was adorned by a wide black stripe bordered in silver. *"Greetings, Imperator."*

"I will deal with you soon enough, Thot Tran. Let me speak to the domo."

Tran's snout-shaped mask dipped, implying condescension. *"I regret the domo is indisposed, Lord Imperator. He asked me to speak with you on his behalf."*

Sozzerozs hissed. "And by what right do *you* address *me*?"

"*Forgive me, Lord Imperator. I am merely carrying out the stated orders of my domo, who sends you his deepest thanks and his most sincere condolences for the deaths of Nizor Szamra and Wazir Togor.*"

He tried not to show his hatred, but his lips curled back, exposing his fangs. "Are mere words supposed to excuse the murders of my kin? How dare you use us as pawns."

"*I seem to recall you and your courtiers were willing participants in our deception.*"

His taloned digits curled into fists. "Your ambassador neglected to mention you would be treating us as targets."

Tran shrugged and spread his arms. "*Please accept my regrets, Lord Imperator. These sacrifices were necessary—and not merely for the sake of verisimilitude.*"

"What reason could you possibly have for treating us as if we were expendable?"

The Breen folded his hands together. "*Since the inception of the Typhon Pact, your Hegemony has been our alliance's weak link. If I may be frank, your past accords with the Federation are a source of concern. Had we not put you up to this summit as a ruse, we suspect you would eventually have sought out such a meeting in earnest. Now, if you or one of your successors should ever entertain that notion, you will have to remember this fiasco—and know that the Federation will be extremely reluctant to ever take you at your word again. So don't think of this as a betrayal, my lord. Consider it our preemptive investment in your loyalty.*"

Sozzerozs imagined seizing Tran's masked head and twisting it off his body with a wet and satisfying crack of breaking bone. *And I thought I couldn't hold the*

Breen in greater contempt. "You didn't trust us to keep our word of honor? *That's* what all this was about?"

Tran chortled and shook his head. *"Far from it, Lord Imperator."*

Awash in moist heat and crimson light, Sozzerozs was as close to relaxed as he had felt since before traveling under false pretenses to Orion. The imperator stretched supine across a basking stone in his private quarters. Across from him, Azarog luxuriated on the stone that until that day had been reserved for Togor. Sozzerozs turned his head to regard the logy Azarog.

"Tell me your thoughts regarding the Rigellian, Safranski."

After a slow blink, Azarog turned his head toward Sozzerozs. "He says little, but when he speaks, he argues to win. He's direct. Unconcerned with trifles." He paused for a slow rattling exhalation. "Unlike the Betazoid, he did not smell of fear."

"I took much the same measure of Bacco." Dark thoughts plagued the imperator. "What I am about to tell you is a vital state secret. I must have your vow of secrecy and faith."

Azarog sat up slowly and faced him. "I swear it upon my life, Imperator."

Sozzerozs sat upright and mirrored Azarog's pose. "Our invitation to the Federation may have begun as a ploy, a diversion to aid the Breen—but in the end I think it became much more." He leaned forward. "The androids who tried to kill us were agents of the Breen. Our so-called allies were prepared to sacrifice us for their own gain—and to ensure the Federation would never again accept our bond of honor. The Breen sought to shed our blood as they made liars of us."

The news brought Azarog to his feet. "How shall we answer their treachery?"

"I promise you, Azarog: the Breen will pay dearly for this betrayal. But now is not the time for us to become careless. Too much depends upon us." He felt Azarog's gaze as he padded across the compartment to a transparent metal viewport that looked out at the cold reaches of the cosmos. "Open a clandestine channel to the Rigellian, Safranski. Make him and his president understand that we will earn back their trust. I will have Gozorra provide you with intelligence regarding the Breen; I want you to share it with the Federation."

With caution, the *zulta-osol* sidled up to Sozzerozs. "I will obey, Lord Imperator—but I would be negligent if I failed to counsel you that such a breach of our pledge to the Pact could have dire consequences—not only for us personally, but for the Hegemony itself."

"I'm aware of the risks. But this is what has to happen." He turned and looked Azarog in the eye. "We joined the Pact because I let avarice and envy cloud my judgment. But what I saw on Orion showed me who our true friends are. I led our people down this ignoble path; I will lead us back to righteousness." He looked back out at the stars and envisioned the shape of the future. "I know we can't withdraw from the Pact yet—but soon, with help from the Federation, we *will* free ourselves from this yoke of iniquity. And on *that* day, Azarog . . . *honor will be served.*"

24

It took all of La Forge's willpower not to wince as he peeled the blackened flesh off the back of Data's neck to make way for a temporary dermal graft. "You're sure this doesn't hurt, Data?"

"Quite sure." Like a child in a barber's chair, Data remained absolutely still on the sloped worktable, while Worf paced slowly behind La Forge. "I register the pressure of contact, but I have been programmed not to react to cosmetic damage in the same way organic beings do."

"Convenient," Worf said.

"More like lucky," La Forge said. Not only did Data's flesh look real, it *felt* real—warm with naturalistic body heat, pliant, and just as elastic as real skin. In the past when he had helped Data make repairs to his previous body's metallic bioplast skin, he had never come close to mistaking it for the real thing. Data's new exterior, on the other hand, made him wonder if his injuries ought to be treated in sickbay by Doctor Crusher. He focused the bioplast fuser to seal the edges of the graft with minimal scarring. "How long will these patches hold, Data?"

"Several weeks at least." He rotated one bare arm

and frowned at its irregular patchwork of mismatched skin tones. "However, I intend to make permanent repairs as soon as I am able to regain access to my ship."

Worf stopped pacing. "I have spoken with Ambassador Císol. Federation Security has released your vessel. You may return to Orion to claim it when you are ready."

Data turned his head toward Worf, interrupting La Forge's repairs. "That will not be necessary, Commander. If you will grant me permission to dock the *Archeus* on the *Enterprise,* I can instruct its AI to file a flight plan and pilot the ship to rendezvous with us in orbit."

It took the Klingon a second to process that. "Permission granted."

"Thank you." He held up one finger to signal La Forge to wait before resuming his work, and he looked away, his focus distant, as if he were gazing through the ship's bulkheads. A few seconds later, his mood brightened. "My ship is en route. Its ETA is eleven minutes."

The first officer shot a curious look at La Forge, then turned half away from him and Data. "Worf to ops."

Glinn Dygan answered over the ship's comm, *"Ops. Go ahead, sir."*

"Clear the aft hangar and inform the FCO that Mister Data's vessel is en route from the planet, ETA eleven minutes. It is to be given priority clearance."

"Understood, sir."

"That is all. Worf out." He turned his always fearsome glare upon La Forge. "How long until you finish here?"

"Almost done." La Forge chose not to be baited into reacting defensively to Worf's brusque queries. He recognized the first officer's impatience for what it was: frustration. After waiting a few seconds to make sure

Worf didn't misinterpret his intentions, he said, "You seem like a man with something on his mind, Commander. Anything I can do to help?"

Worf sighed. "I cannot make sense of the attack at the bank."

La Forge finished his last pass with the fuser and patted Data's shoulder to let him know he could get dressed. Then he looked at Worf. "What about it's bothering you?"

The question started Worf pacing again. "The androids used tricobalt explosives to fight their way in. After Data caught them, we found they each had one bomb left. So why did they waste time sniping the defenders? Why risk entering the safe room at all? Once the door was open, they could have tossed in their bombs and guaranteed the deaths of all inside."

"I don't know." This was the first La Forge had heard of the androids carrying unused explosives, and he floundered to rationalize an explanation tailored to fit the facts. "Maybe they were worried about getting hit by the blast wave?"

The first officer shook his head. "The assassins showed no regard for their safety or survival up to that point. And according to the survivors, the attackers hesitated to fire the killing shot. Why would they freeze when victory was within their grasp?"

His question lingered, unanswered, as Data put on his shirt and La Forge put away his tools. In La Forge's opinion, there was only one logical answer: *Because killing the president wasn't their true objective.* But to raise that possibility would invite an even more troubling question he was unprepared to face: *Then why did they go to all that effort in the attempt?*

He was still pondering the ramifications of that train of thought when his office door slid open, and Lieutenant Elfiki poked her head inside. "Sirs? We're ready out here."

"Thanks, Dina," La Forge said. He ushered Worf and Data out of his office, into the corridor that led to main engineering. At the end of the passageway was the central console, a pair of octagonal tables with interactive surfaces, connected by a pair of back-to-back workstations. Gathered around the console were Elfiki; the ship's assistant chief engineer, Lieutenant Taurik; and subspace communications specialist Ensign Cyriaque Lamar. La Forge, Worf, and Data settled in at three adjacent stations around one of the octagons. The chief engineer nodded at Elfiki. "What have you got?"

The science officer keyed in commands, pulling up scan results on the linked monitors. "With help from Lieutenant Anders, Ensign Lamar identified the frequency used by the black crystal transceivers inside the android's head. I connected the transceiver to our main array, which should give us a general idea of where this brain's signals are coming from."

"Assuming their control center is still transmitting," Lamar said. "It's likely they know we've captured at least one of their androids, so it's possible they might have shut down or changed frequencies, to prevent us from doing what we're about to try."

Elfiki glared across the console at Lamar. "Way to stay positive."

"Let's just get on with it," La Forge said. "Power it up."

He watched as Elfiki keyed in the final activation sequence and brought the captured obsidian transceiver on line. "Okay," she said, observing the results on her tabletop display. "Right now, we're in passive-receiver mode. The Argus Array and the *Starship Osiris* can help us triangulate any signals we pick up, but this might take a while, so just—" Her jaw went slack and her eyes opened wide as the sensor data appeared on her screen.

Her naked shock compelled everyone else to look at their own screens. La Forge almost couldn't believe what he saw. "Dina . . . did we just find the *source* of the control signal?"

"Um . . ." She nodded and shrugged. "I think we did."

Worf indulged his gift for understatement. "That was easy."

"Yeah," La Forge said with open suspicion. "Maybe a bit *too* easy."

Picard entered the observation lounge to find Worf, La Forge, Šmrhová, and Data waiting for him. His three senior officers stood on the far side of the conference table, all bearing the same grim frowns. Data stood alone, on the near side of the table, his expression equally grave. Taking his place at the head of the table, Picard cut to business. "What have you found?"

Worf touched a keypad on the tabletop. "This."

The center screen of the room's master systems display lit up with a map of local space. A star system was highlighted with a bold red dot.

La Forge nodded at the annotated star chart. "Elfiki and Lamar tapped into the frequency used by the androids and found their control center." With a nod he cued Šmrhová to continue.

"Pyrithia IV," the security chief said. "It barely qualifies as Class M. Poor soil and a cold climate made it less than ideal for colonization. It could be terraformed, but so far, no one's bothered to try. Officially, it's unpopulated."

Eyeing the map, Picard was perplexed. "That world lies *inside* Federation space."

"Legally," Data said, "it is a Federation possession. It

was formally claimed sixty-eight years ago, in the Federation's second addendum to the Treaty of Antos."

Šmrhová called up a pair of green arrowhead symbols. "The starships closest to the Pyrithia system are the *Callisto* and the *Nogura*. Both are en route with orders to disrupt the enemy's control signals and seize control of the base, its assets, and its personnel."

"Well done," Picard said. "But I'm not content to leave others to finish what we've started. Now that the *Atlas* has returned to transport the president and her delegation to Cestus III, I want us under way to Pyrithia immediately, and at maximum warp."

A knowing smirk leavened Worf's dour visage. "Course has been plotted and laid in. Ready to execute on your command, Captain."

Once again, Picard was reminded why he had chosen Worf as his first officer.

"Number One . . . make it so."

25

To be paralyzed in the sight of his enemies had long been one of Worf's recurrent nightmares, and there was no moment when he felt so exposed and vulnerable as when he was materializing from a transporter beam en route to a potential combat situation. Engulfed in golden light and white noise, he felt like a brilliant target, a beacon inviting calamity.

The effect faded, sensation returned, and Worf charged.

Šmrhová was at his side, attired in an armored solid-black combat uniform—a relic of the Dominion War—and bracing a phaser rifle against her shoulder. Worf had scorned such accoutrements as crutches, preferring to live or die by his wits, his reflexes, and his courage. His only weapon was a type-2 hand phaser, his only defense a well-honed talent for battle.

Surrounded by security personnel from the *Enterprise*, the *Callisto*, and the *Nogura*, he sprinted forward and easily took the lead. With one shot he blasted the closed portal ahead of the strike team, and when he reached the carbon-scored door, he kicked it in with one mighty thrust of his foot. The deformed sheet of metal broke free, brittle and smoldering, and struck the floor with a dull and hollow bang. Worf was six paces inside the room on the other side, pivoting left and then right in search of a target, before he realized all was deathly still. There was no one there for him to fight— only unmanned computer consoles awash in a torrent of data.

The other members of the strike team flowed past him. In their black field combat uniforms, they were like a dark river coursing past a boulder. It took them less than thirty seconds to fan out ahead of him, leapfrogging past one another while communicating in quick hand signals, before one of them announced, "All clear!"

A stranger's opinion carried no weight with Worf. He waited until Šmrhová returned and approached him to confide, "The site's secure. And you need to see what we found, sir."

"One moment." He tapped his combadge. "Worf to *Enterprise*. Beam down Commander La Forge and Mister Data." Mere seconds after his order, the air shimmered nearby with a new transporter effect, and the engineer and android took shape inside it. As soon as they emerged, Worf nodded to Šmrhová. "Lead the way, Lieutenant."

The lithe brunette led them through a large and apparently central room packed with computers and monitoring stations that showed all manner of telemetry and vital-systems feedback. It struck Worf as overkill to devote so many systems to monitor only four androids.

Then Šmrhová guided them to a long and narrow passageway. Lying on the floor at its threshold was a single body in a Breen military uniform, still masked. A black scorch had consumed most of its back. "We found traces of two more bodies in the facility's incinerator," Šmrhová said, nodding toward a hatchway nearby. "The others are back here."

Worf, La Forge, and Data followed her down the narrow corridor to an airlock. On the other side of its open double doors was a grisly spectacle: two aliens lay naked inside open pods of unknown function, their faces burned away by what Worf surmised had been point-blank disruptor blasts. The *Enterprise*'s security chief slung her weapon. "We'll get you a more precise time of death once the medical unit has a chance to run some tests, but based on my experience, I'd say these two have been dead for less than a day." She glanced back through the airlock. "The one outside looks like she got killed around the same time. Maybe a bit earlier."

La Forge seemed entranced by the machine of black volcanic glass surrounded by four cocoon-like pods. As he drifted closer to inspect its features, Data said to Worf, "I am going to review the base's computer systems and control network." Worf nodded, and Data left.

Šmrhová continued studying the dead bodies. "This still isn't making sense. I've heard of killing one's own people to tie off loose ends, but if that was the reason to kill them, why leave their bodies behind to be discovered?"

"For that matter," Worf said, "why let us find this base? The Breen know how to make self-destruct systems. Why would they let us capture this? How does this help them?"

The security chief shook her head. "I don't know, sir. But I know I don't like it."

"Agreed." He moved to stand behind La Forge, who was kneeling beside one of the open, empty pods. "Have you found anything new?"

The engineer frowned. "Not really. This core system is definitely Tholian, and these pods have a lot of Romulan parts." He stood and poked at the pod's control panel. "And I might not be able to read Breen Standard, but I know it when I see it." He shrugged at Worf. "It's a muddle, just like what we found inside the androids' heads."

Worf turned and looked back through the airlock. Then he asked Šmrhová, "You said the Breen at the end of the hallway was dead before the two in here were killed?"

She nodded. "That's our current thinking."

He looked toward the garbage hatch. "How old were the traces inside the incinerator?"

"Hard to say. A few days at least, I'd think. Why?"

He pointed at the dead bodies. "Neither of these victims was armed. They did not shoot each other, and it could not have been the one outside." He looked around, half expecting to discover some evidence of a concealed recording device spying on their investigation. "Whoever killed them escaped—and deliberately left this facility for us to find."

La Forge was strangely chipper. "Good. What they left behind can radically advance our knowledge of cybernetics and Tholian thoughtwave technology. Looks like a win to me."

Not wanting to spoil La Forge's moment of discovery, Worf held his criticism and walked away, down the corridor that led back to the central control room.

Šmrhová fell into step beside him and lowered her voice for the sake of discretion. "This is just like the clues we were force-fed on Orion. If the Breen are giving away something like this, they must think they have something even bigger to gain."

"Precisely." He stopped, glanced back at La Forge, then looked at Šmrhová. "Rip this lab apart and beam it up to the *Enterprise* for study. Then, send the bodies to Doctor Crusher for autopsy. Just because the Breen want this to distract us, that does not make it worthless."

She nodded. "Yes, sir." They resumed walking. "I have a question."

"Ask."

"Other than the Changelings, have you ever faced a threat as troubling as remote-controlled, Breen-driven android spies that can impersonate anyone they want?"

Worf pondered the enemies he had faced in his day, including the Borg, the Hirogen, the Jem'Hadar, and even Q. "Very few."

"Then let me ask you another question: If you had a resource like this to wield against your enemies, what would have to be at stake to make you willing to give it up?"

He didn't dare speak his answer aloud: *Something that would alter the balance of galactic power—and change the shape of the future.*

Data called out, "Commander Worf! You need to see this immediately." The first officer and security chief hurried to Data and each hovered over one of the android's shoulders. Looking up and back at Worf, Data pointed out details on the screens in front of him. "I have detected a large number of dormant android control signals being received by this facility." He directed their eyes to a screen showing a star chart that included several adjacent sectors. Scores of star systems in half a dozen sectors were highlighted with triangular red icons. "According to this, there are more than a hundred other android infiltrators on dozens of Federation worlds within fifty light-years of this control center."

Šmrhová blanched. Worf clenched his jaw and ground his teeth.

"That's not good," she said.

"No, it is not." He tapped his combadge. "Worf to *Enterprise.*"

Picard replied, *"Go ahead, Number One."*

"Sir. We need to contact Starfleet Command at once. I believe the Breen may be on the verge of launching an invasion."

Littered with loose parts and partitioned by banks of captured computers, the *Enterprise*'s main cargo bay had been transformed into a testing laboratory. Navigating the labyrinth of hardware, Picard had to mind his step. Stray cables crisscrossed his path and somehow linked all these mismatched alien components into a functioning whole.

Occupying the cargo bay's perimeter were more than a dozen of the ship's senior engineering personnel, representing a variety of professional specialties. Most were engaged in hands-on work—moving pieces into place, running cables, or crawling inside open sections of the thrumming machine to work on something inside. A few, including Taurik, the ship's assistant chief engineer, roamed from one engineer to the next, to ask questions, offer advice, or make entries into the duty logs for their inevitable, exhaustive technical reports.

At the center of the maze stood La Forge. The engineer was surrounded on three sides by display screens, holographic projections, and sprawling command consoles. He alternated between earnest jabs with his right hand at the various panels, and checking the tricorder in his left hand to see if he'd induced the slightest degree of measurable change. Looking up, he noted Picard's approach with what seemed like relief. "Quite a catch, eh, Captain?"

"An impressive acquisition, Mister La Forge." He made a show of looking around at the jury-rigged systems. "Are we any closer to knowing the objectives of the hundred-odd androids we detected awaiting orders from this system?"

"Not really. Have they all been located?"

"Yes. Federation Security will have them all in custody within the next twelve hours."

La Forge frowned. "Then I'd say we lucked out. It sounds crazy, but as far as I can tell, those androids don't have drivers. They were powered up and brought on line, but with no one to control them, they're just dead weight. If the Breen had planned ahead, with standby operators and a backup command center, we'd have been in big trouble."

The hypothetical crisis-that-might-have-been troubled Picard, who masked his growing concern. "Have you learned anything else about their control systems?"

La Forge put down his tricorder and gestured at various consoles and components. "We've reverse-engineered the interfaces they built to make the Tholian thoughtwave transmitters compatible with both the Romulan telepresence system and the cybernetic nervous system and sensory receptors of the Soong-type androids. That enabled us to patch the system into our main sensor array." A nervous smile. "That's as far as we've gotten, but it's presented us with some really interesting possibilities."

Something about the way La Forge had said *interesting* made Picard wary. "Such as?"

His prompting drew an anxious shrug from La Forge. "For one thing, the fact that it worked at all is remarkable. But now that we know the Breen controlled these bodies accurately enough across *interstellar distances* to use them for intelligence work means we need to consider this a viable alternative to imbuing android bodies with sentient minds." The prospect clearly excited him. "I mean, think of it, Captain: Instead of risking the lives of away team personnel, or even starship crews, we could build a legion of these bodies and then train personnel to drive them from safe locations. Instead of creating androids to use as slaves, we could build remote-controlled cybernetic avatars with abilities beyond anything an organic body could stand. Used responsibly, this kind of technology could totally change the future of space exploration."

"An intriguing idea," Picard admitted. "But . . . what if it were used *irresponsibly*?"

Confusion wrinkled La Forge's brow. "I—that is . . . What do you mean?"

La Forge's baffled reaction told Picard his chief engineer hadn't even stopped to consider all the ways technology such as what they'd found could be abused. "In theory, Geordi . . . could this technology be used to intercept and spy on private Tholian thoughtwave transmissions?"

Horrified comprehension erased La Forge's jubilant mood. "Yeah. I guess it could."

"And if it can be used to intercept thoughtwaves, can it be used to *block* them?"

The engineer's stare of shock became one of dismay. "Theoretically . . . yes."

Picard looked around at the cargo bay full of confiscated enemy materiel. "Then these are no mere spoils of war, Geordi. In unscrupulous hands, this equipment could be used to cripple the entire Tholian race, to paralyze every last one of its members, across the galaxy."

"In theory, maybe," La Forge said, "but Starfleet wouldn't do something like that."

"Wouldn't they? Before the Ba'ku incident, or the Tezwa affair, I might have agreed with you. But now . . . I'm not so sure." A frown hardened his features. "Never underestimate the influence of fear, Geordi. At times like this, when our way of life is challenged, there will always be those who are ready to sacrifice our principles to feed the bonfire of security."

"Using this as a weapon against the Tholians would be a serious mistake."

"I agree. Not only would it be an act of war—it would be a war *crime*. And that's exactly what I think the Breen are hoping we'll do with this scientific marvel they've abandoned. They want us to give in to fear, to temptation. To do what *they* would do in our place."

La Forge nodded. "You think they left it as a trap."

"I do. But it's more than that. I agree with Worf's original theory: it's also a distraction. Something meant to divert us now, and later lure us into the arms of strife." He grimaced. "Just the sort of cruel cunning I've come to expect of the Breen."

A moment of dark reflection gave La Forge pause. "A distraction from what?" It was clear the question gnawed at him. "If the real threat, or the real objective, is somewhere else, where is it? And what would be worth giving up all of this?"

"Yes," Picard said, his voice muted to a whisper by a sudden insight. "That is the real question, isn't it? There's no point trying to guess what the Breen are distracting us from. The possibilities are too numerous to ever be narrowed down. But the *where*—that might be a question we can answer. If we assume the summit on Orion was part of that diversion, and this discovery was a continuation of it . . ." His memory flashed upon the star map Data had found on Pyrithia IV, that had revealed all the worlds on which the Breen's remote-controlled androids had been detected—and then to another star map he had seen recently.

A surge of intuition energized him. "Mister La Forge, you're with me." He turned, threaded his way back through the subdivided cargo bay, and tapped his com-badge. "Picard to Commander Worf."

"Worf here."

"Number One, meet me and Commander La Forge in the observation lounge. And bring Lieutenant Šmrhová."

26

The door connecting the observation lounge to the
bridge sighed open. Worf and Šmrhová turned to see
Picard stride in, with La Forge right behind him. Before
the captain reached his chair, he was issuing orders.
"Lieutenant, call up the star map showing the locations
of the android avatars." Šmrhová moved to the control
panel for the master systems display, and Picard continued. "Number One, I believe your theory about the
attacks on Orion is entirely correct: we are being *manipulated,* and it's time we learned to what end."

Picard and La Forge sat down, so Worf did the same.
On the other side of the table, Šmrhová stood to one
side of the MSD as the star chart the captain had requested appeared on its center screen. Picard fixed his
steely glare upon the display. "Lieutenant, what strategic assets might the Breen have been targeting on the
worlds where we've detected androids?"

Šmrhová shook her head. "None that we can determine, sir. They're a mix of colonies and homeworlds.
None of them have starbases or industries vital to Federation interests. A few have agricultural resources
that are locally important, but nothing worth this kind
of effort."

Picard used the tabletop's interface to highlight the Pyrithia system on the viewscreen. "This is where we found what appears to be a Breen base that controlled the androids hidden on worlds throughout this sector. Do any of you notice anything odd about the Pyrithia system?"

His question was met by consternated silence. Then Šmrhová blinked at the star map, as if she had just then seen it clearly for the first time. "It's a Federation planet."

"A Federation *possession*," Picard said, gently correcting her. "A fact whose significance was lost on me when Mister Data first pointed it out." He looked at La Forge. "What appears to be that base's operational range for controlling the androids?"

La Forge studied the map, his brow knit with thought. "At least fifty light-years. But based on what I've seen so far, I'd say it could reach a lot farther."

The captain nodded and turned his piercing gaze upon Worf. "What else is within fifty light-years of every system with an android presence, Number One?"

Worf stared at the chart. In his imagination, he envisioned a circle around Pyrithia IV to encompass its transmission range, then he moved that circle to see how far he could shift it and still keep all the affected systems inside its area of effect. "The Fesarian Federation . . . the Ferengi Alliance . . . the Tzekethi Coalition and the Cardassian Union." Only as he brought his gaze back around to close the circle did he notice a small spur of foreign territory jutting into a nearby sector at the farthest edge of the transmission range. "The Breen Confederacy."

"That raises another interesting question," Picard said. "If the value of this technology is that it permits one to infiltrate hostile territory from the safety of one's own space, why did the Breen place their control center nearly forty light-years beyond their own border?"

Šmrhová squinted at the map. "If its range is only fifty light-years, they might have needed to place it that far forward in order to operate inside the Orion Colonies."

"I considered that." Picard frowned. "But then why not prevail upon their allies, the Tzenkethi? They could have placed their control center inside the Coalition's territory, beyond our reach. They would have been free to strike with impunity as far away as Earth itself."

The security chief thought for a moment, then her aspect became as grim as the captain's. "If the base had been inside Breen or Tzenkethi space, we wouldn't have been able to neutralize it without committing an act of war. . . . They *wanted* us to find it."

"More to the point," Picard replied, "they wanted us to find the androids lurking on our worlds—something we couldn't have done without first discovering the base on Pyrithia IV."

La Forge shook his head. "It still doesn't make sense. Why would they want us to find them? What do they gain by burning one of their own intelligence operations?"

The captain looked again at Worf. "Number One?"

Sensing that he was being tested, Worf focused his mind on the question and stared at the star chart on the viewscreen. "The architects of this scheme were *not* concerned about the loss of the androids, or their control apparatus. What mattered to them was how *we* would react to their discovery." He keyed commands into his tabletop interface and augmented the chart on the screen with a new subset of tactical data. "After we located the android infiltrators, Starfleet and Federation Security ordered all available ships and personnel redeployed to capture them. I have updated the star map with a detailed projection of that redeployment's final configuration."

At first, the overlay of new information looked like a chaotic jumble. Then Worf shifted the perspective of the star chart—transitioning from a two-dimensional, top-down view to a dynamic, three-dimensional computer-enhanced animation. The static map took on the quality of a starfield drifting across the main viewscreen of a starship at warp speed—and within moments, the pattern of ship movements in reaction to the alert became clear.

La Forge was aghast. "Is that what it looks like?"

"It is," Worf said. "A tunnel-like region of space, nearly twenty light-years across and fifty-five light-years long—completely empty of patrols by Starfleet or Federation Security. This gap in the Federation's defenses will occur starting in approximately four hours, and it will remain in effect for forty-one hours afterward."

Šmrhová struck a dubious note. "But what's the point of it? There aren't any strategically valuable systems in that area, and with a window that brief, the Breen can't hope to push more than thirty-five to forty light-years into Federation space before we intercept them."

Picard shot a look at Worf, who had already intuited the captain's thinking. Then the captain shifted his gaze toward Šmrhová. "What if the purpose of this diversion is not to move something into our territory," he chided her, "but to smuggle something out?"

Entertaining that suggestion, La Forge and Šmrhová regarded the star chart with new urgency and intensity. The engineer nodded. "That's exactly the corridor you'd need to sneak something out of Federation space—and into the Breen Confederacy."

The security chief pressed her index finger to the viewscreen. "And look what lies at the end of our side of that corridor." She turned her head toward Picard. "The Tirana system. Where the Federation Security vessel *Sirriam* went missing."

Worf's blood ran hot with anger at the realization he and the *Enterprise* had been so close to the enemy's scheme days earlier, only to have been deceived. "That cannot be a coincidence." He looked at Picard. "Whatever the Breen are up to, Captain, I think the answer is there."

With a grim nod of concurrence, Picard stood from his chair. "Agreed. Lieutenant, contact Starfleet Command and warn them to restore patrols of the Breen border. Number One, take us to the Tirana system—maximum warp."

27

"And in a flash of white light," La Forge said with a dramatic flourish, "they were gone." Though the *Enterprise* was hurtling toward what threatened to be a hostile encounter with the Breen in the Tirana system, he had freed up an hour of his time to assist Data with his fine-grade cosmetic repairs, now that they had access to Data's vessel, the *Archeus*. Its claustrophobic interiors, however, felt to La Forge more like a glorified cluster of closets than a starship.

Perched on a stool in a narrow lab, Data kept his head still as he spoke. "The Caeliar sound like a remarkable species. I regret that I missed the opportunity to meet them. As a fully synthetic being myself, I would have found such an interaction . . . *intriguing*."

"Yeah, they were interesting—I'll give them that much. But according to Counselor Troi, they were also kind of a pain in the ass." To pass the time while he worked, La Forge had regaled his old friend with tales of the *Enterprise* crew's exploits during the years between Data's demise and his return. Out of necessity, they had spent most of that time discussing the fate of the Federation's since-vanquished mortal enemy. "Anyway, after the Caeliar 'assimilated' the Borg, they all just up and vanished. Most of the Borg technology that was left behind turned to dust, but I guess the parts that weren't linked to the Collective, like the factory on Mangala, are still lying around." He switched off the dermal fuser and checked his handiwork underneath the hairline on the nape of Data's neck. "Good as new. What's next?"

"We need to recalibrate the chromatic-control circuits in my eyes. They were damaged when an explosion inside the bank briefly overloaded my visual receptors." He selected a pen-shaped ocular recalibrator from the worktable and mustered a genial smile as he handed it to La Forge. "I could do it myself, but it will be easier with your help."

Envy was not an emotion that often afflicted La Forge, but he suffered pangs of covetous admiration for Data's unique assortment of high-tech cybernetic implements. "That's kind of you to say." He took the tool from Data; it seemed to have no moving parts. "What do I do with it?"

Data pointed at one end of the device. "Aim its emitter crystal directly into the pupil of one of my eyes. Then apply gentle pressure to its sides. It will emit a series of photonic pulses that my eyes will use to restore their constituent circuits and relays to their default settings."

"You're the boss." He did as his friend had instructed, and a bright green ray shot from the device, bathing Data's left eye in viridescent light. Minuscule details, such as the capillaries in the whites of Data's eyes, continued to fascinate La Forge. A prismatic swirl within Data's iris quickly turned a radiant hue of emerald.

Data blinked his left eyelid a few times, and La Forge eased his grip on the device, terminating the beam. "Excellent," the android said. "Now my right eye."

La Forge resumed work, admiring the simplicity of the maintenance kit designed and built by Data's creator, Noonien Soong. "If only fixing the warp drive were this easy, I might have time for a hobby." Data's iris flashed green, and he put down the ocular recalibrator.

"As I understand it, your off-duty hours are mostly spoken-for these days." Data smiled at La Forge's surprised double take. "Doctor Crusher told me about your budding romance with Doctor Harstad. She seems very nice, Geordi. I am happy for you."

La Forge laughed. "It didn't take you long to get caught up on ship's gossip, did it?"

Data shrugged. "It looks large from the outside, but the *Enterprise* is a very small place."

"So it is." He looked over his shoulder to check the chrono on the bulkhead. "I wish we had more time. Now that you're back, I'd love to set up a poker game."

A wistful nod conveyed Data's fondness for the senior officers' weekly game of Dealer's Choice. "That *would* be fun. Who has filled the seats left by Captain Riker and Counselor Troi?"

The question struck an unexpected chord of sorrow in La Forge. "Lately, it was Choudhury, Elfiki, and Chen. But after Jas . . ." He found it too difficult to say, *after Jas was killed,* so he skipped over it. "Well, we just kind of forgot about the game."

"I am sorry to hear that."

La Forge looked up and saw genuine sympathy in Data's eyes. He found it reassuring that his friend seemed to have finally integrated human emotions into his life to the point that they now seemed effortless and natural. "I've missed having you around, Data. And not just for poker. Day-to-day life around here just hasn't been the same without you." He sat down on a stool opposite Data's. "I mean . . . I've found a way to get by; life goes on. But after you"—he decided not to hide behind a gentle euphemism—"died . . . there were so many moments when I found myself thinking, 'If only Data were here. He would have loved this.'"

Data nodded. "I understand." He furrowed his brow. "Since my return, I have had to rely on the memories I inherited from my father to bridge the temporal gap in my consciousness. On occasion, it has been easy to lose track of my place in time, to forget that years elapsed in my absence." A goofy smile brightened his youthful face. "On the other hand, it has also been a blessing. Because it often seems to me as if no time has passed between my download into B-4 and my reincarnation inside this body, I have had no time to 'miss' anyone."

His admission made La Forge laugh, not out of mockery but out of true joy. "That's what I love about you, Data: Only *you* could find the silver lining to being dead."

28

The *Enterprise* was at Red Alert as it dropped from warp speed to sublight, and Picard channeled his anxiety into a clenched fist as the airless, reddish-brown orb of Tirana III took shape on the main viewscreen. He looked at Šmrhová. "Tactical. Report."

Her attention alternated between her console and the main viewscreen. "We're picking up energy readings from the surface. Whatever's causing it, it's big."

Something—be it instinct, intuition, or common sense—told Picard this was what he had come to find. "Lock all sensors onto that reading. I want to know what we're dealing with."

"Aye, sir," the security chief said as she kept working.

Next to Picard, Worf seemed ready to leap from his chair. It was obvious he would rather be on his feet, but since Picard was seated, so was he. "Helm," he said, "time to orbit."

Faur answered over her shoulder, "Twenty seconds." On the viewscreen, Tirana III had expanded so that only half of its northern hemisphere was visible.

Low murmurings from the aft stations snared Picard's attention, and he swiveled his chair so he could see Lieutenants Chen and Elfiki working together at the master systems display, which they had reconfigured as an all-purpose sensor analysis station. The two women conferred in excited whispers as they tapped commands into their respective panels. When they noticed that they had Picard's attention, it was the half-Vulcan contact specialist who turned to report. "Sir, we've identified the source of the energy signals on the surface." She relayed a set of schematics and technical information to the main viewscreen, where it appeared on the left side of a split screen. "It's a *Mardiff*-class mining vessel, the *S.S. Basirico,* out of Ramatis."

On the half of the screen opposite the schematics, the planet's ruddy surface snapped into view, revealing a massive industrial vehicle—a vast agglomeration of pipes, reactors, smelting furnaces, refinery systems, and fuel pods, all topped by a comparatively tiny blister of crew accommodations.

Šmrhová looked up from her console. "There are no mining or refinery permits for any vessel named *Basirico.* Whatever that thing's doing here, it's illegal."

Picard leaned forward, certain there was more to this than he was seeing. "Why would the Breen go to this much trouble to hide an illegal mining operation?"

Glinn Dygan turned his chair toward Picard and Worf. "Sirs, the *Basirico* isn't engaged in standard mining or refining operations. They're excavating something, and proceeding with extreme care—which suggests that whatever it is, it's valuable—and fragile."

"Keep scanning," Picard said. "I want to know what they're digging up."

Behind him, Elfiki called out, "Sir? I think we have something. Something huge."

Worf and the captain traded a look of alarm, then they got up and moved in tandem to stand behind Chen and Elfiki. Picard looked at the science officer. "Report, Lieutenant."

"There's a structure underneath the *Basirico*." She called up enhanced sensor images on the large aft screen. "Most of the metallic composites are common to starship construction. What's unusual is its quantum phase signature." Pointing at an ancillary screen, she added, "It's consistent with matter from a known close parallel universe."

Chen cut in, "That's not all, sirs. After we masked the *Basirico* from our sensors, we got a clear shot of some large-scale structures inside the buried ship." She shifted the images in question to the main screen and enlarged them. "They're a pretty close match for the singularity cores the Tzenkethi were using to generate artificial wormholes. Maybe an improved version."

Worf's eyes widened. "Self-contained wormhole propulsion? Is that possible?"

"Not for us." Elfiki gestured at the screen. "But someone in the alternate universe thinks it is." She looked at Worf and Picard. "But, seeing as they crashed in *our* universe, I think it's safe to say they might not have worked out all the bugs yet."

"I've seen enough," Picard said. He turned and strode toward the center of the bridge. "Raise shields, arm all weapons. Glinn Dygan, hail the *Basirico*. Number One, prepare a boarding party. I want that ship seized and its crew arrested."

Dygan made a few quick taps on his console. "Channel open, Captain."

Picard raised his voice and invested it with authority. "Attention, mining vessel *Basirico*. This is Captain Jean-Luc Picard, commanding the Federation *Starship Enterprise*. I order you to cease operations, surrender, and prepare to be boarded. Acknowledge."

Long moments passed without a response.

An alert warbled on Dygan's console. "The *Basirico* is transmitting a distress call."

Then Šmrhová called out, "Vessel uncloaking! Bearing one-eight-two mark one, range two hundred thousand kilometers."

"On-screen," Worf said.

The image on the main viewer switched to an aft angle, revealing the distorted shape of a Breen warship emerging as if from a desert mirage. Tactical data scrolled up the right-hand side of the screen, and Šmrhová announced, "Engine signature matches the Breen cruiser *Mlotek*." She looked up, her countenance grim. "They've raised shields and locked weapons"— she shot a hateful stare at the vessel on the screen— "and they're hailing us."

"Put them on-screen, Lieutenant." Picard turned to face his foe.

A view of the *Mlotek*'s bridge appeared on-screen, its angle so narrow as to reveal nothing except one snout-masked officer and a soft-focus blur in the background. *"I am Thot Raas, commanding the Breen cruiser* Mlotek. *We come to answer the distress call of the vessel on the surface."*

It was such a brazen ploy that its sheer hubris almost took Picard by surprise. Then it made him angry. "Thot Raas, I find your humanitarian motives suspect, at best. How did your vessel come to be in Federation space? Much less in immediate proximity to the *Basirico*?"

"Such petty legal distinctions are irrelevant. We stand ready to defend the innocents on the planet's surface from your unprovoked aggression."

Picard wasn't certain whether he or Worf was more mystified by the Breen commander's irrational challenge. The two Starfleet officers exchanged stunned glances, then looked back at the Breen. "Thot Raas," Picard said, "the vessel on the surface bears a Federation registry, and it's engaged in unlicensed operations on a Federation world. Consequently, the *Basirico* and its crew fall incontrovertibly within our jurisdiction. As for your own ship, its presence here, under cloak, violates several laws and treaties, thereby nullifying your claim to be acting in good faith."

The Breen appeared paralyzed for several seconds. Then he replied, *"You will permit the* Basirico *and its crew to depart this system with its salvage, under our protection. If you continue to threaten them, you will be fired upon."*

"I don't think so." Picard couldn't see the Breen's eyes through that damnable mask, but he was certain that if he could, he would see fear in them. "Its salvage is illegal without a proper license. Furthermore, if its crew members are Federation citizens, they have nothing to fear from me. They'll be afforded every protection available under the law. Unlike you and your vessel—which I will destroy if you don't withdraw at warp speed, with your cloak down, in the next thirty seconds. Do I make myself clear, Thot Raas?"

"If you fire upon this ship, the Breen Confederacy will interpret that as an act of war."

"Your presence here is already an act of war," Picard shot back. "But for the sake of peace, that's an error I'm offering you one last chance to correct."

Thot Raas slowly tilted his head, like a wild enemy regarding its prey. *"Do not interfere, Captain. The civilian vessel will leave with its salvage. This is your last warning."*

The transmission ended, reverting the viewscreen to the enlarged image of the *Basirico* on the surface. A spreading bloom of dust rose up around the mining vessel, all but obscuring it from the *Enterprise*'s visual sensors. Picard sensed the outcome of this crisis would be decided in the next few moments. "Lieutenant Elfiki! What's happening down there?"

"They've snared the starship wreckage in some kind of a grappling frame," she said. "It looks as if they plan to pull it free by lifting off."

Worf confided, "Captain, if they rendezvous with the Breen ship—"

"Dygan," Picard snapped, "order the *Basirico* to cut its engines at once. Make clear that if they fail to comply, we will have no choice but to fire upon them." He turned toward Šmrhová. "Lock forward torpedoes on the *Basirico,* phasers on the *Mlotek.*"

She keyed in the command, then looked up. "The *Mlotek* is hailing us."

"On-screen," Picard said as he faced forward.

The masked head of Thot Raas filled the screen once more. *"Do not try to bluff me, Picard. You will not fire on an unarmed ship full of Federation civilians. Stand down."*

Picard imagined he could see the Breen's desperation, even through that opaque mask. "I've had enough of your games. Enough lies and manipulations. This ends here, now."

He cast a sidelong look at Šmrhová. She frowned. "The *Basirico* is still ascending."

Then he looked at Thot Raas. He wanted the Breen commander to remember the look in his eyes at this moment. "Lieutenant Šmrhová . . . fire torpedoes."

Soft feedback tones trilled from her console. Picard looked back toward the master systems display, whose center screen showed the crimson streaks of photon torpedoes tearing away at full impulse toward Tirana III. Then the five-warhead salvo slammed into the

Basirico, which disappeared in a painfully bright flash of white fire. After the glow of the blast faded, all that remained of the mining ship and its excavated prize was a dark smear of ash and dust obscuring the planet's cinnamon-hued surface.

His eyes cold and his mien adamant, Picard turned back to Thot Raas. "If, as I suspect, that ship was actually an asset of the Typhon Pact, conducting a military operation in Federation space, then its vessel was improperly marked, and its crew was out of uniform, making their presence here a crime of espionage—and an act of war." He took a few slow steps forward as he continued. "On the other hand, if I just ordered the destruction of a legal private Federation vessel and murdered its crew of Federation citizens, I shall have to face a court-martial and answer for my actions to Starfleet and my government. But not before I take this opportunity to blast you and your ship to pieces." He flashed a cold glare at the Breen. "Unless, of course, you wish to disavow your operatives on the surface—and retreat from our space while I'm still willing to permit it. In which case, all this could be excused as a . . . *misunderstanding.*"

The standoff lasted for several seconds of fraught silence.

Then, from the tactical console, Šmrhová declared, "The *Mlotek* has powered down its weapons and lowered its shields."

Thot Raas tilted his head forward at an odd, conciliatory angle. *"Our apologies, Captain. We seem to have involved ourselves in a matter that was not our concern. As it is now resolved, we will resume our course to Tzenkethi space, as permitted under interstellar law."*

"By all means, Thot Raas. And see that your cloak remains off line while you transit our space—as a demonstration of your goodwill. *Enterprise* out."

Dygan cut the channel, and the main viewscreen showed the *Mlotek* reversing course and accelerating away, first at full impulse, and then leaping to warp in a flash of light and color.

Picard's relief at the confrontation's end was tempered by his need to confirm what they had just destroyed. "Number One, secure from Red Alert. Lieutenant Elfiki, send your scans of the parallel-universe wreck to Commander La Forge for analysis. If this is what the Breen thought was worth sacrificing so much to gain, I want to learn all that we can about it."

29

It had been only a few days since Thot Tran had stood at the right hand of the domo, occupying a place of honor that presaged a future bright with possibility. Tonight he stood before Brex with his head bowed and his knee bent, a penitent summoned to face a storm of wrath.

"Do you have any idea what this failure has cost us? Not only within the Pact, but as a people? I placed my trust in you, Tran. And you've repaid me with disgrace."

At the risk of worsening his predicament, Tran dared to speak in his own defense. "Lord Domo, Starfleet has no proof that the mining vessel was under our control, only suspicions it can never verify, thanks to its own violent intervention."

Brex stepped forward and loomed above him. "It doesn't matter. All of local space knows the *Mlotek* was hounded out of Federation territory like a frightened *terlo* cub." The domo circled him as he continued, and as Tran listened, he wondered if Brex meant to kill him. "Billions of *sakto* wasted. An entire intelligence project sacrificed, along with two of our top cyberneticists. We've angered the Orions, enraged the Gorn, tipped our hand to the Romulans, and risked a war with the Federation." He stepped back in front of Tran and towered over him. "And what do we have to show for all this blood and treasure? *Nothing.*"

"It might still be possible to turn this crisis to our advantage."

The domo met Tran's hopeful assertion with bitter skepticism. "How?"

Tran kept his tone neutral. "Before the *Basirico* was destroyed, its crew relayed their scans of the crashed starship to the *Mlotek* for analysis. A rudimentary study of its engines suggests the vessel was capable of creating artificial wormholes, as we suspected."

"Are those scans detailed enough for us to replicate the wormhole drive?"

The accusatory tone of Brex's question left Tran defensive and trepidatious. "No, my lord. There were sensor-blocking minerals in the planet's soil, and it appears the vessel itself incorporated such compounds into its hull and spaceframe."

"Then we know nothing more now than we did before we started." The domo ascended the dais and returned to his elevated power position behind the audience chamber's lectern. He asked with open mockery, "How do you propose we turn this to our advantage, Tran?"

In the silence before Tran's answer, the arctic wind outside the domed chamber howled like *sohii*, the death omens of ancient Paclu legend. "What no one outside the SRD knows is that the crashed vessel's quantum signature confirmed it was from a close parallel universe—one we suspect has been known to the Federation for some time. If we can find a way to reach this alternate universe, we could try to capture one of these vessels intact."

His suggestion seemed to command the domo's attention. After a moment, Brex asked, "What would be the cost to reach this alternate universe? In both time and money?"

"That's difficult to predict, Domo. However, my initial proposal calls for an investment of half a billion *sakto* for a two-year research initiative."

While the domo was still considering Tran's request, the SRD director heard the door of the audience chamber's sole turbolift open behind him. He turned to see Thot Pran and the Confederacy's representative on the Typhon Pact's board of governors, Delegate Gren, walking toward him and Brex. "Greetings," Pran said, his amplified vocoder voice echoing around them. "How convenient to find you both here at this most auspicious moment."

It rankled Tran to see Thot Pran stride into the domo's sanctum as if he were a conqueror. By reflex, he positioned himself between the newcomers and Brex, even though Gren and Pran significantly outranked him in the Confederacy's hierarchical meritocracy. "Explain yourselves."

"I bring the same demand," Gren replied, directing his words over Tran's head at Brex. The delegate held up a data stick. "Domo, this is a formal summons from the Confederate Congress, requesting your appearance before them at midday tomorrow—to face a vote of no confidence." He held out the data stick and waited, his cast defiant and proud.

To Tran's surprise, Brex offered no argument. The domo stepped down from the dais and walked past Tran to face Gren. Then he took the data stick from the delegate's hand. "I have received the summons and will honor my pledge to appear before the Congress."

The leader's acquiescence filled Tran with anxiety.

A new domo would almost certainly want to break with the efforts of a predecessor, especially a project that had spawned so much fury in the highest ranks of the military and the government. "Domo . . ."

Brex cut him off with a raised hand, and Tran obeyed the signal for silence.

Pran stepped forward and all but touched the front of his mask's snout to Brex's. "You have overreached for the last time, Domo Brex. Now you shall answer for your errors of judgment to those who appointed you. And after they strip you of your office . . . I shall look forward to replacing you." He turned his head toward Tran. "And erasing your mistakes."

The supreme commander of the Breen military marched out of the sanctum with Delegate Gren on his heels. They stepped into the turbolift. As the door slid shut, Tran realized he now had far more pressing concerns than his projects at the Special Research Division.

He needed to persuade the future Domo Pran not to have him killed.

"Of all the reasons I might have had to return to Cestus III, this is one I'd hoped I would never see." Nanietta Bacco paused and squinted into the sunlight blazing through the ornate stained-glass windows behind the choir balcony, opposite the lectern. Before her, the pews of the Unitarian church were packed from the front row to the back with mourners of many species and many credos. What they had in common was that they had all loved the late Esperanza Piñiero. *Must keep going,* she told herself. Just as she struggled inwardly to hold fast to a shred of her composure, she clung to the sides of the lectern to keep herself from trembling. Pushing through her grief, she let the words on the padd in front of her carry her onward.

"Four years ago, Esperanza talked me into running for the office of President of the United Federation of Planets—a rhetorical feat for which I never truly forgave her." A mild susurrus of restrained chuckling traveled through the congregation. "But that was her way: she knew what was right, and what had to be done, and one way or another, she made things happen.

"I knew her most of her life. When I first met her, she was just a little girl, living here with her family in Two Rivers. Even then, nothing mattered more to her than fairness. She never feared to stand up to bullies— or her teachers, or her parents. There were so many things to love about Esperanza that I could never name them all: her loyalty, her bravery, her intelligence, her energy. But if I had to name her greatest virtue, I'd say it was her compassion."

Sorrow seized Bacco's throat and misted her eyes, threatening to break down her disguise of dignity, but she held on. As she continued, her padd scrolled the text of her speech, matching the timing of her delivery automatically. "Esperanza fulfilled many roles throughout her life. She was a daughter and a sister; a friend and a confidant. During her years in Starfleet, she rose to the rank of commander, acted as an attaché to Admiral Alynna Nechayev, and served the Federation both in times of peace and in war.

"After she left Starfleet, she came home, eager to serve her fellow citizens any way she could. So it was that one afternoon she strolled into my old office in Pike City, gave me a hug that nearly crushed the life out of me, then said with a smile, 'Governor, can I have a job?'"

A warm laugh of recognition and amusement helped lift the weight of bereavement for a few moments. Then the audience settled, and Bacco resumed her eulogy.

"What could I say? I knew her well enough to know she wouldn't take no for an answer. So I brought her on as a special adviser in interstellar affairs—a job for which she was overqualified, if I say so myself.

"I warned her that politics can be a harsh profession. I've seen it turn the best of people into jaded cynics and partisan mudslingers. But public service brought out the best in Esperanza. It reaffirmed the values she had always held dear. Ensconced in the halls of government, she became more alive to the plight and suffering of others: the persecuted who cry out for justice; the abandoned in need of refuge; the soldiers who all too often are the first ones called upon to risk and sacrifice all they have, or ever will have, simply because they swore an oath.

"Her life's work was not to champion those with power or special connections. It was to give a voice to those who were not heard; to add rungs to the ladder of opportunity; to preserve the dream of the Federation's founding.

"I know that encomiums such as this one are what we've come to expect when someone of note departs this life. Over and again we hear the familiar lyrics of paeans to the passing of a great soul, the hosannas to her decency, her honesty, her modesty. What makes this one different is that, in the case of Esperanza Piñiero, it has the added virtue of being true.

"Sometimes there are two versions of a person's life story—one public, one private; separate and discordant. Not so with Esperanza. Her public and private personas were one and the same. She brought to the political arena no demons, no hidden agenda, no vendettas. She committed herself to this life for one reason only: to serve the best interests of the people. And that was what made her my rock, my touchstone, and my inspiration.

"And yet, I still resisted when she suggested I run for president. I was happy serving as the governor of Cestus III, and the notion of multiplying my responsibilities and my risks a hundredfold, by shifting my arena from the planetary to the interstellar, seemed like more trouble than it was worth. But she persuaded me to run, and to hire her as my campaign manager, not by tempting me with illusions of power, or fantasies of enacting a radical agenda, or delusions of creating some sort of legacy . . . but by making me believe, as she did, that there was so much good we could do, for so many more people, if only we were willing to take on that burden. She talked me into running for president not by appealing to my desires, but by challenging me to give more of myself—more of my energy, my time, my passion, my love.

"She knew what was right, and what had to be done. So she made it happen." A tear rolled from the corner of her eye, and she palmed it from her cheek. "Now she's gone, cut down by an act of senseless murder, at a time when she had so much more left to do. In a moment such as this, it would be easy to give in to the darkness that has filled our souls now that her light has been stolen from us—to lash out and try to repay violence with violence. We must not succumb to that impulse. But that doesn't mean we should be weak. Rather, we should, in unity, face our future as Esperanza would have: with an eye toward a fairer, better, and more peaceful galaxy.

"None of us can accomplish all that alone. But together, we can give one another the strength to celebrate Esperanza for her compassion, her courage, and her conviction—and to honor her with lives that would make her as proud to be our friend as we all were to be hers."

She bowed her head, closed her eyes, and said a silent prayer of farewell. Then she looked out upon a sea of tear-stained eyes, grateful to be among those who had loved her friend as deeply as she had. "Thank you." She picked up her padd and left the lectern to a surge of applause—not a wave of adulation but an upswell of confirmation, gratitude, and support.

The rest of the service passed in a surreal blur, as did the trek to the cemetery, where Esperanza's flag-draped coffin was borne to its final resting place in a riverside plot by two of her brothers, her colleague Safranski, and a trio of Starfleet officers in full dress white uniforms. Standing at attention graveside was a detail of seven more Starfleet officers in dress uniforms, all carrying ancient ceremonial rifles loaded with blank ammunition, a Bolian ensign with a trumpet that had been polished to mirror perfection, and an Efrosian lieutenant wearing a snare drum.

Bacco promised herself she wouldn't cry in public, but then the drummer filled the air with his dry roll of percussive flourish, the trumpeter started to play "Taps," and her eyes burned with welling tears. The first crack of rifle fire broke down her last defense, and she hunched forward and wept into her hands. By the time the third salvo was fired and its last echoes had vanished into the crisp autumn air, Bacco had abandoned all pretense of stoicism.

After the service, she let her protection agents spirit her away from the cemetery to a waiting diplomatic transport, which in turn was set to ferry her to the *Starship Atlas* for the journey back to Earth. As she settled into her private cabin aboard the transport, the door signal intruded softly upon her maudlin solitude. She rubbed her temples and sighed. "Come in."

The door slid open, and Safranski poked his head inside. His manner was wary, as if he expected an ambush. "A moment, Madam President?"

"Get on with it." She beckoned him inside and pointed him toward the chair beside hers.

He stepped inside quickly, and the door shut behind him. As he sat down, she noticed the padd tucked under his arm. "There are two bits of news I thought you'd want to know sooner rather than later." He offered her the padd. "First, we just received this from Praetor Kamemor—via private channels, not the Typhon Pact ambassador."

She took the slim tablet and read the praetor's eloquent, heartfelt letter of condolence. It was no trifling paragraph, no boilerplate perfunctory gesture. It was full of personal details, and its erudition left her with no doubt that it was the genuine work of Gell Kamemor herself.

It was to Safranski's credit, Bacco thought, that he was patient enough to sit and wait in silence for the several minutes she spent reading the missive.

She set the padd on the end table beside her chair. "What's the second item of business?"

"I thought you'd be pleased to know the letter wasn't today's only back-channel contact. I received a personal communiqué from Azarog, the Gorn *zulta-osol*. Apparently, he and Imperator Sozzerozs are serious about continuing the dialogue we started on Orion—and this time they're backing up their words with action: they've started feeding us intelligence regarding the Breen. The first scoop is a heads-up about a no-confidence vote to replace Brex with Pran. It seems the domo's being deposed tomorrow morning."

"That's good." She saw in a glance that Safranski had misunderstood her. "Not that Brex is being suc-

ceeded by a hard-liner like Pran. I mean it's good the
Gorn told us. We still might win them back as allies."
Reflecting on the past several days of tragedy, Bacco
marshaled a bittersweet smile as she remembered the
meaning of the name *Esperanza*.

It meant *hope*.

30

Funky blues-rock fostered a festive atmosphere inside the Happy Bottom Riding Club. The spacious compartment was large enough that most times one could easily sense the curvature of the *Enterprise*'s primary hull from the shape of the lounge's outer bulkheads. Tonight, however, the club was packed with guests—some milling while swilling drinks, some loitering along the buffet of finger foods and delicacies from a dozen different worlds, some dancing in front of the live band. They all had come to bid farewell to Data, who once again was preparing to leave in his ship, the *Archeus*, for some unknown corner of the galaxy.

La Forge stood alone at a deck-to-overhead window, trying and failing to shed his black-dog mood with a Sazerac before facing his departing best friend. Normally, he enjoyed a party as much as anyone, but he failed to see why he should treat Data's latest disappearing act, so soon after the last one, as a cause for celebration.

You're just being selfish now, he castigated himself. *Data's living his life on his own terms, maybe for the first time. You didn't hold it against Will or Deanna when they left to get married and start a new life on the* Titan. *How is this any different?*

He was still grappling with his melancholy when Doctor Tamala Harstad, his inamorata of the past several months, slipped though the crowd to join him at the window. "I thought I might find you hiding over here." She dispelled his emotional storm cloud with a glimpse of her perfect smile, a twinkle in her dark brown eyes, and a warm, tender kiss. Then she took him by his arm and gave him a gingerly tug. "Stop being a stick in the mud and come join the party."

It didn't take much for her to pull him away from the window. As they slipped through the crowded room, he knew that it was because he hadn't really wanted to be alone in the first place—he'd simply wanted someone to care enough to come get him. As she grinned over her shoulder at him, and he smiled back, he knew he'd finally found the perfect person for the job.

She towed him into his circle of friends: Picard, Crusher, Worf, Šmrhová, Chen, Taurik, Elfiki, and Data. "Found him," Harstad boasted, like a hunter returning with a trophy kill.

"Good," Šmrhová deadpanned. "Two more minutes and I'd have sent out a search party."

He raised his drink in a casual salutation. "Sorry about that. I just needed a moment."

Worf put him on the spot: "For what?"

Before he could answer, Elfiki interjected, "Probably drowning his sorrows over not getting to study that wormhole ship the Breen were trying to salvage." She nudged Taurik with her elbow. "Would've been nice to find out what made that thing tick, right?" La Forge kept his poker face steady as he noticed Chen glaring at Elfiki while she was chattering at Taurik. *I'm no expert in relationships,* La Forge mused, *but that looks like hard-core jealousy.*

"I suspect it's for the best we destroyed it," the captain said. "We've only just begun to unlock the potential of slipstream drive. Perhaps we should learn to walk before we try to run." His counsel was affirmed by slow nods of agreement from Worf, Crusher, and La Forge.

To what felt like the group's collective relief, Taurik changed the subject. "If it's not too personal an inquiry, Mister Data, what are your plans after you leave?"

La Forge was curious to see how much private information Data would share in front of officers who, despite being senior personnel aboard the *Enterprise,* were not exactly close friends familiar with his complicated personal history. In the past, Data had been all too willing to overshare, but since his reincarnation, he had become cagy and evasive.

After a fleeting hesitation that implied Data was taking care in choosing his words, he replied, "There is someone I need to find. An old family friend, who I believe possesses information that can help me resolve a problem of great personal significance."

"Data," Crusher said, her voice a gentle protest, "you don't have to do this alone. I'm sure we could persuade Starfleet Command to let us help you if—"

"No, Doctor. I appreciate the gesture, but this is not a matter that concerns Starfleet or the Federation. It would be inappropriate for me to allow this ship and its crew to become involved in my personal affairs." He turned a regretful glance toward La Forge. "I have allowed my private life to intrude on the *Enterprise*'s missions in the past, and never to good result." To Crusher and Picard he added, "In this case, I think it best that I finish my business alone."

"Spoken like a Klingon," Worf said, raising his glass of prune juice to Data.

Picard nodded. "We understand, Data. And I promise we'll respect your wishes—but know that our hopes will always be with you, wherever you go."

The heartfelt sentiment made Data smile. "Thank you, Captain."

Chen took it upon herself to lighten the mood. "Data, I'd love to hear more about your adventures on the *Enterprise*-D! Is it true some lunatic tried to kidnap you for a museum?"

"You must be referring to Kivas Fajo," Data said, strangely eager to regale the young contact specialist. "That is an interesting story. He was a Zibalian collector of rare and unique treasures—and in 2366, he decided that he wanted to add me to his private collection. . . ."

La Forge and the others who had served with Data on the *Enterprise*-D listened as he spun the story with tremendous flair and wit. Watching the younger officers listen in rapt attention almost made the old story sound new again to La Forge, as if the tale had taken on renewed vitality by the simple virtue of having found a fresh audience.

The next hour passed with war stories and small talk, but soon it was clear the party was winding down. Data made the rounds, thanking everyone who had come to wish him well, charming the room with handshakes and easy smiles. *He's come a long way from the Data who never used to know what to say at a party,* La Forge thought as he watched his friend mingle.

By midnight, the Riding Club was all but empty. Only Data, La Forge, Worf, Picard, and Crusher remained. In a remarkably restrained display of insistent courtesy, the captain had shooed away all the junior officers so he and the others could have a few moments alone with Data. They met in a circle around a table by a window in a secluded corner of the lounge.

"Thank you, everyone," Data said. "I will miss you all while I am away."

Picard shook his hand. "*Au revoir,* Mister Data. And remember that if you ever want our help, you need but ask."

As the captain released Data's hand, Crusher stepped forward and embraced the android. "Be careful, Data." As they parted, she gave him a peck on the cheek. "For luck."

The doctor took the captain's hand, and they headed for the door, leaving only Worf, La Forge, and Data. The first officer seemed to be searching for something to say. Then he held out his hand toward Data. As the android reached up to shake it, Worf clasped his friend's forearm in a warrior's grip and cracked a mischievous smile. "*Qapla'.*"

Data gave Worf's arm a single firm shake. "*Qapla'*, Worf."

They released each other, and then Worf made his exit.

"I guess this is it, then," La Forge said.

"I suppose it is." Data's brow creased with concern. "Are you still upset about my decision to continue searching for Emil Vaslovik?"

La Forge sighed. "No. I just hate that we have to keep saying good-bye." He shrugged. "I keep hoping that one of these days you'll come back—to Starfleet . . . to the *Enterprise.*"

"I may yet do those things, Geordi."

"Or you might get killed again. Or just vanish." He shook his head. "Sorry, Data. I'm not trying to jinx you, I swear. But I keep wondering: What if you leave and I never see you again?"

"As Captain Picard might say, this is not good-bye—merely farewell." Data placed a reassuring hand on La Forge's shoulder. "I give you my word: we *will* meet again." He pulled La Forge into a bear hug and gave him a friendly slap on the back, then they stepped apart. "Take care of yourself, Geordi."

There was nothing else to say, and they both knew it. Data offered him one last smile, and then he made his own exit without a backward glance.

As La Forge watched his best friend walk away toward the unknown, he was filled not with sadness or with fear, but with joyful hope.

Data had given La Forge his word, and that was all the engineer had needed.

If he promises we'll meet again . . . we will.

Exhaustion pulled Picard toward his bed, but the peaceful vision of his slumbering son anchored him in place. He leaned in the doorway of René's room and watched the boy's chest rise and fall with the slow rhythm of sleeping breaths. All the times when Picard fretted over his son's safety, or any of what felt to him like a thousand other interrelated details that would determine the shape of the boy's future, fell from his thoughts in moments such as this.

He yawned. As devoutly as he wished he could forgo sleep and spend his nights watching over his son, he knew it was time to rest. "Dream of a better world, *mon fils.*"

Fearful of waking him, Picard padded away with light steps, drifting like a ghost back into his and Beverly's room. Like him, she was dressed for bed; unlike his dark gray flannel pajamas, her nightclothes were pale and diaphanous, barely equal to the demands of propriety—not that it mattered, as she was already half beneath the bedcovers. The lamp above her side was off, and her face was lit by the soft glow of the padd in her hands.

Picard sat down on his side, kicked off his slippers, and rolled over toward Beverly as he pulled the blankets up under his arm. "Work or pleasure?" She lifted her eyes from her reading and shot a suspicious look at him. He nodded at the padd. "Your night reading."

"Crew fitness reports. Nothing puts me to sleep faster." She turned off the padd, then rolled away from him to set it on her end table. "I guess I've had enough." As she returned to her sitting position, he leaned forward for a good-night kiss. She pulled away. "It's late."

"You're still angry with me?"

She sighed. "No. . . . Go to sleep."

Experience told him that her denial was tantamount to a confirmation. "Beverly. I can tell you're upset. Please—tell me why."

"I'm not *upset*." She reclined against her pillows and fixed her forlorn gaze on the ceiling. "If I had to put a word to what I'm feeling, I guess I'd say I'm . . . *troubled*."

He sat up and turned toward her, hoping to draw her out with eye contact, open body language, and a gentle tone of voice. "By what? . . . Is this about what happened on Orion?"

"Of course it is, Jean-Luc." She touched his arm. "I'm not asking you to explain yourself again. I understand *why* you did what you did, protecting me instead of the president." Her blue eyes were shadowed with sorrow and disappointment. "I'm just not sure I can accept it."

Her sentiment wounded him. "Did my decision *offend* you? I love you, Beverly, and I won't apologize for putting your safety and René's first when I make my decisions."

She sat up quickly as she flared with anger. "Do you listen to yourself? That's exactly the kind of sentiment

you used to condemn in your officers when you commanded the *Stargazer*."

"I don't know that I condemned it so much as—"

"Don't try to rewrite history. Jack told me whenever
you read him the riot act for even *suggesting* that my
safety or Wesley's ought to be considered during tactical
situations. So I find it more than a bit hypocritical on your
part when you lay claim to that privilege for yourself."

He'd winced when she invoked the name of her first
husband, Jack Crusher, who had died in the line of duty
under Picard's command thirty years earlier. "What you
call hypocrisy, I call personal growth. It wouldn't be the
first time I had to admit that the beliefs I clung to as a
younger man turned out to be flawed. But if it helps
you to label me a hypocrite, so be it."

Frustrated, Beverly shook her head. "Jean-Luc,
you're not just any member of the crew—you're the
captain. If your judgment is compromised because
you're ready to place your family's safety ahead of accomplishing your missions, that puts this ship and its
crew at risk." A frown deepened the lines on her face.
"Maybe it would be best if René and I left the ship."

"To go where?"

She shrugged. "I don't know. Maybe to a ground assignment with Starfleet Medical. Or even back to civilian life. I could join the staff of a teaching hospital
somewhere. Or open my own practice. Heaven knows
there are plenty of worlds in need of new physicians."

"All right. If that's what you think is best, I'll go with
you."

His answer made her recoil slightly. "What? Are you
serious? You'd resign from Starfleet? Just like that?"

He didn't understand why she was so surprised.
"You seem to think it's a viable path for yourself—why
not for me?"

"Since when are you ready to hang up your uniform?"

Picard almost laughed. "Is it really so difficult to imagine? Maybe you've forgotten, but I almost didn't join Starfleet. When the Academy rejected my first application, I considered taking a scholarship to study at Oxford. If I hadn't been so stubborn about proving myself to Starfleet, I might have made a life for myself in the private sector, or in academia."

His wife signaled her doubts with the elegant rise of an eyebrow. "I find it hard to picture you behind a desk or in front of a classroom."

"Beverly . . . I've been proud to serve as a Starfleet officer. But my career is only a part of who I am. Now that I have you and René, my life has become much larger than I ever thought possible. Being a father has forced me to think ahead not just to tomorrow, or next year, but beyond the end of my lifetime, in ways I never did before. For the sake of my son, I have to think about the future—not just mine, but his, as well. So if you think it's best that we raise our son somewhere other than aboard a starship, I will support your decision without reservation. I am ready to make changes—to live where and how you want. Give the word . . . and we'll go."

Disarmed of her anger by his sincere confession, she tenderly pressed her palm to his cheek. "Just tell me this. What do *you* want to do?"

He smiled and laid his hand over hers. "I want to love my wife and son . . . explore the wonders of the galaxy . . . and command this ship. In *that order*."

The last remnants of her bad mood melted away, letting through a sad smile. She kissed him and touched her forehead to his. "Sounds like a plan."

THREE MONTHS
LATER

EPILOGUE

A lonely pilgrim in the endless night, Data walked through a jungle of bioluminescent flora on a world that had no sun or moon. The telluric rogue planet made its own heat through thermal venting, massive expulsions of superheated gases from its molten core that kept its oceans warm and its dense atmosphere of hydrogen compounds, methane, and carbon dioxide at an ambient temperature sufficient to keep its surface water liquid without boiling it off into space.

Each footfall he took through the thick nonphotosynthetic foliage lit up the ground beneath his feet, as chemicals in the subsurface mosses reacted with faint green pulses to the pressure of his weight. Broad leaves hanging in his path also lit up as he brushed them aside. It was a beautiful sight, one whose charms might once have been lost on him but now filled him with delight and fascination——but also apprehension, because he knew the phenomenon would make his approach visible from a distance, even this deep inside the forest. He had seen no evidence of complex animal life on this world, so he had no concern that he might attract the notice of predators, but he would have preferred not to have his presence betrayed to his quarry.

Ahead of him, the forest thinned. He quickened his pace, pushed through a bramble as sharp as barbed wire, and emerged from the overgrown jungle to find himself standing upon the shore of a lake that stretched for kilometers on either side of him and extended beyond the horizon. There was no wind here; the still air was oppressive in its humidity. Reflected stars sparkled on the lake's unrippled black surface. Two kilometers from shore, rising from its mirror image in the water, stood Data's destination: the Immortal's newest redoubt.

It was one of the most elegant but also one of the most strangely alien structures Data had ever seen: an asymmetrical trio of organically curved towers, each composed of several geodesics—soft transitions between the vertical and horizontal planes—that peeled off from the ground and twisted upward around an open core of space. Their exterior surfaces, translucent skins of hexagons over spiral skeletons with horizontal linkages, evoked for him the notion of a beehive's honeycomb made of pale lavender crystal and pristine white metal that glinted with starlight. Semitransparent habitable bridges linked them and gave the overall structure the aspect of a triple helix. At the water line, the towers flared outward and formed a shared foundation of fluid curves; just below their crown-like apexes, they were fused by insectile arches.

A most elegant design, Data thought with admiration. *Efficient and beautiful at the same time.* He increased the magnification on his visual receptors and studied the structure more closely. Its outer surface sported a number of artistically integrated systems, such as moisture collectors, supersensitive photovoltaic cladding, and wind turbines that even in such becalmed weather still turned slowly, a testament to their near-frictionless operation. Beneath the skins he saw hints of the towers' infrastructure, a series of interlocking dodecahedral metal frames.

In a blink he reset his eyes to their default settings and pondered his options for reaching the naturally moated fortress. *I could walk across the lake bed with little difficulty, but there is no guarantee I will find any ingress to the structure under the water's surface— or that I will find purchase for scaling its exterior.* He began to suspect that his attempt at making a clandestine approach, by beaming down beyond its estimated sensor range and walking to it while shielding his body's presence and energy emissions from detection, might have been a tactical error. *The Immortal has often proved hostile to uninvited guests . . . but considering our history, it is possible he might make an exception for me.*

He took a leap of faith and deactivated his body's sensor-blocking systems.

Then he waited.

Less than a minute later, he noted an ephemeral blink of light that lit up the surfaces of the towers that faced one another around their shared open core. It faded, but seconds later he saw a dim blur backed by a ruddy glow. Whatever it was, it moved swiftly toward him, skimming the black lake without disturbing the water's glass-like surface.

He switched his eyes to night-vision mode. In the pale green twilight, he discerned the empty open-top hovercraft with ease. Examining it in full-spectrum mode, he saw no sign of its forward phaser cannon having been activated, so he stood his ground and awaited its arrival. It halted as it reached the beach less than two meters from him, and then it hovered. He walked toward it, climbed aboard, and sat down in the front seat. As soon as he settled, the craft pivoted about-face and accelerated toward the towers.

Wind tousled his hair into wild tangles as the small craft sped above the lake. The towers quickly dominated his forward view, and as the hovercraft circled around between them to land inside an open parking area, he remained impressed at their sheer scale. *This place could house many tens of thousands if it were located on a populated world,* he noted. *Why would the Immortal desire so vast a structure for his residence?* It was one of many questions that would have to wait for another time. Data knew the Immortal likely harbored innumerable secrets, but he had come here seeking enlightenment about only one.

There was no one to meet him when he disembarked from the hovercraft, but a door that led to the interior of the tower opened as soon as he stepped out of the vehicle. Recognizing the invitation, he crossed the open-air landing area, stepped through the doorway, and wasn't the least bit surprised when the portal closed behind him. In the corridor, he waited for his next cue, and it came in the sound of a lone violin, its melody faint but its siren purpose clear.

The music led him down a curving passageway and into a turbolift, which delivered him to the top floor of the highest tower. He stepped out into an airy level subdivided by curving partitions riddled with open spaces—forms and textures that echoed the towers' exteriors. Following the virtuoso solo through the lavish residential penthouse, he passed freshly carved marble sculptures on classic pedestal columns, and brand-new oil paintings on framed canvases suspended in midair with wires almost too fine to see—all of them works crafted in the style of Leonardo da Vinci, one of the Immortal's many aliases.

Another of the Immortal's hundred-odd *noms de voyage* had been Johannes Brahms, whose only major composition for the violin—Violin Concerto in D Major, opus 77—bore striking and unmistakable similarities to the new concerto whose passionate strains guided Data forward. He reached the outer edge of the penthouse, which was ringed with great sloping windows that looked out on an eternal starry night. Then he passed the final partition and came face-to-face with the musician, who ceased playing as their eyes met.

The woman was youthful and striking in her beauty, with high cheekbones and a pale but flawless complexion. Her long and lustrous hair was the deep red of burnished copper and braided into a long tail that she wore draped over her shoulder. She graced him with a sweet smile, and her cornflower-blue eyes opened wide at the sight of him. "Hello, Data."

He had expected to find her here, and thanks to his inheritance of his father's memories, he had known she would be rejuvenated into the portrait of her long-lost youth—but nothing had prepared him for the profound joy he would feel upon this, the moment of their reunion. Tears filled his eyes, and his lips trembled as he tried to smile back. "Hello, Mother."

Juliana Tainer set aside her violin and bow, got up, and took him in her arms. Wrapping him in a fierce but loving embrace, she peppered his cheek with kisses. "I knew you'd find us someday," she said with more than a trace of her old Irish lilt. "We both did."

"It was not easy." He leaned back to look at her. "First, I had to analyze several decades' worth of financial transactions that fit the profile I had come to associate—"

She pressed her index finger to his lips, silencing him. "Data. It's not important. All that matters is that you're here now, and we're safe."

He looked around the penthouse, searching for any sign of the Immortal, but as far as he could tell, he and his mother were alone. "Where is he?"

"You mean Akharin?" She let go of him and stepped away, toward her instruments. Suddenly, her manner took on a haunted quality. "I don't know."

Masking his concern, he asked in a gentle voice, "Do you know when he will return?"

Tears fell from Juliana's eyes, and this time they were not ones of happiness. "I don't know if he's *ever* coming back, Data."

It was difficult for him to read the turbulent emotions behind her sorrowful display. "Did the two of you have some manner of falling out? Did he abandon you here?"

Wiping her cheeks dry, she snapped, "No, of course not. Nothing like that."

"What, then?" He edged forward, irrationally hoping to bridge their gap of understanding through proximity. "Please, Mother. I have come a long way to find him. I need to know."

Juliana crossed her arms and retreated from him, to stand beside one of the windows and look out at the nightscape. "There's nothing I can tell you that'll help."

"You cannot know that for certain. Any piece of information, however trivial, might prove beneficial." He drifted toward her in slow steps until he was at her back, and then he rested his hands on her shoulders. "Mother, please. Akharin possesses knowledge that I desperately need. It is imperative that I find him, no matter how long it takes, or how far it takes me."

She turned and pressed her hands to his chest. "Don't say that, Data. Just forget about him, and stop trying to find him. I'm begging you—stop looking and let him go."

The emotion behind her fervent plea was an easy one to parse: fear. But her distress was not reason enough for him to desist. He took her by her shoulders. "Why? Tell me why!"

"Because if you don't, the Fellowship of Artificial Intelligence will abduct you, too."

COLD EQUATIONS

CONCLUDES IN BOOK III

THE BODY ELECTRIC

ACKNOWLEDGMENTS

Once again, I shall strive for brevity with my acknowledgments. First, I thank my wife, Kara, for her encouragement and constant support.

Readers of the first book in this trilogy are already aware of this next detail, but for those who might read this book before that one, I'd like to point out that the *Cold Equations* trilogy was conceived as a direct sequel to author Jeffrey Lang's truly exceptional *Star Trek: The Next Generation* novel *Immortal Coil* (2002). Many of this trilogy's coolest ideas either originated in that book, or else would not have been possible without it to build upon.

My thanks also go out to author, editor, and *Star Trek* savant Keith R.A. DeCandido, who vetted the scenes involving President Bacco and her retinue, an ensemble he originated in his *Star Trek* novels *A Time for War, A Time for Peace* and *Articles of the Federation*.

Also worthy of my praise and thanks are the excellent wiki-based reference sites Memory Alpha and Memory Beta, as well as the perpetually useful tome *Star Trek Star Charts* by Geoffrey Mandel. My *Star Trek* brain trust also included author and designer Michael

ACKNOWLEDGMENTS

Okuda, and authors David R. George III and Christopher L. Bennett.

Lastly, thank you, gentle readers, for continuing to keep the dream of *Star Trek* alive, both on screen and in print, in the hope that future generations might also share our desire "to boldly go where no one has gone before."

ABOUT THE AUTHOR

The Mack abides.
Learn more at his website:
www.davidmack.pro